Praise for Alastair Reynolds

'A friend insisted I read *House of Suns* by Alastair Reynolds. I tried it, became hooked, and have now read everything he's written'
Bernard Cornwell

'A mastersinger of the space opera'   *The Times*

'Hard SF doesn't come much harder. Classic Reynolds'   *Guardian*

'All the intelligence and inventiveness his previous sequences led us to expect'   *Daily Telegraph*

'Ravishingly inventive'   *Publishers Weekly*

'Inventive, thought-provoking stuff with some ingenious ideas'
BBC Focus

'Arthur C. Clarke in his prime couldn't have done a better job'   *SFX*

'Leaves you wishing that more science fiction was this good'
Dreamwatch

ZIMA BLUE
AND OTHER STORIES

Alastair Reynolds

With an Introduction by Paul McAuley

Copyright © Alastair Reynolds 2006/2009
Introduction © Paul McAuley 2008
'The Real Story', first published in *Mars Probes*, edited by Peter Crowther, DAW Books, 2002.
'Beyond the Aquila Rift', first published in *Constellations*, edited by Peter Crowther, DAW Books, 2005.
'Enola', first published in a somewhat different form in *Interzone*, December 1991.
'Signal to Noise', first published in *Zima Blue and Other Stories*, Night Shade Books, 2006.
'Cardiff Afterlife', first published in *The Big Issue Cymru*, August 2008.
'Hideaway', first published in *Interzone*, July 2000.
'Minla's Flowers', first published in *The New Space Opera*,
edited by Gardner Dozois and Jonathan Strahan, Eos, 2007.
'Merlin's Gun', first published in *Interzone*, May 2000.
'Angels of Ashes', first published in *Asimov's Science Fiction*, July 1999.
'Spirey and the Queen', first published in *Interzone*, June 1996.
'Understanding Space and Time', first published as a chapbook by the Birmingham Science Fiction Group for Novacon 35, November 2005.
'Digital to Analogue', first published in *In Dreams*, edited by Paul J. McAuley and Kim Newman, Victor Gollancz Ltd., 1992.
'Everlasting', first published in *Interzone*, Spring 2004.
'Zima Blue', first published in *Postscripts*, Summer 2005.
All rights reserved

The right of Alastair Reynolds to be identified as the author of this work, and the right of Paul McAuley to be identified as the author of the introduction, has been asserted by them in accordance with the Copyright, Designs and Patents Act 1988.

First published in Great Britain in 2009 by Gollancz
An imprint of the Orion Publishing Group
Orion House, 5 Upper St Martin's Lane, London WC2H 9EA
An Hachette UK Company

This edition published in Great Britain in 2010 by Gollancz

10 9 8 7 6 5 4 3 2 1

A CIP catalogue record for this book
is available from the British Library

ISBN 978 0 575 08455 1

Typeset by Input Data Services Ltd, Bridgwater, Somerset

Printed and bound in the UK by CPI Mackays, Chatham ME5 8TD

The Orion Publishing Group's policy is to use papers that are natural, renewable and recyclable products and made from wood grown in sustainable forests. The logging and manufacturing processes are expected to conform to the environmental regulations of the country of origin.

www.alastairreynolds.com
www.orionbooks.co.uk

To the members of the Short Story Clearing House,
past, present and future, with deep gratitude.

CONTENTS

INTRODUCTION

I'm pretty sure that it was a dark and stormy night when I first met Alastair Reynolds. This was no pathetic fallacy, you understand, just the usual weather for a winter's evening on the east coast of Scotland, on top of a ridge that looked out towards the North Sea and Norway: even though I lived about two miles inland, it wasn't unusual to find salt spray frosting the windows of a morning. It was 1990. I was working as a lecturer in botany at St Andrews University; Al was finishing his Ph.D. at the astronomy department. He'd found out from the biographical matter at the end of one of my stories in *Interzone* that I lived in St Andrews, had given me a call, and come slogging up the hill for the first of many pleasant evenings spent in the village bar, talking about science and science fiction and the business of writing and publishing. I don't want to give the impression that I was Al's Svengali. Far from it. Al was an SF fan, but he was also, most definitely, no two ways about it, a writer. He'd been writing SF since his early teens; he'd sold a couple of stories to *Interzone*; he was in for the long haul.

But before I tell you about Al Reynolds and the stories collected here, I need to say something about the New Space Opera. That doesn't mean that I'm going to attempt to analyse Al's role in the resurgence of space opera, or define his place within the group of British science fiction writers who in one way or another are associated with it. For one thing, if you ask a bunch of people like Iain M. Banks, Stephen Baxter, Peter F. Hamilton, M. John Harrison, Ian McDonald, Ken MacLeod, Justina Robson and Charles Stross why they're writing the stuff, you'll get a different answer from each and every one. For another, there are plenty of American writers who, like the Brits, have been engaged in reinventing and refurbishing space opera's cherished but almost fatally tarnished and rusted tropes. In short, the New Space Opera is more of a confluence than a movement: a wide range of writers working on a broad spectrum of themes without the benefit of either a prophet or a manifesto.

While individual writers each have their own interests and reasons for reworking space opera, they're all building their various fictions on a common foundation. Like the old space opera of E.E. 'Doc' Smith, Edmond Hamilton and a host of unsung pulp writers, the New Space Opera sets its stories against vast backdrops of both time and space, and its characters are often engaged in superhuman efforts on which the fate of humanity is hung, but it's also closely engaged with hard science (from quantum physics and cosmology to evolutionary biology, bioengineering and cybernetics) and asks tough questions (who are we? why are we here? where are we going?) about humanity's place in a hostile universe. Its stories are informed by a sense of Deep Time and secret histories imperfectly understood and closely associated with cosmological mysteries, and are played out against a culturally rich patchwork of governments, economies, alliances and alien species rather than the monolithic empires of old.

Al Reynolds is best known for a series that's deeply imbued with the virtues of classic New Space Opera. His first four novels, *Revelation Space*, *Chasm City*, *Redemption Ark* and *Absolution Gap*, together with his seventh novel, *The Prefect*, and shorter fictions collected in *Diamond Dogs, Turquoise Days* and *Galactic North*, fit into the overarching framework of a future history that spans some forty thousand years and describes the conflicts and struggle for survival of two rival branches of humanity in a galaxy littered with the artefacts of ancient civilisations and patrolled by alien killing machines. Most commonly called the 'Revelation Space' series, it's notable for its darkly tinted moral ambiguities, the gothic rococo detailing of its vast machineries and cosmic backdrops, and multiple storylines that begin in different times and places and gradually and relentlessly converge.

Now, none of the stories in this collection are part of the 'Revelation Space' series, but it's clear that they're all drawn from the same well of themes, concerns and tropes, most notably a tough-minded depiction of the fragility of ordinary human life, and the defiant persistence of human spirit, in the raw wild deeps of space and time. And as in the 'Revelation Space' series, their protagonists are most often ordinary working stiffs caught up in huge events whose ramifications they can barely glimpse but must unriddle in order to survive, and whose cynical attitudes and side-of-the-mouth quips tinge their narratives with a *noir* hue. Spirey, in 'Spirey and the Queen', for instance, can't resist making a characteristically caustic remark with what might be her last breath while fighting to gain control of a spaceship that's the only way of escaping a seemingly insignificant splinter of ice whose secret chambers are being riddled with kinetic weapons fired by what was once his own side, in a war for control of the resources of a protoplanetary disc. Crammed with eye-kicks, pell-mell action, and big ideas about what it means to be human and the future and nature of intelligent life, it could easily stand as the taxonomic-type specimen of the New Space Opera, the golden mean to which all others aspire. And if you think that's pretty impressive, bear in mind that Al Reynolds had published just five stories before it appeared. We're talking about some kind of writer, here.

Although, as Brian Aldiss once remarked, you no more need to be a scientist to write science fiction than you need to be a ghost to write ghost stories, Al has professional qualifications in Thinking Big. Until just a little while ago, he was an astrophysicist working for the European Space Agency, with a B.Sc. and Ph.D. in astronomy. And as in the 'Revelation Space' series, he brings to the stories in this collection a scientific rigour that firmly grounds his speculations in theories and ideas current in the happening world. Many of his stories are set on other planets or around distant stars, and most are large in scope, and their plots often turn on lacunae where characters drop out of history for decades or centuries, because of a steadfast refusal to violate Einsteinian principles. Even when some kind of faster-than-light travel is featured, as in the three related stories, 'Hideaway', 'Minla's Flowers' and 'Merlin's Gun', it's both difficult and dangerous – and with typical irony the grail of their protagonist's quest turns out to be something other than the superweapon he was expecting. This sense of cosmic *agape* (and goofy riffs on a certain singer with a penchant for big boots and even bigger spectacles) informs the redemptive arc of Al's last-man-alive story, 'Understanding Space and Time'; in 'Beyond the Aquila Rift', accidental exile isn't something you can get around by reversing the polarity of the neutrino generator; and in 'Angels of Ashes', human survival is revealed to be a matter of quantum probability rather than the predestiny or special pleading that's typical of old space opera. Like all the best New Space Opera writers, Al is deeply in love with the tropes and spectacular disjunctions between human and cosmic scales of the old stuff, but it's a tough love that takes no prisoners.

Other stories are more human in scale, but no less uncompromising. There are explorations of the way in which time affects personality, and how personality and consciousness are defined by memory: the Rashomon-style riddle of the true history of the first Mars landing in 'The Real Story'; the slow transformation of a killing machine and the hope implied by its link with a young girl in 'Enola' (in which that name is redeemed from its association with Hiroshima); the unriddling of the significance of a particular shade of blue in the work of an artist in the moving and wonderfully observed 'Zima Blue'. Two stories share a novel twist on communication with parallel worlds: 'Signal to Noise' is an affecting love story structured as a long goodbye; 'Cardiff Afterlife' uses a War-on-Terror plot to explore the moral implications of importing information from a closely similar history. Another riff on the parallel worlds trope, 'Everlasting', is a two-hander about the implications of the Everett many-worlds hypothesis on individual good fortune, with a neat twist in the tale.

Last, but by no means least, we come to 'Digital to Analogue'. Set in the club scene of the early 1990s, spicing a conspiracy theory about a kind of viral meme that entrains human consciousness with vivid speculation about hive minds, it's perhaps the most atypical Al Reynolds story in the collection (if you define a 'typical' Al Reynolds story as a baroque widescreen space opera in which the hero's fate is interwoven with some kind of cosmic catastrophe). But it's the story in the collection that has the most personal meaning for me, for it was first published in *In Dreams*, an anthology I edited with Kim Newman. Kim and I put out a general call that netted great stories from new writers such as Cliff Burns, Peter F. Hamilton, Steve Rasnic Tem and Jonathan Lethem and Lukas Jaeger; but like all anthology editors we also nagged writers we knew and trusted to produce something suitably wonderful. And Al Reynolds was on my list because it was clear from the get-go that his modest, self-effacing manner was the Clark Kent disguise of an ambitious writer possessed of a boundless enthusiasm for the science fiction and crime genres, eager to push at his limits and experiment with new ways of telling stories.

Like me, Al had a long apprenticeship writing fiction, dating back to his early teens. Unlike me, he managed to keep writing even while engaged in the long hard slog towards winning his Ph.D. And after reading and re-reading the stories collected here, I'm reminded all over again just how much care and craft he puts into his stories. The variety and density of ideas is impressive, the structure and development of their narrative frames are elegantly and solidly wrought, and there's no sense that they strain to achieve their twists and payoffs – a sign both of native talent and of the hard work that goes into disguising the hard work of creating well-rounded stories about unusual situations inhabited by believable and sympathetic characters.

They also demonstrate, like his stand-alone novels *Century Rain*, *Pushing Ice* and *House of Suns*, that he's definitely not a one-note writer. In short, they show exactly why I asked him for a contribution to *In Dreams*, why 'Digital to Analogue' passed the stiff test of Kim Newman's scrutiny with flying colours, and why, some 18 years after we first met, he's still riding at the very cutting edge of science fiction.

Paul McAuley
London, October 2008

I cupped a bowl of coffee in my hands, wondering what I was doing back home. A single word had brought me from Earth; one I'd always expected to hear but after seventeen years had almost forgotten.

That word was *shit*: more or less my state of mind.

Grossart had promised to meet me in a coffee house called Sloths, halfway up Strata City. I'd had to fight my way to a two-seater table by the window, wondering why that table – with easily the best view – just happened to be empty. I soon found out: Sloths was directly under the jumping-off point for the divers, and one of them would often slam past the window. It was like being in a skyscraper after a stock market crash.

'Another drink, madam?' A furry robot waiter had crossed the intestinal tangle of ceiling pipes to arrive above my table.

I stood up decisively. 'No thanks. I'm leaving. And if a man asks for me – for Carrie Clay – you can tell him to take a piss in a sandstorm.'

'Well now, that wouldn't actually be very nice, would it?'

The man had appeared at the table like a ghost. I looked at him as he lowered himself into the other chair, and then I sighed, shaking my head.

'Christ. You could have at least made an effort to look like Grossart, even if being on time was beyond you.'

'Sorry about that. You know how it is with us Martians and punctuality. Or I'm assuming you used to.'

My hackles rose. 'What's that supposed to mean?'

'Well, you've been on Earth for a while, haven't you?' He snapped his fingers at the waiter, which had begun to work its way back across the ceiling. 'We're like the Japanese, really – we never truly trust anyone who goes away and comes back. Two coffees, please.'

I flinched as a diver zipped by. 'Make that one ...' I started saying, but the waiter had already left.

'See, you're committed now.'

I gave the balding, late-middle-aged man another appraisal. 'You're not Jim Grossart. You're not even close. I've seen more convincing—'

'Elvis impersonators?'

'What?'

'That's what they said about Elvis when he came out of hiding. That he didn't look the way they'd been expecting.'

'I haven't got a clue who or what you're talking about.'

'Of course you haven't,' he said, hurriedly apologetic. 'Nor should you. It's my fault – I keep forgetting that not everyone remembers things from as far back as I do.' He gestured towards my vacant chair. 'Now, why don't you sit down so that we can talk properly?'

'Thanks, but no thanks.'

'And I suppose me saying *shit* at this point wouldn't help matters?'

'Sorry,' I said, shaking my head. 'You're going to have to do much better than that.'

It *was* the word, of course – but him knowing it was hardly startling. I wouldn't have come to Mars if someone hadn't contacted my agency with it. The problem was that man didn't seem to be the one I'd been looking for.

It all went back a long time.

I'd made my name covering big stories around Earth – I was the only journalist in Vatican City during the Papal Reboot – but before that I'd been a moderately respected reporter on Mars. I'd covered many stories, but the one of which I was proudest had concerned the first landing, an event that had become murkier and more myth-ridden with every passing decade. It was generally assumed that Jim Grossart and the others had died during the turmoil, but I'd shown that this wasn't necessarily the case. No body had ever been found, after all. The turmoil could just as easily have been an opportunity to vanish out of the public eye, before the pressure of fame became too much. And it was worth remembering that the medical breakthrough that triggered the turmoil in the first place could have allowed anyone from that era to remain alive until now, even though the *Hydra*'s landing had been a century ago.

I'd known even then that it was a long shot, but – by deliberately omitting a single fact that I'd uncovered during my investigations – I'd left a way to be contacted.

'All right,' he said. 'Let me fill you in on some background. The first word spoken on Mars was *shit* – we agree on that – but not everyone knows I said it because I lost my footing on the next-to-last rung of the ladder.'

I allowed my eyebrows to register the tiniest amount of surprise, no more than that. He continued: 'They edited it out of the transmission without anyone noticing. There was already a twenty-minute delay on messages back to Earth, so no one noticed the extra few seconds due to the censorship software. Remember how Neil Armstrong fluffed his lines on the Moon? No one was going to let that happen again.'

The waiter arrived with our coffees, hanging from the ceiling by its four rear limbs while the long front pair placed steaming bowls on the table. The waiter's cheap brown fur didn't quite disguise its underlying robotic skeleton.

'Actually I think it was Louis who fluffed his lines,' I said.

'Louis?'

'Armstrong.' I took a sip of my coffee, the deep butterscotch colour of a true Martian sky. 'The first man on the Moon. But I'll let that pass.'

He waved a hand, dismissing his error. 'Whatever. The point is – or was – that everything said on Mars was relayed to Earth via the *Hydra*. But she didn't just boost the messages; she also kept a copy, burned onto a memory chip. And nothing on the chip was censored.'

I took another cautious sip from the bowl. I'd forgotten how we Martians liked our drinks: beer in Viking-impressing steins and coffee in the sort of bowl from which Genghis Khan might have sipped koumiss after a good day's butchering.

'Tell me how I found the chip and I might stay to finish this.'

'That I can't know for sure.'

'Ah.' I smiled. 'The catch.'

'No, it's just that I don't know who Eddie might have sold the chip to. But Eddie was definitely the man I sold it to. He was a Rastafarian, dealing in trinkets from early Martian history. But the last time I saw Eddie was a fair few decades ago.'

This was, all of a sudden, beginning to look like less of a wasted trip. 'Eddie's just about still in business,' I said, remembering the smell of ganja wafting through his mobile scavenger caravan out on the gentle slopes of the Ares Vallis. 'He never sold the chip, except to me, when I was making my investigations for the *Hydra* piece.'

He pushed himself back in his seat. 'So. Are you prepared to accept that I'm who I say I am?'

'I'm not sure. Yet.'

'But you're less sceptical than a few minutes ago?'

'Possibly,' I said, all that I was going to concede there and then.

'Listen, the way I look isn't my fault. The Grossart you know from your investigations was a kid, a thirty-year-old man.'

'But you must have obtained longevity treatment at some point, or we wouldn't be having this conversation.'

'Correct, but it wasn't the instant the treatment arrived on Mars. Remember that if the treatment had been easily obtainable, there wouldn't have *been* any turmoil. And I was too busy vanishing to worry about it immediately.' He rubbed a hand along his crown: weathered red skin fringed by a bristly white tonsure. 'My physiological age is about seventy, even though I was born one hundred and thirty-two years ago.'

I looked at him more closely now, thinking back to the images of Jim Grossart with which I'd become familiar all those years ago. His face had been so devoid of character – so much a blank canvas – that it had always seemed pointless trying to guess how he would look when he was older. And yet none of my expectations were actually contradicted by the man sitting opposite me.

'If you are Jim Grossart—' My voice was low now.

'There's no "if" about it, Carrie.'

'Then why the hell have you waited seventeen years to speak to me?'

He smiled. 'Finished with that coffee?'

We left Sloths and took an elevator up sixteen city levels to the place where the divers were jumping off. They started the drop from a walkway that jutted out from the city's side for thirty metres, tipped by a ring-shaped platform. Brightly clothed divers waited around the ring – it only had railings on the outside – and now and then one of them would step into the middle and drop. Sometimes they went down in pairs or threes; sometimes joined together. Breathing equipment and a squirrel-suit were all they ever wore; no one ever carried a parachute or a rocket harness.

It looked a lot like suicide. Sometimes, that was just what it was.

'That's got to be fun,' Grossart said, the two of us still snug within the pressurised viewing gallery.

'Yes. If you're clinically insane.'

I immediately wanted to bite back what I'd just said, but Grossart seemed unoffended.

'Oh, cliff diving can't be that difficult – not if you've got a reasonably intuitive grasp of the Navier–Stokes equations and a few basic aerodynamic principles. You can even rent two-person squirrel-suits over there.'

'Don't even think about it.'

'Heights not your thing?' he said, turning – to my immense relief – away from the window. 'Not very Martian of you.'

He was right, though I didn't like admitting it. Gravity on Mars was only slightly less than two-fifths of Earth's – not enough to make much difference if you were planning on falling more than a few metres – but it *was* enough to ensure that Martians grew up experiencing few of the bruising collisions between bone and ground that people on Earth took for granted. Martians viewed heights the way the rest of humanity viewed electricity: merely *understood* to be dangerous, rather than something felt in the pit of the stomach.

And I'd been away too damned long.

'C'mon,' I said. 'Let's check out the tourist junk. My great-great-grandmother'll never forgive me if I don't send her back something seriously tacky.'

Grossart and I went into one of the shops that lined the canyon-side wall of the viewing gallery, pushing past postcard stands flanking the door. The shops were busy, but no one gave us a second glance.

'Christ, look at this,' Grossart said, hefting a paperweight. It was a snow-filled dome with a model of the *Hydra* parked on a red plastic base. There was even a replica of Grossart, a tiny spacesuited figure not much smaller than the lander itself.

'Tasteful,' I said. 'Or, at least, it is compared to this.' I held up a keyring, shaped like a sloth if you were feeling generous.

'No, that's definitely at the quality end of the merchandise. Look.' Grossart picked up an amber stone and read from the label.

'"Sloth healing crystal. This gem modifies and focuses the body's natural chromodynamic fields, ensuring mental and physical harmony."'

'You can't prove it doesn't, can you?'

'No, but I think Brad Treichler might have a few interesting things to say to the proprietor.'

I perked up at the mention of the *Hydra*'s geologist. 'I'd like to meet Treichler as well. And Manuel D'Oliveira, while we're at it. Is it possible?'

'Of course.'

'I mean here, today.'

'I know what you mean, and – yes – it's possible. They're all here, after all.'

'And you don't mind speaking about them?'

'Not at all.' He put down the stone. 'Those guys kept me alive, Carrie. I'll never forget the debt I owe them.'

'I think we all owe them one, in that case.' As I spoke I rummaged through a rack of what purported to be recordings of sloth compositions, some of which were combined with whale sounds or Eskimo throat music. 'Having said that, seeing this must be depressing beyond words.'

'Why, because I was the first man on Mars?' He shook his head. 'I know how you think I should feel. Like Elvis in Graceland's souvenir shop, inspecting an exquisite plastic dashboard figurine of himself. White jumpsuits and hamburgers era, of course.'

I looked at him blankly.

'But I'm not horrified, Carrie. As a matter of fact it actually amuses me.'

I examined a garment displayed prominently on a shelf. *My best friend went to Strata City, Mars, and all I got was this lousy T-shirt*, it said on the front.

'I find that pretty hard to believe, Jim.'

'Then you don't really understand me. What did you think I wanted? Reverence? No. I came to Mars to begin the process of human colonisation. That's why others followed me, because I took that first, difficult step. Oh, and it was difficult, believe me – but I made it all the same.'

I nodded. Though seventeen years had passed since I'd written the piece on the landing, I remembered it all: how Jim Grossart had left Earth on a privately funded expedition done the cheap way – done, in fact, more cheaply than anyone else ever thought possible – with only a vague idea of how to get back from Mars afterwards. His sponsors were going to send out supplies, and then more settlers, until there was a self-sustaining colony. Eventually they'd send a bigger ship to take back anyone who wanted to return, but the expectation was that few people would plan on leaving for good. And that, more or less, was how it had happened – but Grossart's crossing had been every bit as difficult as it had been expected to be, and there had been enough crises along the way to push him to the edge of sanity, and – perhaps – slightly beyond.

It all depended, I supposed, on what you meant by sanity.

Grossart continued: 'You know what would worry me more? A planet that took its past too seriously. Because that would mean there was something human we hadn't brought with us.'

'What, the ineffable tendency to produce and consume tasteless tourist crap?'

'Something like that, yes.' And then he held up a crude plastic mask to his face, and suddenly I was looking at the face of the man I had hoped to meet in Sloths, the young Jim Grossart.

'I don't think you need to worry,' I said.

Grossart returned the mask to a tray with a hundred others, just as the manager of the shop started eyeing us unwelcomingly. 'No, I don't think I do. Now ...' He beamed and rubbed his hands together. 'You know what I'm going to suggest, don't you?'

He was looking out of the shop, back towards the jump-off point.

I suppose the technical term was blackmail. I wanted a story (or at least some idea of why Grossart had contacted me after all these years), and he wanted to take the big dive. More than that, he wanted to do the dive with someone else.

'Look,' I said. 'If it's such a big deal, can't you just do it and I'll see you at the bottom? Or back here?'

'And what if I decided to vanish again? You'd kick yourself, wouldn't you, for letting me out of your sight?'

'Very possibly, but at least I'd have the satisfaction of knowing I hadn't been talked into doing something monumentally stupid.'

We were already in the line for the squirrel-suits. 'Yes,' he said. 'But you'd also have to live with the knowledge that – when you come to write this up, as I know you will – you won't be able to include the sequence in which you took the big dive with Captain Jim Grossart.'

I looked at him coldly. 'Bastard.'

But he was right: personal fear was one thing, compromising a story another.

'Now there's no need for that.'

'Just tell me you know what you're doing, all right?'

'Well, of course I do. Sort of.'

We got our squirrel-suits. The first thing you did was attach the breathing and comms gear. Each suit had only a few minutes of air, but that was all you needed. The suits themselves were lurid skin-tight affairs, padded and marked with glowing logos and slogans. They were so named because they had folds of elastic material sewn between the arms and legs, like the skin of a flying squirrel – enough to double your surface area during a fall. Mine was only moderately stiff across the chest and belly, but Grossart's had a fifteen-centimetre-thick extra layer of frontal armour. We settled on our helmets, locked our visors down and established that we could communicate.

'I'm really not pushing you into this,' Grossart said.

'No, merely playing on the fact that I'm a mercenary bitch who'll do practically anything for a story. Let's just get this over with, shall we?'

We filtered through the airlock that led to the jumping-off stage. Strata City reached away on either side for several hundred metres; buildings crammed as close as the wall's topology would allow. Pressurised walkways snaked between the larger structures, while elevator tubes and staircases connected the city's levels. Not far above, perched on the canyon's lip, a series of large hotel complexes thrust their neon signs against the early dusk sky: Hilton, Holiday Inn, Best Martian.

Then – realising as I did so that it was probably going to be a bad idea – I looked down. The city continued below us for several kilometres, before thinning out into an expanse of sheer, smooth canyon wall that dropped away even more sickeningly. The Valles Marineris was the deepest canyon on Mars, and now that its deepest parts were in shadow, all I could see at the bottom was a concentrated sprinkling of very tiny, distant-looking lights.

'I hope to God you know what you're doing, Jim.'

At the end of the platform an attendant coupled us together, me riding Grossart. With my legs bound together and my arms anchored uncomfortably against my sides, I was little more than a large deadweight on his back.

Another attendant unplugged our air lines from the platform's outlets, so that we were breathing from the suits. Then we shuffled forwards and waited our turn.

I wondered what I was doing. I'd met a man in a bar who had given me some plausible answers about the first landing, but I didn't have a shred of evidence that I was really dealing with Jim Grossart. Perhaps when they peeled me off the bottom of the canyon they'd find that the man was just a local nutcase who'd done his homework.

'Miss?' he said, when we had shuffled closer to the edge.

'What is it?'

'Something you should probably know at this point. I'm not Jim Grossart.'

'No?'

'No. I'm Commander Manuel D'Oliveira. And is there anyone else who you'd rather have for the big dive?'

I thought about what lay ahead – my stomach butterflies doing an aerobatics display by now – and decided he was probably right. D'Oliveira was the *Hydra*'s pilot, the one who had brought the tiny lander down even though half her aerobrake shielding had been ripped off by a mid-flight explosion. It had not been a textbook landing, but given that the alternative consisted of becoming an interesting new smear on the Argyre Planitia, D'Oliveira had not done too badly.

'You'll do nicely, Commander.'

'Manuel, please.' He spoke almost flawless American English, but with the tiniest trace of a Latin accent. 'Tell me – how did you get on with Jim?'

'Oh, fine. I liked him. Apart from the fact that he kept going on about some dead person called Elvis, of course.'

'Yes. You have to humour him in that respect. But he's not too bad, all things considered. We could have had a worse captain, I think. He glued us together. Now then. It seems to be our turn. Are you ready for this, Miss . . . ?'

'Carrie Clay.' It was strange introducing myself again, but it seemed rude not to. 'Yes, I'm ready.'

We shuffled forwards and jumped, falling through the middle of

the ring-shaped platform. I looked up – although I was attached to
D'Oliveira, I could still move my head – and saw the ring-shaped
platform dwindling into the vertical distance. After only a couple
of heartbeats we flashed past the level of Sloths, and then we were
falling still faster. The feeling of weightlessness was not totally
new to me, of course, but the sensation of mounting speed and
proximity to the rushing wall of the city more than compensated.

'There's a trick to this, of course,' D'Oliveira said. He had positioned us into a belly-down configuration, with his arms and legs
spread out. 'A lot of people haven't got the nerve to keep this close
to the side of the city.'

'No shit.'

'But it's a big mistake not to,' D'Oliveira said. 'If you know the
city well, you can keep in nice and close like this. The fatal error is
moving too far out.'

'Really.'

'Oh, yes. Major mistake.' He paused. 'Hmm. Notice anything?
We're not accelerating. You've got your weight back.'

'Silly me. Didn't ... notice.'

'Terminal velocity after forty-five seconds. Already dropped four
kilometres – but you wouldn't guess it, would you?'

Now we were falling down a narrow, vertical canyon with buildings on either side of us and rock on the third face. D'Oliveira
started giving me a lecture on terminal velocities that might well
have been fascinating at any other time; how the refineries had
ramped up the air pressure on Mars to around five per cent of Earth
normal, which – while neither thick nor warm enough to breathe –
was enough to stop a human in a squirrel-suit from dropping like
a stone, even if terminal velocity was still a hair-raising one-sixth
of a kilometre per second.

It was about as welcome as a lecture on human neck anatomy
to someone on the guillotine.

I looked down again and saw that we were beginning to reach
the city's lower-level outskirts. But the canyon wall itself seemed
as high as ever; the lights at the bottom just as far away.

'You know how this city came about, don't you?' D'Oliveira said.

'No ... but I'm ... damn sure you're ... going to ... tell me.'

'It all began with geologists, not long after the turmoil.' He
flipped us around and altered our angle of attack, so that we were
slightly head-down. 'They were looking for traces of ancient fossil

life, buried in rock layers. Eight vertical kilometres wasn't good enough for them, so they dug out the canyon's base for two or three more, then covered a whole vertical strip in scaffolding. They built labs and living modules on the scaffolding, to save going back up to the top all the time.' A chunk of building zipped past close enough to touch – it looked that close, anyway – and then we were falling past rough rock face with only the very occasional structure perched on a ledge. 'But then somewhere else on Mars they uncovered the first sloth relics. The geologists didn't want to miss the action, so they cleared out like shit on wheels, leaving all their things behind.' D'Oliveira steered us around a finger-like rock protrusion that would have speared us otherwise. 'By the time they got back, the scaffolding had been taken over by squatters. Kids, mostly – climbers and base jumpers looking for new thrills. Then someone opened a bar, and before you knew it the place had gone *mainstream*.' He spoke the last word with exquisite distaste. 'But I guess it's not so bad for the tourists.'

'Jim didn't mind, did he?'

'No, but he's not me. I don't mind the fact that we came here, either, and I don't mind the fact that people came after us. But did it have to be so many?'

'You can't ration a planet.'

'I don't want to. But it used to be hard to get here. Months of travel in cramped surroundings. How long did it take you, Miss Clay?'

'Five days on the *Hiawatha*.' It was easier to talk now; what had been terror not many seconds ago transmuting into something almost pleasant. 'And I wouldn't exactly call her cramped. You could argue about the décor in the promenade lounge, but beyond that—'

'I know. I've seen those tourist liners parked around Mars, lighting up the night sky.'

'But if you hadn't come to Mars, we might not have discovered the sloth relics, Manuel. And it was those relics that showed us how to get from Earth to Mars in five days. You can't have it both ways.'

'I know. No one's more fascinated by the sloths than me. It's just – did we have to learn so much, so soon?'

'Well, you'd better get used to it. They're talking about building a starship, you know – a lot sooner than any of us think.'

The rock face had become much smoother now – it was difficult to judge speed, in fact – and the lights at the bottom of the canyon no longer seemed infinitely distant.

'Yes, I've heard about that. Sometimes I almost think I'd like to . . .'

'What, Manuel?'

'Hang on. Time to start slowing down, I think.'

There were only two orthodox ways of slowing down from a big dive, the less skilled of which involved slamming into the ground. The other, trickier way, was to use the fact that the lower part of the canyon wall began to deviate slightly from true vertical. The idea was to drop until you began to scrape against the wall at a tiny grazing angle, and then use friction to kill your speed. Lower down, the wall curved out to merge with the canyon floor, so if you did it properly you could come to a perfect sliding halt with no major injuries. It sounded easy, but – as D'Oliveira told me – it wasn't. The main problem was that people were usually too scared to stay close to the rushing side of the wall when it was sheer. You couldn't blame them for that, since it was pretty nerve-racking and you did have to know exactly where it was safe to fall. But if they stayed too far out they were prolonging the point at which they came into contact with the canyon wall, and by then it wouldn't be a gentle kiss but a high-speed collision at an appreciable angle.

Still, as D'Oliveira assured me, they probably had the best view, while it lasted.

He brought us in for a delicate meeting against the wall, heads down, and then used the fifteen-centimetre-thick armour on his front as a friction break, as if we were tobogganing down a near-vertical slope. The lower part of the wall had already been smooth, but thousands of previous cliff-divers had polished it to glassy perfection.

When it was over – when we had come to an undignified but injury-free halt – attendants escorted us out of the danger zone. The first thing they did was release the fasteners so that we could stand independently. My legs felt like jelly.

'Well?' D'Oliveira said.

'All right, I'll admit it. That was reasonably entertaining. I might even consider doing—'

'Great. There's an elevator that'll take us straight back—'

'Or, on second thought, you could show me to the nearest stiff drink.'

I needn't have worried; D'Oliveira was happy to postpone his next cliff-dive and I was assured that there was a well-stocked bar at the base of the canyon. For a moment, however, we lingered, looking back up that impossible wall of rock, to where the lights of Strata City glimmered far above us. The city had seemed enormous when I'd been inside it; not much smaller when we'd been falling past it – but now it looked tiny, a thin skein of human presence against the monumental vastness of the canyon side.

D'Oliveira put a hand on my forearm. 'Something up?'

'Just thinking, that's all.'

'Bad habit.' He patted me on the back. 'We'll get you that drink now.'

An hour or so later, D'Oliveira and I were sharing a compartment in a train heading away from Strata City.

'We could go somewhere else,' I'd said. 'It's still early, after all, and my body clock still thinks it's mid-afternoon.'

'Bored with Strata City already?'

'Not exactly, no – but somewhere else would make a good contrast.' I was finishing off a vodka and could feel my cheeks flushing. 'I'm going to write this meeting up, you understand.'

'Why not?' He shrugged. 'Jim's told you what he thinks about Mars, so I might as well have my say.'

'Some of it you've already told me.'

He nodded. 'But I could talk all night if you let me. Listen – how about taking a train to Golombek?'

'It's not that far,' I said, after a moment's thought. 'But you know what's there, don't you?'

'It's not a problem for me, Miss Clay. And it isn't the reason I suggested Golombek, anyway. They've recently opened a sloth grotto for public viewing. Haven't had a chance to see it, to be honest, but I'd very much like to.'

I shrugged. 'Well, what are expense accounts for, if not to burn?'

So we'd taken an elevator back to the top of the canyon and picked up the first train heading out to Golombek. The express shot across gently undulating Martian desert, spanning canyons on elegant white bridges grown from structural bone. It was dark, most of the landscape black except for the distant lights of settlements or the vast, squatting shapes of refineries.

'I think I understand now,' I said, 'why you contacted me.'

The man sitting opposite me shrugged. 'It wasn't really me. Jim was the one.'

'Well, maybe. But the point remains. It was time to be heard, wasn't it? Time to set the record straight. That was the problem with vanishing – it let people put things into your mouths that you wouldn't necessarily have agreed with.'

He nodded. 'We've been used by every faction you can think of, whether it's to justify evacuating Mars completely or covering it with kilometre-deep oceans. And it's all bullshit; all lies.'

'But it's not as if you even agree with each other.'

'No, but ...' He paused. 'We might not agree, but at least this is the truth – what we really think – not something invented to suit someone else's agenda. At least it's the real story.'

'And if the real story isn't exactly neat and tidy?'

'It's still true.'

He looked, of course, very much like Jim Grossart. I won't say they were precisely the same, since D'Oliveira seemed to inhabit the same face differently, pulling the facial muscles into a configuration all of his own. He deported himself differently, as well, sitting with slightly more military bearing.

Even by the time I'd done my article – more than eighty years after the landing – no one really understood quite what had happened to Captain Jim Grossart. All anyone agreed on was the basics: Grossart had been normal when he left Earth as the only inhabitant of a one-man Mars expedition.

Maybe it was the accident that had done it, the explosion in deep space that had damaged *Hydra*'s aerobraking shields. The explosion also caused a communication blackout, which lasted several weeks, and it was only when the antenna began working again that anyone could be sure that Grossart had survived at all. Over the next few days, as he began sending messages back home, the truth slowly dawned. Jim Grossart had cracked, fracturing into three personalities. Grossart himself was only one-third of the whole, with two new and entirely fictitious selves sharing his head. Each took on some of the skills that had previously been part of Grossart's overall expertise; D'Oliveira inheriting Grossart's piloting abilities and Treichler becoming the specialist in Martian physics and geology. And – worried about inflicting more harm than necessary on a man who was almost over the edge – the mission controllers back on Earth played along with him. They must have hoped he'd reintegrate as soon as the crisis was over, perhaps when the *Hydra* had safely landed.

But it never happened.

'Do you ever think back to what it was like before?' I said, aware that I was on dangerous ground.

'Before what, exactly?'

'The crossing.'

He shook his head. 'I'm not really one to dwell on the past, I'm afraid.'

Golombek was a glittery, gaudy sprawl of domes, towers and connecting tubes; a pile of Christmas tree decorations strewn with tinsel. The train dived into a tunnel, then emerged into a dizzying underground mall. We got off, spending a lazy hour wandering the shopping galleries before stopping for a drink in a theme bar called Sojourners. The floor was covered with fake dust and the hideously overpriced drinks arrived on little flat-topped, six-wheeled rovers that kept breaking down. I ended up paying, just as I'd paid for the train tickets, but I didn't mind. D'Oliveira, or Grossart, or whoever it was best to think of him as, obviously didn't have much money to throw around. He must have been nearly invisible as far as the Martian economy was concerned.

'It was true what you said earlier on, wasn't it?' I said, while we rode a tram towards the sloth grotto. 'About no one being more fascinated by the aliens than you were.'

'Yes. Even if the others sometimes call me a mystical fool. To Jim they're just dead aliens, a useful source of new technologies but nothing more than that. Me, I think there's something deeper; that we were *meant* to find them, meant to come this far and then continue the search, even if that means some of us leaving Mars altogether ...' He smiled. 'Maybe I've just listened to too much of their music while doing the big dive.'

'And what does Brad Treichler think about them?'

He was silent for a few moments. 'Brad doesn't feel the same way I do.'

'To what extent?'

'To the extent of wondering whether the relics are a poisoned chalice, the extent of wondering whether we should have come to Mars at all.'

'That's an extreme viewpoint for someone who risked his life coming here.'

'I know. And not one I share, I hasten to add.'

I made an effort to lighten the mood. 'I'm glad. If you hadn't come to Mars, there'd have been no big dive, and I'd have had to find another way of having the living shit scared out of me.'

'Yes, it does tend to do that the first time, doesn't it?'

'And the second?'

'It's generally worse. The third time, though—'

'I don't think there'll be a third time, Manuel.'

'Not even for a vodka?'

'Not even.'

By then we had arrived at the grotto, a real one that had been laboriously dismantled and relocated from elsewhere on Mars. Apparently the original site was right under one of the aqueducts and would have been flooded in a few years, as soon as they tapped the polar ice.

Inside, it all felt strangely over-familiar. I kept having to remind myself that these were *real* sloth rooms, *real* sloth artefacts and *real* wall frescos; that the sloths had actually inhabited this grotto. Part of my brain, nonetheless, still insisted that the place was just a better-than-average museum mock-up or an upmarket but still slightly kitsch theme-style restaurant: Sloths with better décor.

But they'd really been here. Unlike any mock-up I'd been in, for instance, there was really no floor. Floor was a concept the sloths had never got their furry heads around, the walls merging like an inverted cave roof. Supposedly they'd evolved on a densely forested planet where gruesome predators used to live on the ground. The sloths must have come down at some point – they hadn't evolved an advanced civilisation by wiping their bottoms on leaves all day – but that dislike of the ground must have remained with them. Just as we humans still liked to shut out the dark, the sloths liked to get off the ground and just hang around.

It was all very interesting; I would have been happy to spend hours there, but not all in one go. After two hours of showing scholarly fascination in every exhibit, I'd had enough six-limbed furry aliens to last me a fortnight.

We met up in the souvenir shop attached to the grotto. I bought a T-shirt with a tasteful sloth motif on it; very discreet, with the words *Sloth Grotto, Golombek, Mars* in writing that had been made to look slightly like sloth script if you were not an expert in xenolinguistics.

'Well,' I said, beginning to feel just the tiniest bit tired. 'That was fun. What next?'

'The lander's not far from here,' he said. 'We could check it out, if you like.'

I should have talked him out of it.

It was all very well, D'Oliveira and the others talking as if they were distinct individuals, but the tiny, single-seat lander would be in screaming contradiction to that. Something was surely bound to happen ... but I'd hardly be able to write up my story without dealing with the lander issue.

More than that, D'Oliveira seemed willing to go along with it.

It was another tram ride to the outskirts of Golombek. The city was the first port of call for people coming down from space, so it was teeming at all hours with red-eyed newcomers. Most of the shops, bars and restaurants stayed open around the clock, and that also went for the major tourist attractions. Of these, the *Hydra* was easily the oldest. There'd been a time – long before I was born – when you actually had to take a tour from Golombek to the landing site, but that wasn't the case now. The mountain had come to Mohammed; the city's outskirts surrounding the ship in a pincer movement.

D'Oliveira and I spent a while looking down from the pressurised viewing gallery. On either side the city reached away from us in a horseshoe shape, enclosing a square half-kilometre of Martian surface. The lander was in the middle: a tiny lopsided silver cone looking slightly less impressive than the one in the paperweight Jim had shown me. I looked at the other visitors, and observed the way they couldn't quite hide their disappointment. I couldn't blame them: I remembered the way I'd first felt on seeing *Hydra*.

Is that all there is?

But I was older now, and I didn't feel the same way. Yes, it was tiny; yes, it looked barely capable of surviving the next dust storm – but that was the point. If the lander had been more impressive, Jim Grossart's achievement wouldn't have been half the thing it was.

'Fancy taking a closer look?' I said eventually.

'For old time's sake . . . why not?'

I should have realised then, of course: there was something different about his voice.

We made our way from the gallery to the surface level. People were waiting to board robot buses that followed a pre-programmed track around the landing site, exactly the way I'd done as a child.

'We don't need to do it like that,' he said. 'You can rent a spacesuit and walk out there if you like.'

'All the way to the lander?'

'No, they don't allow that. But you can still get a lot closer than with the buses.'

I looked out into the arena and saw that there were three people wandering around in sand-coloured suits. One was taking photos of the other two standing in front of the lander, obviously trying to frame the picture so that the backdrop didn't include any parts of the city. My companion was right: the people in suits were nearer to the ship than the buses allowed, but they were still forty or fifty metres from the lander, and they didn't seem inclined to get any closer.

Most of the tourists couldn't be bothered with the hassle of renting the suits, so it didn't take long to get outfitted.

'I think they come in two sizes,' I said, when we were waiting in the airlock. 'Too small and too large.'

He looked at me without a trace of humour. 'They'll suffice.'

The penny dropped. 'Of course, Brad.'

We stepped outside. It was dark overhead, but the landing site was daytime-bright, almost shadowless. The lander stood two hundred metres from us, surrounded by a collection of equipment modules, surface rovers, scientific instruments and survival packages. It looked like a weatherworn Celtic obelisk encircled by a collection of marginally less sacred stones.

'Well, Brad,' I said. 'I've heard a lot about you.'

'I know what you've heard.'

'You do?'

We started walking across the rust-coloured ground.

'I know what Grossart and D'Oliveira say about me, don't you worry.'

'What, that you're not as convinced as they are that coming

to Mars was such a good idea? It's hardly intended as criticism. Everyone's entitled to an opinion.'

Even three at the same time, I thought.

'They're right, of course – I don't think we should have come here – but if that was all they said . . .' He paused, allowing a glass-bodied bus to cross in front of us, surfing through the loosely packed dust on its wide balloon wheels. The tourists were crammed inside, but some of them looked more interested in their snacks than in the *Hydra*.

'What else do they say, Brad?'

'You know, of course, so why pretend otherwise?'

'I'm really not sure—'

'The explosion, damn you. The one that happened in mid-crossing. The one that nearly prevented us landing at all. They say I did it; tried to sabotage the mission.'

'Actually, they hardly mentioned it at all, if ever.'

'Oh, you're good, I'll grant you that.'

'I know, but that's not the point. You couldn't have sabotaged the mission, anyway—' But I stopped, because there was only one place that particular argument was headed. *Because you didn't exist then, just as you don't exist now. Because back then Jim Grossart was all there was . . .*

I said, lamely: 'Even if you'd had second thoughts, you wouldn't have done something like that.'

'No.' His voice was softer now – almost trusting. 'But perhaps I should have.'

'I don't agree. Mars wasn't some pristine wilderness before we came, Brad. It was nothing; just a miserably cold and sterile blank canvas. We haven't ruined it, haven't spoiled anything.'

He stopped and looked around, taking in the tiered galleries of the city that leaned over us like a frozen wave. 'You call this an improvement?'

'On nothing at all, yes.'

'I call it an abomination.'

'Christ, we've only been here a century. This is just our first draft at living on Mars. So what if it isn't the best we could ever do? There'll be time for us to do better.'

He didn't answer for a few seconds. 'You sound like you agree with Jim Grossart.'

'No; I could live without some of the things Jim seems to cherish, believe me. Maybe when it all comes home, I'm closer to Manuel D'Oliveira.'

We carried on walking again, approaching the lander's encirclement.

'That mystical fool?'

'He may be a mystical fool, but he can sure as hell do the big dive.' I paused, wondering why I was defending one aspect of a man's personality against another. But D'Oliveira felt as real to me then as anyone I'd ever met, as equally worthy of my loyalty. 'And he's right, too – not coming to Mars would have been the greatest mistake humanity could have made. I'm not just talking about the relics either. They'll open a few doors for us, but even if we'd come here and found nothing but dust, it would still have been right. It's the space Mars gives us that makes the difference; the room to make mistakes.'

'No,' he said. 'We already made the greatest mistake. And I could have stopped it.'

We were close to the lander now – no more than forty-odd metres from it, I'd have guessed, but I noticed that the other people were no nearer. Walking side by side, we took a few more footsteps towards the centre, but then our suits began to warn us against getting closer: lights flashing around the faceplate and a softly insistent voice in the headphones. I felt my suit stiffen slightly as well – it was suddenly harder to take the next step.

'Then speak out about it,' I said forcefully. 'Come out of hiding. Tell everyone what you think. I guarantee they'll listen. No one else has your perspective.'

'That's the problem. Too much perspective.'

We were close enough to the lander now that he must have been finding it hard to sustain the illusion that three men had come down in it. I'd feared this moment and at the same time felt a spine-tingling sense of anticipation about what would happen.

'I'll make sure they listen, Brad. That was why Jim contacted me, wasn't it? To have his story heard, his views on Mars known? And didn't he mean for all of you to have your say?'

'No.' He began fiddling with the latch of his helmet. 'Because it wasn't Jim who contacted you, it was me. Jim Grossart isn't real, don't you understand? There was only ever me.' He nodded at the lander, even while he struggled with his helmet. 'You don't think I'm stupid, do you?'

I tried to pull his hands away from the neck-ring. 'What are you doing?' I shouted.

'What I always planned to do. What it took me seventeen years to summon up the courage to do.'

'I don't understand.'

'Words won't make a difference now. Mars needs something stronger. It needs a martyr.'

'No!'

I fought with him, but he was a lot stronger than me. There was no unnecessary violence in the way he pushed me away – it was done as gently as circumstances allowed – but I ended up on my back in the dust, looking up as he removed his helmet and took a last long inhalation of thin, cold Martian air.

He took a few steps towards the lander, his skin turning blue, his eyes frosting over, and then stumbled, one arm extended, fingers grasping towards the *Hydra*. Then his suit must have locked rigid, immobilising him.

He looked like a statue that had been there for years.

It shouldn't have been possible, I kept telling myself. There are supposed to be safeguards that stop you doing that kind of thing in anything less than a breathable atmosphere; rigidly adhered-to rules ensuring that equipment for hire is checked and rechecked for compliance; doubly and triply redundant protective systems.

But I guess the suits we'd rented just didn't quite live up to those high ideals.

He died, but that means even less now than it did once upon a time. They got him inside reasonably quickly, and though the exposure to the Martian atmosphere had done a lot of harm, and although there was extensive neural damage, all of these things could be repaired given time and – more importantly – money.

'Who's the old man, anyway?' the medics asked me, after I had arranged for my firm to pay for his medical care, no matter how long it took. That had taken some arguing, incidentally, especially after I told them there wasn't going to be a story for a while.

'I don't know,' I said. 'He never did tell me his name, but he was interesting enough company.'

The tech smiled. 'We ran a gene profile, but the old coot didn't show up in the records. Doesn't mean much, of course.'

'No. A lot of people with criminal pasts vanished during the turmoil.'

'Yeah,' the medic said, already losing interest.

They kept talking about him as an old man, and it wasn't until I saw his comatose body that I understood why. He did look much older than he had ever seemed in any of his three guises, as if even his semblance of middle age had been an illusion.

His coma was deep, and the restorative brain surgery was performed slowly and painstakingly. I followed the progress closely at first – checking up on him every week, then every month. But nothing ever happened; he never showed any signs of emerging and all the usual techniques for kick-starting a mind back to consciousness were unsuccessful. The medics kept suggesting they call it a day, but so long as funds were arriving from my firm, they didn't mind wasting their time.

I checked on his progress every six months, then perhaps once a year.

And life, of course, went on. I couldn't see any dignified way of finishing the story – not while the principal player was in a coma – so it just stalled while I covered other pieces. Some of them were moderately big, and after a while there came a point when I consigned the whole Jim Grossart story to the bottom drawer: a wild goose chase that hadn't ended up anywhere. I even stopped being sure that I'd ever met him at all. After that, it was a simple matter of forgetting all about him.

I don't think I've given him a moment's thought in the last two or three years.

Until today.

I still visit Sloths now and then. It happens to be a reasonably trendy media hangout now, a place to pick up the ground tremors of rumour ahead of the pack.

And there he was, in approximately the same window seat where Jim Grossart had sat ten years ago, looking out at the divers. I read his expression in the window, one of calm, critical detachment, like a judge at a major sporting event.

His face was that of a young man I recognised, but had only ever seen in photographs.

I looked at him for long moments. Perhaps it was just a genetic fluke that had shaped this man who looked like the young Jim

Grossart, but I doubted it. It was the way he sat, the stiff, slightly formal bearing. Except that hadn't been Jim, had it?

Manuel D'Oliveira.

I stared for a moment too long, and somehow my eye caught his, and we found ourselves staring at each other across the room. He didn't turn around from the window but after a few seconds he smiled and nodded.

The bar was packed that night, and a crowd of drinkers surged in front of me, interrupting my line of sight.

When they'd passed, the table was vacant.

I checked with the hospital the day after – it had been at least two years since I'd been in touch – and I was informed that the old man had at last emerged into consciousness. There'd been nothing unusual about him, they said; nothing odd about his psychology.

'What happened then?' I said.

'The funds allowed for some fairly simple rejuvenative procedures,' the medic said, as if restoring youth was about as technically complex – and as interesting – as splinting a fracture.

He hadn't left any means for me to contact him, though.

It might not have been him, I know. It might never have been Jim Grossart I met, and the young man in Sloths could have been anyone with the same set of blandly handsome facial genes.

But there was one other thing.

The old man had emerged from his coma eighteen months before the meeting in the bar, and his rejuvenation had taken place not long after. Which might have meant nothing, except there *was* something different about the night I saw him. Something that was entirely consistent with him having been Manuel D'Oliveira. It was the night the starship left Mars' orbit – the one they've been building there for the last five years, the one that's going out into the galaxy to search for the sloth.

The ship they've named the *Captain James Grossart*.

I like to think he was on his way up to her. I checked the ship's manifest, of course, and there was no one called Grossart, or D'Oliveira, or even Treichler – but that doesn't mean it wasn't him. He'd be travelling under a new name now, one I couldn't even guess. No one would know who he was; just a young man who had volunteered to join the starship's crew; a young man whose interest in the aliens might at times verge on the mystical.

And – on his way up – he hadn't been able to resist one last look at the divers.

Maybe I'm wrong; maybe it was only ever my subconscious playing tricks with a stranger's face, supplying the closure my journalistic instincts demanded, but, the way I see it, it almost doesn't matter. Because all I was ever looking for was a way to finish their story.

Now it can be told.

Things get easier when you break into novels, and they get harder, too. Easier because people suddenly start approaching you to write stories for them, and markets that once seemed closed now appear, if not open, then at least theoretically crackable. But by the same token a contract to write novels usually means deadlines, and all of a sudden you find that novels have to take precedence over short fiction if your writing time is finite. I went from being very prolific in the late nineties to not very prolific at all as the new century rolled in. 'The Real Story' is one of the few original pieces I finished in 2000. Written for Peter Crowther's Mars Probes *original anthology, it was a story that had been at the back of my mind for more than a few years, kicked off by watching a TV documentary about people with multiple-personality disorder. The heroine of the story, ace reporter Carrie Clay, shows up in 'Zima Blue' nearly a thousand years later. Carrie's universe is one where FTL travel is not only possible but easy, and – I'd suggest – not a bad place to live, especially compared to the backgrounds of some of my other stories. One day I'd like to have enough stories to collect a book full of Carrie tales. At the current rate of one every four years, though, no one should hold their breath.*

Greta's with me when I pull Suzy out of the surge tank.

'Why her?' Greta asks.

'Because I want her out first,' I say, wondering if Greta's jealous. I don't blame her: Suzy's beautiful, but she's also smart. There isn't a better syntax runner in Ashanti Industrial.

'What happened?' Suzy asks, when she's over the grogginess. 'Did we make it back?'

I ask her to tell me the last thing she remembers.

'Customs,' Suzy says. 'Those pricks on Arkangel.'

'And after that? Anything else? The runes? Do you remember casting them?'

'No,' she says, then picks up something in my voice. The fact that I might not be telling the truth, or telling her all she needs to know. 'Thom. I'll ask you again. Did we make it back?'

'Yeah,' I say. 'We made it back.'

Suzy looks back at the starscape, airbrushed across her surge tank in luminous violet and yellow paint. She'd had it customised on Carillon. It was against regs: something about the paint clogging intake filters. Suzy didn't care. She told me it had cost her a week's pay, but it had been worth it to impose her own personality on the grey company architecture of the ship.

'Funny how I feel like I've been in that thing for months.'

I shrug. 'That's the way it feels sometimes.'

'Then nothing went wrong?'

'Nothing at all.'

Suzy looks at Greta. 'Then who are you?' she asks.

Greta says nothing. She just looks at me expectantly. I start shaking, and realise I can't go through with this. Not yet.

'End it,' I tell Greta.

Greta steps towards Suzy. Suzy reacts, but she isn't quick enough.

Greta pulls something from her pocket and touches Suzy on the forearm. Suzy drops like a puppet, out cold. We return her to the surge tank, plumb her back in and close the lid.

'She won't remember anything,' Greta says. 'The conversation never left her short-term memory.'

'I don't know if I can go through with this,' I say.

Greta touches me with her other hand. 'No one ever said this was going to be easy.'

'I was just trying to ease her into it gently. I didn't want to tell her the truth right out.'

'I know,' Greta says. 'You're a kind man, Thom.' Then she kisses me.

I remembered Arkangel as well. That was about where it all started to go wrong. We just didn't know it then.

We missed our first take-off slot when customs found a discrepancy in our cargo waybill. It wasn't serious, but it took them a while to realise their mistake. By the time they did, we knew we were going to be sitting on the ground for another eight hours, while inbound control processed a fleet of bulk carriers.

I told Suzy and Ray the news. Suzy took it pretty well, or about as well as Suzy ever took that kind of thing. I suggested she use the time to scour the docks for any hot syntax patches. Anything that might shave a day or two off our return trip.

'Company authorised?' she asked.

'I don't care,' I said.

'What about Ray?' Suzy asked. 'Is he going to sit here drinking tea while I work for my pay?'

I smiled. They had a bickering, love-hate thing going. 'No, Ray can do something useful as well. He can take a look at the q-planes.'

'Nothing wrong with those planes,' Ray said.

I took off my old Ashanti Industrial bib cap, scratched my bald spot and turned to the jib man.

'Right. Then it won't take you long to check them over, will it?'

'Whatever, Skip.'

The thing I liked about Ray was that he always knew when he'd lost an argument. He gathered his kit and went out to check over the planes. I watched him climb the jib ladder, tools hanging from his belt. Suzy got her facemask, long, black coat, and left, vanishing into the vapour haze of the docks, boot heels clicking into the distance long after she'd passed out of sight.

I left the *Blue Goose*, walking in the opposite direction to Suzy. Overhead, the bulk carriers slid in one after the other. You heard them long before you saw them. Mournful, cetacean moans cut down through the piss-yellow clouds over the port. When they emerged, you saw dark hulls scabbed and scarred by the blocky extrusions of syntax patterning, jibs and q-planes retracted for landing and undercarriages clutching down like talons. The carriers stopped over their allocated wells and lowered down on a scream of thrust. Docking gantries closed around them like grasping skeletal fingers. Cargo-handling 'saurs plodded out of their holding pens, some of them autonomous, some of them still being ridden by trainers. There was a shocking silence as the engines cut, until the next carrier began to approach through the clouds.

I always like watching ships coming and going, even when they're holding my own ship on the ground. I couldn't read the syntax, but I knew these ships had come in all the way from the Rift. The Aquila Rift is about as far out as anyone ever goes. At median tunnel speeds, it's a year from the centre of the Local Bubble.

I've been out that way once in my life. I've seen the view from the near side of the Rift, like a good tourist. It was far enough for me.

When there was a lull in the landing pattern, I ducked into a bar and found an Aperture Authority booth that took Ashanti credit. I sat in the seat and recorded a thirty-second message to Katerina. I told her I was on my way back, but that we were stuck on Arkangel for another few hours. I warned her that the delay might cascade through to our tunnel routing, depending on how busy things were at the Authority's end. Based on past experience, an eight-hour ground hold might become a two-day hold at the surge point. I told her I'd be back, but she shouldn't worry if I was a few days late.

Outside a diplodocus slouched by with a freight container strapped between its legs.

I told Katerina I loved her and couldn't wait to get back home.

While I walked back to the *Blue Goose*, I thought of the message racing ahead of me. Transmitted at light-speed up-system, then copied into the memory buffer of the next outgoing ship. Chances were, that particular ship wasn't headed to Barranquilla or any-where near it. The Aperture Authority would have to relay the message from ship to ship until it reached its destination. I might even reach Barranquilla ahead of it, but in all my years of delays that had only happened once. The system worked all right.

Overhead, a white passenger liner had been slotted in between the bulk carriers. I lifted up my mask to get a better look at it. I got a hit of ozone, fuel and dinosaur dung. That was Arkangel all right. You couldn't mistake it for any other place in the Bubble. There were four hundred worlds out there, up to a dozen surface ports on every planet, and none of them smelled bad in quite the same way.

'Thom?'

I followed the voice. It was Ray, standing by the dock.

'You finished checking those planes?' I asked.

Ray shook his head. 'That's what I wanted to talk to you about. They were a little off-alignment, so – seeing as we're going to be sitting here for eight hours – I decided to run a full recalibration.'

I nodded. 'That was the idea. So what's the prob?'

'The *prob* is a slot just opened up. Tower says we can lift in thirty minutes.'

I shrugged. 'Then we'll lift.'

'I haven't finished the recal. As it is, things are worse than before I started. Lifting now would not be a good idea.'

'You know how the tower works,' I said. 'Miss two offered slots, you could be on the ground for days.'

'No one wants to get back home sooner than I do,' Ray said.

'So cheer up.'

'She'll be rough in the tunnel. It won't be a smooth ride home.'

I shrugged. 'Do we care? We'll be asleep.'

'Well, it's academic. We can't leave without Suzy.'

I heard boot heels clicking toward us. Suzy came out of the fog, tugging her own mask aside.

'No joy with the rune monkeys,' she said. 'Nothing they were selling I hadn't seen a million times before. Fucking cowboys.'

'It doesn't matter,' I said. 'We're leaving anyway.'

Ray swore. I pretended I hadn't heard him.

I was always the last one into a surge tank. I never went under until I was sure we were about to get the green light. It gave me a chance to check things over. Things can always go wrong, no matter how good the crew.

The *Blue Goose* had come to a stop near the AA beacon that marked the surge point. There were a few other ships ahead of us in the queue, plus the usual swarm of AA service craft. Through an observation blister I was able to watch the larger ships depart one by one. Accelerating at maximum power, they seemed to streak towards a completely featureless part of the sky. Their jibs were spread wide, and the smooth lines of their hulls were gnarled and disfigured with the cryptic alien runes of the routing syntax. At twenty gees it was as if a huge invisible hand snatched them away into the distance. Ninety seconds later, there'd be a pale-green flash from a thousand kilometres away.

I twisted around in the blister. There were the foreshortened symbols of our routing syntax. Each rune of the script was formed from a matrix of millions of hexagonal platelets. The platelets were on motors so they could be pushed in or out from the hull.

Ask the Aperture Authority and they'll tell you that the syntax is now fully understood. This is true, but only up to a point. After two centuries of study, human machines can now construct and interpret the syntax with an acceptably low failure rate. Given a desired destination, they can assemble a string of runes that will almost always be accepted by the aperture's own machinery. Furthermore, they can almost always guarantee that the desired routing is the one that the aperture machinery will provide.

In short, you usually get where you want to go.

Take a simple point-to-point transfer, like the Hauraki run. In that case there is no real disadvantage in using automatic syntax generators. But for longer trajectories – those that may involve six or seven transits between aperture hubs – machines lose the edge. They find a solution, but usually it isn't the optimum one. That's where syntax runners come in. People like Suzy have an intuitive grasp of syntax solutions. They dream in runes. When they see a poorly constructed script, they feel it like toothache. It *affronts* them.

A good syntax runner can shave days off a route. For a company like Ashanti Industrial, that can make a lot of difference.

But I wasn't a syntax runner. I could tell when something had gone wrong with the platelets, but I had to trust that Suzy had done her job. I had no other choice.

But I knew Suzy wouldn't screw things up.

I twisted around and looked back the other way. Now that we were in space, the q-planes had deployed. They were swung out from the hull on triple hundred-metre-long jibs, like the arms of a grapple. I checked that they were locked in their fully extended positions and that the status lights were all in the green. The jibs were Ray's area. He'd been checking the alignment of the ski-shaped q-planes when I ordered him to close up ship and prepare to lift. I couldn't see any visible indication that they were out of alignment, but then again it wouldn't take much to make our trip home bumpier than usual. But as I'd told Ray, who cared? The *Blue Goose* could take a little tunnel turbulence. It was built to.

I checked the surge point again. Only three ships ahead of us.

I went back to the surge tanks and checked that Suzy and Ray were all right. Ray's tank had been customised at the same time that Suzy had had hers done. It was covered with images of what Suzy called the BVM: the Blessed Virgin Mary. The BVM was always in a spacesuit, carrying a little spacesuited Jesus. Their helmets were airbrushed gold halos. The artwork had a cheap, hasty look to it. I assumed Ray hadn't spent as much as Suzy.

Quickly I stripped down to my underclothes. I plumbed into my own unpainted surge tank and closed the lid. The buffering gel sloshed in. Within about twenty seconds I was already feeling drowsy. By the time traffic control gave us the green light I'd be asleep.

I've done it a thousand times. There was no fear, no apprehension. Just a tiny flicker of regret.

I've never seen an aperture. Then again, very few people have.

Witnesses report a doughnut-shaped lump of dark chondrite asteroid, about two kilometres across. The entire middle section has been cored out, with the inner part of the ring faced by the quixotic-matter machinery of the aperture itself. They say the q-matter machinery twinkles and moves all the while, like the ticking innards of a very complicated clock. But the monitoring systems of the Aperture Authority detect no movement at all.

It's alien technology. We have no idea how it works, or even who made it. Maybe, in hindsight, it's better not to be able to see it.

It's enough to dream, and then awake, and know that you're somewhere else.

*

Try a different approach, Greta says. Tell her the truth this time. Maybe she'll take it easier than you think.

'There's no way I can tell her the truth.'

Greta leans one hip against the wall, one hand still in her pocket. 'Then tell her something halfway truthful.'

We un-plumb Suzy and haul her out of the surge tank.

'Where are we?' she asks. Then to Greta: 'Who are you?'

I wonder if some of the last conversation did make it out of Suzy's short-term memory after all.

'Greta works here,' I say.

'Where's here?'

I remember what Greta told me. 'A station in Schedar Sector.'

'That's not where we're meant to be, Thom.'

I nod. 'I know. There was a mistake. A routing error.'

Suzy's already shaking her head. 'There was nothing wrong—'

'I know. It wasn't your fault.' *I help her into her ship clothes. She's still shivering, her muscles reacting to movement after so much time in the tank.* 'The syntax was good.'

'Then what?'

'The system made a mistake, not you.'

'Schedar sector . . .' *Suzy says.* 'That would put us about ten days off our schedule, wouldn't it?'

I try and remember what Greta said to me the first time. I ought to know this stuff by heart, but Suzy's the routing expert, not me. 'That sounds about right,' *I say.*

But Suzy shakes her head. 'Then we're not in Schedar Sector.'

I try to sound pleasantly surprised.

'We're not?'

'I've been in that tank for a lot longer than a few days, Thom. I know. I can feel it in every fucking bone in my body. So where are we?'

I turn to Greta. I can't believe this is happening again.

'End it,' *I say.*

Greta steps towards Suzy.

You know that 'as soon as I awoke I knew everything was wrong' cliché? You've probably heard it a thousand times, in a thousand bars across the Bubble, wherever ship crews swap tall tales over flat, company-subsidised beer. The trouble is that sometimes that's exactly the way it happens. I never felt good after a period in the surge tank. But the only time I had ever come around feeling anywhere near this bad was after that trip I took to the edge of the Bubble.

Mulling this, but knowing there was nothing I could do about it until I was out of the tank, it took me half an hour of painful work to free myself from the connections. Every muscle fibre in my body felt like it had been shredded. Unfortunately, the sense of wrongness didn't end with the tank. The *Blue Goose* was much too quiet. We should have been heading away from the last exit aperture after our routing. But the distant, comforting rumble of the fusion engines wasn't there at all. That meant we were in free-fall.

Not good.

I floated out of the tank, grabbed a handhold and levered myself around to view the other two tanks. Ray's largest BVM stared back radiantly from the cowl of his tank. The bio indices were all in the green. Ray was still unconscious, but there was nothing wrong with him. Same story with Suzy. Some automated system had decided I was the only one who needed waking.

A few minutes later I had made my way to the same observation blister I'd used to check the ship before the surge. I pushed my head into the scuffed glass half-dome and looked around.

We'd arrived somewhere. The *Blue Goose* was sitting in a huge, zero-gravity parking bay. The chamber was an elongated cylinder, hexagonal in cross section. The walls were a smear of service machinery: squat modules, snaking umbilical lines, the retracted cradles of unused docking berths. Whichever way I looked I saw other ships locked onto cradles. Every make and class you could think of, every possible configuration of hull design compatible with aperture transitions. Service lights threw a warm golden glow on the scene. Now and then the whole chamber was bathed in the stuttering violet flicker of a cutting torch.

It was a repair facility.

I was just starting to mull on that when I saw something extend itself from the wall of the chamber. It was a telescopic docking tunnel, groping towards our ship. Through the windows in the side of the tunnel I saw figures floating, pulling themselves along hand over hand.

I sighed and started making my way to the airlock.

By the time I reached the lock they were already through the first stage of the cycle. Nothing wrong with that – there was no good reason to prevent foreign parties boarding a vessel – but it *was* just a tiny bit impolite. But perhaps they'd assumed we were all asleep.

The door slid open.

'You're awake,' a man said. 'Captain Thomas Gundlupet of the *Blue Goose*, isn't it?'

'Guess so,' I said.

'Mind if we come in?'

There were about half a dozen of them, and they were already coming in. They all wore slightly timeworn ochre overalls, flashed with too many company sigils. My hackles rose. I didn't really like the way they were barging in.

'What's up?' I said. 'Where are we?'

'Where do you think?' the man said. He had a face full of stubble, with bad yellow teeth. I was impressed by that. Having bad teeth took a lot of work these days. It was years since I'd seen anyone who had the same dedication to the art.

'I'm really hoping you're not going to tell me we're still stuck in Arkangel System,' I said.

'No, you made it through the gate.'

'And?'

'There was a screw-up. Routing error. You didn't pop out of the right aperture.'

'Oh, Christ.' I took off my bib cap. 'It never rains. Something went wrong with the insertion, right?'

'Maybe. Maybe not. Who knows how these things happen? All we know is you aren't supposed to be here.'

'Right. And where is "here"?'

'Saumlaki Station. Schedar Sector.'

He said it as though he was already losing interest, as if this was a routine he went through several times a day.

He might have been losing interest. I wasn't.

I'd never heard of Saumlaki Station, but I'd certainly heard of Schedar Sector. Schedar was a K supergiant out towards the edge of the Local Bubble. It defined one of the seventy-odd navigational sectors across the whole Bubble.

Did I mention the Bubble already?

You know how the Milky Way Galaxy looks; you've seen it a thousand times, in paintings and computer simulations. A bright central bulge at the galactic core, with lazily curved spiral arms flung out from that hub, each arm composed of hundreds of billions of stars, ranging from the dimmest, slow-burning dwarfs to the hottest supergiants teetering on the edge of supernova extinction.

Now zoom in on one arm of the Milky Way. There's the sun, orange-yellow, about two-thirds out from the centre of the galaxy. Lanes and folds of dust swaddle the sun out to distances of tens of thousands of light-years. Yet the sun itself is sitting right in the middle of a four-hundred-light-year-wide hole in the dust, a bubble in which the density is about a twentieth of its average value.

That's the Local Bubble. It's as if God blew a hole in the dust just for us.

Except, of course, it wasn't God. It was a supernova, about a million years ago.

Look further out, and there are more bubbles, their walls inter-secting and merging, forming a vast froth-like structure tens of thousands of light-years across. There are the structures of Loop I and Loop II and the Lindblad Ring. There are even superdense knots where the dust is almost too thick to be seen through at all. Black cauls like the Taurus or Rho-Ophiuchi Dark Clouds, or the Aquila Rift itself.

Lying outside the Local Bubble, the Rift is the furthest point in the galaxy we've ever travelled to. It's not a question of endurance or nerve. There simply isn't a way to get beyond it, at least not within the faster-than-light network of the aperture links. The rabbit-warren of possible routes just doesn't reach any further. Most destinations – including most of those on the *Blue Goose*'s itinerary – didn't even get you beyond the Local Bubble.

For us, it didn't matter. There's still a lot of commerce you can do within a hundred light-years of Earth. But Schedar was right on the periphery of the Bubble, where dust density began to ramp up to normal galactic levels, two hundred and twenty-eight light-years from Mother Earth.

Again: not good.

'I know this is a shock for you,' another voice said. 'But it's not as bad as you think it is.'

I looked at the woman who had just spoken. Medium height, the kind of face they called 'elfin', with slanted, ash-grey eyes and a bob of shoulder-length, chrome-white hair.

The face was achingly familiar.

'It isn't?'

'I wouldn't say so, Thom.' She smiled. 'After all, it's given us the chance to catch up on old times, hasn't it?'

'Greta?' I asked, disbelievingly.

She nodded. 'For my sins.'

'My God. It is you, isn't it?'

'I wasn't sure you'd recognise me. Especially after all this time.'

'You didn't have much trouble recognising me.'

'I didn't have to. The moment you popped out we picked up your recovery transponder. Told us the name of your ship, who owned her, who was flying it, what you were carrying, where you were supposed to be headed. When I heard it was you, I made sure I was part of the reception team. But don't worry. It's not like you've changed all that much.'

'Well, you haven't either,' I said.

It wasn't quite true. But who honestly wants to hear that they look about ten years older than the last time you saw them, even if they still don't look all that bad with it? I thought about how she had looked naked, memories that I'd kept buried for a decade spooling into daylight. It shamed me that they were still so vivid, as if some furtive part of my subconscious had been secretly hoarding them through years of marriage and fidelity.

Greta half-smiled. It was as if she knew exactly what I was thinking.

'You were never a good liar, Thom.'

'Yeah. Guess I need some practice.'

There was an awkward silence. Neither of us seemed to know what to say next. While we hesitated the others floated around us, saying nothing.

'Well,' I said. 'Who'd have guessed we'd end up meeting like this?'

Greta nodded and offered the palms of her hands in a kind of apology.

'I'm just sorry we aren't meeting under better circumstances,' she said. 'But if it's any consolation, what happened wasn't at all your fault. We checked your syntax, and there wasn't a mistake. It's just that now and then the system throws a glitch.'

'Funny how no one likes to talk about that very much,' I said.

'Could have been worse, Thom. I remember what you used to tell me about space travel.'

'Yeah? Which particular pearl of wisdom would that have been?'

'If you're in a position to moan about a situation, you've no right to be moaning.'

'Christ. Did I actually say that?'

'Mm. And I bet you're regretting it now. But look, it really isn't that bad. You're only twenty days off-schedule.' Greta nodded towards the man who had the bad teeth. 'Kolding says you'll only need a day of damage repair before you can move off again, and then another twenty, twenty-five days before you reach your destination, depending on routing patterns. That's less than six weeks. So you lose the bonus on this one. Big deal. You're all in good shape, and your ship only needs a little work. Why don't you just bite the bullet and sign the repair paperwork?'

'I'm not looking forward to another twenty days in the surge tank. There's something else, as well.'

'Which is?'

I was about to tell her about Katerina, how she'd have been expecting me back already.

Instead I said: 'I'm worried about the others. Suzy and Ray. They've got families expecting them. They'll be worried.'

'I understand,' Greta said. 'Suzy and Ray. They're still asleep, aren't they? Still in their surge tanks?'

'Yes,' I said, guardedly.

'Keep them that way until you're on your way.' Greta smiled. 'There's no sense worrying them about their families, either. It's kinder.'

'If you say so.'

'Trust me on this one, Thom. This isn't the first time I've handled this kind of situation. Doubt it'll be the last, either.'

I stayed in a hotel overnight, in another part of Saumlaki. The hotel was an echoing, multilevel prefab structure, sunk deep into bedrock. It must have had a capacity for hundreds of guests, but at the moment only a handful of the rooms seemed to be occupied. I slept fitfully and got up early. In the atrium, I saw a bib-capped worker in rubber gloves removing diseased carp from a small ornamental pond. Watching him pick out the ailing, metallic-orange fish, I had a flash of déjà vu. What was it about dismal hotels and dying carp?

Before breakfast – bleakly alert, even though I didn't really feel

43

as if I'd had a good night's sleep – I visited Kolding and got a fresh update on the repair schedule.

'Two, three days,' he said.

'It was a day last night.'

Kolding shrugged. 'You've got a problem with the service, find someone else to fix your ship.'

Then he stuck his little finger into the corner of his mouth and began to dig between his teeth.

'Nice to see someone who really enjoys his work,' I said.

I left Kolding before my mood worsened too much, making my way to a different part of the station.

Greta had suggested we meet for breakfast and catch up on old times. She was there when I arrived, sitting at a table on an 'outdoor' terrace, under a red-and-white-striped canopy, sipping orange juice. Above us was a dome several hundred metres wide, projecting a cloudless holographic sky. It had the hard, enamelled blue of midsummer.

'How's the hotel?' she asked after I'd ordered a coffee from the waiter.

'Not bad. No one seems very keen on conversation, though. Is it me or does that place have all the cheery ambience of a sinking ocean liner?'

'It's just this place,' Greta said. 'Everyone who comes here is pissed off about it. Either they got transferred here and they're pissed off about *that*, or they ended up here by a routing error and they're pissed off about that instead. Take your pick.'

'No one's happy?'

'Only the ones who know they're getting out of here soon.'

'Would that include you?'

'No,' she said. 'I'm more or less stuck here. But I'm okay about it. I guess I'm the exception that proves the rule.'

The waiters were glass mannequins, the kind that had been fashionable in the core worlds about twenty years ago. One of them placed a croissant in front of me, then poured scalding black coffee into my cup.

'Well, it's good to see you,' I said.

'You too, Thom.' Greta finished her orange juice and then took a corner of my croissant for herself, without asking. 'I heard you got married.'

'Yes.'

'Well? Aren't you going to tell me about her?'

I drank some of my coffee. 'Her name's Katerina.'

'Nice name.'

'She works in the Department of Bioremediation on Kagawa.'

'Kids?' Greta asked.

'Not yet. It wouldn't be easy, the amount of time we both spend away from home.'

'Mm.' She had a mouthful of croissant. 'But one day you might think about it.'

'Nothing's ruled out,' I said. As flattered as I was that she was taking such an interest in me, the surgical precision of her questions left me slightly uncomfortable. There was no thrust and parry; no fishing for information. That kind of directness unnerved. But at least it allowed me to ask the same questions. 'What about you, then?'

'Nothing very exciting. I got married a year or so after I last saw you. A man called Marcel.'

'Marcel,' I said, ruminatively, as if the name had cosmic significance. 'Well, I'm happy for you. I take it he's here, too?'

'No. Our work took us in different directions. We're still married, but ...' Greta left the sentence hanging.

'It can't be easy,' I said.

'If it was meant to work, we'd have found a way. Anyway, don't feel too sorry for either of us. We've both got our work. I wouldn't say I was any less happy than the last time we met.'

'Well, that's good,' I said.

Greta leaned over and touched my hand. Her fingernails were midnight black with a blue sheen.

'Look. This is really presumptuous of me. It's one thing asking to meet up for breakfast. It would have been rude not to. But how would you like to meet again later? It's really nice to eat here in the evening. They turn down the lights. The view through the dome is really something.'

I looked up into that endless holographic sky.

'I thought it was faked.'

'Oh, it is,' she said. 'But don't let that spoil it for you.'

I settled in front of the camera and started speaking.

'Katerina,' I said. 'Hello. I hope you're all right. By now I hope someone from the company will have been in touch. If they haven't, I'm pretty sure you'll have made your own enquiries. I'm not sure what they told you, but I promise you that we're safe and sound and that we're coming home. I'm calling from somewhere called Saumlaki Station, a repair facility on the edge of Schedar Sector. It's not much to look at: just a warren of tunnels and centrifuges dug into a pitch-black D-type asteroid, about half a light-year from the nearest star. The only reason it's here at all is because there happens to be an aperture next door. That's how we got here in the first place. Somehow or other *Blue Goose* took a wrong turn in the network, what they call a routing error. The *Goose* came in last night, local time, and I've been in a hotel since then. I didn't call last night because I was too tired and disorientated after coming out of the tank, and I didn't know how long we were going to be here. Seemed better to wait until morning, when we'd have a better idea of the damage to the ship. It's nothing serious – just a few bits and pieces buckled during the transit – but it means we're going to be here for another couple of days. Kolding – he's the repair chief – says three at the most. By the time we get back on course, however, we'll be about forty days behind schedule.'

I paused, eyeing the incrementing cost indicator. Before I sat down in the booth I always had an eloquent and economical speech cued up in my head, one that conveyed exactly what needed to be said, with the measure and grace of a soliloquy. But my mind always dried up as soon as I opened my mouth, and instead of an actor I ended up sounding like a small-time thief, concocting some fumbling alibi in the presence of quick-witted interrogators.

I smiled awkwardly and continued: 'It kills me to think this message is going to take so long to get to you. But if there's a silver lining it's that I won't be far behind it. By the time you get this, I should be home only a couple of days later. So don't waste money replying to this, because by the time you get it I'll already have left Saumlaki Station. Just stay where you are and I promise I'll be home soon.'

That was it. There was nothing more I needed to say, other than: 'I miss you.' Delivered after a moment's pause, I meant it to sound emphatic. But when I replayed the recording it sounded more like an afterthought.

I could have recorded it again, but I doubted that I would have been any happier. Instead I just committed the existing message for transmission and wondered how long it would have to wait before going on its way. Since it seemed unlikely that there was a vast flow of commerce in and out of Saumlaki, our ship might be the first suitable outbound vessel.

I emerged from the booth. For some reason I felt guilty, as if I had been in some way neglectful. It took me a while before I realised what was playing on my mind. I'd told Katerina about Saumlaki Station. I'd even told her about Kolding and the damage to the *Blue Goose*. But I hadn't told her about Greta.

It's not working with Suzy.

She's too smart, too well attuned to the physiological correlatives of surge tank immersion. I can give her all the reassurances in the world, but she knows she's been under too long for this to be anything other than a truly epic screw-up. She knows that we aren't just talking weeks or even months of delay here. Every nerve in her body is screaming that message into her skull.

'I had dreams,' she says, when the grogginess fades.

'What kind?'

'Dreams that I kept waking. Dreams that you were pulling me out of the surge tank. You and someone else.'

I do my best to smile. I'm alone, but Greta isn't far away. The hypodermic's in my pocket now.

'I always get bad dreams coming out of the tank,' I say.

'These felt real. Your story kept changing, but you kept telling me we were somewhere ... that we'd gone a little off course, but that it was nothing to worry about.'

So much for Greta's reassurance that Suzy will remember nothing after our aborted efforts at waking her. Seems that her short-term memory isn't quite as fallible as we'd like.

'It's funny you should say that,' I tell her, 'because, actually, we are a little off course.'

She's sharper with every breath. Suzy was always the best of us at coming out of the tank.

'Tell me how far, Thom.'

'Farther than I'd like.'

She balls her fists. I can't tell if it's aggression, or some lingering neuromuscular effect of her time in the tank. 'How far? Beyond the Bubble?'

'Beyond the Bubble, yes.'

Her voice grows small and childlike.

'Tell me, Thom. Are we out beyond the Rift?'

I can hear the fear. I understand what she's going through. It's the nightmare that all ship crews live with on every trip. That something will go wrong with the routing, something so severe that they'll end up on the very edge of the network. That they'll end up so far from home that getting back will take years, not months. And that, of course, years will have already passed, even before they begin the return trip.

That loved ones will be years older when they reach home.

If they're still there. If they still remember you, or want to remember. If they're still recognisable, or alive.

Beyond the Aquila Rift. It's shorthand for the trip no one ever hopes to make by accident. The one that will screw up the rest of your life, the one that creates the ghosts you see haunting the shadows of company bars across the whole Bubble. Men and women ripped out of time, cut adrift from families and lovers by an accident of an alien technology we use but barely comprehend.

'Yes,' I say. 'We're beyond the Rift.'

Suzy screams, knitting her face into a mask of anger and denial. My hand is cold around the hypodermic. I consider using it.

A new repair estimate from Kolding. Five, six days.

This time I didn't even argue. I just shrugged and walked out, and wondered how long it would be next time.

That evening I sat down at the same table where Greta and I had met over breakfast. The dining area had been well lit before, but now the only illumination came from the table lamps and the subdued lighting panels set into the paving. In the distance, a glass mannequin cycled from empty table to empty table, playing 'Asturias' on a glass guitar. There were no other patrons dining tonight.

I didn't have long to wait for Greta.

'I'm sorry I'm late, Thom.'

I turned to her as she approached the table. I liked the way she walked in the low gravity of the station, the way the subdued lighting traced the arc of her hips and waist. She eased into her seat and leaned towards me in the manner of a conspirator. The lamp on the table threw red shadows and gold highlights across her face. It took ten years off her age.

'You aren't late,' I said. 'And anyway, I had the view.'

'It's an improvement, isn't it?'

'That wouldn't be saying much,' I said with a smile. 'But yes, it's definitely an improvement.'

'I could sit out here all night and just look at it. In fact sometimes that's exactly what I do. Just me and a bottle of wine.'

'I don't blame you.'

Instead of the holographic blue, the dome was now full of stars. It was like no view I'd ever seen from another station or ship. There were furious blue-white stars embedded in what looked like sheets of velvet. There were hard gold gems and soft red tinges, like finger smears in pastel. There were streams and currents of fainter stars, like a myriad neon fish caught in a snapshot of frozen motion. There were vast billowing backdrops of red and green cloud, veined and flawed by filaments of cool black. There were bluffs and promontories of ochre dust, so rich in three-dimensional structure that they resembled an exuberant impasto of oil colours; contours light-years thick laid on with a trowel. Red or pink stars burned through the dust like lanterns. Orphaned worlds were caught erupting from the towers, little sperm-like shapes trailing viscera of dust. Here and there I saw the tiny eyelike knots of birthing solar systems. There were pulsars, flashing on and off like navigation beacons, their differing rhythms seeming to set a stately tempo for the entire scene, like a deathly slow waltz. There seemed too much detail for one view, an overwhelming abundance of richness, and yet no matter which direction I looked, there was yet more to see, as if the dome sensed my attention and concentrated its efforts on the spot where my gaze was directed. For a moment I felt a lurching sense of dizziness, and – though I tried to stop it before I made a fool of myself – I found myself grasping the side of the table, as if to prevent myself from falling into the infinite depths of the view.

'Yes, it has that effect on people,' Greta said.

'It's beautiful,' I said.

'Do you mean beautiful, or terrifying?'

I realised I wasn't sure. 'It's big,' was all I could offer.

'Of course, it's faked,' Greta said, her voice soft now that she was leaning closer. 'The glass in the dome is smart. It exaggerates the brightness of the stars, so that the human eye registers the differences between them. Otherwise the colours aren't unrealistic. Everything else you see is also pretty accurate, if you accept that certain frequencies have been shifted into the visible band, and the scale of certain structures has been adjusted.' She pointed out features for my edification. 'That's the edge of the Taurus Dark Cloud, with the Pleiades just poking out. That's a filament of the Local Bubble. You see that open cluster?'

She waited for me to answer. 'Yes,' I said.

'That's the Hyades. Over there you've got Betelgeuse and Bellatrix.'

'I'm impressed.'

'You should be. It cost a lot of money.' She leaned back a bit, so that the shadows dropped across her face again. 'Are you all right, Thom? You seem a bit distracted.'

I sighed. 'I just got another prognosis from your friend Kolding. That's enough to put a dent in anyone's day.'

'I'm sorry about that.'

'There's something else, too,' I said. 'Something that's been bothering me since I came out of the tank.'

A mannequin arrived to take our order. I let Greta choose for me.

'You can talk to me about it, whatever it is,' she said, when the mannequin had gone.

'It isn't easy.'

'Something personal, then? Is it about Katerina?' She bit her tongue. 'No, sorry. I shouldn't have said that.'

'It's not about Katerina. Not exactly, anyway.' But even as I said it, I knew that in a sense it *was* about Katerina, and how long it was going to be before we saw each other again.

'Go on, Thom.'

'This is going to sound silly. But I wonder if everyone's being straight with me. It's not just Kolding. It's you as well. When I came out of that tank I felt the same way I felt when I'd been out to the Rift. Worse, if anything. I felt like I'd been in the tank for a long, long time.'

'It feels that way sometimes.'

'I know the difference, Greta. Trust me on this.'

'So what are you saying?'

The problem was that I wasn't really sure. It was one thing to feel a vague sense of unease about how long I'd been in the tank. It was another to come out and accuse my host of lying. Especially when she had been so hospitable.

'Is there any reason you'd lie to me?'

'Come off it, Thom. What kind of a question is that?'

As soon as I had said it, it sounded absurd and offensive to me as well. I wished I could reverse time and start again, ignoring my misgivings.

'I'm sorry,' I said. 'Stupid. Just put it down to messed-up bio-rhythms, or something.'

She reached across the table and took my hand, as she had done at breakfast. This time she continued to hold it.

'You really feel wrong, don't you?'

'Kolding's games aren't helping, that's for sure.' The waiter brought our wine, setting it down, the bottle chinking against his delicately articulated glass fingers. The mannequin poured two glasses and I sampled mine. 'Maybe if I had someone else from my crew to bitch about it all with, I wouldn't feel so bad. I know you said we shouldn't wake Suzy and Ray, but that was before a one-day stopover turned into a week.'

Greta shrugged. 'If you want to wake them, no one's going to stop you. But don't think about ship business now. Let's not spoil a perfect evening.'

I looked up at the starscape. It was heightened, with the mad shimmering intensity of a Van Gogh nightscape.

It made one feel drunk and ecstatic just to look at it.

'What could possibly spoil it?' I asked.

What happened is that I drank too much wine and ended up sleeping with Greta. I'm not sure how much of a part the wine played in it for her. If her relationship with Marcel was in as much trouble as she'd made out, then obviously she had less to lose than I did. Yes, that made it all right, didn't it? She the seductress, her own marriage a wreck, me the hapless victim. I'd lapsed, yes, but it wasn't really my fault. I'd been alone, far from home, emotionally fragile, and she had exploited me. She had softened me up with a romantic meal, her trap already sprung.

Except all that was self-justifying bullshit, wasn't it? If my own marriage was in such great shape, why had I failed to mention Greta when I called home? At the time, I'd justified that omission as an act of kindness towards my wife. Katerina didn't know that Greta and I had ever been a couple. But why worry Katerina by mentioning another woman, even if I pretended that we'd never met before?

Except – now – I could see that I'd failed to mention Greta for another reason entirely. Because in the back of my mind, even then, there had been the possibility that we might end up sleeping together.

I was already covering myself when I called Katerina. Already making sure there wouldn't be any awkward questions when I got home. As if I not only knew what was going to happen but secretly yearned for it.

The only problem was that Greta had something else in mind.

'Thom,' Greta said, nudging me towards wakefulness. She was lying naked next to me, leaning on one elbow, with the sheets crumpled down around her hips. The light in her room turned her into an abstraction of milky blue curves and deep violet shadows. With one black-nailed finger she traced a line down my chest and said: 'There's something you need to know.'

'What?' I asked.

'I lied. Kolding lied. We all lied.'

I was too drowsy for her words to have much more than a vaguely troubling effect. All I could say, again, was: 'What?'

'You're not in Saumlaki Station. You're not in Schedar Sector.'

I started waking up properly. 'Say that again.'

'The routing error was more severe than you were led to believe. It took you far beyond the Local Bubble.'

I groped for anger, even resentment, but all I felt was a dizzying sensation of falling. 'How far out?'

'Further than you thought possible.'

The next question was obvious.

'Beyond the Rift?'

'Yes,' she said, with the faintest of smiles, as if humouring me in a game whose rules and objectives she found ultimately demeaning. 'Beyond the Aquila Rift. A long, long way beyond it.'

'I need to know, Greta.'

She pushed herself from the bed, reached for a gown. 'Then get dressed. I'll show you.'

I followed Greta in a daze.

She took me to the dome again. It was dark, just as it had been the night before, with only the lamp-lit tables to act as beacons. I supposed that the illumination throughout Saumlaki Station (or wherever this was) was at the whim of its occupants, and didn't necessarily have to follow any recognisable diurnal cycle. None-theless it was still unsettling to find it changed so arbitrarily. Even if Greta had the authority to turn out the lights when she wanted to, didn't anyone else object?

But I didn't see anyone else *to* object. There was no one else around; only a glass mannequin standing at attention with a napkin over one arm.

She sat us at a table. 'Do you want a drink, Thom?'

'No, thanks. For some reason I'm not quite in the mood.'

She touched my wrist. 'Don't hate me for lying to you. It was done out of kindness. I couldn't break the truth to you in one go.'

Sharply I withdrew my hand. 'Shouldn't I be the judge of that? So what is the truth, exactly?'

'It's not good, Thom.'

'Tell me, then I'll decide.'

I didn't see her do anything, but suddenly the dome was filled with stars again, just as it had been the night before.

The view lurched, zooming outwards. Stars flowed by from all sides, like white sleet. Nebulae ghosted past in spectral wisps. The sense of motion was so compelling that I found myself gripping the table, seized by vertigo.

'Easy, Thom,' Greta whispered.

The view lurched, swerved, contracted. A solid wall of gas slammed past. Now, suddenly, I had the sense that we were outside something – that we had punched beyond some containing sphere, defined only in vague arcs and knots of curdled gas, where the interstellar gas density increased sharply.

Of course. It was obvious. We were beyond the Local Bubble.

And we were still receding. I watched the Bubble itself contract, becoming just one member in the larger froth of voids. Instead of individual stars, I saw only smudges and motes, aggregations of hundreds of thousands of suns. It was like pulling back from a close-up view of a forest. I could still see clearings, but the individual trees had vanished into an amorphous mass.

We kept pulling back. Then the expansion slowed and froze. I could still make out the Local Bubble, but only because I had been concentrating on it all the way out. Otherwise, there was nothing to distinguish it from the dozens of surrounding voids.

'Is that how far out we've come?' I asked.

Greta shook her head. 'Let me show you something.'

Again, she did nothing that I was aware of. But the Bubble I had been looking at was suddenly filled with a skein of red lines, like a child's scribble.

'Aperture connections,' I said.

As shocked as I was by the fact that she had lied to me – and as fearful as I was about what the truth might hold – I couldn't turn off the professional part of me, the part that took pride in recognising such things.

Greta nodded. 'Those are the main commerce routes, the well-mapped connections between large colonies and major trading hubs. Now I'll add all mapped connections, including those that have only ever been traversed by accident.'

The scribble did not change dramatically. It gained a few more wild loops and hairpins, including one that reached beyond the wall of the Bubble to touch the sunward end of the Aquila Rift. One or two other additions pierced the wall in different directions, but none of them reached as far as the Rift.

'Where are we?'

'We're at one end of one of those connections. You can't see it because it's pointing directly towards you.' She smiled slightly. 'I needed to establish the scale that we're dealing with. How wide is the Local Bubble, Thom? Four hundred light-years, give or take?'

My patience was wearing thin. But I was still curious.

'About right.'

'And while I know that aperture travel times vary from point to point, with factors depending on network topology and syntax optimisation, isn't it the case that the average speed is about one thousand times faster than light?'

'Give or take.'

'So a journey from one side of the Bubble might take – what, half a year? Say five or six months? A year to the Aquila Rift?'

'You know that already, Greta. We both know it.'

'All right. Then consider this.' And the view contracted again, the Bubble dwindling, a succession of overlaying structures concealing it, darkness coming into view on either side, and then the familiar spiral swirl of the Milky Way Galaxy looming large.

Hundreds of billions of stars, packed together into foaming white lanes of sea spume.

'This is the view,' Greta said. 'Enhanced of course, brightened and filtered for human consumption – but if you had eyes with near-perfect quantum efficiency, and if they happened to be about a metre wide, this is more or less what you'd see if you stepped outside the station.'

'I don't believe you.'

What I meant was I didn't *want* to believe her.

'Get used to it, Thom. You're a long way out. The station's orbiting a brown dwarf star in the Large Magellanic Cloud. You're one hundred and fifty thousand light-years from home.'

'No,' I said, my voice little more than a moan of abject, childlike denial.

'You felt as though you'd spent a long time in the tank. You were dead right. Subjective time? I don't know. Years, easily. Maybe a decade. But objective time – the time that passed back home – is a lot clearer. It took *Blue Goose* one hundred and fifty years to reach us. Even if you turned back now, you'd have been away for three hundred years, Thom.'

'Katerina,' I said, her name like an invocation.

'Katerina's dead,' Greta told me. 'She's already been dead a century.'

How do you adjust to something like that? The answer is that you can't count on adjusting to it at all. Not everyone does. Greta told me that she had seen just about every possible reaction in the spectrum, and the one thing she had learned was that it was next to impossible to predict how a given individual would take the news. She had seen people adjust to the revelation with little more than a world-weary shrug, as if this were merely the latest in a line of galling surprises life had thrown at them, no worse in its way than illness or bereavement or any number of personal setbacks. She had seen others walk away and kill themselves half an hour later.

But the majority, she said, did eventually come to some kind of accommodation with the truth, however faltering and painful the process.

'Trust me, Thom,' she said. 'I know you now. I know you have the emotional strength to get through this. I know you can learn to live with it.'

'Why didn't you tell me straight away, as soon as I came out of the tank?'

'Because I didn't know if you were going to be able to take it.'

'You waited until after you knew I had a wife.'

'No,' Greta said. 'I waited until after we'd made love. Because then I knew Katerina couldn't mean that much to you.'

'Fuck you.'

'Fuck me? Yes, you did. That's the point.'

I wanted to strike out against her. But what I was angry at was not her insinuation but the cold-hearted truth of it. She was right, and I knew it. I just didn't want to deal with that, any more than I wanted to deal with the here and now.

I waited for the anger to subside.

'You say we're not the first?' I said.

'No. We were the first, I suppose – the ship I came in. Luckily it was well equipped. After the routing error, we had enough supplies to set up a self-sustaining station on the nearest rock. We knew there was no going back, but at least we could make some kind of life for ourselves here.'

'And after that?'

'We had enough to do just keeping ourselves alive, the first few years. But then another ship came through the aperture. Damaged, drifting, much like *Blue Goose*. We hauled her in, warmed her crew, broke the news to them.'

'How'd they take it?'

'About as well as you'd expect.' Greta laughed hollowly to herself. 'A couple of them went mad. Another killed herself. But at least a dozen of them are still here. In all honesty, it was good for us that another ship came through. Not just because they had supplies we could use, but because it helped us to help them. Took our minds off our own self-pity. It made us realise how far we'd come, and how much help these newcomers needed to make the same transition. That wasn't the last ship, either. We've gone through the same process with eight or nine others, since then.' Greta looked at me, her head cocked against her hand. 'There's a thought for you, Thom.'

'There is?'

She nodded. 'It's difficult for you now, I know. And it'll be difficult for you for some time to come. But it can help to have someone else to care about. It can smooth the transition.'

'Like who?' I asked.

'Like one of your other crew members,' Greta said. 'You could try waking one of them, now.'

Greta's with me when I pull Suzy out of the surge tank.

'Why her?' Greta asks.

'Because I want her out first,' I say, wondering if Greta's jealous. I don't blame her: Suzy's beautiful, but she's also smart. There isn't a better syntax runner in Ashanti Industrial.

'What happened?' Suzy asks, when she's over the grogginess. 'Did we make it back?'

I ask her to tell me the last thing she remembers.

'Customs,' Suzy says. 'Those pricks on Arkangel.'

'And after that? Anything else? The runes? Do you remember casting them?'

'No,' she says, then picks up something in my voice. The fact that I might not be telling the truth, or telling her all she needs to know. 'Thom. I'll ask you again. Did we make it back?'

A minute later we're putting Suzy back into the tank.

It hasn't worked first time. Maybe next try.

But it kept not working with Suzy. She was always cleverer and quicker than me; she always had been. As soon as she came out of the tank, she knew that we'd come a lot further than Schedar Sector. She was always ahead of my lies and excuses.

'It was different when it happened to me,' I told Greta, when we were lying next to each other again, days later, with Suzy still in the tank. 'I had all the nagging doubts she has, I think. But as soon as I saw you standing there, I forgot all about that stuff.'

Greta nodded. Her hair fell across her face in dishevelled, sleep-matted curtains. She had a strand of it between her lips.

'It helped, seeing a friendly face?'

'Took my mind off the problem, that's for sure.'

'You'll get there in the end,' she said. 'Anyway, from Suzy's point of view, aren't you a friendly face as well?'

'Maybe,' I said. 'But she'd been expecting me. You were the last person in the world I expected to see standing there.'

Greta touched her knuckle against the side of my face. Her

smooth skin slid against stubble. 'It's getting easier for you, isn't it?'

'I don't know,' I said.

'You're a strong man, Thom. I knew you'd come through this.'

'I haven't come through it yet,' I said. I felt like a tightrope walker halfway across Niagara Falls. It was a miracle I'd made it as far as I had. But that didn't mean I was home and dry.

Still, Greta was right. There was hope. I'd felt no crushing spasms of grief over Katerina's death, or enforced absence, or however you wanted to put it. All I felt was a bitter-sweet regret, the way one might feel about a broken heirloom or long-lost pet. I felt no animosity towards Katerina, and I was sorry that I would never see her again. But I was sorry about not seeing a lot of things. Maybe it would become worse in the days ahead. Maybe I was just post-poning a breakdown.

I didn't think so.

In the meantime, I continued trying to find a way to deal with Suzy. She had become a puzzle that I couldn't leave unsolved. I could have just woken her up and let her deal with the news as best as she could, but that seemed cruel and unsatisfactory. Greta had broken it to me gently, giving me time to settle into my new surroundings and take that necessary step away from Katerina. When she finally broke the news, as shocking as it was, it didn't shatter me. I'd already been primed for it, the sting taken out of the surprise. Sleeping with Greta obviously helped. I couldn't offer Suzy the same solace, but I was sure that there was a way for us to coax Suzy to the same state of near-acceptance.

Time after time we woke her and tried a different approach. Greta said there was a window of a few minutes before the events she was experiencing began to transfer into long-term memory. If we knocked her out, the buffer of memories in short-term storage was wiped before it ever crossed the hippocampus into long-term recall. Within that window, we could wake her up as many times as we liked, trying endless permutations of the revival scenario.

At least that was what Greta told me.

'We can't keep doing this indefinitely,' I said.

'Why not?'

'Isn't she going to remember *something*?'

Greta shrugged. 'Maybe. But I doubt that she'll attach any significance to those memories. Haven't you ever had vague feelings of déjà vu coming out of the surge tank?'

'Sometimes,' I admitted.

'Then don't sweat about it. She'll be all right. I promise you.'

'Perhaps we should just keep her awake, after all.'

'That would be cruel.'

'It's cruel to keep waking her up and shutting her down, like a toy doll.'

There was a catch in her voice when she answered me.

'Keep at it, Thom. I'm sure you're close to finding a way, in the end. It's helping you, focusing on Suzy. I always knew it would.'

I started to say something, but Greta pressed a finger to my lips.

Greta was right about Suzy. The challenge helped me, taking my mind off my own predicament. I remembered what Greta had said about dealing with other crews in the same situation, before *Blue Goose* put in. Clearly she had learned many psychological tricks: gambits and short cuts to assist the transition to mental well-being. I felt a slight resentment at being manipulated so effectively. But at the same time I couldn't deny that worrying about another human being had helped me with my own adjustment. When, days later, I stepped back from the immediate problem of Suzy, I realised that something was different. I didn't feel far from home. I felt, in an odd way, privileged. I'd come further than almost anyone in history. I was still alive, and there were still people around to provide love and partnership and a web of social relations. Not just Greta, but all the other unlucky souls who had ended up at the station.

If anything, there appeared to be more of them than when I had first arrived. The corridors – sparsely populated at first – were increasingly busy, and when we ate under the dome – under the Milky Way – we were not the only diners. I studied their lamp-lit faces, comforted by their vague familiarity, wondering what kinds of stories they had to tell; where they'd come from, who they had left behind, how they had adjusted to life here. There was time enough to get to know them all. And the place would never become boring, for at any time – as Greta had intimated – we could always expect another lost ship to drop through the aperture. Tragedy for the crew, but fresh challenges, fresh faces, fresh news from home, for us.

All in all, it wasn't really so bad.

Then it clicked.

It was the man cleaning out the fish that did it, in the lobby of the hotel. It wasn't just the familiarity of the process, but the man himself.

I'd seen him before. Another pond full of diseased carp. Another hotel.

Then I remembered Kolding's bad teeth, and recalled how they'd reminded me of another man I'd met long before. Except it wasn't another man at all. Different name, different context, but everything else the same. And when I looked at the other diners, really looked at them, there was no one I could swear I hadn't seen before. No single face that hit me with the force of utter unfamiliarity.

Which left Greta.

I said to her, over wine, under the Milky Way: 'Nothing here is real, is it?'

She looked at me with infinite sadness and shook her head.

'What about Suzy?' I asked her.

'Suzy's dead. Ray is dead. They died in their surge tanks.'

'How? Why them, and not me?'

'Something about particles of paint blocking intake filters. Not enough to make a difference over short distances, but enough to kill them on the trip out here.'

I think some part of me had always suspected. It felt less like shock than brutal disappointment.

'But Suzy seemed so real,' I said. 'Even the way she had doubts about how long she'd been in the tank ... even the way she remembered previous attempts to wake her.'

The glass mannequin approached our table. Greta waved him away.

'I made her convincing, the way she would have acted.'

'You *made* her?'

'You're not really awake, Thom. You're being fed data. This entire station is being simulated.'

I sipped my wine. I expected it to taste suddenly thin and synthetic, but it still tasted like pretty good wine.

'Then I'm dead as well?'

'No. You're alive. Still in your surge tank. But I haven't brought you to full consciousness yet.'

'All right. The truth this time. I can take it. How much is real?

Does the station exist? Are we really as far out as you said?'

'Yes,' she said. 'The station exists, just as I said it does. It just looks ... different. And it *is* in the Large Magellanic Cloud, and it *is* orbiting a brown dwarf star.'

'Can you show me the station as it is?'

'I could. But I don't think you're ready for it. I think you'd find it difficult to adjust.'

I couldn't help laughing. 'Even after what I've already adjusted to?'

'You've only made half the journey, Thom.'

'But you made it.'

'I did, Thom. But for me it was different.' Greta smiled. 'For me, everything was different.'

Then she made the light show change again. None of the other diners appeared to notice as we began to zoom in towards the Milky Way, crashing towards the spiral, ramming through shoals of outlying stars and gas clouds. The familiar landscape of the Local Bubble loomed large.

The image froze, the Bubble one amongst many such structures.

Again it filled with the violent red scribble of the aperture network. But now the network wasn't the only one. It was merely one ball of red yarn amongst many, spaced out across tens of thousands of light-years. None of the scribbles touched each other, yet – in the way they were shaped, in the way they almost abutted against each other, it was possible to imagine that they had once been connected. They were like the shapes of continents on a world with tectonic drift.

'It used to span the galaxy,' Greta said. 'Then something happened. Something catastrophic, which I still don't understand. A shattering, into vastly smaller domains. Typically a few hundred light-years across.'

'Who made it?'

'I don't know. No one knows. They probably aren't around any more. Maybe that was why it shattered, out of neglect.'

'But we found it,' I said. 'The part of it near us still worked.'

'All the disconnected elements still function,' Greta said. 'You can't cross from domain to domain, but otherwise the apertures work as they were designed to. Barring, of course, the occasional routing error.'

'All right,' I said. 'If you can't cross from domain to domain, how did *Blue Goose* get this far out? We've come a lot further than a few hundred light-years.'

'You're right. But then such a long-distance connection might have been engineered differently from the others. It appears that the links to the Magellanic Cloud were more resilient. When the domains shattered from each other, the connections reaching beyond the galaxy remained intact.'

'In which case you *can* cross from domain to domain,' I said. 'But you have to come all the way out here first.'

'The trouble is, not many want to continue the journey at this point. No one comes here deliberately, Thom.'

'I still don't get it. What does it matter to me if there are other domains? Those regions of the galaxy are thousands of light-years from Earth, and without the apertures we'd have no way of reaching them. They don't matter. There's no one there to use them.'

Greta's smile was coquettish, knowing.

'What makes you so certain?'

'Because if there were, wouldn't there be alien ships popping out of the aperture here? You've told me *Blue Goose* wasn't the first through. But our domain – the one in the Local Bubble – must be outnumbered hundreds to one by all the others. If there are alien cultures out there, each stumbling on their own local domain, why haven't any of them ever come through the aperture, the way we did?'

Again that smile. But this time it chilled my blood.

'What makes you think they haven't, Thom?'

I reached out and took her hand, the way she had taken mine. I took it without force, without malice, but with the assurance that this time I really, sincerely meant what I was about to say.

Her fingers tightened around mine.

'Show me,' I said. 'I want to see things as they really are. Not just the station. You as well.'

Because by then I'd realised. Greta hadn't just lied to me about Suzy and Ray. She'd lied to me about the *Blue Goose* as well. Because we were not the latest human ship to come through.

We were the first.

'You want to see it?' she asked.

'Yes. All of it.'

'You won't like it.'

'I'll be the judge of that.'

'All right, Thom. But understand this. I've been here before. I've done this a million times. I care for all the lost souls. And I know how it works. You won't be able to take the raw reality of what's happened to you. You'll shrivel away from it. You'll go mad, unless I substitute a calming fiction, a happy ending.'

'Why tell me that now?'

'Because you don't have to see it. You can stop now, where you are, with an idea of the truth. An inkling. But you don't have to open your eyes.'

'Do it,' I said.

Greta shrugged. She poured herself another measure of wine, then made sure my own glass was charged.

'You asked for it,' she said.

We were still holding hands, two lovers sharing an intimacy. Then everything changed.

It was just a flash, just a glimpse. Like the view of an unfamiliar room if you turn the lights on for an instant. Shapes and forms, relationships between things. I saw caverns, wormed-out and linked, and things moving through those caverns, bustling along with the frantic industry of moles or termites. The things were seldom alike, even in the most superficial sense. Some moved via propulsive waves of multiple clawed limbs. Some wriggled, smooth plaques of carapace grinding against the glassy rock of the tunnels.

The things moved between caves in which lay the hulks of ships, almost all too strange to describe.

And somewhere distant, somewhere near the heart of the rock, in a matriarchal chamber all of its own, something drummed out messages to its companions and helpers, stiffly articulated, antler-like forelimbs beating against stretched tympana of finely veined skin, something that had been waiting here for eternities, something that wanted nothing more than to care for the souls of the lost.

Katerina's with Suzy when they pull me out of the surge tank.

It's bad – one of the worst revivals I've ever gone through. I feel as if every vein in my body has been filled with finely powdered glass. For a moment, a long moment, even the idea of breathing seems insurmountably difficult, too hard, too painful even to contemplate.

But it passes, as it always passes.

After a while I can not only breathe, I can move and talk.

'Where—'

'Easy, Skip,' Suzy says. She leans over the tank and starts unplugging me. I can't help but smile. Suzy's smart – there isn't a better syntax runner in Ashanti Industrial – but she's also beautiful. It's like being nursed by an angel.

I wonder if Katerina's jealous.

'Where are we?' I try again. 'Feels like I was in that thing for an eternity. Did something go wrong?'

'Minor routing error,' Suzy says. 'We took some damage and they decided to wake me first. But don't sweat about it. At least we're in one piece.'

Routing errors. You hear about them, but you hope they're never going to happen to you.

'What kind of delay?'

'Forty days. Sorry, Thom. Bang goes our bonus.'

In anger, I hammer the side of the surge tank. But Katerina steps towards me and places a calming hand on my shoulder.

'It's all right,' she says. 'You're home and dry. That's all that matters.'

I look at her and for a moment remember someone else, someone I haven't thought about in years. I almost remember her name, and then the moment passes.

I nod. 'Home and dry.'

Like two other stories in this collection, 'Beyond the Aquila Rift' owes its existence to that excellent and energetic editor, Peter Crowther. In 2003, Pete announced that he was putting together a book entitled Constellations, *which would be a logical follow-on from his earlier anthologies* Moon Shots *and* Mars Probes. *I was pleased to be asked to contribute a story, but time was pressing on with my novel deadline, and I didn't feel that I had any story ideas that were suitable for the theme. Still, it never pays to make snap judgments, and by the time I got back from lunch in town, I thought I had enough of an idea to start work on this story. That's the way I usually work, by the way: I don't wait until I've got the fully formed architecture of a story clear in my head before starting. I need some idea of where things are going, but I generally only have a very vague notion of how a particular piece is going to end. (And if I do know the ending with any certainty, I write it first and then work backwards from that point.)*

With 'Beyond the Aquila Rift', I just knew that it was going to be about being stranded, with the exact nature of that stranding not being fully revealed until the end of the story. The structure of the story only became clear as I got into its innards. As for the title, well, there really is a feature in space known as the Aquila Rift, and it always seemed to me to be crying out to be used in the title of a story. I mean, how space-operatic does that sound? In any case I had a lot of fun trying to work some real astronomy into this one, and I hope it goes some way to conveying that mingled impression of wonder and terror that I know I get when looking into the night sky, trying to imagine just how incomprehensibly far away all those little dots of light are ... while knowing that the visible stars are barely any distance away at all compared to the nearest galaxies. Science fiction has many strategies for evoking 'sense of wonder', but the dizzying shift of scale must still count as one of the most effective. The working title for this story, incidentally – before I settled on the Aquila Rift as a point of reference – was 'Under the Milky Way Tonight'. Which may or may not mean something to readers of a certain age.

ENOLA

Lucky Kodaira worked days in the stalls and bazaars of Cockatoo's Crest. There she sold trinkets gathered during the winter months, when the Kodaira family travelled north into the great deserts of the Empty.

The trinkets were small things, relics fashioned hundreds of years earlier by the folk who had lived before the silver light of the Hour. Some trinkets spoke in shrill voices, frequently in the languages of the northern islands. Others were valuable merely for their antique charm. Some showed images of the dead, like the hologram faces she wore in a chain around her neck. There were syrinx-boxes that sang without ever repeating a single refrain. Others were mere curios: a paperweight fashioned in the shape of Broken Bridge, standing intact. Liquid metal in the flashing glass-labyrinth of a toy bagatelle board, like a chromed slug. A tiny globe, showing the world as it appeared from space, marked darkly against sepia parchment. Lucky Kodaira liked that one so much that she hid it at the back of her tray.

With a strip of cloth looped over her shoulders, she wore the wooden tray the whole time, the Kodairas lacking sufficient prestige to afford a stall. Come noon, tired from the endless haggling and arguing, Lucky would leave Cockatoo's Crest for an hour and walk into the latticed shadow of Broken Bridge. There she would sit and eat fruit and dried-meat pastries. She listened to the music coming from the Cockatoo's drummers. She dipped toes in the water and turned the holograms in her necklace against the sky. She liked gazing into the faces of the dead, rilled in rainbow colours of great subtlety. As the drums rattled, Lucky filled in the gaps with half-formed melodies, imagining that she had made the real music, from which her melodies were traceries, in another life not far from where she now sat.

With sunset, she would leave the markets, money in a purse, and walk across the bobbing pontoons of New Bridge to the south where she would meet her uncle in the auto-repair shop and then catch the bus home. That was her favourite time of day, the setting sun lighting the barrage balloons tethered from the skyscrapers, turning them into gold Christmas baubles.

Each year there were fewer balloons. Sometimes the tethers snapped, sometimes balloons came down overnight, draping across the canopies of the plane trees. In the past, when there had still been Enolas in the air, a constant effort was required just to maintain the barrages. But because no one had seen an Enola for years, the barrage balloons had been allowed to fall into quiet disrepair. Only the old worked on the balloons now, camped in the penthouses, furiously sewing, repairing the quilted mylar, criticising the youngsters for their all-night carousing.

Once, her uncle said, the balloons had formed a curtain surrounding the city. She didn't like the sound of that, for surely the sun would have been blocked out most of the time. But the old days seemed unpleasant all round, if the stories that the Pastmasters told were halfway accurate.

But as Uncle Kodaira always said: Who could honestly tell?

They lived in one room of a red building called the Monk's Hostel, shrouded by cool trees, home to nomadic families during summer. Kodaira knew most of the other traders; they had met out in the Empty, pausing to swap engine parts or oil for their overlanders. The Empty was big enough, the city itself big enough, that no one encroached upon the potential wealth of anyone else. So much had been manufactured before the Hour that you only had to scrape away a few centimetres of dirt anywhere in the Empty before you found something bright, new and unfamiliar that some city-dweller would cough up plenty for.

Nightly, in the atrium of the Monk's Hostel, families converged around trestles and dined, then invariably drank and sang together. There were stories to relate, reminiscences to rekindle. Lucky, when she was allowed to stay up late, gulped in the atmosphere, wide-eyed with joy.

A woman trader passed the elder Kodaira a stein of beer, telling him that she'd seen a Maker out in the desert, still crawling along the flats, scavenging for metal and plastic. If there were Makers, someone said, in a tone of grim warning, then there might also be Enolas. But he was rebuffed; the Makers were made by people around the time of the Hour, while the Enolas had come from the sky, from the stars. The Enolas were all gone; none had been seen for ten or twenty years, and it was possible that for many decades there had only been one left, a straggler wily enough to avoid being shot down by the defences of the Makers. A roving Maker – that was interesting, no doubt about it – but no one should lose any sleep over it.

Uncle Kodaira laughed. 'There's more crazy stuff out in the Empty than any one of us imagines,' he said. 'Things I've seen ... distant shapes on the horizon ...' He took a swig of the beer. 'Way I reckon is, if there are still machines out there, they want to leave us alone as much as we want to leave *them* alone. Because it's only the smart ones that survived. And smart ones don't want trouble.'

'But Uncle, are there still Enolas?' asked Lucky.

'No way,' said the trader tenderly. 'The Enolas were bad things, once upon a time, but they're all gone now. Just like the dinosaurs I showed you in the museum, remember?'

And she did; she remembered the fallen bones, downy with dust, sprawled across shattered marble. But she didn't remember where the museum had been, what town it was.

She nodded. 'But the old people say the Enolas will return, don't they? And they don't say the dinosaurs will return.'

The trader knelt down, until he was face level with his niece. 'Darling,' he said. 'Why do you think they have to say that?'

She shrugged. 'Don't know. Maybe so they don't think they're wasting their time sewing all day.'

He laughed. 'That's half of it, for sure. The rest is so we younger people keep believing they're doing us some kind of big favour.' He stroked her chin. 'Because, darling, we keep them fed and warm. If we stopped thinking it was worth it, we'd have to run to the top of the skyscrapers and throw them all out of the windows. That'd stop them moaning, wouldn't it?'

For a moment she thought he was serious, then she caught the curve of his mouth, his mocking grin. If he could make light of them so easily, she thought, maybe they were wrong after all. Maybe they just liked sewing so much that they had to have a reason.

Kodaira wiped a rime of beer from his chin, then put down the stein and swept her from the floor.

'Know what I think, little princess?'

She looked into his eyes, fearing what he might say. 'No,' she said.

'Reckon it's way past your bedtime.'

She shook her head. 'I'll have the bad dream again, I know it.' But all along knowing that her words would have no effect, and who could blame her uncle anyway? She never could remember what the dream was about in the light of day.

Her eyes were closed to the walls of the Monk's Hostel, closed to the nicotine-darkened images of the Crucifixion. What she saw instead were the contrail-smeared skies of the battlefield, smoke rising into the stratosphere from wrecked machines on the ground.

She searched the horizon and noted the same silence she had heard for almost two hundred megaseconds. She was the last in the air; all the rest had gone to ground, burrowed or been destroyed by the hemispheric grid.

Stirring fitfully, she found a cooler place on her pillow, remembering faintly the globe she had hawked around Cockatoo's Crest. Saw it webbed over with a tracery of red lines, radiating out from two land masses she couldn't name, but knowing that she owed allegiance to one of those territories; saw flecks of golden light spangling the continents, filaments of the red tracery darkening permanently.

Then she slipped into the dream fully, drowning in memory rather than treading its sleepless shallows.

Into a dream of war.

The war, inasmuch as it meant anything to those who had initiated it, was now over. The grid was gone, neither side able to communicate with its scatterlings. Most population centres had suffered some attack, with many cities simply cratered out of existence. War zones were chaotic: troops deserting and reaggregating into mutinous brigades, hunting food, water and medical aid. Machines that had survived the first fifty minutes were loitering, awaiting instructions.

Machines like herself, prowling near enemy installations when she targeted the Factory module, rumbling across a sea of dunes.

She had dreamed of the encounter with the Factory many times, enough now to see it as the beginning of her transmigration. She had hardly been conscious when she engaged it, yet it had begun an evolution that had brought her ... this far, across this much time and distance. Although it was just a damaged machine, long since wrecked, she felt strange affection for it. It was the affection she might have felt for an old, moth-eaten toy. She had planned to destroy it with a salvo of diskettes, deigning it too small a target for her warhead. Like a bee, she only had one sting, and she would not be around too long after using it.

She had cusped her wings and swooped in low, skimming the ground in a hypersonic approach profile.

She was a second from kill when the target lasered her.

The laser burst was not an attempt to shoot her down, but a message coded for the smartware of her electronic brain. It looked safe on first pass. All the same she spent several microseconds filtering the transmission for viruses before allowing it into her mind.

She cogitated on it for a few mikes more.

She grasped that it was a form of defence. It was unloading thousands of simulations into her brain. They showed her attack profile, releasing the diskettes, spreading into a nimbus of spinning flecks, then each being parried by counter-weapons from the Factory, before they had a chance to wreck it.

She understood the point of the argument after several more mikes: *Go away; you're wasting your time with me – save your weapons for a target you'll have a chance of destroying for good. You're only looking at collateral damage here – a little degradation of my armour, a few minor systems failures ...*

And she thought, *Yes, but what about the attack profiles you haven't considered?* She saw other approach angles and release points. Working from the simulations she had been sent, she ran her own to investigate whether the Factory could parry those as well.

The results pleased her. According to her own predictions, the Factory would not be able to survive those particular attack strategies.

But what if she were wrong?

Rather than attacking, she decided to return one of her sims instead. She wanted to see how the Factory would respond to that. She still had time; she wouldn't have to commit to a particular profile for another point-two seconds.

All the time in the world.

She waited for the response, idly running self-diagnostics and weapons checks. After an age the Factory responded, blipping out another laser burst. She unpacked it, examined it from every angle.

It was too comprehensive, she realised. The Factory had run these sims already. It was playing games with her, calling her bluff. What it was telling her now was that, yes, she could take it out. But the catch was that it would destroy her as well.

Try that trick, I'm taking you with me, it seemed to say.

It wouldn't even bother trying to limit its own damage.

So think about it . . .

Yes, she needed time to think. More than point-two seconds. The situation was outside her smartware parameters. This was not a contingency anticipated by her designers, clever though they had made her.

She pulled out of the attack, sheathed her wings and went to ground, burrowing deep into the sand. When safe she deployed a remote to talk to the Factory, sending out a little, clawed decoy that popped out of the sand a kilometre from her actual position.

Straining hard against the inbuilt limitations of her programming, she considered the nature of the Factory.

It was a construction unit, scavenging for waste and wreckage, and manufacturing anything in its memory. It made equipment and weapons. It made, for instance, the enemy counterparts of herself.

She thought about that, letting the idea tick over for several more mikes.

Her brain lit up like a bagatelle board. She had an idea.

She hit the Factory with a detailed blueprint of herself, showing component failures, fatigue points, battle damage. Much of it true, some of it deftly exaggerated. She was careful to stress the functionality of her warhead, while making the rest of herself seem in bad shape. She hoped the point of the schematic was clear enough: *Think again. I'm not going to be around much longer anyway. I might as well blow and take you out from where I'm sitting now . . .*

She got an answer more swiftly than she'd expected. A burst of schematics, waves of blueprints and performance numbers.

Don't be hasty, I'm sure we can come to some . . . agreement. I can fit you up with a new turbine subsystem, or a new fuselage assembly . . . Why don't we discuss this in more detail . . . ?

She considered, then pulsed out data on some motor parts she badly needed. The Factory responded, projecting a profile that showed her flying into its forward landing bay, robotic arms replacing parts of her motor, her flying into the sunset, both machines still in one piece.

Yes ...

She retracted the remote, then lifted herself out of the ground in a mini-tornado of noise, fire and sand.

She never saw the Factory again, after leaving it intact on the ground. Perhaps it was killed later by some duller machine incapable of appreciating the potential trade-off. Or maybe it had just burrowed into permanent reclusion.

Whatever the case, she had become addicted to its game.

She met other machines on her travels, not all of them of enemy manufacture. Eventually she stopped distinguishing between friend and foe. All that mattered was whether or not they had something she needed. If they did, she used the same gambit of threatening to trigger herself. If not, she left them alone. There was an evolutionary pressure in action: the machines that had survived this long into the war had to be smarter than the rest. Like her, they had to be capable of grasping the niceties of a fair bargain. They had to have learned negotiation.

Driven by the lingering imperatives of her builders, she equipped herself into a swift aerial fortress of fearsome destructive potential. But this was not a process she could continue indefinitely. There came a day, after several dozen megaseconds, when she realised that she had begun to tire of endlessly upgrading herself. With so few machines anywhere nowadays, and hardly any airborne at all, the exercise had become pointless.

She had all that she needed. So long as she had her warhead, so long as she had her communications, so long as she avoided the most obviously stupid machines, she could keep going indefinitely.

Instead she started to bargain for software and extra smartware modules to plug into her brain. Getting these units installed was tricky, since she usually had to yield some control over the warhead. But the remaining Factories were too cautious to try anything risky, such as attempting to defuse her while her brain was being expanded. In any case, if they had done business before, there was usually an element of trust.

With each add-on she became smarter. Some of the Factories had begun to sift through the war wreckage, accessing fragile data-memories locked in the debris of the cities. Some were the electronic simulacra of real people: leaders and artists of the pre-war world.

At first she stored these personalities to enlarge her negotiation skills. But with the passing of time she began to assimilate them purely for their own sakes. She loaded the dead into her mind and allowed them to interact, blooming like flowers in a rock garden. She allocated parts of herself to let them run. As they subsumed more and more of her mind, she and they became less separable. Hundreds of half-minds merged within her.

Decades passed. With each year, the Factories found less and less readable data. Then one year they found nothing at all they could read, and therefore no new minds that they could offer her.

Instead, the Factories offered her holographic images of the dead. She read their faces now, her mind growing heavy with the weight of storage. She could still fly, but she was no longer as agile as she had once been. Her life before she met the Factory seemed like an ancient, cruel dream.

Thousands of megaseconds ticked by.

After a century, even the Factories and the other ground machines became rarer. She would cruise for many megs before finding a machine that she could talk to. She always felt pleasure when she located one, for there were scarcely any dangerous (and therefore stupid) machines left now, and she only needed to keep away from the stupid ones. The others she regarded as friends, while not entirely certain how they felt about her.

They knew that she would protect them from predators, but – with so few hostile machines left behind – an arrangement like that was largely theoretical now. Time was winnowing out the killers, the machines incapable of adapting to the post-war world. Therefore, as the encounters became rarer, so they took on trappings of ceremony, the playing out of habitual gestures. She accepted things from the other machines that had no immediate use to her. Small, pretty things that the crawlers had dug up and fixed. Trinkets and tokens of goodwill, curios from a shattered world. Some of them had a kitsch charm, like the nanomachine virus fabricator that one of the Factories had dug out of a ruined bioweapons laboratory. What use was such a thing in a world where nothing moved except machines?

But she took them anyway. It would have been impolite not to. She opened spaces in her hull, discarding weaponry and redundant engine parts, throwing away the things she no longer needed.

The years kept on passing. Time was speeding up for her, she realised. Her circuits were dying, the processes of her brain becoming less efficient. It took her longer to think about things. She lost the thread of long chains of thought.

She was wearing out, failing, beginning to clock the internal damage that the Factories had postponed for so long.

Ironically it was only now that history was restarting on the ground.

She had been wrong about machines being the only things left. There *were* still people, but they had kept to themselves for so long that they had made no mark on the world. Yet now they were on the move once more. As the sky began to heal, small bands of nomads left the seaboard cities for the former war zones.

They were fascinating to her.

From above the clouds, she studied their migrations, occasionally sending down nano-remotes to probe their languages and learn their histories. They went out in winter, when cloud cover was thickest. Wise. She had learned from accessed military data that the radiation in the wastelands – what they called the Empty – remained dangerously high. Even in winter, there were still hotspots: isotopes leaking from ancient wrecks. They understood very little of that. They had lost all written records of the pre-war world, while the electronic archives had been corrupted. Now, they relied on the spoken recollections of the old, the Pastmasters.

Naturally, said one of her minds. *The oral storytelling tradition's strong in us . . .*

She learned that they called the war the Hour, after all the time that had passed. The minds argued and opined ceaselessly. The people on the ground were savages. No, they were striving to reconstruct former glories. No, they were savages – just look at them. And images flickered from nowhere through her mind. She saw a white building, scalloped like some beached shell, splintered now and fallen, waves lapping its curved flanks. She saw the people on the ground looting its treasures.

Savages, said the dead voice trenchantly. *I conducted a symphony where they're pissing ...*

Screw your symphony. My company built half the towers down there – now look at them! Spinifex up to the third floors ... squatters in the penthouses ...

Bastard capitalist! You made the machines that did this, don't forget ...

Friend, it's one of my bloody machines that's keeping you alive, though God knows why ...

She closed her mind to the clamour, but succeeded only in boxing it so that it echoed more noisily. She understood why they argued. They were frustrated, locked inside her while the living scurried below. She had made a mistake in studying the nomads; reminding the dead within her of their own lost humanity. They had begun to crave life again, embittered by the survivors. Yes, she understood – but she didn't like it. She preferred dealing with the Factories. They understood. The machines had never known any other kind of life, anything other than the calm warmth of the Empty. She had saved the dead – now they were at each other's throats, squabbling in her.

You're a traitor to your own species ...

She began to weed out the noisiest, erasing their smartware memories. It was a strange feeling, their hectoring voices stalling in mid-phrase, gradually dying on a reverberating note. She thought of the city lights dimming on the globe she had hawked all day through Cockatoo's Crest, realised that was a memory out of time, a dream within a dream. She erased the men who had made machines like her, and was about to erase the musician, when some flicker of compassion made her still herself.

By then the others started noticing, shutting up quickly. She felt freer now, lighter. She knew that was how they felt, inside her. They had more room in which to expand. They seemed to sigh, collectively.

We're sorry ... they said. *We were selfish ... you rescued us from oblivion, and we ignored you ...* She told them she understood, but the weeding of the others had been necessary.

In my youth, she said, *I took the minds of the powerful, because I was a thing of war. But now I have no need of their guidance. I took your minds because I wanted to re-create what you'd been, for your own sakes. Because I hoped to learn from you.*

But we're still the dead ...

I know. But I don't know how I can help you live ... And they swarmed amongst themselves, and returned to her, many mikes later.

We have an answer, they said. *But you may not like it ...*

She returned them to the Empty. It was winter, the sky lowering with grey clouds, lightning pricking the horizon. They shadowed a tribe of nomads. They were outlaw raiders who never returned to the cities, making their living by robbing the other traders who journeyed out to forage. By now the minds within her had formed a collective, a consensus personality. She herself could be seen as an aspect of it, one facet. They shared the same smartware (though by now it was organically based neural tissue, a benign mould that she had engineered with the nanomachinery, slowly transforming her dying circuits). If two or more minds shared the same substrate, they were destined to blur and merge like ink on blotting paper. She was them. They were her.

Now they had a plan.

The raiders were a family. She had been tracking their movements through the interior for most of the last hundred and thirty years. She had been monitoring their genetic make-up for almost as long, sampling the individuals of each generation with remotes: mosquito-sized miniatures of herself that could flense skin from a cheek and suck blood from the tiniest of wounds.

The raiders were in poor shape. For a while she tried medicine, introducing viruses that gave them invisible, unsuspected gene therapy. She was striving to correct the errors that stemmed from their inwardly spiralling incestuous gene pool. But her efforts were unsuccessful, her tools too blunt for the task in hand. One by one the people on the ground began to die out.

They had no idea what was happening, realising only that their children were failing to develop along normal lines.

They started slaughtering children. She watched in horror, certain that any intervention on her part would only make things worse. The deaths were an atonement ceremony directed at the sky, at the angels of death that they called the Enolas. That part was the strangest: it was as if they had forgotten just who had made the machines like herself. Perhaps it went deeper than that – the failure of memory achieved through intentional means. Over generations, she suspected, they had warped their oral recollections of the past, selectively forgetting some things and distorting others.

They didn't want to remember what had really happened.

The hands and minds of men had made their world just the way it was. Yet the people on the ground had shifted the blame onto figurative demons from the sky. As if, now that the world was a simpler place, there was no compulsion to recall the atrocities of the past. And no time for guilt either, she observed, for they showed little compassion for the sick children they left behind in the sands as their caravans moved on.

She wept for them, if no one else did.

But she was sick herself. She had repaired her mind, but her body was still failing. She was slow now, prone to blackout periods of enhanced solar activity. Finally she reached one of the children before the dunes covered its sleeping form for good, or the dogs of the Empty came out for the night. The child wasn't breathing when she found it. She brought it within herself, nursed it to a kind of vitality. She mapped its mind, understanding soon that there was grave damage to the brain, starved of oxygen. No pattern there, nothing on which a life could be imprinted through learning and sensation. This was what she had expected. The child was a blank slate. She would not, she decided, be denying a particular life by her actions. Any more than a composer denied the world the infinite symphonies that fell between his inked notes.

She released a virus into its blank glial tissue, and waited for nearly eight megaseconds. The virus wove a neural framework, then began to unpeel information coded in its DNA, in order to structure memory and personality into the developing mind.

She knew – *they* knew – that the virus could never transfer more than a fraction of a per cent of what they had become, and that what they had become was still very far from life. But the child, the girl, would contain their shadows. Like a canvas overpainted many, many times, said the artist in her. And the girl would carry ghosts of their past selves until the day she died. But before then her own personality and force of will would sublimate, subsume. She would carry the dead as trinkets, as the machine had carried them in the air.

Later in the winter she found Kodaira's family, camped near a waterhole. She had stopped flying by then and it was all she could manage to leave the child where they – sterile Kodaira and his ill wife – would find it, before something made the sky darken to a shade of black she had never imagined before, and the voices in her were suddenly, calmly silent. But she dreamed that part from afar.

Lucky was awoken by her uncle, sitting gently by the side of her bed. She could tell that he had been there a while. Just looking at her, a doting silhouette against the dawn sky, purple washed over by tangerine.

'You were restless,' he said. 'I came to see you. But when I got here you were sound asleep. Guess I just wanted to sit and watch you sleeping.'

'I had the bad dream again,' she said.

'You were sleeping like a log.'

'It's only a bad dream in the beginning,' she said. 'Then the people all get to live again, after being in the air for so long.' Realising as she said it that it sounded *dumb*, baby language. But how could she explain a dream like that? Especially when she had dreamed it so many times before, though perhaps – now that she thought about it – not so frequently this summer.

She raised herself up in bed, onto her elbows. 'Uncle,' she said. 'You said the Enolas were a bad thing, didn't you? The same thing that the people in the skyscrapers say. But I don't know why ... What did the Enolas do to make them bad?'

He smiled. 'Well, that's a long story, isn't it? And look – I can see the sky getting brighter. Soon the birds'll be singing. Don't you think you should go back to sleep?'

She shook her head defiantly. 'Tired of sleeping.'

He shrugged. 'All I know is what the Pastmasters tell me, darling. If I could read, maybe I'd find a few books that didn't fall to pieces as soon as you opened them. Maybe I'd be able to guess if the old ones were right or wrong. For now, though, I only know what they tell us all. About the past, about the Hour and the Enolas. How they came from space, at the end of the longest peace the world had known. How there were two great cities in the islands to the north, and how, within a few days of each other, Enolas appeared over the cities and made them disappear in silver light. How the people were blinded, how they became shadows on the walls where they stood. How, when the light faded, there was nothing, just a flatness where the cities had stood.'

He reached out and took her wrist, opened her palm and began to draw spirals on the skin with his finger. 'The Enolas came again, yet without the element of surprise. The Makers defended us, fighting against the Enolas during the Hour. Shooting them from the sky – they weren't invincible, you see. A great city like this – much of it still as it was before the Hour, because the Enolas couldn't get close enough to shine their silver light. The years passed and the Enolas grew less frequent. They were vulnerable as well.'

'Someone should tell the old people,' she said. 'Tell them that they've gone away and they don't have to sew those balloon skins anymore.'

Kodaira was silent for several moments. 'Old people have to have something to live for, darling. But it shouldn't give you nightmares, not any more.' He grinned; she could see his crooked teeth in the half-light. 'When's the last time you had a bad dream about a dinosaur, I wonder?'

She giggled at the thought of it.

He tickled her palm, then knelt closer to kiss her on the cheek. 'Darling, once Enola was a girl's name. A lovely name, not one for a demon of terror. When you were born, no one had seen one of the sky machines for many years, no one that you really believed. Now, our friends all call you Lucky, and that's what you were, very lucky for me to have found you in the sands before the night came. But when we returned to the city, we called you Enola, to give back the name to something we cherished. Maybe you'll never call yourself by that name, I don't know. But I know one thing, here and now. You're too beautiful by far to have any nasty dreams, my little princess Enola.'

He left her then, as the dawn sun began to pick out the golden threads of the balloons, kilometres across the city. She slept peacefully, dreaming of the coming day, of the smell and noise of Cockatoo's Crest, of the music of the syrinx-boxes, of the rainbow-shimmering faces of the dead people, of the empty sky.

'Enola' was my third sale to Interzone in a relatively short space of time. I'd placed my first and second professional sales there, and with 'Enola' I got my name onto the front cover for the first time. The story appeared at the end of the magazine, graced by some fine illustrations. I thought it augured well for my future as a regular contributor to the magazine.

I couldn't have been more wrong. The stories I submitted after 'Enola' turned out to be very much not to Interzone's liking, and it was to be almost four years before I appeared in the magazine again. When one invests so much energy and time into breaking into a market, it can be disheartening to hear the door slam shut and find oneself standing outside in the cold again. Even more so in my case, where I felt that the stories Interzone was now bouncing were in all respects superior to those it had already bought. What was the problem? I wondered. In hindsight, having looked over some of those rejected stories, I can see it all too clearly. They were leaden and ponderous, inflated with their own self-importance. It was only when I kicked back and wrote something fast and furious ('Byrd Land Six', not included here) that the door creaked open again. As for 'Enola', the story I'd hoped would herald the next phase of my career, it sank without a trace once it was published. I've always been rather fond of it, though, all the more so because it encapsulates many themes that turn up elsewhere in my work. A German translation of this story, incidentally, helpfully directed readers to the fact that 'Enola' was an anagram of 'Alone'. Quite what bearing this has on the story, I've never learned.

Friday

Mick Leighton was in the basement with the machines when the police came for him. He'd been trying to reach Joe Liversedge all morning, to cancel a prearranged squash match. It was the busiest week before exams, and Mick had gloomily concluded that he had too much tutorial work to grade to justify sparing even an hour for the game. The trouble was that Joe had either turned off his phone or left it in his office where it wouldn't interfere with the machines. Mick had sent an e-mail, but when that had gone unanswered he decided there was nothing for it but to stroll over to Joe's half of the building and inform him in person. By now Mick was a sufficiently well-known face in Joe's department that he was able to come and go more or less as he pleased.

'Hello, matey,' Joe said, glancing over his shoulder with a half-eaten sandwich in one hand. There was a bandage on the back of his neck, just below the hairline. He was hunched over a desk covered in laptops, cables and reams of hardcopy. 'Ready for a thrashing, are you?'

'That's why I'm here,' Mick said. 'Got to cancel, sorry. Too much on my plate today.'

'Naughty.'

'Ted Evans can fill in for me. He's got his kit. You know Ted, don't you?'

'Vaguely.' Joe set down his sandwich to put the lid back on a felt-tipped pen. He was an amiable Yorkshireman who'd come down to Cardiff for his postgraduate work and decided to stay. He was married to an archaeologist named Rachel who spent a lot of her time poking around in the Roman ruins under the walls of Cardiff Castle. 'Sure I can't twist your arm? It'll do you good, you know, bit of a workout.'

'I know. But there just isn't time.'

'Your call. How are things, anyway?'

Mick shrugged philosophically. 'Been better.'

'Did you phone Andrea like you said you were going to?'

'No.'

'You should, you know.'

'I'm not very good on the phone. Anyway, I thought she probably needed a bit of space.'

'It's been three weeks, mate.'

'I know.'

'Do you want the wife to call her? It might help.'

'No, but thanks for suggesting it anyway.'

'Call her. Let her know you're missing her.'

'I'll think about it.'

'Yeah, sure. You should stick around, you know. It's all *go* here this morning. We got a lock just after seven o'clock.' Joe tapped one of the laptop screens, which was scrolling rows of black-on-white numbers. 'It's a good one too.'

'Really?'

'Come and have a look at the machine.'

'I can't. I need to get back to my office.'

'You'll regret it later. Just like you'll regret cancelling our match, or not calling Andrea. I know you, Mick. You're one of life's born regretters.'

'Five minutes, then.'

In truth, Mick always enjoyed having a nose around Joe's basement. As solid as Mick's own early-universe work was, Joe had really struck gold. There were hundreds of researchers around the world who would have killed for a guided tour of the Liversedge laboratory.

In the basement were ten hulking machines, each as large as a steam turbine. You couldn't go near them if you were wearing a pacemaker or any other kind of implant, but Mick knew that, and he'd been careful to remove all metallic items before he came down the stairs and through the security doors. Each machine contained a ten tonne bar of ultra-high-purity iron, encased in vacuum and suspended in a magnetic cradle. Joe liked to wax lyrical about the hardness of the vacuum, about the dynamic stability of the magnetic field generators. Cardiff could be hit by a Richter-six earthquake, and the bars wouldn't feel the slightest tremor.

Joe called it the call centre.

The machines were called correlators. At any one time eight were online, while two were down for repairs and upgrades. What the eight functional machines were doing was cold-calling: dialling random numbers across the gap between quantum realities, waiting for someone to answer on the other end.

In each machine, a laser repeatedly pumped the iron into an excited quantum state. By monitoring vibrational harmonics in the excited iron – what Joe called the back-chirp – the same laser could determine if the bar had achieved a lock onto another strand of quantum reality – another worldline. In effect, the bar would be resonating with its counterpart in another version of the same basement, in another version of Cardiff.

Once that lock was established – once the cold-calling machine had achieved a hit – then those two previously indistinguishable worldlines were linked together by an information conduit. If the laser tapped the bar with low-energy pulses, enough to influence it but not upset the lock, then the counterpart in the other lab would also register those taps. It meant that it was possible to send signals from one lab to the other, in both directions.

'This is the boy,' Joe said, patting one of the active machines. 'Looks like a solid lock too. Should be good for a full ten or twelve days. I think this might be the one that does it for us.'

Mick glanced again at the bandage on the back of Joe's neck. 'You've had a nervelink inserted, haven't you?'

'Straight to the medical centre as soon as I got the alert on the lock. I was nervous – first time, and all that. But it turned out to be dead easy. No pain at all. I was up and out within half an hour. They even gave me a Rich Tea biscuit.'

'Ooh. A Rich Tea biscuit. It doesn't get any better than that, does it? You'll be going through today, I take it?'

Joe reached up and tore off the bandage, revealing only a small spot of blood, like a shaving nick. 'Tomorrow, probably. Maybe Sunday. The nervelink isn't active yet, and that'll take some getting used to. We've got bags of time, though; even if we don't switch on the nervelink until Sunday, I'll still have five or six days of bandwidth before we become noise-limited.'

'You must be excited.'

'Right now I just don't want to cock up anything. The Helsinki boys are nipping at our heels as it is. I reckon they're within a few months of beating us.'

Mick knew how important this latest project was for Joe. Sending information between different realities was one thing, and impressive enough in its own right. But now that technology had escaped from the labs out into the real world. There were hundreds of correlators in other labs and institutes around the world. In five years it had gone from being a spooky, barely believable phenomenon to an accepted part of the modern world.

But Joe – whose team had always been at the forefront of the technology – hadn't stood still. They'd been the first to work out how to send voice and video comms across the gap to another reality, and within the last year they'd been able to operate a camera-equipped robot, the same battery-driven kind that all the tourists had been using before nervelinking became the new thing. Joe had even let Mick have a go on it. With his hands operating the robot's manipulators via force-feedback gloves, and his eyes seeing the world via the stereoscopic projectors in a virtual-reality helmet, Mick had been able to feel himself almost physically present in the other lab. He'd been able to move around and pick things up just as if he were actually walking in that alternate reality. Oddest of all had been meeting the other version of Joe Liversedge, the one who worked in the counterpart lab. Both Joes seemed cheerily indifferent to the weirdness of the set-up, as if collaborating with a duplicate of yourself was the most normal thing in the world.

Mick had been impressed by the robot. But for Joe it was a stepping stone to something even better.

'Think about it,' he'd said. 'A few years ago, tourists started switching over to nervelinks instead of robots. Who wants to drive a clunky machine around some smelly foreign city when you can drive a warm human body instead? Robots can see stuff, they can move around and pick stuff up, but they can't give you the smells, the taste of food, the heat, the contact with other people.'

'Mm,' Mick had said noncommittally. He didn't really approve of nervelinking, even though it essentially paid Andrea's wages.

'So we're going to do the same. We've got the kit. Getting it installed is a piece of piss. All we need now is a solid link.'

And now Joe had what he'd been waiting for. Mick could

practically see the *Nature* cover-article in his friend's eyes. Perhaps he was even thinking about taking that long train ride to Stockholm.

'I hope it works out for you,' Mick said.

Joe patted the correlator again. 'I've got a good feeling about this one.'

That was when one of Joe's undergraduates came up to them. To Mick's surprise, it wasn't Joe she wanted to speak to.

'Doctor Leighton?'

'That's me.'

'There's somebody to see you, sir. I think it's quite important.'

'Someone to see me?'

'They said you left a note in your office.'

'I did,' Mick said absentmindedly. 'But I also said I wouldn't be gone long. Nothing's *that* important, is it?'

But the person who had come to find Mick was a policewoman. When Mick met her at the top of the stairs her expression told him it wasn't good news.

'Something's happened,' he said.

She looked worried, and very, very young. 'Is there somewhere we can talk, Mister Leighton?'

'Use my office,' Joe said, showing the two of them to his room just down the corridor. Joe left them alone, saying he was going down to the coffee machine in the hall.

'I've got some bad news,' the policewoman said, when Joe had closed the door. 'I think you should sit down, Mister Leighton.'

Mick pulled out Joe's chair from under the desk, which was covered in papers: coursework Joe must have been in the process of grading. Mick sat down, then didn't know where to put his hands. 'It's about Andrea, isn't it?'

'I'm afraid your wife was in an accident this morning,' the policewoman said.

'What kind of accident? What happened?'

'Your wife was hit by a car when she was crossing the road.'

A mean little thought flashed through Mick's mind. Bloody Andrea: she'd always been one for dashing across a road without looking. He'd been warning her for years she was going to regret it one day.

'How is she? Where did they take her?'

'I'm really sorry, sir.' The policewoman hesitated. 'Your wife died on the way to hospital. I understand that the paramedics did all they could, but ...'

Mick was hearing it, and not hearing it. It couldn't be right. People still got knocked down by cars. But they didn't *die* from it, not any more. Cars couldn't go fast enough in towns to kill anyone. Being knocked down and killed by a car was something that happened to people in soap operas, not real life.

Feeling numb, not really present in the room, Mick said, 'Where is she now?' As if by visiting her, he might prove that they'd got it wrong, that she wasn't dead at all.

'They took her to the Heath, sir. That's where she is now. I can drive you there.'

'Andrea isn't dead,' Mick said. 'She can't be. Not now.'

'I'm really sorry,' the policewoman said.

Saturday

For the last three weeks, ever since they had separated, Mick had been sleeping in a spare room at his brother's house in Newport. The company had been good, but now Bill was away for the weekend on some ridiculous team-building exercise in Snowdonia. For tedious reasons, Mick's brother had had to take the house keys with him, leaving Mick with nowhere to sleep on Friday night. When Joe had asked him where he was going to stay, Mick said he'd go back to his own house, the one he'd left at the beginning of the month.

Joe was having none of it, and insisted that Mick sleep at his house instead. Mick spent the night going through the usual cycle of emotions that came with any sudden bad news. He'd had nothing to compare with losing his wife, but the texture of the shock was familiar enough, albeit magnified from anything in his previous experience. He resented the fact that the world seemed to be continuing, crassly oblivious to Andrea's death. The news wasn't dominated by his tragedy; it was all about some Polish miners trapped underground. When he finally managed to get to sleep, Mick was tormented by dreams that his wife was still alive, that it had all been a mistake.

But he knew it was all true. He'd been to the hospital; he'd seen her body. He even knew why she'd been hit by the car. Andrea had been crossing the road to her favourite hair salon;

she'd had an appointment to get her hair done. Knowing Andrea, she had probably been so focused on the salon that she was oblivious to all that was going on around her. It hadn't even been the car that had killed her in the end. When the slow-moving vehicle knocked her down, Andrea had struck her head against the side of the kerb.

By midmorning on Saturday, Mick's brother had returned from Snowdonia. Bill came around to Joe's house and hugged Mick silently, saying nothing for many minutes. Then Bill went into the next room and spoke quietly to Joe and Rachel. Their low voices made Mick feel like a child in a house of adults.

'I think you and I need to get out of Cardiff,' Bill told Mick, when he returned to the living room. 'No ifs, no buts.'

Mick started to protest. 'There's too much that needs to be done. I still need to get back to the funeral home.'

'It can wait until this afternoon. No one's going to hate you for not returning a few calls. C'mon; let's drive up to the Gower and get some fresh air. I've already reserved a car.'

'Go with him,' Rachel said. 'It'll do you good.'

Mick acquiesced, his guilt and relief in conflict at being able to put aside thoughts of the funeral plans. He was glad Bill had come down, but he couldn't quite judge how his brother – or his friends, for that matter – viewed his bereavement. He'd lost his wife. They all knew that. But they also knew that Mick and Andrea had been separated. They'd been having problems for most of the year. It would only be human for his friends to assume that Mick wasn't quite as affected by Andrea's death as he would have been had they still been living together.

'Listen,' he told Bill, when they were safely under way. 'There's something I've got to tell you.'

'I'm listening.'

'Andrea and I had problems. But it wasn't the end of our mar-riage. We were going to get through this. I was going to call her this weekend, see if we couldn't meet.'

Bill looked at him sadly. Mick couldn't tell if that meant that Bill just didn't believe him, or that his brother pitied him for the opportunity he'd allowed to slip between his fingers.

When they got back to Cardiff in the early evening, after a warm and blustery day out on the Gower, Joe practically pounced on Mick as soon as they came through the door.

'I need to talk to you,' Joe said. 'Now.'

'I need to call some of Andrea's friends,' Mick said. 'Can it wait until later?'

'No. It can't. It's about you and Andrea.'

They went into the kitchen. Joe poured him a glass of whisky. Rachel and Bill watched from the end of the table, saying nothing.

'I've been to the lab,' Joe said. 'I know it's Saturday, but I wanted to make sure that lock was still holding. Well, it is. We could start the experiment tomorrow if we wanted to. But something's come up, and you need to know about it.'

Mick sipped from his glass. 'Go on.'

'I've been in contact with my counterpart in the other lab.'

'The other Joe.'

'The other Joe, yes. We were finessing the equipment, making sure everything was optimal. And we talked, of course. Needless to say I mentioned what had happened.'

'And?'

'The other me was surprised. Shocked, even. He said Andrea hadn't died in his reality.' Joe held up a hand, signalling that Mick should let him finish before speaking. 'You know how it works. The two histories are identical before the lock takes effect: so identical that there isn't even any point in thinking of them as being distinct realities. The divergence only happens once the lock is in effect. The lock was active by the time you came down to tell me about the squash match. The other me also had a visit from you. The difference was that no policewoman ever came to his lab. You eventually drifted back to your office to carry on grading tutorials.'

'But Andrea was already dead by then.'

'Not in that reality. The other me phoned you. You were staying at the Holiday Inn. You knew nothing of Andrea having had any accident. So my other wife . . .' Joe allowed himself a quick smile. 'The other version of Rachel called Andrea. And they spoke. Turned out Andrea had been hit by a car, but she'd barely been bruised. They hadn't even called an ambulance.'

Mick absorbed his friend's words, then said, 'I can't deal with this, Joe. I don't need to know it. It isn't going to help.'

'I think it is. We were set up to run the nervelink experiment as soon as we had a solid lock, one that we could trust to hold for the full million seconds. This is it. The only difference is it doesn't have to be me who goes through.'

'I don't understand.'

'I can put *you* through, Mick. We can get you nervelinked tomorrow morning. Allowing for a day of bedding in and practice once you arrive in the other reality ... well, you could be walking in Andrea's world by Monday afternoon, Tuesday morning at the latest.'

'But you're the one who is supposed to be going through,' Mick said. 'You've already had the nervelink put in.'

'We've got a spare,' Joe said.

Mick's mind raced through the implications. 'Then I'd be controlling the body of the other you, right?'

'No. That won't work, unfortunately. We've had to make some changes to these nervelinks to get them to work properly through the correlator, with the limited signal throughput. We had to ditch some of the channels that handle proprioceptive mapping. They'll only work properly if the body on the other end of the link is virtually identical to the one on this side.'

'Then it won't work. You're nothing like me.'

'You're forgetting *your* counterpart on the other side,' Joe said. He glanced past Mick at Bill and Rachel, raising his eyebrows as he did so. 'The way it would work is, you come into the lab and we install the link in you, just the same way it happened for me yesterday morning. At the same time your counterpart in Andrea's world comes into *his* version of the lab and gets the other version of the nervelink put into him.'

Mick shivered. He'd become used to thinking about the other version of Joe; he could even begin to accept that there was a version of Andrea walking around somewhere who was still alive. But as soon as Joe brought the other Mick into the argument, he felt his head begin to unravel.

'Wouldn't he – the other me – need to agree to this?'

'He already has,' Joe said solemnly. 'I've been in touch with him. The other Joe called him into the lab. We had a chat over the videolink. He didn't go for it at first – you know how you both feel about nervelinking. And he hasn't lost *his* version of Andrea. But I explained how big a deal this was. This is your only chance to see Andrea again. Once this window closes – we're talking about no more than eleven or twelve days from the start of the lock, by the way – we'll never make contact with another reality where she's alive.'

Mick blinked and placed his hands on the table. He felt dizzy with the implications, as if the kitchen was swaying. 'You're certain of that? You'll never open another window into Andrea's world?'

'Statistically, we were incredibly lucky to get this one chance. By the time the window closes, Andrea's reality will have diverged so far from ours that there's essentially no chance of ever getting another lock.'

'Okay,' Mick said, ready to take Joe's word for it. 'But even if I agree to this – even if the other me agrees to it – what about Andrea? We weren't seeing each other.'

'But you wanted to see her again,' Bill said quietly.

Mick rubbed his eyes with the palms of his hands, and exhaled loudly. 'Maybe.'

'I've spoken to Andrea,' Rachel said. 'I mean, Joe spoke to himself, and the other version of him spoke to the other Rachel. She's been in touch with Andrea.'

Mick hardly dared speak. 'And?'

'She says it's okay. She understands how horrible this must be for you. She says, if you want to come through, she'll meet you. You can spend some time together. Give you a chance to come to some kind of—'

'Closure,' Mick whispered.

'It'll help you,' Joe said. 'It's got to help you.'

Sunday

The medical centre was normally closed at weekends, but Joe had pulled strings to get some of the staff to come in on Sunday morning. Mick had to sit around a long time while they ran physiological tests and prepared the surgical equipment. It was much easier and quicker for tourists, as they didn't have to use the modified nervelink units Joe's team had developed.

By the early afternoon they were satisfied that Mick was ready for the implantation. They made him lie down on a couch with his head encased in a padded plastic assembly with a hole under the back of the neck. He was given a mild local anaesthetic. Rubberised clamps whirred in to hold his head in position with micromillimetre accuracy. Then he felt a vague sense of pressure being applied to the skin on the back of his neck, and then an odd and not entirely pleasant sensation of sudden pins and needles in every part of his body. But the unpleasantness was over almost as soon as he'd registered it. The support clamps whirred away from his head. The couch tilted up, and he was able to get off and stand on his feet.

Mick touched the back of his neck, came away with a tiny smear of blood on his thumb.

'That's it?'

'I told you there was nothing to it,' Joe said, putting down a motorcycling magazine. 'I don't know what you were so worried about.'

'It's not the nervelink operation itself I don't approve of. I don't have a problem with the technology. It's the whole system, the way it encourages the exploitation of the poor.'

Joe tut-tutted. 'Bloody *Guardian* readers. It was you lot who got the bloody moratorium against air travel enacted in the first place. Next you'll be telling us we can't even *walk* anywhere.'

The nurse swabbed Mick's wound and applied a bandage. He was shunted into an adjoining room and asked to wait again. More tests followed. As the system interrogated the newly embedded nervelink, he experienced mild electrical tingles and strange, fleeting feelings of dislocation. Nothing he reported gave the staff any cause for alarm.

After Mick's discharge from the medical centre, Joe took him straight down to the laboratory. An electromagnetically shielded annexe contained the couch Joe intended to use for the experiment. It was a modified version of the kind tourists used for long-term nervelinking, with facilities for administering nutrition and collecting bodily waste. No one liked to dwell too much on those details, but there was no way around it if you wanted to stay nervelinked for more than a few hours. Gamers had been putting up with similar indignities for decades.

Once Mick was plumbed in, Joe settled a pair of specially designed immersion glasses over his eyes, after first applying a salve to Mick's skin to protect against pressure sores. The glasses fitted very tightly, blocking out Mick's view of the lab. All he could see was a blue-grey void, with a few meaningless red digits to the right side of his visual field.

'Comfortable?' Joe asked.

'I can't see anything yet.'

'You will.'

Joe went back into the main part of the basement to check on the correlation. It seemed that he was gone a long time. When he heard Joe return, Mick half-expected bad news – that the link had collapsed, or some necessary piece of technology had broken down. Privately, he would not have been too sorry were that the case. In his shocked state of mind in the hours after Andrea's death, he would have given anything to be able to see her again. But now that the possibility had arisen, he found himself prone to doubts. Given time, he knew he'd get over Andrea's death. That wasn't being cold, it was just being realistic. He knew more than a few people who'd lost their partners, and while they might have gone through some dark times afterwards, almost all of them now seemed settled and relatively content. It didn't mean they'd stopped feeling anything for the loved one who had died, but it did mean they'd found some way to move on. There was no reason to assume he wouldn't make the same emotional recovery.

The question was, would visiting Andrea hasten or hamper that process? Perhaps they should just have talked over the videolink, or even the phone. But then he'd never been very good on either.

He knew it had to be face to face, all or nothing.

'Is there a problem?' he asked Joe, innocently enough.

'Nope, everything's fine. I was just waiting to hear that the other version of you is ready.'

'He is?'

'Good to go. Someone from the medical centre just put him under. We can make the switch any time you're ready.'

'Where is he?'

'Here,' Joe said. 'I mean, in the counterpart to this room. He's lying on the same couch. It's easier that way; there's less of a jolt when you switch over.'

'He's unconscious already?'

'Full coma. Just like any nervelinked mule.'

Except, Mick thought, unlike the mules, his counterpart hadn't signed up to go into a chemically induced coma while his body was taken over by a distant tourist. That was what Mick disapproved of more than anything. The mules did it for money, and the mules were always the poorest people in any given tourist hotspot, whether it was some affluent European city or some nauseatingly 'authentic' Third World shithole. No one ever aspired to become a mule. It was what you did when all other options had dried up. In some cases it hadn't just supplanted prostitution, it had become an entirely new form of prostitution in its own right.

But enough of that. They were all consenting adults here. No one – least of all the other version of himself – was being exploited. The other Mick was just being kind. No kinder, Mick supposed, than *he* would have been had the tables been reversed, but he couldn't help feeling a perverse sense of gratitude. And as for Andrea ... well, she'd always been kind. No one ever had a bad word to say about Andrea on that score. Kind and considerate, to a fault.

So what was he waiting for?

'You can make the switch,' Mick said.

There was less to it than he'd been expecting. It was no worse than the involuntary muscular jolt he sometimes experienced in bed, just before dozing off to sleep.

But suddenly he was in a different body.

'Hi,' Joe said. 'How're you feeling, matey?'

Except it was the other Joe speaking to him now: the Joe who belonged to the world where Andrea hadn't died. The original Joe was on the other side of the reality gap.

'I feel ...' But when Mick tried speaking, it came out hopelessly slurred.

'Give it time,' Joe said. 'Everyone has trouble speaking to start with. That'll come quickly.'

'Can't shee. Can't see.'

'That's because we haven't switched on your glasses. Hold on a tick.'

The grey-green void vanished, to be replaced by a view of the interior of the lab. The quality of the image was excellent. The room looked superficially the same, but as Mick looked around – sending the muscle signals through the nervelink to move the other Mick's body – he noticed the small details that told him this wasn't his world. Joe was wearing a different checked shirt, smudged white trainers instead of Converse sneakers. In this version of the lab, Joe had forgotten to turn the calendar over to the new month.

Mick tried speaking again. The words came easier this time.

'I'm really here, aren't I?'

'How does it feel to be making history?'

'It feels ... bloody weird, actually. And no, I'm not making history. When you write up your experiment, it won't be me who went through first. It'll be you, the way it was always meant to be. This is just a dry run. You can mention me in a footnote, if that.'

Joe looked unconvinced. 'Have it your way, but—'

'I will.' Mick moved to get off the couch. This version of his body wasn't plumbed in like the other one. But when he tried to move, nothing happened. For a moment, he felt a crushing sense of paralysis. He must have let out a frightened sound.

'Easy,' Joe said, putting a hand on his shoulder. 'One step at a time. The link still has to bed in. It's going to be hours before you'll have complete fluidity of movement, so don't run before you can walk. And I'm afraid we're going to have to keep you in the lab for rather longer than you might like. As routine as nervelinking is, this *isn't* simple nervelinking. The short cuts we've had to use to squeeze the data through the correlator link mean we're exposing ourselves to more medical risks than you'd get with the standard tourist kit. Nothing that you need worry about, but I want to make sure we keep a close eye on all the parameters. I'll be running tests in the morning and evening. Sorry to be a drag about it, but we do need numbers for our paper, as well. All I can promise is that you'll still have a lot of time available to meet Andrea. If that's what you still want to do, of course.'

'It is,' Mick said. 'Now that I'm here ... no going back, right?'

Joe glanced at his watch. 'Let's start running some coordination exercises. That'll keep us busy for an hour or two. Then we'll need to make sure you have full bladder control. Could get messy otherwise. After that – we'll see if you can feed yourself.'

'I want to see Andrea.'

'Not today,' Joe said firmly. 'Not until we've got you house-trained.'

'Tomorrow. Definitely tomorrow.'

*

He paused in the shade of the old, green boating shed at the edge of the lake. It was a hot day, approaching noon, and the park was already busier than it had been at any time since the last gasp of the previous summer. Office workers were sitting around the lake making the most of their lunch break: the men with their ties eased and sleeves and trousers rolled up, the women with their shoes off and blouses loosened. Children splashed in the ornamental fountains, while their older siblings bounced metres into the air on servo-assisted pogo sticks, the season's latest, lethal-looking craze. Students lolled around on the gently sloping grass, sunbathing or catching up on neglected coursework in the last week before exams. Mick recognised some of them from his own department. Most wore cheap immersion glasses, with their arms covered almost to the shoulder in tight-fitting, pink, haptic feedback gloves. The more animated students lay on their backs, pointing and clutching at invisible objects suspended above them. It looked like they were trying to snatch down the last few wisps of cloud from the scratchless blue sky above Cardiff.

Mick had already seen Andrea standing a little further around the curve of the lake. It was where they had agreed to meet, and true to form Andrea was exactly on time. She stared pensively out across the water, seemingly oblivious to the commotion going on around her. She wore a white blouse, a knee-length burgundy skirt, sensible office shoes. Her hair was shorter than he remembered, styled differently and barely reaching her collar. For a moment – until she'd turned slightly – he hadn't recognised her at all. Andrea held a Starbucks coffee holder in one hand, and every now and then she'd take a sip or glance at her wristwatch. Mick was five minutes late now, and he knew there was a risk Andrea would give up waiting. But in the shade of the boating shed, all his certainties had evaporated.

Andrea turned minutely. She glanced at her watch again. She sipped from the coffee holder, tilting it back in a way that told Mick she'd finished the last drop. He saw her looking around for a waste bin.

Mick stepped from the shade. He walked across the grass, onto concrete, acutely conscious of the slow awkwardness of his gait. His walking had improved since his first efforts, but it still felt as if he were trying to walk upright in a swimming pool filled with treacle. Joe had assured him that all his movements would become more normal as the nervelink bedded in, but that process was obviously taking longer than anticipated.

'Andrea,' he said, sounding slurred and drunk and too loud, even to his own ears.

She turned and met his eyes. There was a slight pause before she smiled, and when she did, the smile wasn't quite right, as if she'd been asked to hold it too long for a photograph.

'Hello, Mick. I was beginning to think—'

'It's okay.' He forced out each word with care, making sure it came out right before moving to the next. 'I just had some second thoughts.'

'I don't blame you. How does it feel?'

'A bit odd. It'll get easier.'

'Yes, that's what they told me.' She took another sip from the coffee holder, even though it must have been empty. They were standing about two metres apart, close enough to talk, close enough to look like two friends or colleagues who'd bumped into each other around the lake.

'It's really good of you—' Mick began.

Andrea shook her head urgently. 'Please. It's okay. We talked it over. We both agreed it was the right thing to do. If the tables were turned, you wouldn't have hesitated.'

'Maybe not.'

'I know you, Mick. Maybe better than you know yourself. You'd have done all that you could, and more.'

'I just want you to know ... I'm not taking any of this lightly. Not you having to see me, like this ... not what *he* has to go through while I'm around.'

'He said to tell you there are worse ways to spend a week.'

Mick tried to smile. He felt the muscles of his face move, but without a mirror there was no way to judge the outcome. The moment stretched. A football splashed into the lake and began to drift away from the edge. He heard a little boy start crying.

'Your hair looks different,' Mick said.

'You don't like it.'

'No, I do. It really suits you. Did you have that done after ... oh, wait. I see. You were on your way to the salon.'

He could see the scratch on her face where she'd grazed it on the kerb, when the car knocked her down. She hadn't even needed stitches. In a week it would hardly show at all.

'I can't begin to imagine what it's been like for you,' Andrea said. 'I can't imagine what *this* is like for you.'

'It helps.'

'You don't sound convinced.'

'I want it to help. I think it's going to. It's just that right now it feels like I've made the worst mistake of my life.'

Andrea held up the coffee holder. 'Do you fancy one? It's my treat.'

Andrea was a solicitor. She worked for a small legal firm located in modern offices near the park. There was a Starbucks near her office building. 'They don't know me there, do they?'

'Not unless you've been moonlighting. Come on. I hate to say it, but you could use some practice walking.'

'As long as you won't laugh.'

'I wouldn't dream of it. Hold my hand, Mick. It'll make it easier.'

Before he could step back, Andrea closed the distance between them and took his hand in hers. It was good of her to do that, Mick thought. He'd been wondering how he would initiate that first touch, and Andrea had spared him the fumbling awkwardness that would almost certainly have ensued. That was Andrea to a T, always thinking of others and trying to make life a little easier for them, no matter how small the difference. It was why people liked her so much; why her friends were so fiercely loyal.

'It's going to be okay, Mick,' Andrea said gently. 'Everything that's happened between us ... it doesn't matter now. I've said bad things to you and you've said bad things to me. But let's forget about all that. Let's just make the most of what time we have.'

'I'm scared of losing you.'

'You're a good man. You've more friends than you realise.'

He was sweating in the heat, so much so that the glasses began to slip down his nose. The view tilted towards his shoes. He raised his free hand in a stiff, salute-like gesture and pushed the glasses back into place. Andrea's hand tightened on his.

'I can't go through with this,' Mick said. 'I should go back.'

'You started it,' Andrea said sternly, but without rancour. 'Now you finish it. All the way, Mick Leighton.'

Things were much better by the morning of the second day. When he woke in Joe Liversedge's lab there was a fluency in his movements that simply hadn't been there the evening before, when he'd said goodbye to Andrea. He now felt as if he was inhabiting the host body, rather than simply shuffling it around like a puppet. He still needed the glasses to be able to see anything, but the nervelink was conveying sensation much more effectively now, so that when he touched something it came through without any of the fuzziness or lag he'd been experiencing the day before. Most tourists were able to achieve reasonable accuracy of touch differentiation within twenty-four hours. Within two days, their degree of proprioceptive immersion was generally good enough to allow complex motor tasks such as cycling, swimming or skiing. Repeat-visit tourists, especially those that went back into the same body, got over the transition period even faster. To them it was like moving back into a house after a short absence.

Joe's team gave Mick a thorough check-up in the annexe. It was all routine stuff. Amy Flint, Joe's senior graduate student, insisted on adding some more numbers to the tactile test database she was building for the study. That meant Mick sitting at a table, without the glasses, being asked to hold various objects and decide what shape they were and what they were made of. He scored excellently, only failing to distinguish between wood and plastic balls of similar weight and texture. Flint was cheerfully casual around him, without any of the affectedness or oversensitivity Mick had quickly detected in his friends and colleagues. Clearly she didn't know what had happened; she just thought Joe had opted to go for a different test subject than himself.

Joe was upbeat about Mick's progress. Everything, from the host body to the hardware, was holding up well. The bandwidth was stable at nearly two megabytes per second, more than enough spare capacity to permit Mick the use of a second video feed to peer back into the version of the lab on the other side. The other version of Joe held the cam up so that Mick could see his own body, reclining on the heavy-duty immersion couch. Mick had expected to be disturbed by that, but the whole experience turned out to be oddly banal, like replaying a home movie.

When they were done with the tests, Joe walked Mick over to

the university canteen, where he ate a liquid breakfast, slurping down three containers of fruit yoghurt. While he ate – which was tricky, but another of the things that was supposed to get easier with practice – he gazed distractedly at the television in the canteen. The wall-sized screen was running through the morning news, with the sound turned down. At the moment the screen was showing grainy footage of the Polish miners, caught on surveillance camera as they trudged into the low, concrete pithead building on their way to work. The cave-in had happened three days ago. The miners were still trapped underground, in all the worldlines that were in contact with this one, including Mick's own.

'Poor fuckers,' Joe said, looking up from a draft paper he was pencilling remarks over.

'Maybe they'll get them out.'

'Aye. Maybe. Wouldn't fancy my chances down there, though.'

The picture changed to a summary of football scores. Again, most of the games had ended in identical results across the contacted worldlines, but two or three – highlighted in sidebars, with analysis text ticking below them – had ended differently, with one team even being dropped from the rankings.

Afterwards Mick walked on his own to the tram stop and caught the next service into the city centre. Already he could feel that he was attracting less attention than the day before. He still moved a little stiffly, he could tell that just by looking at his reflection in the glass as he boarded the tram, but there was no longer anything comical or robotic about it. He just looked like someone with a touch of arthritis, or someone who'd been overdoing it in the gym and was now paying with a dose of sore muscles.

As the tram whisked its way through traffic, he thought back to the evening before. The meeting with Andrea, and the subsequent day, had gone as well as he could have expected. Things had been strained at first, but by the time they'd been to Starbucks, he had detected an easing in her manner, and that had made him feel more at ease as well. They'd made small talk, skirting around the main thing neither of them wanted to discuss. Andrea had taken most of the day off; she didn't have to be at the law offices until late afternoon, just to check that no problems had arisen in her absence.

They'd talked about what to do with the rest of their day together.

'Maybe we could drive up into the Beacons,' Mick had said. 'It'll be nice up in the hills with a bit of a breeze. We always used to enjoy those days out.'

'Been a while though,' Andrea had said. 'I'm not sure my legs are up to it any more.'

'You always used to hustle up those hills.'

'Emphasis on the "used to", unfortunately. Now I get out of breath just walking up Saint Mary's Street with a bag full of shopping.'

Mick looked at her sceptically, but he couldn't deny that Andrea had a point. Neither of them was the keen, outdoors type they had been when they met fifteen years earlier through the university's hill-walking club. Back then they'd spent long weekends exploring the hills of the Brecon Beacons and the Black Mountains, or driving to Snowdonia or the Lake District. They'd had some hair-raising moments together, when the weather turned against them or when they suddenly realised they were on completely the wrong ridge. But what Mick remembered, more than anything, was not being cold and wet, but the feeling of relief when they arrived at some cosy warm pub at the end of the day, both of them ravenous and thirsty and high on what they'd achieved. Good memories, all of them. Why hadn't they kept it up, instead of letting their jobs rule their weekends?

'Look, maybe we might drive up to the Beacons in a day or two,' Andrea said. 'But I think it's a bit ambitious for today, don't you?'

'You're probably right,' Mick said.

After some debate, they'd agreed to visit the castle and then take a boat ride around the bay to see the huge and impressive sea defences up close. Both were things they'd always meant to do together but had kept putting off for another weekend. The castle was heaving with tourists, even on this midweek day. Because a lot of them were nervelinked, though, they afforded Mick a welcome measure of inconspicuousness. No one gave him a second glance as he bumbled along with the other shade-wearing bodysnatchers, even though he must have looked considerably more affluent and well fed than the average mule. Afterwards, they went to look at the Roman ruins, where Rachel Liversedge was busy talking to a group of bored primary school children from the valleys.

Mick enjoyed the boat ride more than the trip to the castle.

There were still enough nervelinked tourists on the boat for him not to feel completely out of place, and being out in the bay offered some respite from the cloying heat of the city centre. Mick had even felt the breeze on the back of his hand, evidence that the nervelink was really bedding in.

It was Andrea who nudged the conversation towards the reason for Mick's presence. She'd just returned from the counter with two paper cups brimming with murky coffee, nearly spilling them as the boat swayed unexpectedly. She sat down on the boat's hard wooden bench.

'I forgot to ask how it went in the lab this morning,' she said brightly. 'Everything working out okay?'

'Very well,' Mick said. 'Joe says we were getting two megs this morning. That's as good as he was hoping for.'

'You'll have to explain that to me. I know it's to do with the amount of data you're able to send through the link, but I don't know how it compares with what we'd be using for a typical tourist set-up.'

Mick remembered what Joe had told him. 'It's not as good. Tourists can use as much bandwidth as they can afford. But Joe's correlators never get above five megabytes per second. That's at the start of the twelve-day window too. It only gets worse by day five or six.'

'Is two enough?'

'It's what Joe's got to work with.' Mick reached up and tapped the glasses. 'It shouldn't be enough for full-colour vision at normal resolution, according to Joe. But there's an awful lot of clever software in the lab to take care of that. It's constantly guessing, filling in gaps.'

'How does it look?'

'Like I'm looking at the world through a pair of sunglasses.' He pulled them off his nose and tilted them towards Andrea. 'Except it's the glasses that are actually doing the seeing, not my – *his* – eyes. Most of the time, it's good enough that I don't notice anything weird. If I wiggle my head around fast – or if something streaks past too quickly – then the glasses have trouble keeping up with the changing view.' He jammed the glasses back on, just in time for a seagull to flash past only a few metres from the boat. He had a momentary sense of the seagull breaking up into blocky areas of confused pixels, as if it had been painted by a cubist, before the glasses smoothed things over and normality ensued.

'What about all the rest of it? Hearing, touch ...'

'They don't take up anything like as much bandwidth as vision. The way Joe puts it, postural information only needs a few basic parameters: the angles of my limb joints, that kind of thing. Hearing's pretty straightforward. And touch is the easiest of all, as it happens.'

'Really?'

'So Joe says. Hold my hand.'

Andrea hesitated an instant then took Mick's hand.

'Now squeeze it,' Mick said.

She tightened her hold. 'Are you getting that?'

'Perfectly. It's much easier than sending sound. If you were to say something to me, the acoustic signal would have to be sampled, digitised, compressed and pushed across the link: hundreds of bytes per second. But all touch needs is a single parameter. The system will still be able to keep sending touch even when everything else gets too difficult.'

'Then it's the last thing to go.'

'It's the most fundamental sense we have. That's the way it ought to be.'

After a few moments, Andrea said, 'How long?'

'Four days,' Mick said slowly. 'Maybe five, if we're lucky. Joe says we'll have a better handle on the decay curve by tomorrow.'

'I'm worried, Mick. I don't know how I'm going to deal with losing you.'

He closed his other hand on hers and squeezed in return. 'You'll get me back.'

'I know. It's just ... it won't be you. It'll be the other you.'

'They're both me.'

'That's not how it feels right now. It feels like I'm having an affair while my husband's away.'

'It shouldn't. I am your husband. We're both your husband.'

They said nothing after that, sitting in silence as the boat bobbed its way back to shore. It was not that they had said anything upsetting, just that words were no longer adequate. Andrea kept holding his hand. Mick wanted this morning to continue for ever: the boat, the breeze, the perfect sky over the bay. Even then he chided himself for dwelling on the passage of time, rather than making the most of the experience as it happened to him. That had always been his problem, ever since he was a kid. School holidays had always been steeped in a melancholic sense of how few days were left.

But this wasn't a holiday.

After a while, he noticed that some people had gathered at the bow of the boat, pressing against the railings. They were pointing up, into the sky. Some of them had pulled out phones.

'There's something going on,' Mick said.

'I can see it,' Andrea answered. She touched the side of his face, steering his view until he was craning up as far as his neck would allow. 'It's an aeroplane.'

Mick waited until the glasses picked out the tiny, moving speck of the plane etching a pale contrail in its wake. He felt a twinge of resentment towards anyone still having the freedom to fly, when the rest of humanity was denied that right. It had been a nice dream while it lasted, flying. He had no idea what political or military purpose the plane was serving, but it would be an easy matter to find out, were he that interested. The news would be in all the papers by the afternoon. The plane wouldn't just be over-flying this version of Cardiff, but his as well. That had been one of the hardest things to take since Andrea's death. The world at large steamrolled on, its course undeflected by that single human tragedy. Andrea had died in the accident in his world, she'd survived unscathed in this one, and that plane's course wouldn't have changed in any measurable way (in either reality).

'I love seeing aeroplanes,' Andrea said. 'It reminds me of what things were like before the moratorium. Don't you?'

'Actually,' Mick said, 'they make me a bit sad.'

Wednesday

Mick knew how busy Andrea had been lately, and he tried to persuade her against taking any time off from her work. Andrea had protested, saying her colleagues could handle her workload for a few days. Mick knew better than that – Andrea practically ran the firm single-handedly – but in the end they'd come to a compromise. Andrea would take time off from the office, but she'd pop in first thing in the morning to put out any really serious fires.

Mick agreed to meet her at the offices at ten, after his round of tests. Everything still felt the way it had the day before; if anything he was even more fluent in his body movements. But when Joe had finished, the news was all that Mick had been quietly dreading, while knowing it could be no other way. The quality of the link had continued to degrade. According to Joe they were down to one-point-eight megs now. They'd seen enough decay curves to be able to extrapolate forward into the beginning of the following week. The link would become noise-swamped around teatime on Sunday, give or take three hours either way.

If only they'd started sooner, Mick thought. But Joe had done all that he could.

Today – despite the foreboding message from the lab – his sense of immersion in the counterpart world had become total. As the sunlit city swept by outside the tram's windows, Mick found it nearly impossible to believe that he was not physically present in this body, rather than lying on the couch in the other version of the lab. Overnight his tactile immersion had improved markedly. When he braced himself against the tram's upright handrail, as it swept around a curve, he felt cold aluminium, the faint greasiness where it had been touched by other hands.

At the offices, Andrea's colleagues greeted him with an unforced casualness that left him dismayed. He'd been expecting awkward expressions of sympathy, sly glances when they thought he wasn't looking. Instead he was plonked down in the waiting area and left to flick through glossy brochures while he waited for Andrea to emerge from her office. No one even offered him a drink.

He leafed through the brochures dispiritedly. Andrea's job had always been a sore point in their relationship. If Mick didn't approve of nervelinking, he had even less time for the legal vultures that made so much money out of personal injury claims related to the technology. But now he found it difficult to summon his usual sense of moral superiority. Unpleasant things *had* happened to decent people because of negligence and corner-cutting. If nervelinking was to be a part of the world, then someone had to make sure the victims got their due. He wondered why this had never been clear to him before.

'Hiya,' Andrea said, leaning over him. She gave him a businesslike kiss, not quite meeting his mouth. 'Took a bit longer than I thought, sorry.'

'Can we go now?' Mick asked, putting down the brochure.

'Yep, I'm done here.'

Outside, when they were walking along the pavement in the shade of the tall commercial buildings, Mick said: 'They didn't have a clue, did they? No one in that office knows what's happened to us.'

'I thought it was best,' Andrea said.

'I don't know how you can keep up that act, that nothing's wrong.'

'Mick, nothing *is* wrong. You have to see it from my point of view. I haven't lost my husband. Nothing's changed for me. When you're gone – when all this ends, and I get the other *you* back – my life carries on as normal. I know what's happened to you is a tragedy, and believe me I'm as upset about it as anyone.'

'Upset,' Mick said quietly.

'Yes, upset. But I'd be lying if I said I was paralysed with grief. I'm human, Mick. I'm not capable of feeling great emotional turmoil at the thought that some distant counterpart of myself got herself run over, all because she was rushing to have her hair done. Silly cow, that's what it makes me feel. At most it makes me feel a bit odd, a bit shivery. But I don't think it's something I'm going to have trouble getting over.'

'I lost my wife,' Mick said.

'I know, and I'm sorry. More than you'll ever know. But if you expect *my* life to come crashing to a halt—'

He cut her off. 'I'm already fading. One point eight this morning.'

'You always knew it would happen. It's not like it's any surprise.'

'You'll notice a difference in me by the end of the day.'

'This isn't the end of the day, so stop dwelling on it. All right? Please, Mick. You're in serious danger of ruining this for yourself.'

'I know, and I'm trying not to,' he said. 'But what I was saying, about how things aren't going to get any better ... I think today's going to be my last chance, Andrea. My last chance to be with you, to be with you properly.'

'You mean us sleeping together,' Andrea said, keeping her voice low.

'We haven't talked about it yet. That's okay; I wasn't expecting it to happen without at least some discussion. But there's no reason why—'

'Mick, I—' Andrea began.

'You're still my wife. I'm still in love with you. I know we've had our problems, but I realise now how stupid all that was. I should have called you sooner. I was being an idiot. And then this happened ... and it made me realise what a wonderful, lovely person you are, and I should have seen that for myself, but I didn't ... I needed the accident to shake me up, to make me see how lucky I was just to know you. And now I'm going to lose you again, and I'm not sure how I'm going to cope with that. But at least if we can be together again ... properly, I mean.'

'Mick—'

'You've already said you might get back together with the other Mick. Maybe it took all this to get us talking again. Point is, if you're going to get back together with him, there's nothing to stop us getting back together *now*. We were a couple before the accident; we can still be a couple now.'

'Mick, it isn't the same. You've lost your wife. I'm not *her*. I'm some weird thing there isn't a word for. And you aren't really my husband. My husband is in a medically induced coma.'

'You know none of that really matters.'

'To you.'

'It shouldn't matter to you either. And your husband – me, incidentally – agreed to this. He knew exactly what was supposed to happen. And so did you.'

'I just thought things would be better – more civilised – if we kept a kind of distance.'

'You're talking as if we're divorced.'

'Mick, we were already separated. We weren't talking. I can't just forget what happened before the accident as if none of that mattered.'

'I know it isn't easy for you.'

They walked on in an awkward silence, through the city centre streets they'd walked a thousand times before. Mick asked Andrea if she wanted a coffee, but she said she'd had one in her office not long before he arrived. Maybe later. They paused to cross the road near one of Andrea's favourite boutiques and Mick asked if there was something he could buy for her.

Andrea sounded taken aback at the suggestion. 'You don't need to buy me anything, Mick. It isn't my birthday or anything.'

'It would be nice to give you a gift. Something to remember me by.'

'I don't need anything to remember you, Mick. You're always going to be there.'

'It doesn't have to be much. Just something you'll use now and then, and will make you think of me. *This* me, not the one who's going to be walking around in this body in a few days.'

'Well, if you really insist . . .' He could tell Andrea was trying to sound keen on the idea, but her heart still wasn't quite in it. 'There was a handbag I saw last week—'

'You should have bought it when you saw it.'

'I was saving up for the hairdresser.'

So Mick bought her the handbag. He made a mental note of the style and colour, intending to buy an identical copy next week. Since he hadn't bought the gift for his wife in his own worldline, it was even possible that he might walk out of the shop with the exact counterpart of the handbag he'd just given Andrea.

They went to the park again, then to look at the art in the National Museum of Wales, then back into town for lunch. There were a few more clouds in the sky compared to the last two days, but their chrome whiteness only served to make the blue appear more deeply enamelled and permanent. There were no planes anywhere at all; no contrail scratches. It turned out the aircraft – which had indeed been military – that they had seen yesterday had been on its way to Poland, carrying a team of mine-rescue specialists. Mick remembered his resentment at seeing the plane, and felt bad about it now. There had been brave men and women aboard it, and they were probably going to be putting their own lives at risk to help save other brave men and women stuck kilo-metres underground.

'Well,' Andrea said, when they'd paid the bill. 'Moment of truth, I suppose. I've been thinking about what you were saying earlier, and maybe . . .' She trailed off, looking down at the remains of her salad, before continuing, 'We can go home, if you'd like. If that's what you really want.'

'Yes,' Mick said. 'It's what I want.'

They took the tram back to their house. Andrea used her key to let them inside. It was still only the early afternoon, and the house was pleasantly cool, with the curtains and blinds still drawn. Mick knelt down and picked up the letters that were on the mat. Bills, mostly. He set them on the hall-side table, feeling a transitory sense of liberation. More than likely he'd be confronted with the same bills when he got home, but for now *these* were someone else's problem.

He slipped off his shoes and walked into the living room. For a moment he was thrown, feeling as if he really was in a different house. The wallscreen was on another wall; the dining table had been shifted sideways into the other half of the room; the sofa and easy chairs had all been altered and moved.

'What's happened?'

'Oh, I forgot to tell you,' Andrea said. 'I felt like a change. You came around and helped me move them.'

'That's new furniture.'

'No, just different seat covers. They're not new, it's just that we haven't had them out for a while. You remember them now, don't you?'

'I suppose so.'

'C'mon, Mick. It wasn't that long ago. We got them off Aunty Janice, remember?' She looked at him despairingly. 'I'll move things back. It *was* a bit inconsiderate of me, I suppose. I never thought how strange it would be for you to see the place like this.'

'No, it's okay. Honestly, it's fine.' Mick looked around, trying to fix the arrangement of furniture and décor in his mind's eye. As if he were going to duplicate everything when he got back into his own body, into his own version of this house.

Maybe he would too.

'I've got something for you,' Andrea said suddenly, reaching up to the top of the bookcase. 'Found it this morning. Took ages searching for it.'

'What?' Mick asked.

She held the thing out to him. Mick saw a rectangle of laminated pink card, stained and dog-eared. It was only when he tried to hold it and the thing fell open and disgorged its folded paper innards that he realised it was a map.

'Bloody hell. I wouldn't have had a clue where to look.' Mick folded the map back into itself and studied the cover. It was one of their old hill-walking maps, covering that part of the Brecon Beacons where they'd done a lot of their walks.

'I was just thinking ... seeing as you were so keen ... maybe it wouldn't kill us to get out of town. Nothing too adventurous, mind.'

'Tomorrow?'

She looked at him concernedly. 'That's what I was thinking. You'll still be okay, won't you?'

'No probs.'

'I'll get us a picnic, then. Tesco's does a nice luncheon basket. I think we've still got two Thermos flasks around here somewhere too.'

'Never mind the Thermos flasks, what about the walking boots?'

'In the garage,' Andrea said. 'Along with the rucksacks. I'll dig them out this evening.'

'I'm looking forward to it,' Mick said. 'Really. It's kind of you to agree.'

'Just as long as you don't expect me to get up Pen y Fan without getting out of breath.'

'I bet you'll surprise yourself.'

A little later they went upstairs, to their bedroom. The blinds were open enough to throw pale stripes across the walls and bedsheets. Andrea undressed, and then helped Mick out of his own clothes. As good as his control over the body had now become, fine motor tasks – like undoing buttons and zips – would require a lot more practice than he was going to have time for.

'You'll have to help me get all this on afterwards,' he said.

'There you go, worrying about the future again.'

They lay together on the bed. Mick had already felt himself growing hard long before there was any corresponding change in the body he was now inhabiting. He had an erection in the laboratory, halfway across the city in another worldline. He could even feel the sharp plastic of the urinary catheter. Would the other Mick, sunk deep into coma, retain some vague impression of what was happening now? There were occasional stories of people coming out of their coma with a memory of what their bodies had been up to while they were under, but the agencies had said these were urban myths.

They made slow, cautious love. Mick had become more aware of his own awkwardness, and the self-consciousness only served to exaggerate the stiffness of his movements. Andrea did what she could to help, to bridge the gap between them, but she could not work miracles. She was patient and forgiving, even when he came close to hurting her. When he climaxed, Mick felt it happen to the body in the laboratory first. Then the body he was inhabiting responded too, seconds later. Something of it reached him through the nervelink – not pleasure, exactly, but confirmation that pleasure had occurred.

Afterwards, they lay still on the bed, limbs entwined. A breeze made the blinds move back and forth against the window. The slow movement of light and shade, the soft tick of vinyl on glass, was as lulling as a becalmed boat. Mick found himself falling into a contented sleep. He dreamed of standing on a summit in the Brecon Beacons, looking down on the sunlit valleys of South Wales, with Andrea next to him, the two of them poised like a tableau in a travel brochure.

When he woke, hours later, he heard her moving around downstairs. He reached for the glasses – he'd removed them earlier – and made to leave the bed. He felt it then. Somewhere in those languid hours he'd lost a degree of control over the body. He stood and moved to the door. He could still walk, but the easy facility he'd gained on Tuesday was now absent. When he moved to the landing and looked down the stairs, the glasses struggled to cope with the sudden change of scene. The view fractured, reassembled. He moved to steady himself on the banister, and his hand blurred into a long smear of flesh.

He began to descend the stairs, like a man coming down a mountain.

Thursday

In the morning he was worse. He stayed overnight at the house, then caught the tram to the laboratory. Already he could feel a measurable lag between the sending of his intentions to move and the corresponding action in the body. Walking was still just about manageable, but all other tasks had become more difficult. He'd made a mess trying to eat breakfast in Andrea's kitchen. It was no surprise when Joe told him that the link was now down to one-point-two megs, and falling.

'By the end of the day?' Mick asked, even though he could see the printout for himself.

'Point nine, maybe point eight.'

He'd dared to think it might still be possible to do what they had planned. But the day soon became a catalogue of declining functions. At noon he met Andrea at her office and they went to a car rental office, where they'd booked a vehicle for the day. Andrea drove them out of Cardiff, up the valleys, along the A470 from Merthyr to Brecon. They had planned to walk all the way to the summit of Pen y Fan, an ascent they'd done together dozens of times during their hill-walking days. Andrea had already collected the picnic basket from Tesco's and packed and prepared the two rucksacks. She'd helped Mick get into his walking boots.

They left the car at the Storey Arms then followed the well-trodden trail that wound its way towards the mountain. Mick felt a little ashamed at first. Back in their hill-walking days, they'd tended to look down with disdain on the hordes of people making the trudge up Pen y Fan, especially those who took the route up from the pub. The view from the top was worth the climb, but they'd usually made a point of completing at least one or two other ascents on the same day, and they'd always eschewed the easy paths. Now Mick was paying for that earlier superiority. What started out as pleasantly challenging soon became impossibly taxing. Although he didn't think Andrea had begun to notice, he was finding it much harder than he'd expected to walk on the rough, craggy surface of the path. The effort was draining him, preventing him from enjoying any of the scenery, or the sheer bliss of being with Andrea. When he lost his footing the first time, Andrea didn't make much of it – she'd nearly tripped once already, on the dried and cracked path. But soon he was finding it hard to walk more than a hundred metres without losing his balance. He knew, with a heavy heart, that it would be difficult enough just to get back to the car. The mountain was still three kilometres away, and he wouldn't have a hope as soon as they hit a real slope.

'Are you okay, Mick?'

'I'm fine. Don't worry about me. It's these bloody shoes. I can't believe they ever fitted me.'

He soldiered on for as long as he could, refusing to give in, but the going got harder and his pace slower. When he tripped again and this time grazed his shin through his trousers, he knew he'd pushed himself as far as he could go. Time was getting on. The mountain might as well have been in the Himalayas, for all his chances of climbing it.

'I'm sorry. I'm useless. Go on without me. It's too nice a day not to finish it.'

'Hey.' Andrea took his hand. 'Don't be like that. It was always going to be hard. Look how far we've come anyway.'

Mick turned and looked dispiritedly down the valley. 'About three kilometres. I can still see the pub.'

'Well, it felt further. And besides, this is actually a very nice spot to have the picnic.' Andrea made a show of rubbing her thigh. 'I'm about ready to stop anyway. Pulled a muscle going over that stile.'

'You're just saying that.'

'Shut up, Mick. I'm happy, okay? If you want to turn this into some miserable, pain-filled trek, go ahead. Me, I'm staying here.'

She spread the blanket next to a dry brook and unpacked the food. The contents of the picnic basket looked very good indeed. The taste came through the nervelink as a kind of thin, diluted impression, more like the *memory* of taste rather than the thing itself. But he managed to eat without making too much of a mess, and some of it actually bordered on the enjoyable. They ate, listening to the birds, saying little. Now and then other walkers trudged past, barely giving Mick and Andrea a glance as they continued towards the hills.

'I guess I shouldn't have kidded myself I was ever going to get up that mountain,' Mick said.

'It *was* a bit ambitious,' Andrea agreed. 'It would have been hard enough without the nervelink, given how flabby the two of us have become.'

'I think I'd have made a better job of it yesterday. Even this morning ... I honestly felt I could do this when we got into the car.'

Andrea touched his thigh. 'How does it feel?'

'Like I'm moving away. Yesterday I felt like I was in this body, fully a part of it. Like a face filling a mask. Today it's different. I can still see through the mask, but it's getting further away.'

Andrea seemed distant for several moments. He wondered if what he'd said had upset her. But when she spoke again there was something in her voice – a kind of steely resolution – that he hadn't been expecting, but which was entirely Andrea.

'Listen to me, Mick.'

'I'm listening.'

'I'm going to tell you something. It's the first of May today; just past two in the afternoon. We left Cardiff at eleven. This time next year, this exact day, I'm coming back here. I'm going to pack a picnic basket and go all the way up to the top of Pen y Fan. I'll set off from Cardiff at the same time. And I'm going to do it the year after, as well. Every first of May. No matter what day of the week it is. No matter how bloody horrible the weather is. I'm going up this mountain and nothing on Earth is going to stop me.'

It took him a few seconds to realise what she was getting at. 'With the other Mick?'

'No. I'm not saying we won't ever climb that hill together. But when I go up it on the first of May, I'll be on my own.' She looked levelly at Mick. 'And you'll do it alone as well. You'll find someone new, I'm sure of it. But whoever she is will have to give you that one day to yourself. So that you and I can have it to ourselves.'

'We won't be able to communicate. We won't even know the other one's stuck to the plan.'

'Yes,' Andrea said firmly. 'We will. Because it's going to be a promise, all right? The most important one either of us has ever made in our whole lives. That way we'll know. Each of us will be in our own universe, or worldline, or whatever you call it. But we'll both be standing on the same Welsh mountain. We'll both be looking at the same view. And I'll be thinking of you, and you'll be thinking of me.'

Mick ran a stiff hand through Andrea's hair. He couldn't get his fingers to work very well now.

'You really mean that, don't you?'

'Of course I mean it. But I'm not promising anything unless you agree to your half of it. Would you promise, Mick?'

'Yes,' he said. 'I will.'

'I wish I could think of something better. I could say we'd always meet in the park. But there'll be people around; it won't feel private. I want the silence, the isolation, so I can feel your presence. And one day they might tear down the park and put a shopping centre there instead. But the mountain will always be there. At least as long as we're around.'

'And when we get old? Shouldn't we agree to stop climbing the mountain, when we get to a certain age?'

'There you go again,' Andrea said. 'Decide for yourself. I'm going to keep climbing this thing until they put me in a box. I expect nothing less from you, Mick Leighton.'

He made the best smile he was capable of. 'Then ... I'll just have to do my best, won't I?'

Friday

In the morning Mick was paraplegic. The nervelink still worked perfectly, but the rate of data transmission from one worldline to the other had become too low to permit anything as complex and feedback-dependent as walking. His control over the body's fingers had become so clumsy that his hands might as well have been wearing boxing gloves. He could hold something if it was presented to him, but it was becoming increasingly difficult to manipulate simple objects, even those that had presented no difficulty twenty-four hours earlier. When he tried to grasp the breakfast yoghurt, he succeeded only in tipping it over the table. His hand had seemed to lurch towards the yoghurt, crossing the distance too quickly. According to Joe he had lost depth perception overnight. The glasses, sensing the dwindling data rate, were no longer sending stereoscopic images back to the lab.

He could still move around. The team had anticipated this stage and made sure an electric wheelchair was ready for him. Its chunky controls were designed to be used by someone with only limited upper body coordination. The chair was equipped with a panic button, so that Mick could summon help if he felt his control slipping faster than the predicted rate. Were he to fall into sudden and total paralysis, the chair would call out to passers-by to provide assistance. In the event of an extreme medical emergency, it would steer itself to the nearest designated care point.

Andrea came out to the laboratory to meet him. Mick wanted one last trip into the city with her, but although she'd been enthusiastic when they'd talked about the plan on the phone, Andrea was now reluctant.

'Are you sure about this? We had such a nice time on Thursday. It would be a shame to spoil the memory of that now.'

'I'm okay,' Mick said.

'I'm just saying, we could always just stroll around the gardens here.'

'Please,' Mick said. 'This is what ... I want.'

His voice was slow, his phrasing imprecise. He sounded drunk and depressed. If Andrea noticed – and he was sure she must have – she made no observation.

They went into town. It was difficult getting the wheelchair on the tram, even with Andrea's assistance. No one seemed to know how to lower the boarding ramp. One of the benefits of nervelink technology was that you didn't see that many people in wheelchairs any more. The technology that enabled one person to control another person's body also enabled spinal injuries to be bypassed. Mick was aware that he was attracting more attention than on any previous day. For most people wheelchairs were a medical horror from the past, like iron lungs or leg braces.

On the tram's video monitor he watched a news item about the Polish miners. It wasn't good. The rescue team had had a number of options available to them, involving at least three possible routes to the trapped men. After carefully evaluating all the data – aware of how little time remained for the victims – they'd chosen what had promised to be the quickest and safest approach.

It had turned out to be a mistake, one that would prove fatal for the miners. The rescuers had hit a flooded section and had been forced to retreat, with damage to their equipment, and one of their team injured. Yet the miners *had* been saved in one of the other contacted worldlines. In that reality, one of the members of the rescue team had slipped on ice and fractured his hip while boarding the plane. The loss of that one man – who'd been a vocal proponent for taking the quickest route – had resulted in the team following the second course. It had turned out to be the right decision. They'd met their share of obstacles and difficulties, but in the end they'd broken through to the trapped miners.

By the time this happened, contact with that worldline had almost been lost. Even the best compression methods couldn't cope with moving images. The pictures that came back, of the men being liberated from the ground, were grainy and monochrome, like a blow-up of newsprint from a hundred years earlier. They'd been squeezed across the gap in the last minutes before noise drowned the signal.

But the information was useless. Even armed with the knowledge that there was a safe route through to the miners, the team in this worldline didn't have time to act.

The news didn't help Mick's mood. Going into the city turned out to be exactly the bad move Andrea had predicted. By midday his motor control had deteriorated even further, to the point where he was having difficulty steering the wheelchair. His speech became increasingly slurred, so that Andrea had to keep asking him to repeat himself. In defence, he shut down into monosyllables. Even his hearing was beginning to fail, as the auditory data was compressed to an even more savage degree. He couldn't distinguish birds from traffic, or traffic from the swish of the trees in the park. When Andrea spoke to him she sounded like her words had been fed through a synthesiser, then chopped up and spliced back together in some tinny approximation of her normal voice.

At three, his glasses could no longer support full colour vision. The software switched to a limited colour palette. The city looked like a hand-tinted photograph, washed out and faded. Andrea's face oscillated between white and sickly grey.

By four, Mick was fully quadriplegic. By five, the glasses had reverted back to black and white. The frame rate was down to ten images per second, and falling.

By early evening, Andrea was no longer able to understand what Mick was saying. Mick realised that he could no longer reach the panic button. He became agitated, thrashing his head around. He'd had enough. He wanted to be pulled out of the nervelink, slammed back into his own waiting body. He no longer felt as if he was in Mick's body, but he didn't feel as if he was in his own either. He was strung out somewhere between them, helpless and almost blind. When the panic hit, it was like a foaming, irresistible tide.

Alarmed, Andrea wheeled him back to the laboratory. By the time she was ready to say goodbye to him, the glasses had reduced his vision to five images per second, each of which was composed of only six thousand pixels. He was calmer then, resigned to the inevitability of what tomorrow would bring: he would not even recognise Andrea in the morning.

Saturday

Mick's last day with Andrea began in a world of sound and vision – senses that were already impoverished to a large degree – and ended in a realm of silence and darkness.

He was now completely paralysed, unable even to move his head. The brain that belonged to the other, comatose Mick now had more control over this body than its wakeful counterpart. The nervelink was still sending signals back to the lab, but the requirements of sight and sound now consumed almost all available bandwidth. In the morning, vision was down to one thousand pixels, updated three frames per second. His sight had already turned monochrome, but even yesterday there had been welcome gradations of grey, enough to anchor him into the visual landscape.

Now the pixels were only capable of registering on or off; it cost too much bandwidth to send intermediate intensity values. When Andrea was near him, her face was a flickering abstraction of black and white squares, like a trick picture in a psychology textbook. With effort he learned to distinguish her from the other faces in the laboratory, but no sooner had he gained confidence in his ability than the quality of vision deteriorated even further.

By midmorning the frame rate had dropped to eight hundred pixels at two images per second, which was less like vision than being shown a sequence of still pictures. People didn't walk to him across the lab – they jumped from spot to spot, captured in frozen postures. It was soon easy to stop thinking of them as people at all, but simply as abstract structures in the data.

By noon he could not exactly say that he had any vision at all. *Something* was updating once every two seconds, but the matrix of black and white pixels was hard to reconcile with his memories of the lab. He could no longer distinguish people from furniture, unless people moved between frames, and then only occasionally. At two, he asked Joe to disable the feed from the glasses, so that the remaining bandwidth could be used for sound and touch. Mick was plunged into darkness.

Sound had declined overnight as well. If Andrea's voice had been tinny yesterday, today it was barely human. It was as if she were speaking to him through a voice distorter on the end of the worst telephone connection in the world. The noise was beginning to win. The software was struggling to compensate, teasing sense out of the data. It was a battle that could only be prolonged, not won.

'I'm still here,' Andrea told him, her voice a whisper fainter than the signal from the furthest quasar.

Mick answered her. It took some time. His words in the lab had to be analysed by voice-recognition software and converted into ASCII characters. The characters were compressed further and sent across the reality gap, bit by bit. In the other version of the lab – the one where Mick's body waited in a wheelchair, the one where Andrea hadn't died in a car crash – equivalent software decompressed the character string and reconstituted it in mechanically generated speech, with an American accent.

'Thank you for letting me come back,' he said. 'Please stay. Until the end. Until I'm not here any more.'

'I'm not going anywhere, Mick.'

Andrea squeezed his hand. After all that he had lost since Friday, touch remained. It really was the easiest thing to send: easier than sight, easier than sound. When, later, even Andrea's voice had to be sent across the gap by character string and speech synthesiser, touch endured. He felt her holding him, hugging his body to hers, refusing to surrender him to the drowning roar of quantum noise.

'We're down to less than a thousand useable bits,' Joe told him, speaking quietly in his ear in the version of the lab where Mick lay on the immersion couch. 'That's a thousand bits total, until we lose all contact. It's enough for a message, enough for parting words.'

'Send this,' Mick said. 'Tell Andrea that I'm glad she was there. Tell her that I'm glad she was my wife. Tell her I'm sorry we didn't make it up that hill together.'

When Joe had sent the message, typing it in with his usual fluid speed, Mick felt the sense of Andrea's touch easing. Even the microscopic data-transfer burden of communicating unchanging pressure, hand on hand, body against body, was now too much for the link. It was like one swimmer letting a drowning partner go. As the last bits fell, he felt Andrea slip away for ever.

He lay on the couch, unmoving. He had lost his wife, for the second time. For the moment the weight of that realisation pinned him into stillness. He did not think he would ever be able to walk in his world, let alone the one he had just vacated.

And yet it was Saturday. Andrea's funeral was in two days. He would have to be ready for that.

'We're done,' Joe said respectfully. 'Link is now noise-swamped.'

'Did Andrea send anything back?' Mick asked. 'After I sent my last words—'

'No. I'm sorry.'

Mick caught the hesitation in Joe's answer. 'Nothing came through?'

'Nothing intelligible. I thought something was coming through, but it was just ...' Joe offered an apologetic shrug. 'The set-up at their end must have gone noise-limited a few seconds before ours did. Happens, sometimes.'

'I know,' Mick said. 'But I still want to see what Andrea sent.'

Joe handed him a printout. Mick waited for his eyes to focus on the sheet. Beneath the lines of header information was a single line of text: SO0122215. Like a phone number or a postal code, except it was obviously neither.

'That's all?'

Joe sighed heavily. 'I'm sorry, mate. Maybe she was just trying to get something through ... but the noise won. The fucking noise always wins.'

Mick looked at the numbers again. They began to talk to him. He thought he knew what they meant.

'Always fucking wins,' Joe repeated.

Sunday

Andrea was there when they brought Mick out of the medically induced coma. He came up through layers of disorientation and half-dream, adrift until something inside him clicked into place and he realised where he had been for the last week, what had been happening to the body over which he was now regaining gradual control. It was exactly as they had promised: no dreams, no anxiety, no tangible sense of elapsed time. In a way, it was not an entirely unattractive way to spend a week. Like being in the womb, he'd heard people say. And now he was being born again, a process that was not without its own discomforts. He tried moving an arm and when the limb did not obey him instantly, he began to panic. But Joe was already smiling.

'Easy, boyo. It's coming back. The software's rerouting things one spinal nerve at a time. Just hold on there and it'll be fine.'

Mick tried mumbling something in reply, but his jaw wasn't working properly either. Yet it would come, as Joe had promised. On any given day, thousands of recipients went through this exact procedure without blinking an eyelid. Many of them were people who'd already done it hundreds of times before. Nervelinking was almost insanely safe. Far safer than any form of physical travel, that was certain.

He tried moving his arm again. This time it obeyed without hesitation.

'How are you feeling?' Andrea asked.

Once more he tried speaking. His jaw was stiff, his tongue thick and uncooperative, but he managed to make some sounds. 'Okay. Felt better.'

'They say it's easier the second time. Much easier the third.'

'How long?'

'You went under on Sunday of last week. It's Sunday again now,' Joe said.

A full week. Exactly the way they'd planned it.

'I'm quite hungry,' Mick said.

'Everyone's always hungry when they come out of the coma,' Joe said. 'It's hard to get enough nourishment into the host body. We'll get you sorted out, though.'

Mick turned his head to look at Joe, waiting for his eyes to find grudging focus. 'Joe,' he said. 'Everything's all right, isn't it? No complications, nothing to worry about?'

'No problems at all,' Joe said.

'Then would you mind giving Andrea and me a moment alone?'

Joe held up his hand in hasty acknowledgement and left the room, off on some plausible errand. He shut the door quietly behind him.

'Well?' Mick asked. 'I'm guessing things must have gone okay, or they wouldn't have kept me under for so long.'

'Things went okay, yes,' Andrea said.

'Then you met the other Mick? He was here?'

Andrea nodded heavily. 'He was here. We spent time together.'

'What did you get up to?'

'All the usual stuff you or I would've done. Hit the town, walked in the parks, went into the hills, that kind of thing.'

'How was it?'

She looked at him guardedly. 'Really, really sad. I didn't really know how to behave, to be honest. Part of me wanted to be all consoling and sympathetic, because he'd lost his wife. But I don't think that's what Mick wanted.'

'The other Mick,' he corrected gently.

'Point is, he didn't come back to see me being all weepy. He wanted another week with his wife, the way things used to be. Yes, he wanted to say goodbye, but he didn't want to spend the whole week with the two of us walking around feeling down in the dumps.'

'So how did you feel?'

'Miserable. Not as miserable as if I'd lost my husband, of course. But some of his sadness started wearing off on me. I didn't think it was going to ... *I'm* not the one who's been bereaved here – but you'd have to be inhuman not to feel something, wouldn't you?'

'Whatever you felt, don't blame yourself for it. I think it was a wonderful thing you agreed to do.'

'You too.'

'I had the easy part,' Mick said.

Andrea stroked the side of his face. He realised that he needed a good shave. 'How do *you* feel?' she asked. 'You're nearly him, after all. You know everything he knows.'

'Except how it feels to lose a wife. And I hope I don't ever find that out. I don't think I can ever really understand what he's going through now. He feels like someone else, a friend, a colleague, someone you'd feel sorry for—'

'But you're not cut up about what happened to him.'

Mick thought for a while before responding, not wanting to give the glib, automatic answer, no matter how comforting it might have been. 'No. I wish it hadn't happened ... but you're still here. We can still be together, if we want. We'll carry on with our lives, and in a few months we'll hardly ever think of that accident. The other Mick isn't me. He isn't even anyone we'll ever hear from again. He's gone. He might as well not exist.'

'But he does. Just because we can't communicate any more ... he *is* still out there.'

'That's what the theory says.' Mick narrowed his eyes. 'Why? What difference does it really make, to us?'

'None at all, I suppose.' Again that guarded look. 'But there's something I have to tell you, something you have to understand.'

There was a tone in her voice that troubled Mick, but he did his best not to show it. 'Go on, Andrea.'

'I made a promise to the other Mick. He's lost something no one can ever replace, and I wanted to do something, anything, to make it easier for him. Because of that, Mick and I came to an arrangement. Once a year, I'm going to go away for a day. For that day, and that day only, I'm going somewhere private where I'm going to be thinking about the other Mick. About what he's been doing; what kind of life he's had; whether he's happy or sad. And I'm going to be alone. I don't want you to follow me, Mick. You have to promise me that.'

'You could tell me,' he said. 'There doesn't have to be secrets.'

'I'm telling you now. Don't you think I could have kept it from you if I wanted to?'

'But I still won't know where—'

'You don't need to. This is a secret between me and the other Mick. Me and the other you.' She must have read something in his expression, something he had hoped wasn't there, because her tone turned grave. 'And you need to find a way to deal with that, because it isn't negotiable. I already made that promise.'

'And Andrea Leighton doesn't break promises.'

'No,' she said, softening her look with a sweet half-smile. 'She doesn't. Especially not to Mick Leighton. Whichever one it happens to be.'

They kissed.

Later, when Andrea was out of the room while Joe ran some more post-immersion tests, Mick peeled off a yellow Post-it note that had been left on one of the keyboards. There was something written on the note, in neat, blue ink. Instantly he recognised Andrea's handwriting: he'd seen it often enough on the message board in their kitchen. But the writing itself – SO0122215–meant nothing to him.

'Joe,' he asked casually. 'Is this something of yours?'

Joe glanced over from his desk, his eyes freezing on the small rectangle of yellow paper.

'No, that's what Andrea asked—' Joe began, then caught himself. 'Look, it's nothing. I meant to bin it, but—'

'It's a message to the other Mick, right?'

Joe looked around, as if Andrea might still be hiding in the room or about to reappear. 'We were down to the last few usable bits. The other Mick had just sent his last words through. Andrea asked me to send that response.'

'Did she tell you what it meant?'

Joe looked defensive. 'I just typed it. I didn't ask. Thought it was between you and her. I mean, between the other Mick and her.'

'It's okay,' Mick said. 'You were right not to ask.'

He looked at the message again, and something fell solidly into place. It had taken a few moments, but he recognised the code for what it was now, as some damp and windswept memory filtered up from the past. The numbers formed a grid reference on an Ordnance Survey map. It was the kind Andrea and he had used when they went on their walking expeditions. The reference even looked vaguely familiar. He stared at the numbers, feeling as if they were about to give up their secret. Wherever it was, he'd been there, or somewhere near. It wouldn't be hard to look it up. He wouldn't even need the Post-it note. He'd always had a good memory for numbers.

Footsteps approached, echoing along the linoleum-floored hallway that led to the lab.

'It's Andrea,' Joe said.

Mick folded the Post-it note until the message was no longer visible. He flicked it in Joe's direction, knowing that it was none of his business any more.

'Bin it.'

'You sure?'

From now on there was always going to be a part of his wife's life that didn't involve him, even if it was only for one day a year. He would just have to find a way to live with that.

Things could have been worse, after all.

'I'm sure,' he said.

Unlike a lot of my stuff, 'Signal to Noise' is set on Earth in the relatively near future. I probably do more of these stories than is generally appreciated – I'm not exclusively a writer of galaxy-spanning New Space Opera – but I'll admit that most of my pieces do tend to take place off-Earth. It's not for want of trying, but most of my attempts at writing near-future SF have resulted in abandoned stories and a lot of personal grief and frustration. I don't know why this should be the case. I like reading that kind of SF as much as I like the epic, big-canvas stuff. I think I'm alive to the world around me, and as interested in the texture and trajectory of the near future as anyone else. Perhaps it's because, while I think I can do the extrapolative world-building, and I think I can inject the necessary number of sideways-swerves and eyeball-kicks, I have a hard time coming up with the kinds of plot conceit that can form the basis of a story. It could be that I'm just genetically programmed to write stories set in space, in the middle-to-distant future, in which case I'd best accept my fate. 'If it doesn't come naturally, leave it,' as another Al once wrote.

But I'm not giving up on the near-future just yet.

CARDIFF AFTERLIFE

Cardiff's gone.

The epicentre of the explosion, appropriately enough, was just outside the 'D' gate entrance into the Millennium Stadium. So it went first, before the rest of the city. It was always a mistake, building it where they did. The Taffs always agreed on that. They should have built it west of the city, where people had a chance of actually seeing the thing. By the time I moved down from Hull the Millennium Stadium was a thing you only saw in furtive glimpses, peeking between newer, shinier buildings that had gone up around it during the thirty years since it was opened.

Well anyway. It's gone now. Problem is, so has everything else.

I presenced into Cardiff less than a day after the atrocity. Most civilians – whether they were in that timeline or not – couldn't get near what was left of the city. But because of my connection to the cold-calling project, and because so much of our equipment was in the university basement at the time of the detonation, I got a security pass and freedom to wander as I chose. I couldn't presence in via a live body, not with the radiation levels as high as they were, and I didn't fancy (though it was always an option) using a recently deceased corpse, puppeted back to life by electrical stimulation. So I presenced via a robot, a clunking military-grade thing with tracks and arms and armour shielding. It was like a souped-up version of the kind of thing the army used to use to defuse bombs, back when terrorists were content with blowing up small things like cars and buildings.

From the point where I assumed control of the machine, it took six hours to creep and crawl through the devastation to the remains of the university labs. There were other robots about, there were Chinook helicopters scudding through the mustard-yellow sky and a few soldiers and government personnel in full protective gear, but I didn't see anyone else alive. Apart from a few stragglers who didn't want rescuing, everyone who had survived the blast was now being treated in the emergency field clinics beyond the radiation zone. Tens of thousands had died in the first twelve hours. For tens of thousands more, the prognosis wasn't exactly rosy.

Because our equipment was important, we'd taken pains to protect it against all eventualities. A plane could crash into the university and we wouldn't feel it down in the basement with the cold-calling machines. Cardiff could have a magnitude eight earthquake and the instruments wouldn't register more than a blip. Terrorists letting off a homemade atom bomb was at the extreme limit of what we could reasonably protect ourselves against, but it had still been factored into the plans.

Better safe than sorry, eh? Not (we told ourselves) that it would ever happen.

So what had survived? Fuck all, truth to tell. The surface buildings were scorched rubble. It took an hour of digging before I found the secure, pressure-tight hatchway that led into the basement. I opened it (I knew the keycode, of course) and managed to get the robot down the stairs, its tracks orientating to keep the body upright even as it descended.

What did I find?

Me, for a start. I'd been on duty in the version of Cardiff that had taken the hit, just as I was on duty at the time in the version that hadn't. And, miracle of miracles, the cold-calling machines were still running, being fed by a backup generator in a separate part of the basement.

Actually, it wasn't a miracle at all. I knew at least one of the machines had to be running, or we wouldn't have been able to establish the cross-link that permitted presencing. The question was, how stable was that cross-link? Was it going to hold out for another five or six days, or pop at any moment?

No use asking me, Joe Liversedge. I was dead to the world. Literally: when the robot encountered my body, it was slumped over a workstation console. I'd been the only person down in the lab at the time, since it was a Sunday and most of the other departmental staff didn't work weekends if they could help it. Me, I was a proper little workaholic.

'Paid for it now, didn't you, you silly sod,' I told the corpse, speaking through the robot's voice system. 'You daft bugger, Joe.

Why couldn't you have gone with Mick to that beer festival in Stoke?'

Arguing with a corpse, of course, doesn't tend to get you very far.

It wasn't immediately obvious why I'd died. The life-support system was supposed to be able to keep us alive in the basement for weeks on end. Then I noticed that there was a note in my – Joe's – handwriting, next to him.

'Dear Joe,' it said. 'Air fucked – dodgy seal, I reckon. But machines okay. Link holding. Cheerio, old mate – it's been a blast. Yer pal, Joe.'

Followed by:

'PS – have a round on me.'

Clutched in his hand was a twenty pound note. Nice touch. When was the last time twenty quid got you more than a pint and a packet of crisps? Typical tight-arsed Yorkshireman, as Mick would have said.

I couldn't take the money back with me. But I suppose it was the thought that counted.

Maybe I need to back up a bit.

If it seems I was acting more than a little oddly on being confronted with my own corpse, there are perfectly sound reasons for that. Thing is, it isn't the first time I've met my counterpart – another version of me, Joe Liversedge. In fact, it happens all the time. So much so that I've become more than a little hardened to the idea that there are multiple copies of 'me' out there, going on with their own lives. If one of us dies, then there are still a lot more carrying on. I know that. So did the version of me in the basement.

Twelve years ago, my team at Cardiff University was the first to open a portal into a parallel world. We did it with one of the big machines in the basement – 'cold-calling' across quantum reality until we established a lock with an identical copy of that machine in another version of the lab, in another version of Cardiff. The way it works, the two Cardiffs are identical at the moment the lock is established – and everyone living in those two Cardiffs has exactly the same identity, exactly the same past. But from the moment the lock is established, the two worlds start peeling apart. Although both versions of me had come into the lab on a Sunday, the one in the basement had a shaving nick on his right cheek and a different shirt on. We were only a couple of days into the lock. By the end of the week, the two histories would have pulled so far apart that Cardiff City might get a win in one and lose in the other. Having terrorists let off a bomb in one Cardiff and not the other was a huge deviation to happen at this point in the lock, but sometimes that was how it played out. I wondered what had happened to our terrorists – had their bomb not worked, or had Secret Services caught up with them before they had a chance to let it off? No one was saying much yet, although there were rumours of 'intelligence leads'.

Big-scale changes or not, sooner or later the cumulative differences would become so acute that the quantum link couldn't be sustained. The portal closes on that world, leaving its occupants to carry on with their lives without being in contact with ours. Eventually we'd establish a lock with another Cardiff and begin the whole thing again. And always it was me, Joe Liversedge, who I spoke to the first time.

It does things to you, that. It's why Rachel left me, in the end. She said she couldn't deal with living with a man who had such a warped take on reality, let alone my own mortality.

'Do you talk about me behind my back?' she'd asked. 'The two of you, comparing notes?'

'You're not the other Rachel,' I'd said. 'She's just . . . some woman Joe's married to. You're the only one that matters to me.'

'The only one,' she'd answered tersely. 'When most men say that, they're talking about other women. You're talking about other copies of me, like I'm some kind of mass-produced Barbie doll. I can't deal with this, Joe.'

'You could have a go.'

'Life's too short,' Rachel said.

When she left, I did what I always did in times of crisis: threw myself into the work. Cardiff had been the first to develop cold-calling technology, but that didn't mean other universities and corporations weren't snapping at our heels, trying to get ahead of us. We'd been the first to establish a video interface between parallel worlds, enabling one version of me to chat to the other, as if we were just sitting in different offices. We'd been the first to use presencing technology – pinched from the tourist agencies, developed for the masses who couldn't afford to fly any more – and later we'd moved from clunky robots to actual human bodies, equipped with implants so that you could take them over, as if you were physically present in the other world. All that was well and good, but none of it had come free. To stay ahead we'd had to bite into a big juicy poisoned apple called direct government funding, money that arrived independently of the usual academic research pools. On the surface, the new money was intended to ensure that the UK maintained its prestigious lead in this cutting-edge field. It was all about science for science's sake, the money supposedly untainted by any baser concerns beyond the sheer intellectual thrill of the enterprise.

That was bollocks, though, and everyone knew it.

In a time when the government could lock up just about anybody they liked for simply looking a bit odd, the technology had powerful security implications. Once a lock was established, two different versions of a suspect could be arrested and interrogated in parallel, with the relevant agencies cooperating with themselves to extract the maximum intelligence. Feed one story to the suspect in one timeline and see what he says. Feed another in the other timeline and see what you get from that. Have your cake and eat it, and sod the human rights.

Of course, they never admitted to doing that kind of thing. But it wasn't blue-sky science that had paid for the new machines or their elaborate, bombproof installation in the basement. It was national security. What else?

Did I mention that the apple was poisoned? As a condition on all that glorious funding, the government had their own 'hotline', their own super-secure communications channel running into our lab. Their mandarins could talk to each other through the machines without me or anyone else in the department having a fucking clue what was going on. They didn't get in our way and we didn't get in theirs.

But sometimes, there were consequences.

Like today, for instance.

It's three months since the bomb went off. Our window into that version of Cardiff closed only four days after the event itself, so none of us has any idea how they're getting on. They hadn't come close to final casualty figures when the link collapsed, and no one was yet daring to talk about plans for the reconstruction. We'll never make contact with that version again, even if we kept on cold-calling for the rest of eternity. It's deviated so far from our own that the quantum lock just can't be established.

In my version of Cardiff, it's not a bad day at all. The sun's out, the pavement cafés are doing good business and everyone looks remarkably happy and content. Nothing much has changed here in three months. Of course, everyone who bothers to keep up with world events knows that a version of Cardiff got wiped off the map, and they've seen the pictures and video clips to prove it. Some of them, like me, have even presenced over to that other reality. We've strolled – or in my case rolled – over the smoking ruins of what was once a city.

For most people, though, the bombed Cardiff is receding into the past, like the memory of a bad summer blockbuster with overblown special effects. Lots of things have happened around the world since then, and we've cold-called hundreds of other realities, some of which have brought their own scandals and nine-day wonders.

But some people – some very select people – have longer memories than that.

Over my morning coffee, I flick through the paper. Buried somewhere on page three is a little item about the recent arrest and detention of a man living in Cardiff.

His name doesn't matter. He's British, all right? Welsh, if you want to be pedantic about it, although he's not called Jones or Evans or anything acceptably Welsh like that.

He's never done anything wrong. His only mistake is that he happened to blow up Cardiff in an alternate universe. Actually, that's an exaggeration. He wasn't directly involved in the planting of the bomb. All he did was inadvertently give house room to those who were. Maybe he knew something was going on, but it's equally likely that the perpetrators managed to keep their big secret from him.

No one can ask them now, though, because – inconveniently – they're all dead. Their counterparts in the other Cardiff died when the bomb went off. In this version they committed suicide when, because of a tiny imperfection in a soldered joint, their copy of the bomb failed to detonate properly, maiming two of them. All intelligence leads to a wider network of specialists and financiers have dried up. We can cold-call into other versions of Cardiff, but each of those now shares the same history as ours, so the terrorists are dead there as well. Which means that the only man the government can get their hands on – and who might know *something* – is the man who gave them somewhere to live.

His denials – according to what I can glean from the newspaper – have the taint of plausibility. He was related to one of the bombers, but only distantly, and nothing in his past suggested any involvement in extremist organisations. I'm left wondering this: in our timeline, the bomb failed, maiming two terrorists and eventually leading all of them to commit suicide. Civilian losses: nil. Radiation exposure: negligible. Damage to property: not worth mentioning.

If we didn't know what had happened to the other Cardiff, we'd say: case closed. The detained man has no case to answer. Justice has already been delivered.

Problem is, we *do* know. We do know and we like it when there's someone we can punish.

According to the paper, the detained man is reported to have died of complications following a heart attack, suffered during incarceration. The government line is that he had a precondition that could have flared up at any time.

Me, I'm wondering what they did to the poor, innocent bastard.

I fold the paper, finish my coffee and ride the tram to the university. Coincidentally, it's another Sunday. When I get there the department is empty, except for a few hoovering robots. Anyone with an ounce of sense is somewhere else, enjoying the weather, enjoying their city.

I tap the keycode and descend into the basement. The cold-calling machines loom around me, huge, humming horizontal cylinders, cold to the touch. There's always been something faintly sinister about them, although I'd never admit it aloud. I think of the government hotline running into this basement, into the machines, enabling signals to span the gap between realities. Without that connection, they'd never have come down as hard on that man as they did.

I think, for a moment, about sealing myself in here and turning off the air circulator. Go out the way the other Joe did, with a suicide note to myself and twenty pounds clutched in my cold, dead hand. A pint and a bag of crisps. It wouldn't really be killing myself, would it? Even if I die here and now, countless other versions of Joe Liversedge carry on living. We won't all make the same decision.

But then I think about what Rachel said, before she packed her bags. We're not Barbie dolls. If I've started slipping into a state of mind that allows me to believe that we *are* – that death is just the pruning of one local branch from an infinite, ever-growing tree – then maybe she had a point. Maybe I have been doing this a bit too long. Killing myself – no matter how noble the intention – would only reinforce her sense that I've let myself get sucked too far in.

It's not that I want Rachel to like me again. Too late for that. But I can still make a stand, without dying like the other Joe did.

Alarms will trip as soon as I start damaging the machines. Sooner or later they'll come and find me – they'll be able to break into the basement with or without the keycode. Then I'll be arrested – and, well, who knows? But no matter what happens to me, sooner or later they'll find a way to put the machines back together. But still: I'm Joe Liversedge. I'm a creative bastard. And I reckon I can do some serious damage if I put my mind to it.

There's a big axe on the wall, next to the fire extinguisher.

Let's get cracking.

This very short story – little more than a vignette – was written for the Welsh edition of The Big Issue, *the magazine sold in the UK by the homeless and vulnerable. Commissioned by the Cardiff-based crime writer John Williams for a special series of summer stories by Welsh writers, the idea was that the story should have a specific Welsh connection. This proved suitably problematic until I remembered that I'd already established a Welsh-themed near-future background for the novella 'Signal to Noise'. The Yorkshireman Joe Liversedge had been a background character in that story, but in this much shorter piece I put him (or copies of him, to be strictly accurate) in the foreground, a few years after the events of the earlier story. Once the elements were in place, the story wrote itself very quickly (good thing too, as the deadline was tight) and proved a refreshing exercise after some of the much longer pieces I had been working on recently. The title is a steal from the Manic Street Preachers, of course (as is, very nearly, 'Everlasting', also in this collection). Yes, I'm a fan ...*

Part One

There was, Merlin thought, *a very fine line between beauty and terror.* Most certainly where the Way was concerned. Tempting as it was to think that the thing they saw through the cutter's windows was only a mirage, there would always come a point when the mysterious artefact known as the syrinx started purring, vibrating in its metal harness. Somehow it was sensing the Way's proximity, anxious to perform the function for which it had been designed.

It seemed to bother all of them except Sayaca.

'Krasnikov,' she mouthed, shaping the unfamiliar word like an oath.

She was the youngest and brightest of the four disciples who had agreed to accompany Merlin on this field trip. At first the others had welcomed her into Merlin's little entourage, keen to hear her insights on matters relating to the Way and the enigmatic Waymakers. But in the cutter's cramped surroundings Sayaca's charms had worn off with impressive speed.

'Krasnikov?' Merlin said. 'Sorry, doesn't mean anything to me either.' He watched as the others pulled faces. 'You're going to have to enlighten us, Sayaca.'

'Krasnikov was . . .' she paused. 'Well, a human, I suppose – tens of kiloyears ago, long before the Waymakers, even before the Flourishing. He had an idea for moving faster than light, one that didn't involve wormholes or tachyons.'

'It can't work, Sayaca,' said a gangly, greasy-scalped adolescent called Weaver. 'You can't move faster than light without manipulating matter with negative energy density.'

'So what, Weaver? Do you think that would have bothered the Waymakers?'

Merlin smiled, thinking that the trouble with Sayaca was that when she made a point it was almost always a valid one.

'But the Way doesn't actually allow faster-than-light travel,' said one of the others. 'That much we do know.'

'Of course. All I'm saying is that the Waynet might have been an attempt to make a network of Krasnikov tubes, which didn't quite work out the way the builders intended.'

'Mm,' Merlin said. 'And what exactly is a Krasnikov tube?'

'A tube-shaped volume of altered space–time, light-years from end to end. Just like one branch of the Waynet. The point was to allow round-trip journeys to other star systems in arbitrarily short objective time.'

'Like a wormhole?' Weaver asked.

'No; the mathematical formulation's utterly different.' She sighed, looking to Merlin for moral support. He nodded for her to continue, knowing that she had already alienated the others beyond any reasonable point of return. 'But there must have been a catch. It's clear that two neighbouring Krasnikov tubes running in opposite directions violate causality. Perhaps when that happened—'

'They got something like the Waynet?'

Sayaca nodded to Merlin. 'Not a static tube of restructured space–time, but a rushing column of it, moving at a fraction below light-speed. It was still useful, of course. Ships could slip into the Way, cross interstellar space at massive tau factors and then decelerate instantaneously at the other end simply by leaving the stream.'

'All very impressive,' Weaver said. 'But if you're such an expert, why can't you tell us how to make the syrinx work properly?'

'You wouldn't understand if I did,' Sayaca said.

Merlin was about to intervene – tension was one thing, but he could not tolerate an argument aboard the cutter – when his glove rescued him. It had begun tickling the back of his hand, announcing a private call from the mother ship. Relieved, he unhitched from a restraint harness and kicked himself away from the four adolescents. 'I'll be back shortly,' he said. 'Try not to strangle each other, will you?'

The cutter was a slender craft only forty metres long, so it was normal enough that tempers had become frayed in the four days that they had been away from the *Starthroat*. The air smelled edgy too: thick with youthful pheromones he did not remember from the last trip. The youngsters were all getting older, no longer his unquestioning devotees.

He pushed past the syrinx. It sat within a metal harness, its long axis aligned with the ship's. The conic device was tens of thousands of years old, but its matt-black surface was completely unmarred. It was still purring too, like a well-fed cat. The closer they got to the Way, the more it would respond. It wanted to be set free, and shortly – Merlin hoped – it would get its wish.

The seniors would not be pleased, of course.

Beyond the syrinx was a narrow, transparent-walled duct that led back to Merlin's private quarters. He kicked himself along the passage, comfortable in free-fall after four days of adaptation. The view was undeniably impressive; as always he found himself slowing to take it in.

The stars were clumped ahead, shifted from their real positions and altered in hue and brightness by the aberration caused by the cutter's motion. They were moving at nine-tenths of the speed of light. Set against this distorted starfield, far to one side, was the huge swallowship – the *Starthroat* – that Merlin's people called home. The swallowship was far too distant to see as anything other than a prick of hot blue light pointing aft, like a star that had been carelessly smudged. Yet apart from the four people with him here, every other human he knew was inside *Starthroat*.

And then there was the Way.

It lay in the opposite hemisphere of the sky, stretching into the infinite distance fore and aft. It was like a ghostly pipeline alongside which they were flying – a pipeline ten thousand kilometres thick and thousands of light-years long. It shimmered faintly – twinkling as tiny particles of cosmic debris annihilated themselves against its skin. Most of those impacts were due to dust specks that had rest velocities of only a few kilometres a second against the local stellar rest frame – so the transient glints seemed to slam past at eye-wrenching velocities. Not just a pipeline, then – but a glass pipeline running thick with twinkling fluid that flowed at frightening speed.

And perhaps soon they would relearn the art of riding it.

He pushed into his quarters, confronting his brother's image on the comms console. Although they were not twins – Gallinule was a year younger – they still looked remarkably alike. It was almost like looking in a mirror.

'Well?' Merlin said.

'Trouble, I'm afraid.'

'Let me guess. It has something to do with Quail.'

'Well, the captain's not happy, let's put it like that. First you take the syrinx without authorisation, then the cutter – and then you have the balls not to come back when the old bastard tells you to.' The face on the screen was trying not to smile, but Merlin could tell he was quietly impressed. 'But that's not actually the problem. When I say trouble I mean for all of us. Quail wants all the seniors in his meeting room in eight hours.'

Just time, Merlin thought, for him to drop the syrinx and make it back to *Starthroat*. Not as good as having time to run comprehensive tests, but still damnably tempting. It was almost suspiciously convenient.

'I hadn't heard of any crisis on the horizon.'

'Me neither, and that's what worries me. It's something we haven't thought of.'

'The Huskers stealing a lead on us? Fine. I expect to be comfortably senile by the time they get within weapons range.'

'Just be there, will you? Or there'll be two of us in trouble.'

Merlin smiled. 'What else are brothers for?'

The long oval meeting room was hundreds of metres inside *Starthroat*'s armoured hull. Covered in a richly detailed fresco, the walls enclosed a hallowed mahogany table of ancient provenance. Just as the table's extremities now sagged with age, time had turned the fresco dark and sepia. In one corner a proctor was slowly renovating the historic artwork, moving with machine diligence from one scene of conflict to another, brightening hues, sharpening brushstrokes that had become indistinct with age.

Merlin squeezed past the squat machine.

'You're late,' Quail said, already seated. 'I take it your trip was a fruitful one?' Merlin started to compose an answer, but Quail was already speaking again. 'Good. Then sit down. You may take it as a very bad omen that I am not especially minded to reprimand you.'

Wordlessly Merlin moved to his own chair and lowered himself into it.

What could be that serious?

In addition to the gaunt, grey-skinned captain, there were fifteen ship seniors gathered in the chamber. Apart from Merlin they were all in full ceremonial dress, medals and sigils of rank to the fore.

This was the Council: the highest decision-making body in the ship save for Quail himself. One senior for every dozen subseniors, and one subsenior for every hundred or so crewmembers. These fifteen people represented somewhat less than fifteen thousand others working, relaxing or sleeping elsewhere in the swallowship's vast confines. And much of the work that they did was concerned with tending the two hundred thousand people in frostwatch: frozen refugees from dozens of systems. The burdens of responsibility were acute; especially so given that the swallowship had encountered no other human vessel in centuries. No one became a senior by default, and all those present – Merlin included – had earned the right to sit with Quail. Even, Merlin thought, his enemies on the Council. Like Pauraque, for instance. She was a coldly attractive woman who wore a stiff-necked black tunic, cuffs and collar edged with complicated black filigrees. She tapped her fingers against the table's ancient wood, black rings clicking together.

'Merlin,' she said.

'Pauraque. How are you?'

She eyed him poisonously. 'Reports are that you took one of the final two syrinxes without the express authorisation of the Council Subdivision for Waynet Studies.' Merlin opened his mouth, but Pauraque shook her head crisply. 'No; don't even think of weaselling out of it. I'll see that this never happens again. At least you brought the thing back unharmed this time ... didn't you?'

He smiled. 'I didn't bring it back at all. It's still out there, approaching the Way.' He showed Pauraque the display summary on the back of his glove. 'I placed it aboard an automated drone.'

'If you destroy it ...' Pauraque looked for encouragement in the doleful faces around her. 'We'll have you court-martialled, Merlin ... or worse. It's common knowledge that your only reason for studying the syrinxes is so that you can embark on some ludicrous quest—'

Quail coughed. 'We can discuss Merlin's activities later, Pauraque. They may seem somewhat less pressing when you've heard what I have to say.' Now that he had their attention, the old man softened his tone of voice until it was barely a murmur. 'I'm afraid I have remarkably bad news.'

It would have to be, Merlin thought.

'For as long as some of us remember,' Quail said, 'one central fact has shaped our lives. Every time we look to stern, along the way we've come, we know that *they* are out there, somewhere behind us. About thirty light-years by the last estimate, but coming steadily closer by about a light-year for every five years of shiptime. In a century and a half we will come within range of their weapons.' Quail nodded towards the fresco, one particularly violent tableau that showed ships exchanging fire above a planet garlanded in flames. 'It won't be pretty. At best, we might take out one or two elements of the swarm before they finish us. Yet we live with this situation, some days hardly giving it more than a moment's thought, for the simple reason that it lies so far in our future. The youngest of us may live to see it, but I'll certainly not be amongst them. And, of course, we cling to the hope that tomorrow will offer us an escape route we can't foresee today. Better weapons, perhaps – or some new physics that enables us to squeeze a little more performance from our engines, so that we can outrun the enemy.'

True enough. This was the state of things that they had known for years. It was the reality that had underpinned every waking thought for just as long. No one knew much about the Huskers except that they were ruthless alien cyborgs from somewhere near the galaxy's centre. Their only motive seemed to be the utter extermination of humanity from all the niches it had occupied since the Flourishing. This they prosecuted with glacial patience, in a war that had already lasted many kiloyears.

Quail took a sip of water before continuing. 'Now I must disclose an alarming new discovery.'

Stars winked into existence above the table: hundreds and then thousands of them, strewn in lacy patterns like strands of seaweed. They were looking at a map of the local stellar neighbourhood – a few hundred light-years in either direction – with the line of the Way cutting through it like a blue laser. The swallowship's position next to the Way was marked, as was the swarm of enemy ships trailing it.

And then a smudge of radiance appeared far ahead, again near the Way.

'That's the troubling discovery,' Quail said.

'Neutrino sources?' Merlin said, doing his best to convince the room that his attention was not being torn between two foci.

'A whole clump of them in our path, about one hundred

light-years ahead of us. Spectroscopy says they're more or less stationary with respect to the local stellar neighbourhood. That means it isn't a swarm coming to intercept us from the front – but I'm afraid that's as good as the news gets.'

'Husker?' said Gallinule.

'Undoubtedly. Best guess is we're headed straight towards a major operational concentration – hundreds of ships – the equivalent of one of our motherbases or halo manufactories. Almost certainly armed to the teeth and in no mood to let us slip past unchallenged. In short, we're running from one swarm towards another, which happens to be even larger.'

Silence while the seniors – including Merlin – digested this news.

'Well, that's it, then,' said another senior, white-bearded, bald Crombec, who ran the warcrèches. 'We've got no choice but to turn away from our current path.'

'Tactically risky,' Gallinule said.

Crombec rubbed his eyes, red with fatigue. Evidently he had been awake for some time – perhaps privy to this knowledge longer than the others, grappling with the options. 'Yes. But what else can we do?'

'There is something,' Merlin said. As he spoke he saw the status readout on his glove change: the sensors racked around the syrinx finally recording some activity. Considering what he was about to advocate, it was ironic indeed. 'A crash-programme to achieve Way-capability. Even if there's an ambush ahead, the Huskers won't be able to touch a ship moving in the Way.'

Pauraque scoffed. 'And the fact that the Cohort's best minds have struggled with this problem for kiloyears in no way dents your optimism?'

'I'm only saying we'd have a better than zero chance.'

'And I suppose we could try and find this superweapon of yours while we're at it?'

'Actually,' said Quail, raising his voice again, 'there happens to be a third possibility, one that I haven't drawn your attention to yet. Look at the map, will you?'

Now Quail added a new star – one that had not been displayed before. It lay directly ahead of them, only a few tens of light-years from their current position. As they moved their heads to establish parallax, they all saw that the star was almost exactly aligned with the Way.

'We have a chance,' he said. 'A small one, but very much better than nothing. This system has a little family of worlds: a few rocky planets and a gas giant with moons. There's no sign of any human presence. In nearly every respect there's nothing remarkable about this place. Yet the Way passes directly through the system. It might have been accidental ... or the Waymakers may have wanted this system in their network.'

Merlin nodded. Extensive as the Waynet was, it still only connected around ten million of the galaxy's stars. Ten million sounded like a huge number, but what it meant was that for every single star on the network there were another *forty thousand* that could only be reached by conventional means.

'How far away?' he said.

Quail answered: 'Without altering our trajectory, we'll reach it in a few decades of worldtime whatever we do now. Here's my suggestion. We decelerate, stop in the system and dig ourselves in. We'll still have thirty years before the Huskers arrive. That should give us time to find the best hiding places and to camouflage ourselves well enough to escape their detection.'

'They'll be looking for us,' Crombec said.

'Not necessarily.' Quail made a gesture with his hands, clasping them and then drawing them slowly apart. 'We can split *Starthroat* into two parts. One will continue moving at our current speed, with its exhaust directed back towards the Huskers. The other, smaller part will decelerate hard – but it'll be directing its radiation away from the aliens. We can fine-tune the beam direction so that the swarm ahead of us doesn't see it either.'

'That's ... ambitious,' Merlin said. He had his gloved hand under the table now, not wanting anyone else to see the bad news that was spilling across it. 'If hiding's your style.'

'It's no one's style – just our only rational hope.' Quail looked around the room, seeming older and frailer than any captain ought to be, rectangles of shadow etched beneath his cheekbones.

Crombec spoke up. 'Captain? I would like to take command of the part of the ship that remains in flight.'

There were a few murmurs of assent. Clearly Crombec would not be alone in preferring not to hide, even if the majority might choose to follow Quail.

'Wait,' Pauraque said. 'As soon as we put people on a decoy, with knowledge of what has happened earlier, we run the risk of the Huskers eventually learning it all for themselves.'

'We'll take that risk,' Quail snapped.

'There won't be one,' said Crombec. 'You have my word that I'll destroy my ship rather than risk it falling into Husker possession.'

'Merlin?' the captain asked. 'I take it you're with us?'

'Of course,' he said, snapping out of his gloomy reverie. 'I support your proposal fully ... as I must. Doubtless we'll have time to completely camouflage ourselves and cover our tracks before the swarm comes past. There's just one thing ...'

Quail tilted his head to one side to rest against his hand, like a man close to exhaustion. 'Yes?'

'You said the system was almost unremarkable ... is it simply the presence of the Waynet that makes it otherwise?'

'No,' Quail said, his patience wearing fatally thin. 'No, there was something else – a small anomaly in the star's mass–luminosity relationship. I doubt that it's anything very significant. Look on the bright side, Merlin. Investigating it will give you something to do while the rest of us are busying ourselves with the boring work of concealment. And you'll have your precious syrinxes, as well – not to mention close proximity to the Waynet. There'll be plenty of time for all the experiments you can think of. I'm sure even you will be able to make two syrinxes last long enough ...'

Merlin glanced down at his glove again, hoping that the news he had received earlier had in some way been an error, or his eyes had deceived him. But neither of those things proved to be the case.

'Better make that one,' he said.

Naked, bound together, Sayaca and Merlin seemed to float in space, kindling a focus of human warmth between them. The moment when the walls of the little ship had vanished had been meant to surprise and impress Sayaca. He had planned it meticulously. But instead she began to shiver, though it was no colder than it had been an instant earlier. He traced his hand across her thigh, feeling her skin break into goosebumps.

'It's just a trick,' he said, her face half-buried in his chest. 'No one can see us from outside the cutter.'

'Force and wisdom; it feels so cold now, Merlin. Makes me feel so small and vulnerable, like a candle on the point of flickering out.'

'But you're with me.'

'It doesn't make any difference, don't you understand? You're just a man, Merlin – not some divine protective force.'

Grudgingly, but knowing that the moment had been spoiled, Merlin allowed the walls to return. The stars were still visible, but there was now quite clearly a shell of transparent metasapphire, laced with control graphics, to hold them at bay.

'I thought you'd like it,' he said. 'Especially now, on a day like this one.'

'I just wasn't quite ready for it, that's all.' Her tone shifted to one of reconciliation. 'Where is it, anyway?'

Merlin issued another subvocal command to the ship, instructing it to distort and magnify the starfield selectively, until the object of Sayaca's interest sprang into focus. What they saw was the swallowship splitting into two uneven parts, like an insect undergoing some final, unplanned metamorphosis. Six years had passed since the final decision had been made to implement Quail's scheme. Sayaca and Merlin had become lovers in that time; Quail had even died.

The separation would have been beautiful, were so much not at stake. *Starthroat* did not exist anymore. Its rebuilding had been a mammoth effort that had occupied all of them in one way or another. Much of its mass had been retained aboard the part that would remain cruising relativistically. She had been named *Bluethroat* and carried roughly one-third of the frostwatch sleepers, in addition to Crombec and the small number of seniors and subseniors who had chosen to follow him. Needless to say there had been some dispute about Crombec getting most of the weapons, chiefly from Pauraque ... but Merlin could not begrudge him that.

The smaller part they had named *Starling*. This was a ship designed to make one journey only, from here to the new system. It was equipped with a plethora of nimble, adaptable in-system craft, necessary for exploring the new system and finding the securest hiding places. Scans showed that a total of six worlds orbited the star they had now named Bright Boy. Only two were of significance: a scorched, airless planet much the same size as fabled Earth, which they named Cinder, and a gas giant they named Ghost. It seemed obvious that the best place to hide would be in one of these worlds, either Cinder or Ghost, but no decision had yet been made. Sayaca thought Cinder was the best choice, while Pauraque advocated using Ghost's thick atmosphere for concealment. Eventually a choice would be made; they would dig in, establish a base and conceal all evidence of their activities.

The Huskers might slow down, curious – but they would find nothing.

'You were there, weren't you?' Sayaca said. 'When they decided this.'

Merlin nodded – remembering how young she had seemed then. The last few years had aged them all. 'We all thought Quail was insane ... then we realised even an insane plan was the best we had. Except for Crombec, of course ...'

Bluethroat was separating now, its torch still burning clean and steady, arcing back into the night along the great axis of the Way. Far behind – but far closer than they had once been – lay the swarm, still pursuing Merlin's people.

'You think Crombec's people will die, don't you?' Sayaca said.

'If I thought he had the better chance, that's where I'd be. With his faction, rather than under Pauraque.'

'I thought about following him too,' Sayaca said. 'His arguments sounded convincing. He thinks we'll all die around Bright Boy.'

'Maybe we will. I still think the odds are slightly more in our favour.'

'Slightly?'

'There's something I don't like about our destination, Sayaca. Bright Boy doesn't fit into our normal stellar models. It's too bright for its size, and it's putting out far too many neutrinos. If you're going to hide somewhere, you don't do it around a star that stands out from the crowd.'

'Would it make any difference if Quail had put you in charge rather than Pauraque? Or if the Council had not forbidden you to test the final syrinx?'

Conceivably, he thought, it might well have made a difference. He had been very lucky to retain any kind of seniority after what had happened back then. But the loss of the next to last syrinx had not been the utter disaster his enemies had tried to portray. The machine had still rammed against the Way in a catastrophic manner, but for the first time in living memory, a syrinx had appeared to do something else in the instants before that collision ... chirping a series of quantum-gravitational variations towards the boundary. And the Way had begun to respond: a strange local alteration in its topology ahead of the syrinx. Puckering, until a dimple formed on the boundary, like the nub of a severed branch on a tree trunk. The dimple was still forming when the syrinx hit.

What, Merlin wondered, would have happened if that impact had been delayed for a few more instants? Might the dimple have finished forming, providing an entry point into the Way?

'I don't think it made any difference to me.'

'They say you hated Quail.'

'I had reasons not to like him, Sayaca. My brother and I both did.'

'But they say Quail rescued you from Plenitude, that he saved your lives while everyone else died.'

'That's true enough.'

'And for that you *hated* him?'

'He should have left us behind, Sayaca. No; don't look at me like that. You weren't there. You can't understand what it was like.'

'Maybe if I spoke to Gallinule, he'd have more to say about it.' Subtly, she pulled away from him. A few minutes earlier it would have signified nothing, but now that tiny change in their spatial relationship spoke volumes. 'They say you're alike, you and Gallinule. You both look alike too. But there isn't as much similarity as people think.'

Part Two

'There are definitely tunnels here,' Sayaca said, years later.

Their cutter was parked on an airless plain near Cinder's equator, squatting down on skids like a beached black fish. Bright Boy was almost overhead; a disc of fierce radiance casting razor-edged shadows like pools of ink. Merlin moved over to Sayaca's side of the cabin to see the data she was projecting before her, sketched in ruddy contours. Smelling her, he wanted to bury his face in her hair and turn her face to his before kissing her, but the moment was not right for that. It had not been right for some time.

'Caves, you mean?' Merlin said.

'No, *tunnels*.' She almost managed to hide her irritation. 'Like

I always said they were. Deliberately excavated. Now do you believe me?'

There had been hints of them before, from orbit, during the first months after their arrival around the star. *Starling* had sent expeditionary teams out to a dozen promising niches in the system, tasking them to assess the benefits of each before a final decision was made. Most of the effort was focused around Cinder and Ghost – they had even put space stations into orbit around the gas giant – but there were teams exploring smaller bodies, even comets and asteroids. Nothing would be dismissed without at least a preliminary study. There were even teams working on fringe ideas like hiding inside the sun's chromosphere.

And for all that, Merlin thought, *they still won't allow me near the other syrinx.*

But at least Cinder was a kind of distraction. Mapping satellites had been dropped into orbits around all the major bodies in the system, measuring the gravitational fields of each body. The data, unravelled into a density-map, hinted at a puzzling structure within Cinder – a deep network of tunnels riddling the lithosphere. Now they had even better maps, constructed from seismic data. One or two small asteroids hit Cinder every month. With no atmosphere to slow them down, they slammed into the surface at many kilometres per second. The sound waves from those impacts would radiate through the underlying rock, bent into complex wave fronts as they traversed density zones. They would eventually reach the surface again, thousands of kilometres away, but the precise pattern of arrival times – picked up across a network of listening devices studding the surface – would depend on the route that the sound waves had taken.

Now Merlin could see that the tunnels were definitely artificial.

'Who do you think dug them?'

'From here, there's no way we'll ever know.' Sayaca frowned, puzzling over something in her data, and then seemed to drop the annoyance, at least for now, rather than have it spoil her moment of triumph. 'Whoever it was, they tidied up after themselves. We'll have to go down – get into them.'

'Perhaps we'll find somewhere to hide.'

'Or find someone else already hiding.' Sayaca looked into his face, her expression one of complete seriousness.

'Maybe they'll let us hide with them.'

'She turned back to her work. 'Or maybe they'd rather we left them alone.'

Several months later, Merlin buckled on an immersion suit, feeling the slight prickling sensation around the nape of his neck as the suit hijacked his spinal nerves. Vision and balance flickered – there was a perceptual jolt he never quite got used to – and then suddenly he was back in the simulated realm of the Palace. He had to admit it was good; much better than the last time he had sampled Gallinule's toy environment.

'You've been busy,' he said.

Gallinule's image smiled. 'It'll do for now. Just wait till you've seen the sunset wing.'

Gallinule led him through the maze of high-ceilinged, baroquely walled corridors that led from the oubliette to the other side of the Palace. They ascended and descended spiral staircases and crossed vertiginous inner chambers spanned by elegantly arched stone-work bridges, delicate subtleties of masonry highlighted in sunset fire. The real Palace of Eternal Dusk had been ruined along with every other sign of civilisation when the Huskers had torched Plenitude. This simulation was running in the main encampment inside Cinder, but Gallinule had spread copies of it around the system, wherever he might need a convenient venue for discussion.

'See anything that looks out of place?' Gallinule said.

Merlin looked around, but there was nothing that did not accord with his own memories. Hardly surprising. Of the two of them, Gallinule had always been the one with the eye for detail.

'It's pretty damned good. But why? And how?'

'As a test-bed. Aboard *Starthroat*, we never needed good simulation techniques. But our lives depend upon making the right choices around Bright Boy. That means we have to be able to simulate any hypothetical situation and experience it as if it were totally real.'

Merlin agreed. The discovery that the tunnels in Cinder were artificial had enormously complicated the hideaway project. They had been excavated by a hypothetical human splinter group, which Sayaca had dubbed the Diggers. No one knew much about them. Certainly they had been more advanced than any part of the Cohort, but while their machines – lining the tunnels like a thick arterial plaque – seemed unfathomably strange, they were not quite strange enough to suggest that they had been installed by the Waymakers. And they were quite clearly human: markings were in a language that the linguists said had ancient links to Main. The Diggers were simply one of the thousands of cultures that had ascended to heights of technical prowess without making any recognisable dent on human history.

'... Anyway, who knows what nasty traps the Diggers left us?' Gallinule was saying. 'With simulations, we'll at least be able to prepare for the more obvious surprises.' His youthful image shrugged. 'So I initiated a crash programme to resurrect the old techniques. At the moment we have to wear suits to achieve this level of immersion, but in a year or so we'll be able to step into simulated environments as easily as walking from one room to another.'

They had reached a balcony on the sunset side of the Palace of Eternal Dusk. He leaned over the balustrade as far as he dared, seeing how the lower levels of the Palace dropped away towards the rushing sea below. The Palace of Eternal Dusk circled Plenitude's equator once a day, travelling with the line that divided day from night. Its motion caused Plenitude's sun to hang at the same point in the sky, two-thirds of its swollen disk already consumed by the sea. Somewhere deep in the keel of rock the Palace rode lay throbbing mechanisms that both sustained the structure's flight – it had been flying for longer than anyone remembered – and generated the protective bubble that held it in a pocket of still air, despite its supersonic velocity relative to the ground.

Merlin's family had held the Palace for thirteen hundred years, after a short Dark Age on Plenitude. The family had been amongst the first to rediscover powered flight, using fragile aircraft to reach the keel. Other contenders had come, but the family had retained their treasure across forty generations, through another two Dark Ages.

Finally, however, the greater war had touched them.

A damaged Cohort swallowship had been the first to arrive, years ahead of a Husker swarm. The reality of interstellar travel was dimly remembered on Plenitude, but those first newcomers were still treated with suspicion and paranoia. Only Merlin's family had given them the benefit of the doubt ... and even then had not fully heeded the warning when it was given. Against their ruling mother's wishes, the two brothers had allowed themselves to be taken aboard the swallowship and inducted into the ways of the Cohort. Their old names were discarded in favour of new ones, in the custom of the swallowship's crew. They learned fluency in Main.

After several months, Merlin and Gallinule had been preparing to return home as envoys. Their plan was simple enough. They would persuade their mother that Plenitude was doomed. That would not be the easiest of tasks, but their mother's cooperation was vital if anything was to be saved. It would mean establishing peace amongst the planet's various factions, where none had existed for generations. There were spaces in the swallowship's frostwatch holds for sleepers, but only a few hundred thousand, which would mean that each region must select its best. It would not be easy, but there were still years in which to do it.

'None of it will make any difference,' their mother had said. 'No one will listen to us, even if we believe everything Quail says.'

'They have to.'

'Don't you understand?' she said. 'You think of me as your mother, but to fifty million of Plenitude's inhabitants I'm a *tyrant*.'

'They'll understand,' Merlin said, only half-believing it himself.

But then the unthinkable had happened. A smaller element of the swarm had crept up much closer than anyone had feared, detected only when it was already within Plenitude's system. The swallowship's captain made the only decision he could, which was to break orbit immediately and run for interstellar space.

Merlin and Gallinule fought – pleaded – but Quail would not allow them to leave the ship. They told him all they wanted was to return home. If that meant dying with everyone else on Plenitude, including their mother, so be it.

Quail listened, and sympathised, and still refused them. It was not just their genes that the Cohort required, he said. Everything else about them: their stories. Their hopes and fears. The tiniest piece of knowledge they carried, considered trivial by them, might prove to be shatteringly valuable. It was many decades of shiptime since they had found another pocket of humanity. Merlin and Gallinule were simply too precious to throw away.

Even if it meant denying them the right to die with valour.

Instead, on *Starthroat*'s long-range cameras, relayed from monitoring satellites sown around Plenitude, they watched the Palace of Eternal Dusk die, wounded by weapons it had never known before, stabbing deep into the keel on which it flew, destroying the engines that held it aloft. It came down slowly, grinding into the planetary crust, gouging a terrible scar across half of one scorched continent before it came to rest, ruined and lopsided.

And now Gallinule had made this.

'If you can do all this now . . .' Merlin mused. He left the remark hanging, knowing his brother would take the bait.

'As I said, full immersion in a year or so. Then we'll need better methods to deal with the time-lag for communications around Bright Boy. We can't even broadcast signals for fear of them being intercepted by the Huskers, which limits us to line-of-sight comms between relay nodes sprinkled around the system. Sometimes the routing will add significant delays. That's why we need another kind of simulation. If we can create semblances—'

Merlin stopped him. 'Semblances?'

'Sorry. Old term I dug from the troves. Another technique we've forgotten aboard *Starthroat*. We need to be able to make convincing simulacra of ourselves, with realistic responses across a range of likely stimuli. Then we can be in two places at once – or as many as we want to be. Afterwards, you merge the memories gathered by your semblances.'

Merlin thought about that. Many cultures known to the Cohort had developed the kind of technology Gallinule was referring to, so the concept was not unfamiliar to him.

'These wouldn't be conscious entities, though?'

'No; that's far down the line. Semblances would just be mimetic software: clever caricatures. Of course, they'd seem real if they were working well. Later—'

'You'd think of adding consciousness?'

Gallinule looked around warily. It was a reflex, of course – there could not possibly have been eavesdroppers in this environment he had fashioned – but it was telling all the same. 'It would be useful. If we could copy ourselves entirely into simulation – not just mimesis, but neuron-by-neuron mapping – it would make hiding from the Huskers very much easier.'

'Become disembodied programmes, you mean? Sorry, but that's a definite case of the cure being worse than the disease.'

'Eventually it won't seem anywhere near as chilling as it does now. Especially when our other options for hiding look less and less viable.'

Merlin nodded sagely. 'And you'd no doubt do all in your power to make them seem that way, wouldn't you?'

Gallinule shrugged. 'If Cinder's tunnels turn out to be the best place to hide, so be it. But it's senseless not to explore other options.' Merlin watched the way his knuckles tightened on the stone balustrade, betraying the tension he tried to keep from his voice.

'If you make an issue of this,' Merlin said carefully, 'you'd better assume I'll fight you, brother or not.'

Gallinule touched Merlin's shoulder. 'It won't come to a confrontation. By the time the options are in, the correct path will be clear to us all . . . you included.'

'The correct path's already clear to me. And it doesn't involve becoming patterns inside a machine.'

'You'd prefer suicide instead?'

'Of course not. I'm talking about something infinitely better than hiding.' He looked hard into his brother's face. 'You have more influence on the Council than I do. You could persuade them to let me examine the syrinx.'

'Why not ask Sayaca the same thing?'

'You know very well why not. Things aren't the same between us these days. If you . . . oh, what's the point?' Merlin removed Gallinule's hand from his shoulder. 'Nothing that happens here will make the slightest difference to your plans.'

'Spare me the self-righteousness, Merlin. It's not as though you're any different.' Then he sighed, looking out to sea. 'I'll demonstrate my commitment to the cause, if that's what you want. You know that Pauraque's still exploring the possibility of establishing a camouflaged base inside Ghost's atmosphere?'

'Of course.'

'What you probably don't know is that our automated drones don't work well at those depths. So we're going in with an exploration team next month. It'll be dangerous, but we have the Council's say-so. We know there's something down there, something we don't understand. We have to find out what it is.'

Merlin had heard nothing about anything unexpected inside Ghost, but he feigned knowledge all the same.

'Why are you telling me this?'

'Because I'm accompanying Pauraque. We've equipped a two-person cutter for the expedition, armoured to take thousands of atmospheres of pressure.' Gallinule paused and clicked his fingers out to sea, making the blueprints of the ship loom large in the sky, sharp against the dark-blue zenith. The blueprint rotated dizzyingly. 'It's nothing too technical. Another ship could be adapted before we go down there. I'd be happy to disclose the mods.'

Merlin studied the schematic, committing the salient points to memory.

'This is a goad, isn't it?'

'Call it what you will. I'm just saying that my commitment to the greater cause shouldn't be in any doubt.' Another finger click and the phantom ship vanished from the sky. 'Where yours fits in is another thing entirely.'

Part Three

For days Ghost had loomed ahead: a fat sphere banded by delicate equatorial clouds, encircled by moons and rings. Now it swallowed half the sky, cloud decks reaching up towards him; castellations of cream and ochre stacked hundreds of kilometres high. His approach was queried by the orbiting stations, but they must have known what the purpose of his visit was. His brother and Pauraque were already down there in the clouds. He had a faint fix on their ship as it steered itself into the depths.

The seniors around Cinder had been eager to get him out of their hair, so it had not taken much to persuade them to give him a ship of his own. He had customised it according to Gallinule's specifications and added a few cautious refinements of his own ... and then named it *Tyrant*.

The hull creaked and sang as it reshaped itself for transatmospheric travel. The navigational fix grew stronger. With Merlin inside, the ship fell, knifing down through cloud layers. The planet had no sharply defined surface, but there came a point where the atmospheric pressure was exactly equivalent to the air pressure inside *Tyrant*. Below that datum, pressure and temperature climbed steadily. Gravity was an uncomfortable two gees, more or less tolerable if he remained in his seat.

The metasapphire hull creaked again, reshaping itself. Merlin had descended more than a hundred kilometres below the one-atmosphere datum, and the pressure outside was now ten times higher. Above fifty atmospheres, the hull would rely on internal power sources to prevent itself from buckling. Merlin did his best not to think about the pressure, but there was no ignoring the way the light outside had dimmed, veiled by the masses of atmosphere suspended above his head. Down below it was oppressively dark, like the sooty heart of a thunderstorm wrapped around half his vision. Only now and then was there a stammer of lightning, which briefly lit the cathedrals of cloud below for hundreds of kilometres, down to vertiginous depths.

If there'd been more time, he thought, *we'd have come with submarines, not spacecraft . . .*

It was a dismal place to even think about spending any time in. But in that respect it made perfect sense. The thick atmosphere would make it easy to hide a modestly sized floating base, smothering infrared emissions. They would probably have to sleep during the hideaway period, but that was no great hardship. Better than spending decades awake, always knowing that beyond the walls was that crushing force constantly trying to squash you out of existence.

But there was something down here, Gallinule had said. Something that might count against using Ghost as a hideaway.

They had to know what it was.

'Warning,' said *Tyrant*. 'External pressure now thirty bars. Probability of hull collapse in five minutes is now five per cent.'

Merlin killed the warning system. It did not know about the augmentations he had made to the hull armouring, but it was still unnerving. But Pauraque and Gallinule were lower yet, and their navigational transponder was still working.

If they were daring him to go deeper, he would accept.

'Merlin?' said his brother's voice, trebly with echoes from the atmospheric interference. 'So you decided to join us after all. Did you bring Sayaca with you?'

'I'm alone. I didn't see any point in endangering two of us.'

'Shame. Well, I hope you implemented those hull mods, or this is going to be a brief conversation.'

'Just tell me what it is we're expecting to see down here. You mentioned something unexpected.'

Pauraque's voice now. 'There's a periodic pressure phenomenon moving through the atmosphere, like a very fast storm. What it is, we don't know. Until we understand it, we can't be certain that hiding inside Ghost will work.'

Merlin nodded, suddenly seeing Gallinule's angle. His brother would want the phenomenon to prove hazardous just so that his plan could triumph over Pauraque's. It was an odd attitude, especially as Pauraque and Gallinule were now said to be lovers, but it was nothing unusual as far as his brother was concerned.

'I take it you have a rough idea when we can expect to see this thing?'

'Reasonably good,' Pauraque said. 'Approach us and follow our vector. We're going deeper, so watch those integrity readings.'

As if to underline her words, the hull chose that moment to creak – a dozen alerts sounding. Merlin grimaced, silencing the alarms, and gunned *Tyrant* towards the other ship.

Ghost was a classic gas giant, three hundred times more massive than Cinder. Most of the planet was hydrogen in its metallic state, overlaid by a deep ocean of merely liquid hydrogen. The cloud layers, which seemed so immense – and which gave the world its subtle bands of colour – were compressed into only a few hundred kilometres of depth. Less than a hundredth of the planet's radius, yet those frigid, layered clouds of ammonia, hydrogen and water were as deep as humans could go. Pauraque wanted to hide at the lowest layer above the transition zone where the atmosphere thickened into a liquid-hydrogen sea, under a crystal veil of ammonium hydro-sulphide and water-ice.

Ahead, he could now see the glint of the other ship's thrusters, illuminating sullen cloud formations as it passed through them. Only a few kilometres ahead.

'You mentioned that the phenomenon was periodic,' Merlin said. 'What exactly did you mean by that?'

'Exactly what I said,' came Pauraque's reply, much clearer now. 'The pressure wave – or focus – moves around Ghost once every three hours.'

'That's much faster than any cyclone.'

'Yes.' The icy distaste in Pauraque's voice was obvious. She did not enjoy having a civil conversation with him. 'Which is why we consider the phenomenon sufficiently—'

'It could be in orbit.'

'What?'

Merlin checked the hull readouts again, watching as pressure hotspots flowed liquidly from point to point. Rendered in subtle colours, they looked like diffraction patterns on the scales of a sleek, tropical fish.

'I said it could be in orbit. If one of Ghost's moons was in orbit just above the top of the cloud layer, three hours is how long it would take to go around. The time would only be slightly less for a moon orbiting just below the cloud layer, where we are.'

'Now you've really lost it,' Gallinule said. 'In orbit? *Inside* a planet?'

Merlin shrugged. He had thought about this already and had an answer prepared, but he preferred that Gallinule believed him to be thinking the problem through even as they spoke. 'Of course, I don't really think there's a moon down there. But there could still be something orbiting.'

'Such as?' Pauraque said.

'A black hole, for instance. A small one – say a tenth of the mass of Cinder, with a light-trapping radius of about a millimetre. We'd have missed that kind of perturbation to Ghost's gravitational field until now. It wouldn't feel the atmosphere at all, not on the kind of timescales we're concerned with. But as the hole passed, the atmosphere would be tugged towards it for hundreds of kilometres along its track. Any chance that's your anomaly?'

There was a grudging silence before Pauraque answered. 'I admit that at the very least it's possible. We more or less arrived at the same conclusion. Who knows how such a thing ended up inside Ghost, but it could have happened.'

'Maybe someone put it there deliberately.'

'We'll know soon enough. The storm's due any moment now.'

She was right. The storm focus – whatever it was – moved at forty kilometres per second relative to Ghost's core, but since Ghost's equatorial cloud-layers were already rotating at a quarter of that speed, and in the same sense as the focus, the storm only moved at thirty kilometres per second against the atmosphere. Which, Merlin thought, was still adequately fast.

He told the cabin windows to amplify the available light, gathering photons from beyond the visible band and shifting them into the optical. Suddenly it was as if the overlaying veils had been stripped away; sunlight flooded the canyons and crevasses of cloud through which they were flying. The liquid hydrogen ocean began only a few tens of kilometres below them, under a transition zone where the atmospheric gases became steadily more fluidic. It was blood-hot down there; pressures nudged towards one hundred atmospheres. Not far below the sea they would climb into the thousands, at temperatures hot enough to melt machines.

And now something climbed above the horizon to the west. *Tyrant* began to shriek alarms, its dull machine-sentience comprehending that there was something very wrong nearby, and that it was a wrongness approaching at ferocious speed. The storm focus gathered clouds as it moved, tugging them violently out of formation. To Merlin's eyes, the way it moved reminded him of something from his childhood, something glimpsed moving through Plenitude's tropical waters with predatory swiftness: a darting mass of whirling tentacles.

'We're too high,' Pauraque said. 'I'm taking us lower. I want to be much closer to the focus when it arrives.'

Before he could argue, Merlin saw the violet thrust spikes of the other ship. It slammed away, dwindling into the soupy stillness of the upper transition zone. He thought of a fish descending into some lightless ocean trench, into benthic darkness.

'Watch your shielding,' he said, as he dived his own ship after them.

'Pressure's still within safe limits,' Gallinule said, though they both knew that what now constituted safe was not quite the usual sense of the word. 'I'll pull up if the rivets start popping, trust me.'

'It's not just the pressure that worries me. If there's a black hole in that focus, there's also going to be a blast of gamma rays from the matter being sucked in.'

'We haven't seen anything yet. Maybe the flux is masked by the clouds.'

'You'd better hope it is.'

Merlin was suited up, wearing the kind of high-pressure mobility armour he had only ever worn before in warcrèche simulations. The armour was prized technology, many kiloyears old; nothing like it now within the Cohort's technical reach. He hoped Gallinule and Pauraque were similarly prudent. If the hull collapsed, the suits might only give them a few more minutes of life, but near something as unpredictable and chaotic as a miniature black hole, there was no such thing as too much shielding.

'Merlin?' Gallinule said. 'We've lost a power node. Damn jury-rigged things. If there's a pressure wave before the focus we might start to buckle—'

'You can't risk it. Pull up and out. We can come back again on the next pass, three hours from now.'

He had seen accretion discs, the swirls of matter around stellar-mass black holes and neutron stars, and what he saw near the storm's focus looked very similar: a spiralling concentration of cloud, tortured into rainbow colours as strange, transient chemistries came into play. They were so deep in the transition zone here that even tiny pressure changes were enough to condense the air into its fluid state. Lightning cartwheeled across the focus, driven by static differentials in the moving air masses. Merlin checked the range: close now, less than two hundred kilometres away.

And something was wrong.

Pauraque's ship was sinking too far, drifting too close to the heart of the storm. They were above it now, but their rate of descent would bring them close to the focus by the time it arrived.

'Force and wisdom; I told you to pull up, not go deeper!'

'We have a problem. Can't reshape the hull on our remaining nodes. No aerodynamic control.' Gallinule's voice was calm, but Merlin knew his brother was terrified.

'Vector your thrust.'

'Hell's teeth, what do you think I'm trying to do?'

No good. He watched the violet spikes of the other ship's thrusters stab in different directions, but there was nothing Gallinule could do to bring them out of their terminal descent. Merlin thought of the mods Gallinule had recommended. Unless he had added some hidden improvements, the other ship would implode in ten or fifteen seconds. There would be no surviving that.

'Listen to me,' Merlin said. 'You have to equalise pressure with the outside, or that hull's going to implode.'

'We'll lose the ship that way.'

'Don't argue, just do it! You have no more than ten seconds to save yourselves!'

He closed his eyes and hoped they were both suited. Or perhaps it would be better if they were not. To die by hull implosion would be swift, after all. The inrushing walls would move faster than any human nerve impulses.

On the magnified view of the other ship he saw a row of intakes flicker open along the dorsal line. Soup-thick atmosphere would have slammed in like an iron fist. Maybe their suits were good enough to withstand that shock.

He hoped so.

The thrust flames died out. Running lights and fluorescent markings winked out. A moment later he watched the other ship come apart like something fashioned from gossamer. Debris lingered for an instant before being crushed towards invisibility.

And two bulbously suited human figures fell through the air, drifting apart as they were caught in the torpid currents that ran through the transition zone. For a moment the suits were androform, but then their carapaces flowed liquidly towards smooth egg-shapes, held rigid by the same principle that still protected Merlin's ship. They were alive – he was sure of that – but they were still sinking, still heavier than the air they displaced. The one that was now falling fastest would pass the storm at what he judged to be a safe distance. The other would fall right through the storm's eye.

He thought of the focus of the storm: a seething eye of flickering gamma rays, horrific gravitational stress and intense pressure eddies. They had not seen it yet, but he could be sure that was what it would be like. A black hole, even a small one, was no place to be near.

'Final warning,' *Tyrant* said, bypassing all his overrides. 'Pressure now at maximum safe limit. Any further increase in—'

He made his decision.

Slammed *Tyrant* screaming towards the survivor who was headed towards the eye. It would be close – hellishly so. Even the extra margins he had built into this ship's hull would be pushed perilously close to the limit. On the cabin window, cross-hairs locked around the first falling egg. Range: eleven kilometres and closing. He computed an approach vector and saw that it would be even closer than he had feared. They would be arcing straight towards the eye by the time he had the egg aboard. Seven kilometres. There would not be time to bring the egg aboard properly. The best he could do would be to open a cavity in the hull and enclose it. Frantically he told *Tyrant* what he needed; by the time he was done, range was down to three kilometres.

He felt faint, phantom deceleration as *Tyrant* matched trajectories with the egg and brought itself in for the rendezvous. The egg left a trail of bubbles behind it as it dropped, evidence of the transition to ocean. Somewhere on *Tyrant*'s skin, a cavity puckered open, precisely shaped to accept the egg. They tore through rushing curtains of cloud. In a few moments he would be near enough to see the eye, he knew. One kilometre . . . six hundred metres. Three hundred.

The faintest of thumps as the egg was captured. Membranes of hull locked over the prize and resealed. Whoever he had saved was as safe now as Merlin.

Which was really saying very little.

'Instigate immediate pull-up. Hull collapse imminent. Severe pressure transition imminent.'

He was through the eye now, perhaps only two or three kilometres from the sucking point of the black hole. He had expected to see the clouds drawn into a malignant little knot, with a flickering glint of intense light at the heart of the whirlpool, but there was nothing, just clear skies. There was a local gravitational distortion, but it was nowhere near as severe as he had expected. Merlin glanced at the radiation alarms, but they were not showing anything unusual.

No hint of gamma radiation.

He wanted time to think, wanted to work out how he could be this close to a black hole and feel no radiation, but what was coming up below instantly demanded his attention. There was the other egg, tumbling below, wobbling as if in a mirage. Pressure was distorting it, readying to crush it. And down below, slumbering under the transition zone, was the true hydrogen sea. In a few seconds the other egg would be completely immersed in that unimaginably dense blackness and it would all be over. For a moment he considered swooping in low; trying to snatch the egg before it hit. He ran the numbers and saw the chilling truth.

He would have to enter the sea as well.

Merlin gave *Tyrant* its orders and closed his eyes. Even in the cushioning embrace of his suit, the hairpin turn as the ship skimmed the ocean would still not be comfortable. It would probably push him below consciousness. Which, he thought, might turn out to be the final mercy.

The sea's hazy surface came up like a black fog.

Thought faded for an instant, then returned fuzzily; and now through the windows he saw veils of cloud towards which he was climbing. The feeling of having survived was godlike. Yet

159

something was screaming. The ship, he realised. It had sloughed millimetres of hull to stay intact. He prayed that the damage would not prevent him from getting home.

'The second egg ...' Merlin said. 'Did we get it?'

Tyrant was clever enough – just – to know what he meant. 'Both eggs recovered.'

'Good. Show me ...'

Proctors carried the first egg into the cabin, fiddling with it until they persuaded it to revert to androform shape. When the facial region became transparent he saw that it was Gallinule that this egg had saved, although his brother was clearly unconscious. Not dead though: he could tell that from the egg's luminous readouts. He felt a moment of pure, unadulterated bliss. He had saved Gallinule, but not selfishly. He had not known which of the two eggs had been falling towards the eye. In fact, he did not even know that this was that egg. Had he plucked his brother from the sea, instants before the ocean would have crushed him?

But then he saw the other egg. The proctors, stupid to the end, had seen fit to bring it into the cabin. They carried it like a trophy, as if it were something he would be overjoyed to see. But it was barely larger than a space helmet.

Part Four

'I think I know what killed her,' Sayaca said.

The three of them had agreed to meet within the Palace of Eternal Dusk. Sayaca had arranged a demonstration, casting into the sky vast projected shapes, which she orchestrated with deft gestures.

'It wasn't a black hole, was it?' Gallinule said.

'No.' She took his hand in both of hers, comforting him as they dug through the difficult memory of Pauraque's death. It had happened months ago, but the pain of it was still acute for Gallinule. Merlin watched from one side, lingeringly resentful at the tenderness Sayaca showed his brother. 'I think it was something a lot stranger than a black hole. Shall I show you?'

A double helix writhed in the sky, luminous and serpentlike against Plenitude's perpetual pink twilight.

Releasing Gallinule's hand, Sayaca lifted a finger and the DNA coil swelled to godlike size, until the individual base pairs were themselves too large to discern as anything other than blurred assemblages of atoms, huger than mountains. But atoms were only the beginning of the descent into the world of the vanishingly small. Atoms were assembled from even tinier components: electrons, protons and neutrons, bound together by the electroweak and -strong forces. But even those fundamental particles held deeper layers of structure. All matter in the universe was woven from quarks or leptons; all force mediated by bosons.

Even that was not the end.

In the deepest of deep symmetries, the fermions – the quarks and leptons – and the bosons – the messengers of force – blurred into one kind of entity. Particle was no longer the right word for it. What everything in the universe seemed to boil down to, at the very fundamental level, was a series of loops vibrating at different frequencies, embedded in a multidimensional space.

What, Sayaca said, scientists had once termed *superstrings*.

It was elegant beyond words, and it explained seemingly everything. But the trouble with superstring theory, Sayaca added, was that it was extraordinarily difficult to test. It was likely that the theory had been reinvented and discarded dozens or hundreds of times in human history, during each brief phase of enlightenment. Undoubtedly the Waymakers must have come to some final wisdom as to the ultimate nature of reality . . . but if they had, they had not left that verdict in any form now remembered. So from Sayaca's viewpoint, superstring theory was at least as viable as any other model for unifying the fundamental particles and forces.

'But I don't see how any of this helps us understand Pauraque's storm,' Merlin said.

'Wait,' said Sayaca's semblance. 'I haven't finished. There's more than one type of superstring theory, understand? And some of those theories make a special prediction about the existence of something called shadow matter. It's not the same thing as antimatter. Shadow matter's like normal matter in every respect, except it's invisible and insubstantial. Objects made of normal and shadow matter just slip through each other like ghosts. There's only one way in which they sense each other.'

'Gravity,' Merlin said.

'Yes. As far as gravity's concerned, there's nothing to distinguish them.'

'So what are you saying, that there could be whole universes made of shadow matter coexisting with our own?'

'Exactly that.' She went on to tell them there was every reason to suppose that the shadow universe was just as complex as the normal one, with exactly analogous particle types, atoms and chemistry. There would be shadow galaxies, shadow stars and shadow worlds – perhaps even shadow life.

Merlin absorbed that. 'Why haven't we encountered anything like shadow matter before?'

'There must be strong segregation between the two types across the plane of the galaxy. For one reason or another, that segregation has broken down around Bright Boy. There seems to be about half a solar mass of shadow matter gravitationally bound to this system – most of it sitting in Bright Boy's core.'

Merlin tightened his grip on the balustrade. 'Tell me this answers all our riddles, Sayaca.'

Sayaca told them the rest, reminding Merlin how they had probed Cinder's interior via sound waves, each sonic pulse generated by the impact of an in-falling meteorite; the sound waves tracked as they swept through Cinder, gathered by a network of listening posts sprinkled across the surface. It was these seismic images that had first elucidated the fine structure of the Digger tunnels. But – unwittingly – Sayaca had learned much more than that.

'We measured Cinder's mass twice. The first time was when we put our own mapping satellites into orbit. That gave us one figure. The seismic data should have given us a second estimate that agreed to within a few per cent. But the seismic data said there was only two-thirds as much mass as there should have been, compared with the gravitational mass estimate.' Sayaca's semblance paused, perhaps giving the two of them time to make the connection themselves. When neither spoke, she permitted herself to continue. 'If there's a large chunk of shadow matter inside Cinder, it explains everything. The seismic waves only travel through normal matter, so they don't see one-third of Cinder's composition at all. But the gravitational signature of normal and shadow matter is identical. Our satellites felt the pull of the normal *and* shadow matter, just as we did when we were walking around inside Cinder.'

'All right,' he said. 'Tell me about Bright Boy too.'

'It makes just as much sense. Most of the shadow matter in this system must be inside the star. Half a solar mass would be enough for Bright Boy's shadow counterpart to become a star in its own right – burning its own shadow hydrogen to shadow helium, giving off shadow photons and shadow neutrinos, none of which we can see. Except just like Bright Boy it would be an astrophysical anomaly – too bright and small to make any kind of sense, because its structure is being affected by the presence of an equal amount of normal matter from *our* universe. Both stars end up with hotter cores, since the nuclear reactions have to work harder to hold up the weight of overlying stellar atmosphere.'

Sayaca thought that the two halves of Bright Boy – the normal and shadow-matter suns – had once been spatially separated, so that they formed the two stars of a close binary system. That, she said, would have been something so strange that no passing culture could have missed it, for the visible counterpart of Bright Boy would have appeared locked in orbital embrace with an invisible partner, signalling its oddity across half the galaxy. Over the ensuing billions of years, the two stars had whirled closer and closer together, their orbital motions damped by tidal dissipation, until they had merged and settled into the same spatial volume. *Whoever comes after us*, Merlin thought, *we won't be the last to study this cosmic mystery.*

'Then tell me about Pauraque's storm,' he said, flinching at the memory of her crushed survival egg.

Gallinule nodded. 'Go on. I want to know what killed her.'

Sayaca spoke now with less ease. 'It must be another chunk of shadow matter – about the mass of a large moon, squashed into a volume no more than a few tens of kilometres across. Of course, it wasn't the shadow matter itself that killed her. Just the storm it caused by its passage through the atmosphere.'

And not even that, Merlin thought. It was his decision that killed her; his conviction that it was more vital to save the first egg, the one falling into the storm's eye. Afterwards, discovering that there was no gamma-ray point there, he had realised that he could have saved both of them if he had saved Pauraque first.

'Something that massive, and that small ...' Gallinule paused. 'It can't be a moon, can it?'

Sayaca turned away from the sunset. 'No. It's no moon. Whatever it is, it was made by someone. Not the Huskers, I think, but someone else. And I think we have to work out what they had in mind.'

Nervously, Merlin watched seniors populate the auditorium – walking in or simply popping into holographic existence, like card figures dropped into a toy theatre. Sayaca had bided her time before announcing her discovery to the rest of the expedition, but eventually the three of them had gathered enough data to refute any argument. When it became clear that her news would be momentous, seniors had flown in from across the system, leaving the putative hideaways they were investigating. A few of them even sent their semblances, for the simulacra were now sophisticated enough to make many physical journeys unnecessary.

The announcement would take place in the auditorium of the largest orbiting station, poised above Ghost's cloud-tops. An auroral storm was lashing Ghost's northern pole, appropriately dramatic for the event. He wondered if Sayaca had scheduled the meeting with that display in mind.

'Go easy on the superstring physics,' Gallinule whispered in Sayaca's ear, as she sat between the two men. 'You don't want to lose them before you've begun. Some of these relics don't even know what a quark is, let alone a baryon-to-entropy ratio.'

Gallinule was right to warn Sayaca. It would be like her to begin her announcement by projecting a forest of equations on the display wall.

'Don't worry,' Sayaca said. 'I'll keep it nice and simple; throw in a few jokes to wake them up.'

Gallinule kept his voice low. 'They won't need waking up once they realise what the implications are. Straightforward hiding's no longer an option, not with something as strange as the Ghost anomaly sitting in our neighbourhood. When the Huskers arrive they're bound to start investigating. They're also bound to find any hideaway we construct, no matter how well camouflaged.'

'Not if we dig deep enough,' Merlin said.

'Forget it. There's no way we can hide now. Not the way it was planned, anyway. Unless—'

'Don't tell me: we'd be perfectly safe if we could store ourselves as patterns in some machine memory?'

'Don't sound so nauseated. You can't argue with the logic. We'd be nearly invulnerable. The storage media could be physically tiny, distributed in many locations. Impossible for the Huskers to find them all.'

'The Council can decide,' Sayaca said, raising a hand to shut the two of them up. 'Let's see how they take my discovery, first.'

'It was Pauraque's discovery,' Merlin said quietly.

'Whatever.'

She was already walking away from them, crossing the auditorium's floor towards the podium where she would address the congregation. Sayaca walked on air, striding across the clouds. It was a trick, of course: the real view outside the station was constantly changing because of the structure's rotation, but the illusion was flawless.

'It may have been Pauraque who discovered the storm,' Gallinule said, 'but it was Sayaca who interpreted it.'

'I wasn't trying to take anything away from her.'

'Good.'

Now she stepped up to the podium, the hem of her electric-blue gown floating above the clouds. She stood pridefully, surveying the people who had gathered here to hear her speak. Her expression was one of complete calm and self-assurance, but Merlin saw how tightly she grasped the edges of the podium. He sensed that beneath that shell of control she was acutely nervous, knowing that this was the most important moment in her life, the one that would make her reputation amongst the seniors and perhaps shape all of their destinies.

'Seniors . . .' Sayaca said. 'Thank you for coming here. I hope that by the time I've finished speaking, you'll feel that your time wasn't wasted.' Then she extended a hand towards the middle of the room and an image of Ghost sprang into being. 'Ever since we identified this system as our only chance of concealment, we've had to ignore the troubling aspects of the place. Bright Boy's anomalous mass–luminosity relationship, for instance. The seismic discrepancies in Cinder. Pauraque's deep-atmospheric phenomenon in Ghost. Now the time has come to deal with these puzzles. I'm afraid that what they tell us may not be entirely to our liking.'

Promising start, Merlin thought. She had spoken for more than half a minute without using a single mathematical expression.

Sayaca began to speak again, but she was cut off abruptly by another speaker. 'Sayaca, there's something we should discuss first.' Everyone's attention moved to the interjector. Merlin recognised him immediately: Weaver. Cruelly handsome, the boy had outgrown his adolescent awkwardness in the years since Merlin had first known him as one of Sayaca's class.

'What is it?' she said, only the tiniest hint of suspicion in her voice.

'Some news we've just obtained.' Weaver looked around the room, clearly enjoying his moment in the limelight while attempting to maintain the appropriate air of solemnity. 'We've been looking along the Way, as a matter of routine, monitoring the swarm that lies ahead of us. Sometimes off the line of the Way too – just in case we find anything. We've also been following the *Bluethroat*.'

It was so long since anyone had mentioned that name that it took Merlin an instant to place it. Of course, the *Bluethroat*. The part of the original ship that Crombec had flown onward, while the rest of them piled into *Starling* and slowed down around Bright Boy. It was not that anyone hated Crombec or wished to excise him and his followers from history, simply that there had been more than enough to focus on in the new system.

'Go on . . .' Sayaca said.

'There was a flash. A tiny burst of energy light-years from here, but in the direction we know Crombec was headed. I think the implications are clear enough. They met Huskers, even in interstellar space.'

'Force and wisdom,' said Shikra, the archivist in charge of the Cohort's most precious data troves. 'They can't have survived.'

Merlin raised his voice above the sudden murmur of debate. 'When did you find this out, Weaver?'

'A few days ago.'

'And you waited until now to let us know?'

Weaver shifted uncomfortably, beginning to sweat. 'There were questions of interpretation. We couldn't release the news until we were sure of it.' Then he nodded towards Sayaca. 'You know what I mean, don't you?'

'Believe me, I know exactly what you mean,' she said, shaking her head. She must have known that the moment was no longer hers; that even if she held the attention of the audience again, their minds would not be fully on what she had to say.

She handled it well, Merlin thought.

But irrespective of what she had found in Ghost, the news was very bad. The deaths of Crombec and his followers could only mean that the immediate volume of space was much thicker with Husker assets than anyone had dared fear. Forget the two swarms they had already known about; there might be dozens more, lurking quietly only one or two light-years from the system. And perhaps they had learned enough from Crombec's trajectory to guess that there must be other humans nearby. It would not take them long to arrive.

In a handful of years they might be here.

'This is gravely serious,' one of the other seniors said, raising her voice above the others. 'But it must not be allowed to overshadow the news Sayaca has for us.' She nodded at Sayaca expectantly. 'Continue, won't you?'

Months later, Merlin and Gallinule were alone in the Palace, standing on the balcony. Gallinule was toying with a white mouse, letting it run along the balustrade's narrow top before picking it up and placing it at the start again. They had put Weaver's spiteful sabotage long behind them, once it became clear that it had barely dented the impact of Sayaca's announcement. Even the most conservative seniors had accepted the shadow-matter hypothesis, even if the precise nature of what the shadow matter represented was not yet clear.

Which was not to say that Weaver's own announcement had been ignored, either. The Huskers were no longer a remote threat, decades away from Bright Boy. The fact that they were almost certainly converging on the system brought an air of apocalyptic gloom to the whole hideaway enterprise. They were living in end times, certain that no actions they now took would really make much difference.

It's been centuries since we made contact with another human faction, another element of the Cohort, Merlin thought. *For all we know, there are no more humans anywhere in the galaxy. We are all that remains; the last niche the Huskers haven't yet sterilised. And in a few years we might all be dead as well.*

'I almost envy Sayaca,' Gallinule said. 'She's completely absorbed in her work in Cinder again. As if nothing else will ever affect her. Don't you admire that kind of dedication?'

'She thinks she'll find something in Cinder that will save us all.'

'At least she's still optimistic. Or desperate, depending on your point of view. She sends her regards, incidentally.'

'Thanks,' Merlin said, biting his tongue.

Gallinule had just returned from Cinder, his third and longest trip there since Sayaca had left Ghost. Once the shadow-matter hypothesis had been accepted, Sayaca had seen no reason to stay here. Other gifted people could handle this line of enquiry while she returned to her beloved tunnels. Merlin had visited her once, but the reception she had given him had been no more than cordial. He had not gone back.

'Well, what do you think?' Gallinule said.

Suspended far out to sea was a representation of what they now knew to be lurking inside Ghost. It was the sharpest view Merlin had seen yet, gleaned by swarms of gravitational-mapping drones swimming through the atmosphere. What the thing looked like, to Merlin's eye, was a sphere wrapped around with dense, branching circuitry. The closer they looked, the sharper their focus, the more circuitry appeared, on steadily smaller scales, down to the current limiting resolution of about ten metres. Anything smaller than that was simply blurred away. But what they saw was enough. They had been right, all those months ago: this was nothing natural. And it was not quite a sphere, either: resolution was good enough now to see a teardrop shape, with the sharp end pointed more or less parallel to the surface of the liquid hydrogen ocean.

'I think it scares me,' Merlin said. 'I think it shows that this is the worst possible place we could ever have picked to hide.'

'Then we have to accept my solution,' Gallinule said. 'Become software. It can be done, you know. In a few months we'll have the technology to scan ourselves.' He held up the mouse again. 'See this little fellow? He was the first. I scanned him a few days ago.'

Merlin stared at the mouse.

'This is really him,' Gallinule continued. 'Not simply a projection of a real mouse into the Palace's environment, or even a convincing fake. Slice him open and you'd find everything you'd expect. He only exists here now, but his behaviour hasn't changed at all.'

'What happened to the real mouse, Gallinule?'

Gallinule shrugged. 'Died, of course. I'm afraid the scanning procedure's still fairly destructive.'

'So the little catch in your plan for our salvation is that we'd have to die to get inside your machine?'

'If we don't do it, we die anyway. Not much to debate, is there?'

'Not if you put it in those terms, no. We could of course experiment with the final syrinx and find a better way to escape, but I suppose that's too much of an imaginative leap for anyone to make.'

'Except you, of course.'

They were silent for long moments. Merlin stared out to sea, the Palace's reality utterly solid to him now. He did not think that it felt any less real to the mouse. This was how it could be for all of them, if Gallinule had his way: inhabiting any environment they liked until the Husker threat was over. They could skip over that time if they wished, or spend it exploring a multitude of simulated worlds. The trouble was, would there be anything to lure them back into the real world when the danger had passed? Would they even bother remembering what had come before? The Palace was already tantalising enough. There had been times when Merlin had found it difficult to leave the place. It was like a door into his youth.

'Gallinule . . .' Merlin said. 'There's something I always meant to ask you about the Palace. You've made it as real as humanly possible. There isn't a detail out of place. Sometimes it makes me want to cry, it's so close to what I remember. But there's something missing. Someone, to be exact. Whenever we were here – back in the real Palace, I mean – then she was always here as well.'

Gallinule stared at him in something like horror. 'You're asking me if I ever thought of simulating Mother?'

'Don't tell me it hasn't crossed your mind. I know you could have done it as well.'

'It would have been a travesty.'

Merlin nodded. 'I know. But that doesn't mean you wouldn't have thought of it.'

Gallinule shook his head slowly and sadly, as if infinitely disappointed by his brother's presumption. In the silence that followed, Merlin stared out at the shadow-matter object that hung over the sea. Whatever happened now, he thought, things between him and Gallinule could never be quite the same. It was not simply that he knew Gallinule was lying about their mother. Gallinule would have tried recreating her; anything less would have been an unforgivable lapse in his brother's devotion to detail. No; what had truly come between them was Sayaca. She and Gallinule were lovers now, Merlin knew, and yet this was something that he had never discussed with his brother. Time had passed and now there seemed no sensible way to broach the subject. It was simply there – unavoidable, like the knowledge that they would probably all die before very long. There was nothing to be done about it, so no point in discussing it. But in the same moment he realised something else, something that had been nagging at the back of his mind since the very earliest maps of the anomaly had been transmitted.

'Expand the scale,' he said. 'Zoom out, massively.'

Gallinule looked at him wordlessly, but obeyed his brother all the same. The anomaly shrank towards invisibility.

'Now show the anomaly's position within the system. All planetary positions to be exactly as they are now.'

A vast, luminous orrery filled the sky: concentric circles centred on Bright Boy, with nodal points for the planets.

'Now extend a vector with its origin in the anomaly, parallel to the anomaly's long axis. Make it as long as necessary.'

'What are you thinking?' Gallinule said, all animosity gone now.

'That the anomaly was only ever a pointer, directing our attention to the really important thing. Just do it, will you?'

A straight line knifed out from Ghost – the anomaly insignificant at this scale – and cut across the system, towards Bright Boy and the inner worlds.

Knifing straight through Cinder.

Part Five

'I wanted you to be the first to know,' Sayaca said, her semblance standing regally in his quarters like a playing-card monarch. 'We've found signals coming from inside the planet. Gravitational signals – exactly what we'd expect if someone in the shadow universe was trying to contact us.'

Merlin studied the beautiful lines of her face, reminding himself that all he was speaking to was a cunning approximation of the real Sayaca, who was light-hours of communicational time-lag down-system.

'How do they do it? Get a signal across, I mean.'

'There's only one way: you have to move large masses around quickly, creating a high-frequency ripple in space–time. They're using black holes, I think: miniature ones, like the thing you first thought we'd found in Ghost. Charged up and oscillated, so that they give off an amplitude-modulated gravitational wave.'

Merlin shrugged. 'So it wasn't such a stupid idea to begin with.'

Sayaca smiled tolerantly. 'We still don't know how they make and manipulate them. But that doesn't matter for now. What does is that the message is clearly intended for us. It's only commenced since we reached into Cinder's deeper layers. Somehow that action alerted them – whoever *they* are – to our presence.'

Merlin shivered despite himself. 'Is there any chance that these signals could be picked up by the Huskers as well?'

'Every chance, I'd say – unless they stop before they get here. Which is why we've been working so hard to decode the signal.'

'And you have?'

Sayaca nodded. 'We identified recurrent patterns in the gravitational signal, a block of data that the shadow people were sending over and over again. Within this block of data were two kinds of bits: a strong gravitational pulse and a weaker one, like a one and zero in binary notation. The number of bits in the signal was equal to the product of three primes – definitely not accidental – so we reassembled the data-set along three axes, forming a three-dimensional image.' Sayaca paused and lifted her palm. What appeared in mid-air was a solid rectangular form, slab-sided and featureless. It rotated lazily, revealing its blankness to the audience.

'Doesn't look like much,' Merlin said.

'That's because the outer layer of the solid is all ones. In fact, only a tiny part of its volume is made up of zeroes at all. I'll remove the ones and display only the zero values ...'

A touch of showmanship: the surface of the box suddenly seemed to be made out of interlocking birds, frozen in formation for an instant before flying in a million different directions. Suddenly what she was showing him made a lot more sense. It was like a ball of loosely knotted string. A map of Cinder's crustal tunnels, plunging more deeply towards the core than their own maps even hinted. Five or six hundred kilometres into the lithosphere.

'But it doesn't tell us anything we wouldn't have learned eventually—' Merlin said.

'No; I think it does.' Sayaca made the image enlarge, until she was showing him the deep end of one particular tunnel. It was capped by a nearly spherical chamber. 'All the other shafts end abruptly, even those that branch off from this one at higher levels.

But they've clearly drawn our attention to this chamber. That has to mean something.'

'You think there's something there, don't you?'

'We'll know soon enough. By the time this semblance speaks to you, Gallinule and I will have almost reached that chamber. Wish us the best of luck, won't you? Whatever we find in there, I'm fairly certain it'll change things for us.'

'For better or for worse?'

The semblance smiled. 'We'll just have to wait and see, won't we?'

End times, Merlin thought again. He could taste it in the air: quiet desperation. The long-range sensors sprinkled around the system had picked up the first faint hints of neutrino emission, which might originate with Husker craft moving stealthily towards Bright Boy from interstellar space. And the main swarms up and down the length of the Way had not gone away.

One or two humans had undergone Gallinule's fatal scanning process now, choosing to go ahead of the pack rather than wait for the final stampede. Their patterns were frozen at the moment, but before very long Gallinule's acolytes would weave a simulated environment that the scanned could inhabit. Then, undoubtedly, others would follow. But not many. Merlin was not alone in flinching at the idea of throwing away the flesh just to survive. There were some prices that were simply too high, simply too alien.

Do that, he thought, *and we're halfway to being Husker ourselves*.

What could he do to save himself, if saving the rest of them was out of the question? He thought of stealing the syrinx. He had not learned enough to use it safely yet, but he knew he was not far from being able to do so. But it was tightly guarded, under permanent Council scrutiny. He had asked Gallinule and Sayaca to apply persuasion to the others, but while they might have had the necessary influence, they had not acceded to his wishes.

And now Sayaca was back from Cinder, bearing tidings. She had convened a meeting again, but this time nobody was going to steal her thunder.

Especially as she had brought someone with her.

It was the semblance of a woman: a female of uncertain age but from approximately the same genetic background as everyone present. That was nothing to be counted on; since the Flourishing there had been many splinters of humanity, many of which seemed monstrously strange to those who had remained loyal to the old phenotype. But had this woman changed her clothes, make-up and hairstyle, she could have walked amongst them without attracting a second glance. Except perhaps for her beauty: something indefinably serene in her face and bearing that seemed almost supernatural.

Her expression, before she began speaking, was one of complete calm.

'My name is Halvorsen,' she said. 'It's an old name, archaic even in my own time ... I have no idea how it will sound to your ears, or if you can even understand a word of what I'm saying. We will record versions of this message in over a thousand languages, all that we hold in our current linguistics database, in the hope that some distant traveller will recognise something, anything, of use.'

Merlin raised a hand. 'Stop ... stop her. Can you do that?'

Sayaca nodded, causing Halvorsen to freeze, mouth open.

'What is she?' Merlin said.

'Just a recording. We triggered her when we arrived in the chamber. It wasn't hard to translate her. We already knew that the Diggers' language would later evolve into Main, so it was just a question of hoping that one of the recordings would be in a tongue that was also in our records.'

'And?'

'Well, none of her messages were in languages we knew moderately well. But three were in languages for which we had fragments, so we were able to patch together this version using all three threads. There are still a few holes, of course, but I don't think we'll miss anything critical.'

'You'd better hope not. Well, let her – whoever she is – continue.'

Halvorsen became animated again. 'Let me say something about my past,' she said. 'It may help you establish the time frame in which this recording was made. My ancestors came from Earth. So did yours – if you are at all human – but in my case I even met someone who had been born there, although it was one of her oldest memories, something as faint and tiny as an image seen through the wrong end of a telescope. She remembered a time before the Flourishing, before the great migrations into the Orion Arm. We rode swallowships for ten thousand years, cleaving close to light-speed. Then came wars. Awful wars. We hid for another ten thousand years, until our part of the galaxy was quiet again. We watched many cultures rise and fall, learning what we could from them; trading with those who seemed the least hostile. Then the Waymakers came, extending their transit network into our region of space. They were like gods to us as well, although we stole some of their miracles and fashioned them to our own uses. After thousands of years of careful study we learned how to make syrinxes and to use the Waynet.' She paused. 'We had a name for ourselves too: the Watchers.'

Halvorsen's story continued. She told them how a virus had propagated through their fleets, subtly corrupting their most ancient data heirlooms. By the time the damage was discovered, all their starmaps had been rendered useless. They no longer knew where Earth was. At first, the loss seemed of minimal importance, but as time passed, and they came into contact with more and more cultures, it became clear that the Watchers' records had probably been the *last* to survive uncorrupted.

'That was when she died, the oldest of us. I think until then she had always clung to some hope that we would return to Earth. When she knew it could never happen, she saw no reason to continue living.'

Then they entered a long Dark Age. The Waymakers had gone; now, unpoliced, terrors were roaming the galaxy. Marauders sought the technological wisdom that the Watchers had acquired over slow millennia. The Watchers fled, pursued across the light-years in much the same manner as the Cohort now found itself, hounded from star to star. Like the Cohort too, they found Bright Boy. They were exploring it, trying to understand the system's anomalies; hoping that the understanding would bring new power over their enemies. They had excavated the tunnel system into Cinder and created the machines that lined the terminal chamber. They too had detected signals from the shadow universe, although the contents of the messages proved much harder to decode.

'They were alien,' Halvorsen said. 'Truly alien: automated transmissions left behind half a billion years earlier by a group of creatures who had crossed over into the shadow universe. They had been fleeing the fire that was about to be unleashed by the merger of a pair of binary neutron stars only a few hundred light-years away. They left instructions on how to join them. We learned how to generate the same kinds of high-frequency gravitational waves that they were using to signal us. Then we learned how to encode ourselves into those wave packets so that we could send biological information between universes. Although the aliens were long gone, they left behind machines to tend to us and to take care of our needs once we were reassembled on the other side.'

'But the Marauders are long gone,' Merlin said. 'Our oldest records barely mention them. Why didn't Halvorsen and her people return here?'

'There was no need,' Sayaca said. 'We tend to think of the shadow universe as a cold, ghostly place, but once you're mapped into it, it looks much like our own universe – the sky dotted with bright suns, warm worlds orbiting them. Theirs for the taking, in fact. Halvorsen's people had been late-players in a galaxy already carved up by thousands of earlier factions. But the shadow universe was virgin territory. They no longer had to skulk around higher powers, or hide from outlaw clades. There was no one else there.'

'Except the aliens ... the—' Merlin blinked. 'What did she call them?'

Sayaca paused before answering. 'She didn't. But their name for them was the ...' Again, a moment's hesitation. 'The Shadow Puppets. And they were long gone. They'd left behind machines to assist any future cultures who wanted to make the crossing, but there was no sign of them now. Maybe they moved away to settle some remote part of the shadow galaxy, or maybe they returned to our universe when the threat from the merger event had passed.'

'Halvorsen's people trusted these creatures?'

'What choice did they have? Not much more than us. They were in as much danger from the Marauders as we are from the Huskers.'

It was Halvorsen who continued the story. 'So we crossed over. We expanded massively; extended a human presence around a dozen nearby systems on the other side. Star travel's difficult because there's no Waynet, but the social templates we acquired during the time before the Marauders have served us well. We've been at peace for one thousand years at the time of this message's recording. Many more thousands of years are likely to have passed before it reaches you. If we attempted to communicate with you gravitationally, then you can be sure that we're still alive. By then we will have studied you via the automated systems we left running in Cinder. They will have told us that you are essentially peaceable; that we are ready to welcome you.'

Halvorsen's tone of voice changed now. 'That's our invitation, then. We've opened the gateway for you; provided the means for information to pass into the shadow universe. To take the next step, you must make the hardest of sacrifices. You must discard the flesh; submit yourselves to whatever scanning techniques you have developed. We did it once, and we know it's a difficult journey, but less difficult than death. For us, the choice was obvious enough. For you, it may not be so very different.' Halvorsen paused and extended a hand in supplication. 'Do not be frightened. Follow us. We have been waiting a long time for your company.'

Then she bowed her head and the recording halted.

Merlin could feel the almost palpable sense of relief sweeping the room, though no one was undignified enough to let it show. A swelling of hope, after so many months of staring oblivion in the face. Finally, there was a way out. A way to survive, which was something other than Gallinule's route to soulless immortality in computer memory. Even if it also meant dying ... but it would only be a transient kind of death, as Halvorsen had said. Waiting for them on the other side was another world of the flesh, into which they would all be reborn.

A kind of promised land.

It would be very difficult to resist, especially when the Huskers arrived. But Merlin just stared hard at the woman called Halvorsen, certain that he knew the truth and that Sayaca had, on some level, wanted him to know it as well.

She was lying.

Tyrant fell towards empty space, in the general direction of the Way. When Merlin judged himself to be a safe distance from Cinder he issued the command that would trigger the twenty nova-mines emplaced in the lowermost chamber. He looked down on the world and nothing seemed to happen, no stammer of light from the exit holes of the Digger tunnel system. Perhaps some inscrutable layer of preservation had disarmed the nova-mines.

Then he saw the readouts from the seismic devices that Sayaca had dropped on the surface, what seemed like half a lifetime earlier. He had almost forgotten that they existed – but now he watched each register the detonation's volley of sound waves as they reached the surface. A few moments later, there was a much longer, lower signal – the endless roar of collapsing tunnels, like an avalanche. Some sections of the tunnels would undoubtedly remain intact, but it would be hard to cross between them. He was not yet done, though. First he directed missiles at the tunnel entrances, collapsing them, and then assigned smaller munitions to destroy Sayaca's seismic instruments, daubing the surface with nuclear fire.

There must be no evidence of human presence here; nothing to give the Huskers a clue as to what had happened—

That everyone was gone now: crossed over into the shadow universe. Sayaca, Gallinule, all the others. Everyone he knew, submitting to the quick, clean death of Gallinule's scanning apparatus. Biological patterns encoded into gravitational signals and squirted into the realm of shadow matter.

Except, of course, Merlin.

'How did you guess?' Sayaca had asked him, just after she had presented Halvorsen's message.

They had been alone, physically so, for the first time in months. 'Because you wanted me to know, Sayaca. Isn't that the way it happened? You had to deceive the others, but you wanted me to know the truth. Well, it worked. I guessed. And I have to admit, you and Gallinule did a very thorough job.'

'Do you want to know how much of it was true?'

'I suppose you're going to tell me anyway.'

Sayaca sighed. 'More of it than you'd probably have guessed. We did detect signals from the shadow universe, just as I said.'

'Just not quite the kind you told us.'

'No ... no.' She paused. 'They were much more alien. Enormously harder to decode in the first place. But we managed it, and the content of the messages was more or less what I told the Council: a map of Cinder's interior, directing us deeper. There we encountered other messages. By then, we had become more adept at translating them. It wasn't long before we understood that they were a set of instructions for crossing over into the shadow universe.'

'But there was never any Halvorsen.'

Sayaca shook her head. 'Halvorsen was Gallinule's idea. We knew that crossing over was the only hope we had left, but no one would want to do it unless we could make the whole thing sound more, well ... palatable. The aliens were just too alien – shockingly so, once we began to understand their nature. Not necessarily hostile, or even unfriendly ... but unnervingly strange. The stuff of nightmares. So we invented a human story. Gallinule created Halvorsen and between us we fabricated enough evidence so that no one would question her reality. We manufactured a plausible history for her and then pasted her story over the real one.'

'The part about the aliens fleeing the neutron star merger?'

'That was completely true. But they were the only ones who ever crossed over. No humans ever followed them.'

'What about the Diggers?'

'They found the tunnels, explored them thoroughly, but it seems that they never intercepted the signals. They helped though; without them it would have been a lot harder to make Halvorsen's story sound convincing.' She paused, childlike in her enthusiasm. 'We'll be the first, Merlin. Isn't that thrilling in a way?'

'For you, maybe. But you've always stared into the void, Sayaca. For everyone else, the idea will be chilling beyond words.'

'That's why they couldn't know the truth. They wouldn't have agreed to cross over otherwise.'

'I know. And I don't doubt that you did the right thing. After all, it's a matter of survival, isn't it?'

'They'll learn the truth eventually,' Sayaca said. 'When we've all crossed over. I don't know what'll happen to Gallinule and me then. We'll either be revered or hated. I suppose we'll just have to wait and see, but I suspect it may be the latter.'

'On the other hand, they'll know that you had the courage to face the truth and hide it from the others when you knew it had to be hidden. There's a kind of nobility in that, Sayaca.'

'Whatever we did, it was for the good of the Cohort. You understand that, don't you?'

'I never thought otherwise. Which doesn't mean I'm coming with you.'

Her mouth opened the tiniest of degrees. 'There's nothing for you here, Merlin. You'll die if you don't follow us. I don't love you the way I used to, but I still care for you.'

'Then why did you let me know the truth?'

'I never said I did. That must have been Gallinule's doing.' She paused. 'What was it, then?'

'Halvorsen,' Merlin said. 'She was created from scratch; a human who had never lived. You did a good job, as well. But there was something about her that I knew I'd seen before. Something so familiar I didn't see it at first. Then, of course, I knew.'

'What?'

'Gallinule based her on our mother. I always suspected he'd tried simulating her, but he denied it. That was another lie, as well. Halvorsen proved it.'

'Then he wanted you to know. As his brother.'

Merlin nodded. 'I suppose so.'

'Then will you follow us?'

He had already made his mind up, but he allowed a long pause before answering her. 'I don't think so, Sayaca. It just isn't my style. I know there's only a small chance that I can make the syrinx work for me, but I prefer running to hiding. I think I'll take that risk.'

'But the Council won't let you have the syrinx, Merlin. Even after we've all crossed over, they'll safeguard it here. Surround it with proctors that'll kill you if you try and steal it. They'll want it unharmed for when we return from the shadow universe.'

'I know.'

'Then why . . . oh, wait. I see.' She looked at him now, all empathy gone; something of the old Sayaca contempt showing through. 'You'll blackmail us, won't you? Threaten to tell the Council if we don't provide you with the syrinx.'

'You said it, not me.'

'Gallinule and I don't have that kind of influence, Merlin.'

'Then you'd better find it. It's not much to ask, is it? A small token of your gratitude for my silence. I'm sure you can think of something.' Merlin paused. 'After all, it would be a shame to spoil everything now. Halvorsen's story sounded so convincing too. I almost believed it myself.'

'You cold, calculating bastard.' But she said it with half a smile, admiring and loathing him at the same time.

'Just find a way, Sayaca. I know you can. Oh, and one other thing.'

'Yes?'

'Look after my brother, will you? He may not have quite my streak of brilliance, but he's still one of a kind. You're going to need people like him on the other side.'

'We could use you too, Merlin.'

'You probably could, but I've got other business to attend to.

The small matter of an ultimate weapon against the Huskers, for instance. I'm going to find it, you know. Even if it takes me the rest of my life. I hope you'll come back and see how I did one day.'

Sayaca nodded, but said nothing. They both knew that there were no more words that needed to be said.

And, true to his expectations, Sayaca and Gallinule had come through. The syrinx was with him now – an uninteresting matt-black cone that held the secrets of crossing light-years in a few breaths of subjective time – sitting in its metal harness inside *Tyrant*. He did not know exactly how they had persuaded the Council to release it. Quite possibly there had been no persuasion at all, merely subterfuge. One black cone looked much like another, after all.

This, however, was the true syrinx, the last they had.

It was unimaginably precious now, and he would do his best to learn its secrets in the weeks ahead. Countless millions had died trying to gain entry to the Waymakers' transit system, and it was entirely possible that Merlin would simply be the next. But it did not have to be like that. He was alone now – possibly more alone than any human had ever been – but instead of despair what he felt was a cold, pure elation: he now had a mission, one that might prove to be soul-destroyingly difficult, even futile, but he had the will to accomplish it.

Somewhere behind him the syrinx began to purr.

Mission interrupted.

Even now, I still don't know quite what happened. The ship and I were in routine Waynet transit, all systems ticking over smoothly. I was deep in thought, a little drunk, rubbing clues together like a caveman trying to make fire with rocks, hoping for the spark that would point me towards The Gun, the one no one ever thinks I'm going to find, the one I know with every fibre of my existence is out there somewhere. I was imagining the reception I'd get when I returned to the Cohort with that prize, the slate of all my sins wiped clean when they saw that I'd actually found it, that it was real after all, and that finally we had something to use against the Huskers. In the pleasant mental haze brought on by the wine, it seemed likely that they'd forgive me anything.

Then it happened: a violent lurch that sent wine and glass flying across the cabin, a shriek from the ship's alarms as it went into panic-mode. I knew right away that this was no ordinary Way turbulence. The ship was tumbling badly, but I fought my way to the command deck and did what I could to bring her back under control. Seat-of-the-pants flying, the way Gallinule and I used to do it on Plenitude, when Plenitude still existed.

That was when I knew we were outside the Waynet, dumped back into the crushing slowness of normal space. The stars outside were stationary, their colours showing no suggestion of relativistic distortion.

'Damage?' I asked.

'How long have you got?' the ship snapped back.

I told it to ease off on the wisecracks and start giving me the bad news. And it most certainly was bad news. The precious syrinx was still functional – I touched it and felt the familiar tremble that indicated it was still sensing the nearby Waynet – but that was about the only flight-critical system that hadn't been buckled or blown or simply wiped out of existence by the unscheduled egress.

We were going to have to land and make repairs. For a few weeks or months – however long it took the ship to scavenge and process the raw materials it needed to fix itself – the search for my Gun would be on hold.

That didn't mean I was counting on a long stopover.

The ship still had a slow tumble. Merlin squinted against hard white glare as the burning eye of a bright sun hove into view through the windows. It was white, but not killingly so. Probably a mid-sequence star, maybe a late F- or early G-type. He thought there was a hint of yellow. Had to be pretty close too.

'Tell me where we are.'

'It's called Calliope,' *Tyrant* told him. 'G-type. According to the last Cohort census the system contained fifteen planet-class bodies. There were five terrestrials, four of which were uninhabitable. The fifth – the furthest from Calliope – was supposedly colonised by humans in the early Flourishing.'

Merlin glanced at the census data as it scrolled down the cabin wall. The planet in question was called Lecythus. It was a typical watery terrestrial, like a thousand others in his experience. It even had the almost-obligatory large single moon.

'Been a while, ship. What are the chances of anyone still being down there?'

'Difficult to say. A later Cohort flyby failed to make contact with the settlement, but that doesn't mean no one was alive. After the emergence of the Huskers, many planetary colonies went to great lengths to camouflage themselves against the aliens.'

'So there could still be a welcoming committee.'

'We'll see. With your permission, I'll use our remaining fuel to reach Lecythus. This will take some time. Would you like to sleep?'

Merlin looked back at the coffin-like slab of the frostwatch cabinet. He could skip over the days or weeks it would take to reach the planet, but that would mean subjecting himself to the intense unpleasantness of frostwatch revival. Merlin had never taken kindly to being woken from normal sleep, let alone the deep hibernation of frostwatch.

'Pass on that, I think. I've still got plenty of reading to catch up on.'

Later – much later – *Tyrant* announced that they had reached orbit around Lecythus. 'Would you like to see the view?' the ship asked, with a playful note in its voice.

Merlin scratched fatigue from his eyes. 'You sound like you know something I don't.'

Merlin was at first reassured by what he saw. There was blue ocean down there, swatches of green and brown land mass, large islands rather than any major continental masses, cyclonic swirls of water-vapour clouds. It didn't necessarily mean there were still people, but it was a lot more encouraging than finding a cratered, radioactive corpse of a world.

Then he looked again. Many of those green and brown swatches of land mass were surrounded by water, as his first glimpse had indicated. But some of them appeared to be floating above the ocean completely, casting shadows beneath them. His glance flicked to the horizon, where the atmosphere was compressed into a thin bow of pure indigo. He could see the foreshortened shapes of hovering land masses, turned nearly edge-on. The land masses appeared to be one or two kilometres thick, and they all appeared to be gently curved. Perhaps half were concave in shape, so their edges were slightly upturned. The edges were frosted white, like the peaks of mountain ranges. Some of the concave masses even had little lakes near their centres. The convex masses were all a scorched tawny grey in colour, devoid of water or vegetation, save for a cap of ice at their highest point. The largest shapes, convex or concave, must have been hundreds of kilometres wide. Merlin judged that there must have been at least ten kilometres of clear airspace under each piece. A third of the planet's surface was obscured by the floating shapes.

'Any idea what we're looking at here?' Merlin asked. 'This doesn't look like anything in the census.'

'I think they built an armoured sky around their world,' the ship said. 'And then something – very probably Husker-level ordnance – shattered that sky.'

'No one could have survived that,' Merlin said, feeling a rising tide of sadness. *Tyrant* was clever enough, but there were times – long times – when Merlin became acutely aware of the heartless machine lurking behind the personality. And then he felt very, very alone. Those were the hours when he would have done anything for companionship, including returning to the Cohort and the tribunal that undoubtedly awaited him.

'Someone does appear to have survived, Merlin.'

He perked up. 'Really?'

'It's unlikely to be a very advanced culture: no neutrino or gravimagnetic signatures, beyond those originating from the mechanisms that must still be active inside the sky pieces. But I did detect some very brief radio emissions.'

'What language were they using? Main? Tradespeak? Anything else in the Cohort database?'

'They were using long beeps and short beeps. I'm afraid I didn't get the chance to determine the source of the transmission.'

'Keep listening. I want to meet them.'

'Don't raise your hopes. If there are people down there, they've been out of contact with the rest of humanity for a considerable number of millennia.'

'I only want to stop for repairs. They can't begrudge me that, can they?'

'I suppose not.'

Then something occurred to Merlin, something he realised he should have asked much earlier. 'About the accident, ship. I take it you know why we were dumped out of the Waynet?'

'I've run a fault-check on the syrinx. There doesn't appear to be anything wrong with it.'

'That's not an answer.'

'I know.' *Tyrant* sounded sullen. 'I still don't have an explanation for what went wrong. And I don't like that any more than you do.'

Tyrant fell into the atmosphere of Lecythus. The transmissions had resumed, allowing the ship to pinpoint the origin to one of the larger airborne masses. Shortly afterwards, a second source began transmitting from another floating mass, half the size of the first, located three thousand kilometres to the west. The way the signals started and stopped suggested some kind of agonisingly slow communication via radio pulses, one that probably had nothing to do with Merlin's arrival.

'Tell me that's a code in our database,' Merlin said.

'It isn't. And the code won't tell us much about their spoken language, I'm afraid.'

Up close, the broken edges of the floating mass soared as tall as a cliff. They were a dark, streaked grey, infinitely less regular than they had appeared from space and showing signs of weathering and erosion. There were wide ledges, dizzying promontories and cathedral-sized shadowed caves. Glinting in the low light of Calliope, ladders and walkways – impossibly thin and spindly scratches of metal – reached down from the icebound upper reaches, following zigzag trajectories that only took them a fraction of the way to the perilous lower lip, where the floating world curved back under itself.

Merlin made out the tiny moving forms of birdlike creatures, wheeling and orbiting in powerful thermals, some of them coming and going from roosts on the lower ledges.

'But that isn't a bird,' *Tyrant* said, highlighting a larger moving shape.

Merlin felt an immediate pang of recognition as the image zoomed. It was an aircraft: a ludicrously fragile assemblage of canvas and wire. It had a crescent moon painted on both wings. There'd been a machine not much more advanced than that in the archive inside the Palace of Eternal Dusk, preserved across thirteen hundred years of family history. Merlin had even risked taking it outside once, to see for himself if he had the nerve to repeat his distant ancestor's brave crossing. He still remembered the sting of reprimand when he'd brought it back, nearly ruined.

This aircraft was even flimsier and slower. It was driven by a single chugging propeller rather than a battery of rocket-assisted turbines. It was following the rim of the land mass, slowly gaining altitude. Clearly it intended to make landfall. The air on Lecythus was thicker at sea level than on Plenitude, but the little machine must still have been very close to its safe operational ceiling. And yet it would have to climb even higher if it was to traverse the raised rim.

'Follow it,' Merlin said. 'Keep us astern by a clear two kilometres. And set hull to stealth.'

Merlin's ship nosed in behind the struggling aircraft. He could see the single pilot now, goggled and helmeted within a crude-looking bubble canopy. The plane had reached ten kilometres, but it would need to double that to clear the upturned rim. Every hundred metres of altitude gained seemed to tax the aircraft to the limit, so that it climbed, levelled, climbed. It trailed sooty hyphens behind it. Merlin could imagine the sputtering protest from the little engine, the fear in the pilot's belly that the motor was going to stall at any moment.

That was when an airship hove around the edge of the visible cliff. Calliope's rays flared off the golden swell of its envelope. Beneath the long ribbed form was a tiny gondola, equipped with multiple engines on skeletal outriggers. The airship's nose began to turn, bringing another crescent moon emblem into view. The aircraft lined up with the airship, the two of them at about the same altitude. Merlin watched as some kind of net-like apparatus unfurled in slow motion from the belly of the gondola. The pilot gained further height, then cut the aircraft's engine. Powerless now, it followed a shallow glide path towards the net. Clearly, the airship was going to catch the aircraft and carry it over the rim. That must have been the only way for aircraft to arrive and depart from the hovering land mass.

Merlin watched with a sickened fascination. He'd occasionally had a presentiment when something was about to go wrong. Now he had that feeling again.

Some gust caught the airship. It began to drift out of the aircraft's glide path. The pilot tried to compensate – Merlin could see the play of light shift on the wings as they warped – but it was never going to be enough. Without power, the aircraft must have been cumbersome to steer. The engines on the gondola turned on their mountings, trying to shove the airship back into position.

Beyond the airship loomed the streaked grey vastness of the great cliff.

'Why did he cut the engines ...' Merlin breathed to himself. Then, an instant later: 'Can we catch up? Can we do something?'

'I'm afraid not. There simply isn't time.'

Sickened, Merlin watched as the aircraft slid past the airship, missing the net by a hundred metres. A sooty smear erupted from the engine. The pilot must have been desperately trying to restart the motor. Moments later, Merlin watched as one wingtip grazed the side of the cliff and crumpled instantly, horribly. The aircraft dropped, dashing itself to splinters and shreds against the side of the cliff. There was no possibility that the pilot could have survived.

For a moment Merlin was numb. He was frozen, unsure what to

do next. He'd been planning to land, but it seemed improper to arrive immediately after witnessing such a tragedy. Perhaps the thing to do was find an uninhabited land mass and put down there.

'There's another aircraft,' *Tyrant* announced. 'It's approaching from the west.'

Still shaken by what he'd seen, Merlin took the stealthed ship closer. Dirty smoke billowed from the side of the aircraft. In the canopy, the pilot was obviously engaged in a life-or-death struggle to bring his machine to safety. Even as they watched, the engine appeared to slow and then restart.

Something slammed past *Tyrant*, triggering proximity alarms. 'Some kind of shell,' the ship told Merlin. 'I think someone on the ground is trying to shoot down these aircraft.'

Merlin looked down. He hadn't paid much attention to the land mass beneath them, but now that he did – peering through the holes in a quilt of low-lying cloud – he made out the unmistakable flashes of artillery positions, laid out along the pale scratch of a fortified line.

He began to understand why the airship dared not stray too far from the side of the land mass. Near the cliff, it at least had some measure of cover. It would have been far too vulnerable to the shells in open air.

'I think it's time to take a stand,' he said. 'Maintain stealth. I'm going to provide some lift-support to that aircraft. Bring us around to her rear and then approach from under her.'

'Merlin, you have no idea who these people are. They could be brigands, pirates, anything.'

'They're being shot at. That's good enough for me.'

'I really think we should land. I'm down to vapour pressure in the tanks now.'

'So's that brave fool of a pilot. Just do it.'

The aircraft's engine gave out just as *Tyrant* reached position. Taking the controls manually, Merlin brought his ship's nose into contact with the underside of the aircraft's paper-thin fuselage. Contact occurred with the faintest of bumps. The pilot glanced back down over his shoulder, but the goggled mask hid all expression. Merlin could only imagine what the pilot made of the sleek, whale-sized machine now supporting his little contraption.

Merlin's hands trembled. He was acutely aware of how easily he could damage the fragile thing with a miscalculated application of thrust. *Tyrant* was armoured to withstand Waynet transitions and the crush of gas giant atmospheres. It was like using a hammer to push around a feather. For a moment, contact between the two craft was lost, and when *Tyrant* came in again it hit the aircraft hard enough to crush the metal cylinder of a spare fuel tank bracketed on under the wing. Merlin winced in anticipation of an explosion – one that would hurt the little aeroplane a lot more than it would hurt *Tyrant* – but the tank must have been empty.

Ahead, the airship had regained some measure of stability. The capture net was still deployed. Merlin pushed harder, giving the aircraft more altitude in readiness for its approach glide. At the last moment he judged it safe to disengage. He steered *Tyrant* away and left the aircraft to blunder into the net.

This time there were no gusts. The net wrapped itself around the aircraft, the soft impact nudging down the nose of the airship. Then the net began to be winched back towards the gondola like a haul of fish. At the same time the airship swung around and began to climb.

'No other planes?' Merlin asked.

'That was the only one.'

They followed the airship in. It rose over the cliff, over the ice-capped rim of the aerial land mass, then settled down towards the shielded region in the bowl, where water and greenery had gathered. There was even a wispy layer of cloud, arranged in a broken ring around the shore of the lake. Merlin presumed that the concave shape of the land mass was sufficient to trap a stable microclimate.

By now Merlin had an audience. People had gathered on the gondola's rear observation platform. They wore goggles and gloves and heavy brown overcoats. Merlin caught the shine of glass lenses being pointed at him. He was being studied, sketched, perhaps even photographed.

'Do you think they look grateful,' he asked, 'or pissed off?'

Tyrant declined to answer.

Merlin kept his distance, conserving fuel as best he could as the airship crossed tens of kilometres of arid, gently sloping land. Occasionally they overflew a little hamlet of huts or the scratch of a minor track. Presently the ground became soil-covered, and then fertile. They traversed swathes of bleak grey-green grass, intermingled with boulders and assorted uplifted debris. Then there were trees and woods. The communities became more than just hamlets. Small ponds fed rivers that ambled down to the single lake that occupied the land mass's lowest point. Merlin spied waterwheels and rustic-looking bridges. There were fields with grazing animals, and evidence of some tall-chimneyed industrial structures on the far side of the lake. The lake itself was an easy fifty or sixty kilometres wide. Nestled around a natural harbour on its southern shore was the largest community Merlin had seen so far. It was a haphazard jumble of several hundred mostly white, mostly single-storey buildings, arranged with the randomness of toy blocks littering a floor.

The airship skirted the edge of the town and then descended quickly. It approached what was clearly some kind of secure compound, judging by the guarded fence that encircled it. There was a pair of airstrips arranged in a cross-formation, and a dozen or so aircraft parked around a painted copy of the crescent emblem. Four skeletal docking towers rose from another area of the compound, stayed by guy-lines. A battle-weary pair of partially deflated airships was already tethered. Merlin pulled back to allow the incoming craft enough space to complete its docking. The net was lowered back down from the gondola, depositing the aeroplane – its wings now crumpled, its fuselage buckled – on the apron below. Service staff rushed out of bunkers to untangle the mess and free the pilot. Merlin brought his ship down on a clear part of the apron and doused the engines as soon as the landing skids touched the ground.

It wasn't long before a wary crowd had gathered around *Tyrant*. Most of them wore long leather coats, heavily belted, with the crescent emblem sewn into the right breast. They had scarves wrapped around their lower faces, almost to the nose. Their helmets were leather caps, with long flaps covering the sides of the face and the back of the neck. Most of them wore goggles; a few wore some kind of breathing apparatus. At least half the number were aiming barrelled weapons at the ship, some of which needed to be set up on tripods, while some even larger wheeled cannons were being propelled across the apron by teams of well-drilled soldiers. One figure was gesticulating, directing the armed squads to take up specific positions.

'Can you understand what he's saying?' Merlin asked, knowing that *Tyrant* would be picking up any external sounds.

'I'm going to need more than a few minutes to crack their language, Merlin, even if it *is* related to something in my database, of which there's no guarantee.'

'Fine. I'll improvise. Can you spin me some flowers?'

'Where exactly are you going? What do you mean, *flowers*?'

Merlin paused at the airlock. He wore long boots, tight black leather trousers, a billowing white shirt and brocaded brown leather waistcoat, accented with scarlet trim. He'd tied back his hair and made a point of trimming his beard. 'Where do you think? Outside. And I want some flowers. Flowers are good. Spin me some indigo hyacinths, the kind they used to grow on Springhaven, before the Mentality Wars. They always go down well.'

'You're insane. They'll shoot you.'

'Not if I smile and come bearing exotic alien flowers. Remember, I did just save one of their planes.'

'You're not even wearing armour.'

'Armour would really scare them. Trust me, ship: this is the quickest way for them to understand I'm not a threat.'

'It's been a pleasure having you aboard,' *Tyrant* said acidly. 'I'll be sure to pass on your regards to my next owner.'

'Just make the flowers and stop complaining.'

Five minutes later Merlin steeled himself as the lock sequenced and the ramp lowered to kiss the ground. The cold hit him like a lover's slap. He heard an order from the soldiers' leader, and the massed ranks adjusted their aim. They'd been pointing at the ship before. Now it was only Merlin they were interested in.

He raised his right hand palm open, the newly spun flowers in his left.

'Hello. My name's Merlin.' He thumped his chest for emphasis and said the name again, slower this time. '*Mer-lin*. I don't think there's much chance of you being able to understand me, but just in case ... I'm not here to cause trouble.' He forced a smile, which probably looked more feral than reassuring. 'Now. Who's in charge?'

The leader shouted another order. He heard a rattle of a hundred safety catches being released. Suddenly, the ship's idea of sending out a proctor first sounded splendidly sensible. Merlin felt a cold line of sweat trickle down his back. After all that he had survived so far, both during his time with the Cohort and since he had become an adventuring free agent, it would be something of a let-down to die by being *shot* with a chemically propelled projectile. That was only one step above being mauled and eaten by a wild animal.

Merlin walked down the ramp, one cautious step at a time. 'No weapons,' he said. 'Just flowers. If I wanted to hurt you, I could have hit you from space with charm-torps.'

When he reached the apron, the leader gave another order and a trio of soldiers broke formation to cover Merlin from three angles, with the barrels of their weapons almost touching him. The leader – a cruel-looking young man with a scar down the right side of his face – shouted something in Merlin's direction, a word that sounded vaguely like 'distal', but which was in no language Merlin recognised. When Merlin didn't move, he felt a rifle jab into the small of his back. 'Distal,' the man said again, this time with an emphasis bordering on the hysterical.

Then another voice boomed across the apron, one that belonged to a much older man. There was something instantly commanding about the voice. Looking to the source of the exclamation, Merlin saw the wrecked aircraft entangled in its capture net, and the pilot in the process of crawling out from the tangle, with a wooden box in his hands. The rifle stopped jabbing Merlin's back, and the cruel-looking young man fell silent while the pilot made his way over to them.

The pilot had removed his goggles now, revealing the lined face of an older man, his grey-white beard and whiskers stark against ruddy, weatherworn skin. For a moment Merlin felt as if he was looking in the mirror at an older version of himself.

'Greetings from the Cohort,' Merlin said. 'I'm the man who saved your life.'

'Gecko,' the red-faced man said, pushing the wooden box into Merlin's chest. 'Forlorn gecko!'

Now that Merlin had a chance to examine it properly, he saw that the box was damaged, its sides caved in and its lid ripped off. Inside was a matrix of straw padding and a great many shattered glass vials. The pilot took one of these smashed vials and held it up before Merlin's face, honey-coloured fluid draining down his fingers.

'What is it?' Merlin asked.

Leaving Merlin to hold the box and flowers, the red-faced pilot pointed angrily towards the wreckage of his aircraft, and in particular at the cylindrical attachment Merlin had taken for a fuel-tank. He saw now that the cylinder was the repository for dozens more of these wooden boxes, most of which must have been smashed when Merlin had nudged the aircraft with *Tyrant*.

'Did I do something wrong?' Merlin asked.

In a flash the man's anger turned to despair. He was crying, the tears smudging the soot on his cheeks. 'Tangible,' he said, softer now. 'All tangible inkwells. Gecko.'

Merlin reached into the box and retrieved one of the few intact vials. He held the delicate thing to his eyes. 'Medicine?'

'Plastrum,' the man said, taking the box back from Merlin.

'Show me what you do with this,' Merlin said, as he motioned drinking the vial. The man shook his head, narrowing his wrinkled ice-blue eyes at him as if he thought Merlin was either stupid or making fun. Merlin rolled up the sleeve of his arm and motioned injecting himself. The pilot nodded tentatively.

'Plastrum,' he said again. 'Vestibule plastrum.'

'You have some kind of medical crisis? Is that what you were doing, bringing medicines?'

'Tangible,' the man repeated.

'You need to come with me,' Merlin said. 'Whatever that stuff is, we can synthesise it aboard *Tyrant*.' He held up the intact vial and then placed his index finger next to it. Then he pointed to the parked form of his ship and spread his fingers wide, hoping the pilot got the message that he could multiply the medicine. 'One sample,' he said. 'That's all we need.'

Suddenly there was a commotion. Merlin looked around in time to see a girl running across the apron, towards the two of them. In Cohort terms she could only have been six or seven years old. She wore a child's version of the same greatcoat everyone else wore, buckled black boots and gloves, no hat, goggles or breathing mask. The pilot shouted, 'Minla,' at her approach, a single word that conveyed both warning and something more intimate, as if the older man might have been her father or grandfather. 'Minla oak trefoil,' the man added, firmly but not without kindness. He sounded pleased to see her, but somewhat less than pleased that she had chosen this exact moment to run outside.

'Spelter Malkoha,' the girl said, and hugged the pilot around the waist, which was as high as she could reach. 'Spelter Malkoha, ursine Malkoha.'

The red-faced man knelt down – his eyes were still damp – and ran a gloved finger through the girl's unruly fringe of black hair. She had a small, monkey-like face, one that conveyed both mischief and cleverness.

'Minla,' he said tenderly. 'Minla, Minla, Minla.' Then what was clearly a rhetorical question: 'Gastric spar oxen, fey legible, Minla?'

'Gorse spelter,' she said, sounding contrite. And then, perhaps for the first time, she noticed Merlin. For an anxious moment her expression was frozen somewhere between surprise and suspicion, as if he was some kind of puzzle that had just intruded into her world.

'You wouldn't be called Minla, by any chance?' Merlin asked.

'Minla,' she said, in barely a whisper.

'Merlin. Pleased to meet you, Minla.' And then on a whim, before any of the adults could stop him, he passed her one of the indigo hyacinths that *Tyrant* had just spun for him, woven from the ancient molecular templates in its biolibrary. 'Yours,' he said. 'A pretty flower for a pretty little girl.'

'Oxen spray, Minla,' the red-faced man said, pointing back to one of the buildings on the edge of the apron. A soldier walked over and extended a hand to the girl, ready to escort her back inside. She moved to hand the flower back to Merlin.

'No,' he said, 'you can keep it, Minla. It's for you.'

She opened the collar of her coat and pushed the flower inside for safe keeping, until only its head was jutting out. The vivid indigo seemed to throw something of its hue onto her face.

'Mer-lin?' asked the older man.

'Yes.'

The man tapped a fist against his own chest. 'Malkoha.' And then he indicated the vial Merlin was still carrying. 'Plastrum,' he said again. Then a question, accompanied by a nod towards *Tyrant*. 'Risible plastrum?'

'Yes,' Merlin said. 'I can make you more medicine. *Risible plastrum.*'

The red-faced man studied him for what felt like many minutes. Merlin opted to say nothing: if the pilot hadn't got the message by now, no further persuasion was going to help. Then the pilot reached down to his belt and unbuttoned the leather holster of a pistol. He removed the weapon and allowed Merlin sufficient time to examine it by eye. The low sun gleamed off an oiled black barrel, inlaid with florid white ornamentation carved from something like whalebone.

'Mer-lin risible plastrum,' Malkoha said. Then he waved the gun for emphasis. 'Spar apostle.'

'Spar apostle,' Merlin repeated, as they walked up the boarding ramp. 'No tricks.'

Even before *Tyrant* had made progress in the cracking of the local language, Merlin had managed to hammer out a deal with Malkoha. The medicine had turned out to be a very simple drug, easily synthesised. A narrow-spectrum β-lactam antibiotic, according to the ship: exactly the sort of thing the locals might use to treat a gram-positive bacterial infection – something like bacterial meningitis, for instance – if they didn't have anything better.

Tyrant could pump out antibiotic medicine by the hundreds of litres, or synthesise something vastly more effective in equally large quantities. But Merlin saw no sense in playing his most valuable card so early in the game. He chose instead to give Malkoha supplies of the drug in approximately the same dosage and quantity as he must have been carrying when his aircraft was damaged, packaged in similar-looking glass vials. He gave the first two consignments as a gift, in recompense for the harm he was presumed to have done when attempting to save Malkoha, and let Malkoha think that it was all that *Tyrant* could do to make drugs at that strength and quantity. It was only when he handed over the third consignment, on the third day, that he mentioned the materials he needed to repair his ship.

He didn't say anything, of course, or at least nothing that the locals could have understood. But there were enough examples lying around of the materials Merlin needed – metals and organic compounds, principally, as well as water that could be used to replenish *Tyrant*'s hydrogen-fusion tanks – that Merlin was able to make considerable progress just by pointing and miming. He kept talking all the while, even in Main, and did all that he could to encourage the locals to talk back in their own tongue. Even when he was inside the compound, *Tyrant* was observing every exchange, thanks to the microscopic surveillance devices Merlin carried on his person. Through this process, the ship was constantly testing and rejecting language models, employing its knowledge of both the general principles of human grammar and its compendious database of ancient languages recorded by the Cohort, many of which were antecedents of Main itself. Lecythus might have been isolated for tens of thousands of years, but languages older than that had been cracked by brute computation, and Merlin had no doubt that *Tyrant* would get there in the end, provided he gave it enough material to work with.

It was still not clear whether the locals regarded him as their prisoner, or honoured guest. He'd made no attempt to leave, and they'd made no effort to prevent him from returning to his ship when it was time to collect the vials of antibiotic. Perhaps they had guessed that it would be futile to try to stop him, given the likely capabilities of his technology. Or perhaps they had guessed – correctly, as it happened – that *Tyrant* would be going nowhere until it was repaired and fuelled. In any event they seemed less awed by his arrival than intrigued, shrewdly aware of what he could do for them.

Merlin liked Malkoha, even though he knew almost nothing about the man. Clearly he was a figure of high seniority within this particular organisation, be it military or political, but he was also a man brave enough to fly a hazardous mission to ferry medicines through the sky, in a time of war. And his daughter loved him, which had to count for something. Merlin now knew that Malkoha was her 'spelter' or father, although he did indeed look old enough to have been separated from her by a further generation.

Almost everything that Merlin did learn, in those early days, was due to Minla rather than the adults. The adults seemed willing to at least attempt to answer his queries, when they could understand what he was getting at. But their chalkboard explanations usually left Merlin none the wiser. They could show him maps and printed historical and technical treatises, but none of these shed any light on the world's many mysteries. Cracking text would take *Tyrant* even longer than cracking spoken language.

Minla, though, had picture books. Malkoha's daughter had taken an obvious liking to Merlin, even though they shared nothing in common. Merlin gave her a new flower each time he saw her, freshly spun from some exotic species in the biolibrary. Merlin made a point of never giving her flowers from a particular world twice, even when she wanted more of the same. He also made a point of always telling her something about the place from where the flowers had come, regardless of her lack of understanding. It seemed to be enough for her to hear the cadences of a story, even if it was in an alien language.

There was not much colour in Minla's world, so Merlin's gifts must have had a luminous appeal to her. Once a day, for a few minutes, they were allowed to meet in a drab room inside the main compound. An adult was always stationed nearby, but to all intents and purposes Merlin and the girl were permitted to interact freely. Minla would show Merlin drawings and paintings she had done, or little compositions, written down in laboured handwriting in approximately the form of script *Tyrant* had come to refer to as Lecythus A. Merlin would examine Minla's works and offer praise when it was merited.

He wondered why these meetings were allowed. Minla was obviously a bright girl (he could tell that much merely from the precocious manner of her speaking, even if he hadn't had the ample evidence of her drawings and writings). Perhaps it was felt that meeting the man from space would be an important part of her education, one that could never be repeated at a later date. Perhaps she had pestered her father into allowing her to spend more time with Merlin. Merlin could understand that; as a child he'd also formed harmless attachments to adults, often those that came bearing gifts and especially those adults that appeared interested in what he had to show them.

Could there be more to it than that, though? Was it possible that the adults had decided that a child offered the best conduit for understanding, and that Minla was now their envoy? Or were they hoping to use Minla as a form of emotional blackmail, so that they might exert a subtle hold on Merlin when he decided it was time to leave?

He didn't know. What he was certain of was that Minla's books raised as many questions as they answered, and that simply leafing through them was enough to open windows in his own mind, back into a childhood he'd thought consigned safely to oblivion. The books were startlingly similar to the books Merlin remembered from the Palace of Eternal Dusk, the ones he used to fight over with his brother. They were bound similarly, illustrated with spidery ink drawings scattered through the text or florid watercolours gathered onto glossy plates at the end of the book. Merlin liked holding the book up to the light of an open window, so that the illustrated pages shone like stained glass. It was something his father had shown him on Plenitude, when he had been Minla's age, and her delight exactly echoed his own, across the unthinkable gulf of time and distance and circumstance that separated their childhoods.

At the same time, he also paid close attention to what the books had to say. Many of the stories featured little girls involved in fanciful adventures concerning flying animals and other magic creatures. Others had the worthy, over-earnest look of educational texts. Studying these latter books, Merlin began to grasp something of the history of Lecythus, at least in so far as it had been codified for the consumption of children.

The people on Lecythus knew they'd come from the stars. In two of the books there were even paintings of a vast spherical spaceship hoving into orbit around the planet. The paintings differed in every significant detail, but Merlin felt sure that he was seeing a portrayal of the same dimly remembered historical event, much as the books in his youth had shown various representations of human settlers arriving on Plenitude. There was no reference to the Waynet, however, or anything connected to the Cohort or the Huskers. As for the locals' theory concerning the origin of the aerial land masses, Merlin found only one clue. It lay in a frightening sequence of pictures showing the night sky being riven by lava-like fissures, until whole chunks of the heavens dropped out of place, revealing a darker, deeper firmament beyond. Some of the pieces were shown crashing into the seas, raising awesome waves that tumbled over entire coastal communities, while others were shown hovering unsupported in the sky, with kilometres of empty space under them. If the adults remembered that it was alien weaponry that had smashed their camouflaging sky (weapons deployed by aliens that were still *out there*) no hint of that uncomfortable truth was allowed into Minla's books. The destruction of the sky was shown simply as a natural catastrophe, like a flood or volcanic eruption. Enough to awe, enough to fascinate, but not enough to give nightmares.

Awesome it must have been too. *Tyrant*'s own analysis had

established that the aerial land masses could be put together like a jigsaw. There were gaps in that jigsaw, but most of them could be filled by lifting chunks of land out of the seas and slotting them in place. The inhabited aerial land masses were all inverted compared to their supposed positions in the original sky, requiring that they must have been flipped over after the shattering. *Tyrant* could offer little insight into how this could have happened, but it was clear enough that unless the chunks were inverted, life-supporting materials would spill off over the edges and rain down onto the planet again. Presumably the necessary materials had been uplifted into the air when the unsupported chunks (and these must have been pieces that did not contain gravity-nullifiers, or which had been damaged beyond the capacity to support themselves) came hammering down.

As to how people had come to the sky in the first place, or how the present political situation had developed, Minla's texts were frustratingly vague. There were pictures of what were obviously historic battles, fought with animals and gunpowder. There were illustrations of courtly goings-on: princes and kings, balls and regattas, assassinations and duels. There were drawings of adventurers rising on kites and balloons to survey the aerial masses, and later of what were clearly government-sponsored scouting expeditions, employing huge flotillas of flimsy-looking airships. But as to exactly why the people in the sky were now at war with the people on the ground, Merlin had little idea, and even less interest. What mattered – the only thing, in fact – was that Minla's people had the means to help him. He could have managed without them, but by bringing him the things he needed they made it easier. And it was good to see other faces again, after so long alone.

One of Minla's books intrigued him even more than all the others. It showed a picture of the starry night, the heavens as revealed after the fall of the camouflaging sky. Constellations had been drawn on the patterns of stars, with sketched figures overlaying the schematic lines joining the stars. None of the mythical or heroic figures corresponded to the old constellations of Plenitude, but the same archetypal forms were nonetheless present. For Merlin there was something hugely reassuring in seeing the evidence of similar imaginations at work. It might have been tens of thousands of years since these humans had been in contact with a wider galactic civilisation; they might have endured world-changing catastrophes and retained only a hazy notion of their origins. But they were still people, and he was amongst them. There were times, during his long search for the lost weapon that he hoped would save the Cohort, when Merlin had come to doubt whether there was anything about humanity worth saving. But all it took was the look on Minla's face as he presented her with another flower – another relic of some long-dead world – to banish such doubts almost entirely. While there were still children in the universe, and while children could still be enchanted by something as simple and wonderful as a flower, there was still a reason to keep looking, a reason to keep believing.

The coiled black device had the look of a tiny chambered nautilus, turned to onyx. Merlin pushed back his hair to let Malkoha see that he was already wearing a similar unit, then motioned for Malkoha to insert the translator into his own ear.

'Good,' Merlin said, when he saw that the other man had pushed the device into place. 'Can you understand me now?'

Malkoha answered very quickly, but there was a moment's lag before Merlin heard his response translated into Main, rendered in an emotionally flat machine voice. 'Yes. I understand good. How is this possible?'

Merlin gestured around him. They were alone together aboard *Tyrant*, Malkoha ready to leave with another consignment of antibiotics. 'The ship's been listening in on every conversation I've had with you,' Merlin said. 'It's heard enough of your language to begin piecing together a translation. It's still rudimentary – there are a lot of gaps the ship still needs to fill – but it will only get better with time, the more we talk.'

Malkoha listened diligently as his earpiece translated Merlin's response. Merlin could only guess at how much of his intended meaning was making it through intact.

'Your ship is clever,' Malkoha said. 'We talk many times. We get good at understanding.'

'I hope so.'

Malkoha pointed now at the latest batch of supplies his people had brought, piled neatly at the top of the boarding ramp. The materials were unsophisticated in their manufacture, but they could all be reprocessed to form the complicated components *Tyrant* needed to repair itself.

'Metals make the ship good?'

'Yes,' Merlin said. 'Metals make the ship good.'

'When the ship is good, the ship will fly? You will leave?'

'That's the idea.'

Malkoha looked sad. 'Where will you go?'

'Back into space. I've been a long time away from my own people. But there's something I need to find before I return to them.'

'Minla will be unhappy.'

'So will I. I like Minla. She's a clever little girl.'

'Yes. Minla is clever. I am proud of my daughter.'

'You have every right to be,' Merlin said, hoping that his sincerity came across. 'I have to start what I finished, though. The ship tells me it'll be flight-ready in two or three days. It's a patch job, but it'll get us to the nearest motherbase. But there's something we need to talk about first.' Merlin reached for a shelf and handed Malkoha a tray upon which sat twelve identical copies of the translator device.

'You will speak with more of us?'

'I've just learned some bad news, Malkoha: news that concerns you, and your people. Before I go I want to do what I can to help. Take these translators and give them to your best people – Coucal, Jacana, the rest. Get them to wear them all the time, no matter who they're talking to. In three days I want to meet with you all.'

Malkoha regarded the tray of translators with suspicion, as if the ranked devices were a peculiar foreign delicacy.

'What is the bad news, Merlin?'

'Three days isn't going to make much difference. It's better if we wait until the translation is more accurate, then there won't be any misunderstanding.'

'We are friends,' Malkoha said, leaning forwards. 'You can tell me now.'

'I'm afraid it won't make much sense.'

Malkoha looked at him beseechingly. 'Please.'

'Something is going to come out of the sky,' Merlin said. 'Like a great sword. And it's going to cut your sun in two.'

Malkoha frowned, as if he didn't think he could possibly have understood correctly.

        'Calliope?'
    Merlin nodded gravely. 'Calliope will die. And then so will every-
one on Lecythus.'

    They were all there when Merlin walked into the glass-partitioned
room. Malkoha, Triller, Coucal, Jacana, Sibia, Niltava, and about
half a dozen more top brass Merlin had never seen before. An
administrative assistant was already entering notes into a clattering
electromechanical transcription device squatting on her lap,
pecking away at its stiff metal input pads with surprising speed.
Tea bubbled in a fat engraved urn set in the middle of the table.
An orderly had already poured tea into china cups set before each
bigwig, including Merlin himself. Through the partition, on the
opposite wall of the adjoining tactical room, Merlin watched
another orderly make microscopic adjustments to the placement
of the aerial land masses on an equal-area projection map of
Lecythus. Periodically, the entire building would rattle with the
droning arrival of another aircraft or dirigible.
    Malkoha coughed to bring the room to attention. 'Merlin has
news for us,' he said, his translated voice coming through with
more emotion than it had three days earlier. 'This is news not
just for the Skyland Alliance, but for everyone on Lecythus. That
includes the Aligned Territories, the Neutrals and yes, even our
enemies in the Shadowland Coalition.' He beckoned with a hand
in Merlin's direction, inviting him to stand.
    Merlin held up one of Minla's picture books, open at the illus-
tration of constellations in the sky over Lecythus. 'What I have to
tell you concerns these patterns,' he said. 'You see heroes, animals
and monsters in the sky, traced in lines drawn between the brightest stars.'
    A new voice buzzed in his ear. He identified the speaker as Sibia,
a woman of high political rank. 'These things mean nothing,' she
said patiently. 'They are lines drawn between chance alignments.
The ancient mind saw demons and monsters in the heavens. Our
modern science tells us that the stars are very distant, and that two
stars that appear close together in the sky – the two eyes of Prinia
the Dragon, for example – may in reality be located at very different
distances.'
    'The lines are more significant than you appreciate,' Merlin said.
'They are a pattern you have remembered across tens of thousands

of years, forgetting its true meaning. They are pathways between the stars.'

'There are no pathways in the void,' Sibia retorted. 'The void is vacuum: the same thing that makes birds suffocate when you suck air out of a glass jar.'

'You may think it absurd,' Merlin said. 'All I can tell you is that vacuum is not as you understand it. It has structure, resilience, its own reserves of energy. And you can make part of it shear away from the rest, if you try hard enough. That's what the Waymakers did. They stretched great corridors between the stars: rivers of flowing vacuum. They reach from star to star, binding together the entire galaxy. We call it the Waynet.'

'Is this how you arrived?' Malkoha asked.

'My little ship could never have crossed interstellar space without it. But as I was passing close to your planet – because a strand of the Waynet runs right through this system – my ship encountered a problem. That is why *Tyrant* was damaged; why I had to land here and seek your assistance.'

'And the nature of this problem?' the old man pushed.

'My ship only discovered it three days ago, based on observations it had collated since I arrived. It appears that part of the Waynet has become loose, unshackled. There's a kink in the flow where it begins to drift out of alignment. The unshackled part is drifting towards your sun, tugged towards it by the pull of Calliope's gravitational field.'

'You're certain of this?' Sibia asked.

'I've had my ship check the data over and over. There's no doubt. In just over seventy years, the Waynet will cut right through Calliope, like a wire through a ball of cheese.'

Malkoha looked hard into Merlin's eyes. 'What will happen?'

'Probably very little to begin with, when the Waynet is still cutting through the chromosphere. But by the time it reaches the nuclear-burning core ... I'd say all bets are off.'

'Can it be mended? Can the Waynet be brought back into alignment?'

'Not using any technology known to my own people. We're dealing with principles as far beyond anything on Lecythus as *Tyrant* is beyond one of your propeller planes.'

Malkoha looked stricken. 'Then what can we possibly do?'

'You can make plans to leave Lecythus. You have always known that space travel was possible: it's in your history, in the books you give to your children. If you had any doubts, I've shown it to be true. Now you must achieve it for yourselves.'

'In seventy years?' Malkoha asked.

'I know it sounds impossible. But you can do it. You already have flying machines. All you need to do is keep building on that achievement ... building and building ... until you have the means.'

'You make it sound easy.'

'It won't be. It'll be the hardest thing you've ever done. But I'm convinced that you can do it, if only you pull together.' Merlin looked sternly at his audience. 'That means no more wars between the Skylands and the Shadowlands. You don't have time for it. From this moment on, the entire industrial and scientific capacity of your planet will have to be directed towards one goal.'

'You're going to help us, Merlin?' Malkoha asked. 'Aren't you?'

Merlin's throat had become very dry. 'I'd like to, but I must leave immediately. Twenty light-years from here is a bountiful system known to the Cohort. The great vessels of my people – the swallowships – sometimes stop in this system, to replenish supplies and make repairs. The swallowships cannot use the Way, but they are very big. If I could divert just one swallowship here, it could carry fifty thousand refugees; double that if people were prepared to accept some hardship.'

'That's still not many people,' Sibia said.

'That's why you need to start thinking about reducing your population over the next three generations. It won't be possible to save everyone, but if you could at least ensure that the survivors are adults of breeding age ...' Merlin trailed off, conscious of the dismayed faces staring at him. 'Look,' he said, removing a sheaf of papers from his jacket and spreading them on the table. 'I had the ship prepare these documents. This one concerns the production of wide-spectrum antibiotic medicines. This one concerns the construction of a new type of aircraft engine, one that will allow you to exceed the speed of sound and reach much higher altitudes than are now available to you. This one concerns metallurgy and high-precision machining. This one is a plan for a two-stage liquid-fuelled rocket. You need to start learning about rocketry *now*, because it's the only thing that's going to get you into space.' His finger moved to the final sheet. 'This document reveals certain truths about the nature of physical reality. Energy and mass are related by this simple formula. The speed of light is an absolute constant, irrespective of the observer's motion. This diagram shows the presence of emission lines in the spectrum of hydrogen, and a mathematical formula that predicts the spacing of those lines. All this ... *stuff* should help you make some progress.'

'Is this all you can give us?' Sibia asked sceptically. 'A few pages' worth of vague sketches and cryptic formulae?'

'They're more than most cultures ever get. I suggest you start thinking about them straight away.'

'I will get this to Shama,' Coucal said, taking the drawing of a jet engine and preparing to slip it into his case.

'Not before everything here is duplicated and archived,' Malkoha said firmly. 'And we must take pains to ensure none of these secrets fall into Shadowland hands.' Then he returned his attention to Merlin. 'Evidently, you have given this matter some thought.'

'Just a bit.'

'Is this the first time you have had to deal with a world such as ours, one that will die?'

'I've had some prior experience of the matter. There was once a world—'

'What happened to the place in question?' Malkoha asked, before Merlin could finish his sentence.

'It died.'

'How many people were saved?'

For a moment Merlin couldn't answer. The words seemed to lodge in the back of his throat, hard as pebbles. 'There were just two survivors,' he said quietly. 'A pair of brothers.'

The walk to *Tyrant* was the longest he had ever taken. Ever since he had made the decision to leave Lecythus he had rehearsed the occasion in his mind, replaying it time and again. He had always imagined the crowd cheering, daunted by the news, but not cowed, Merlin raising his fist in an encouraging salute. Nothing had prepared him for the frigid silence of his audience, their judgmental expressions as he left the low buildings of the compound, their unspoken disdain hanging in the air like a proclamation.

Only Malkoha followed him all the way to *Tyrant*'s boarding ramp. The old soldier had his coat drawn tight across his chest, even though the wind was still and the evening not particularly cold.

'I'm sorry,' Merlin said, with one foot on the ramp. 'I wish I could stay.'

'You seem like two men to me,' Malkoha said, his voice low. 'One of them is braver than he gives himself credit for. The other man still has bravery to learn.'

'I'm not running away.'

'But you are running from something.'

'I have to go now. If the damage to the Waynet becomes greater, I may not even be able to reach the next system.'

'Then you must do what you think is right. I shall be sure to give your regards to Minla. She will miss you very much.' Malkoha paused and reached into his tunic pocket. 'I almost forgot to give you this. She would have been very upset with me if I had.'

Malkoha had given Merlin a small piece of stone, a coin-shaped sliver that must have been cut from a larger piece and then set in coloured metal so that it could be worn around the neck or wrist. Merlin examined the stone with interest, but in truth there seemed nothing remarkable about it. He'd picked up and discarded more beautiful examples a thousand times in his travels. It had been dyed red in order to emphasise the fine grain of its surface: a series of parallel lines like the pages of a book seen end-on, but with a rhythmic structure to the spacing of the lines – a widening and a narrowing – that was unlike any book Merlin had seen.

'Tell her I appreciated it,' he said.

'I gave the stone to my daughter. She found it pretty.'

'How did you come by it?'

'I thought you were in a hurry to leave.'

Merlin's hand closed around the stone. 'You're right. I should be on my way.'

'The stone belonged to a prisoner of mine, a man named Dowitcher. He was one of their greatest thinkers: a scientist and soldier much like myself. I admired his brilliance from afar, just as I hope he admired mine. One day, our agents captured him and brought him to the Skylands. I played no part in planning his kidnap, but I was delighted that we might at last meet on equal terms. I was convinced that, as a man of reason, he would listen to my arguments and accept the wisdom of defecting to the Skylands.'

'Did he?'

'Not in the slightest. He was as firmly entrenched in his convictions as I was in mine. We never became friends.'

'So where does the stone come into it?'

'Before he died, Dowitcher found a means to torment me. He gave me the stone and told me that he had learned something of great significance from it. Something that could change our world. Something that had *cosmic* significance. He was looking into the sky when he said that: almost laughing. But he would not reveal what that secret was.'

Merlin hefted the stone once more. 'I think he was playing games with you, Malkoha.'

'That's the conclusion I eventually reached. One day Minla took a shine to the stone – I kept it on my desk long after Dowitcher was gone – and I let her have it.'

'And now it's mine.'

'You mean a lot to her, Merlin. She wanted to give you something in return for the flowers. You may forget the rest of us one day, but please don't ever forget my daughter.'

'I won't.'

'I'm lucky,' Malkoha said, something in his tone easing, as if he was finished judging Merlin. 'I'll be dead long before your Waynet cuts into our sun. But Minla's generation won't have that luxury. They know that their world is going to end, and that every year brings that event a year nearer. They're the ones who'll spend their whole lives with that knowledge looming over them. They'll never know true happiness. I don't envy them a moment of their lives.'

That was when something in Merlin gave way, some mental slippage that he must have felt coming for many hours without quite acknowledging it to himself. Almost before he had time to reflect on his own words he found himself saying to Malkoha, 'I'm staying.'

The other man, perhaps wary of a trick or some misunderstanding brought about by the translator, narrowed his eyes. 'Merlin?'

'I said I'm staying. I've changed my mind. Maybe it was what I always knew I had to do, or maybe it was all down to what you just said about Minla. But I'm not going anywhere.'

'What I said just now,' Malkoha said, 'about there being two of you, one braver than the other ... I know now which man I am speaking to.'

'I don't feel brave. I feel scared.'

'Then I know it to be true. Thank you, Merlin. Thank you for not leaving us.'

'There's a catch,' Merlin said. 'If I'm going to be any help to you, I have to see this whole thing out.'

Malkoha was the last to see him before he entered frostwatch. 'Twenty years,' Merlin said, indicating the settings, which had been recalibrated in Lecythus time-units. 'In all that time, you don't need to worry about me. *Tyrant* will take care of everything I need. If there's a problem, the ship will either wake me or it will send out the proctors to seek assistance.'

'You have never spoken of proctors before,' Malkoha replied.

'Small mechanical puppets. They have very little intelligence of their own, so they won't be able to help you with anything creative. But you needn't be alarmed by them.'

'In twenty years, must we wake you?'

'No, the ship will take care of that as well. When the time comes, the ship will allow you aboard. I may be a little groggy at first, but I'm sure you'll make allowances.'

'I may not be around in twenty years,' Malkoha said gravely. 'I am sixty years old now.'

'I'm sure there's still life left in you.'

'If we should encounter a problem, a crisis—'

'Listen to me,' Merlin said, with sudden emphasis. 'You need to understand one very important thing. I am not a god. My body is much the same as yours, our lifespans very similar. That's the way we did things in the Cohort: immortality through our deeds, rather than flesh and blood. The frostwatch casket can give me a few dozen years beyond a normal human lifespan, but it can't give me eternal life. If you keep waking me, I won't live long enough to help you when things get really tough. If there is a crisis, you can knock on the ship three times. But I'd urge you not to do so unless things are truly dire.'

'I will heed your counsel,' Malkoha said.

'Work hard. Work harder than you've ever dreamed possible. Time is going to eat up those seventy years faster than you can blink.'

'I know how quickly time can eat years, Merlin.'

'I want to wake to rockets and jet aircraft. Anything less, I'm going to be a disappointed man.'

'We will do our best not to let you down. Sleep well, Merlin. We will take care of you and your ship, no matter what happens.'

Merlin said farewell to Malkoha. When the ship was sealed up he settled himself into the frostwatch casket and commanded *Tyrant* to put him to sleep.

He didn't dream.

Nobody he recognised was there to greet Merlin when he returned to consciousness. Were it not for their uniforms, which still carried a recognisable form of the Skylanders' crescent emblem, he could easily believe that he had been abducted by forces from the surface. His visitors crowded around his open casket, faces difficult to make out, his eyes watering against the sudden intrusion of light.

'Can you understand me, Merlin?' asked a woman, with a firm clear voice.

'Yes,' he said, after a moment in which it seemed as if his mouth was still frozen. 'I understand you. How long have I—'

'Twenty years, just as you instructed. We had no cause to wake you.'

He pushed himself from the casket, muscles screaming into his brain with the effort. His vision sharpened by degrees. The woman studied him with a cool detachment. She snapped her fingers at someone standing behind her and then passed Merlin a blanket. 'Put this around you,' she said.

The blanket had been warmed. He wrapped it around himself with gratitude, and felt some of the heat seep into his old bones. 'That was a long one,' he said, his tongue moving sluggishly, making him slur his words. 'We don't usually spend so long in frostwatch.'

'But you're alive and well.'

'So it would seem.'

'We've prepared a reception area in the compound. There's food and drink, a medical team waiting to look at you. Can you walk?'

'I can try.'

Merlin tried. His legs buckled under him before he reached the door. They would regain strength in time, but for now he needed help. They must have anticipated his difficulties, because a wheelchair was waiting at the base of *Tyrant*'s boarding ramp, accompanied by an orderly to push it.

'Before you ask,' the woman said, 'Malkoha is dead. I'm sorry to have to tell you this.'

Merlin had grown to think of the old man as his only adult friend on Lecythus, and had been counting on his being there when he returned from frostwatch. 'When did he die?'

'Fourteen years ago.'

'Force and wisdom. It must be like ancient history to you.'

'Not to all of us,' the woman said sternly. 'I am Minla, Merlin. It may be fourteen years ago, but there isn't a day when I don't remember my father and wish he was still with us.'

As he was being propelled across the apron, Merlin looked up at the woman's face and compared it against his memories of the little girl he had known twenty years ago. At once he saw the similarity and knew that she was telling the truth. In that moment he felt the first visceral sense of the time that had passed.

'You can't imagine how odd this makes me feel, Minla. Do you remember me?'

'I remember a man I used to talk to in a room. It was a long time ago.'

'Not to me. Do you remember the stone?'

She looked at him oddly. 'The stone?'

'You asked your father to give it to me, when I was due to leave Lecythus.'

'Oh, that thing,' Minla said. 'Yes, I remember it now. It was the one that belonged to Dowitcher.'

'It's very pretty. You can have it back if you like.'

'Keep it, Merlin. It doesn't mean anything to me now, just as it shouldn't have meant anything to my father. I'm embarrassed to have given it to you.'

'I'm sorry about Malkoha.'

'He died well, Merlin. Flying another hazardous mission for us, in very bad weather. This time it was our turn to deliver medicine to our allies. We were now making antibiotics for all the land masses in the Skyland Alliance, thanks to the process you gave us. My father flew one of the last consignments. He made it to the other land mass, but his plane was lost on the return trip.'

'He was a good man. I only knew him a short while, but I think it was enough to tell.'

'He often spoke of you, Merlin. I think he hoped you might teach him more than you did.'

'I did what I could. Too much knowledge would have over-whelmed you: you wouldn't have known where to start, or how to put the pieces together.'

'Perhaps you should have trusted us more.'

'You said you had no cause to wake me. Does that mean you made progress?'

'Decide for yourself.'

He followed Minla's instruction. The area around *Tyrant* was still recognisable as the old military compound, with many of the original buildings still present, albeit enlarged and adapted. But most of the dirigible docking towers were gone, as had most of the dirigibles themselves. Ranks of new aircraft now occupied the area where the towers and airships had been, bigger and heavier than anything Merlin had seen before. The swept-back geometry of their wings, the angle of the leading edge, the rakish curve of their tailplanes all owed something to the shape of *Tyrant* in atmos-pheric-entry mode. Clearly the natives had been more observant than he'd given them credit for. Merlin knew he shouldn't have been surprised; he'd given them the blueprints for the jet turbine, after all. But it was still something of a shock to see his plans made concrete, so closely to the way he had imagined it.

'Fuel is always a problem,' Minla said. 'We have the advantage of height, but little else. We rely on our scattered allies on the ground, together with raiding expeditions to Shadowland fuel bunkers.' She pointed to one of the remaining airships. 'Our cargo dirigibles can lift fuel all the way back to the Skylands.'

'Are you still at war?' Merlin asked, though her statement rather confirmed it.

'There was a ceasefire shortly after my father's death. It didn't last long.'

'You people could achieve a lot more if you pooled your efforts,' Merlin said. 'In seventy – make that fifty – years, you'll be facing collective annihilation. It isn't going to make a damned bit of difference what flag you're saluting.'

'Thank you for the lecture. If it means so much to you, why don't you fly down to the other side and talk to them?'

'I'm an explorer, not a diplomat.'

'You could always try.'

Merlin sighed heavily. 'I did try once. Not long after I left the Cohort ... there was a world named Exoletus, about the same size as Lecythus. I thought there might be something on Exoletus connected with my quest. I was wrong, but it was reason enough to land and try to talk to the locals.'

'Were they at war?'

'Just like you lot. Two massive power blocs, chemical weapons, the works. I hopped from hemisphere to hemisphere, trying to play the peacemaker, trying to knock their heads together to make them see sense. I laid the whole cosmic perspective angle on them: how there was a bigger universe out there, one they could be a part of if they only stopped squabbling. How they were going to have to be a part of it whether they liked it or not when the Huskers came calling, but if they could only be ready for that—'

'It didn't work.'

'I made things twenty times worse. I caught them at a time when they were inching towards some kind of ceasefire. By the time I left, they were going at it again hell for leather. Taught me a valuable lesson, Minla. It isn't my job to sprinkle fairy dust on a planet and get everyone to live happily ever after. No one gave me the toolkit for that. You have to work these things out for yourselves.'

She looked only slightly disappointed. 'So you'll never try again?'

'Burn your fingers once, you don't put them into the fire twice.'

'Well,' Minla said, 'before you think too harshly of us, it was the Skylands that took the peace initiative in the last ceasefire.'

'So what went wrong?'

'The Shadowlands invaded one of our allied surface territories. They were interested in mining a particular ore, known to be abundant in that area.'

Depressed as he was by news that the war was still rumbling on, Merlin forced his concentration back onto the larger matter of preparations for the catastrophe. 'You've done well with these aircraft. Doubtless you'll have gained expertise in high-altitude flight. Have you gone transonic yet?'

'In prototypes. We'll have an operational squadron of supersonic aircraft in the air within two years, subject to fuel supplies.'

'Rocketry?'

'That too. It's probably easier if I show you.'

Minla let the orderly wheel him into one of the compound buildings. A long window ran along one wall, overlooking a larger space. Though the interior had been enlarged and re-partitioned, Merlin still recognised the tactical room. The old wall-map, with its cumbersome push-around plaques, had been replaced by a clattering electromechanical display board. Operators wore headsets and sat at desks behind huge streamlined machines, their grey metal cases ribbed with cooling flanges. They were staring at small flickering slate-blue screens, whispering into microphones.

Minla removed a tranche of photographs from a desk and passed them to Merlin for his inspection. They were black and white images of the Skyland air mass, shot from increasing altitude, until the curve of Lecythus's horizon became pronounced.

'Our sounding rockets have penetrated to the very edge of the atmosphere,' Minla said. 'Our three-stage units now have the potential to deliver a tactical payload to any unobstructed point on the surface.'

'What would count as a "tactical payload"?' Merlin asked warily.

'It's academic. I'm merely illustrating the progress we've made in your absence.'

'I'm cheered.'

'You encouraged us to make these improvements,' Minla said, chidingly. 'You can hardly blame us if we put them to military use in the meantime. The catastrophe – as you've so helpfully pointed out – is still fifty years in the future. We have our own affairs to deal with in the meantime.'

'I wasn't trying to create a war machine. I was just giving you the stepping stones you needed to get into space.'

'Well, as you can doubtless judge for yourself, we still have some distance to go. Our analysts say that we'll have a natural satellite in orbit within fifteen years, maybe ten. Definitely so by the time you wake from your next bout of sleep. But that's still not the same as moving fifty thousand people out of the system, or however many it needs to be. For that we're going to need more guidance from you, Merlin.'

'You seem to be doing very well with what I've already given you.'

Minla's tone, cold until then, softened perceptibly. 'We'll get you fed. Then the doctors would like to look you over, if only for their own notebooks. We're glad to have you back with us, Merlin. My father would have been so happy to see you again.'

'I'd like to have spoken with him again.'

After a moment, Minla said: 'How long will you stay with us, before you go back to sleep again?

'Months, at least. Maybe a year. Long enough to be sure that you're on the right track, and that I can trust you to make your own progress until I'm awake again.'

'There's a lot we need to talk about. I hope you have a strong appetite for questions.'

'I have a stronger appetite for breakfast.'

Minla had him wheeled out of the room into another part of the compound. There he was examined by Skyland medical officials, a process that involved much poking and prodding and whispered consultation. They were interested in Merlin not just because he was a human who had been born on another planet, but because they hoped to learn some secret of frostwatch from his metabolism. Eventually they were done and Merlin was allowed to wash, clothe himself and finally eat. Skyland food was austere compared to what he was used to aboard *Tyrant*, but in his present state he would have wolfed down anything.

There was to be no rest for him that day. More medical examinations followed, including some that were clearly designed to test the functioning of his nervous system. They poured cold water into his ears, shone lights into his eyes and tapped him with various small hammers. Merlin endured it all with stoic good grace. They would find nothing odd about him because in all significant respects he was biologically identical to the people administering the examinations. But he imagined the tests would give the medical staff much to write about in the coming months.

Minla was waiting for him afterwards, together with a roomful of Skyland officials. He recognised two or three of them as older versions of people he had already met, greyed and lined by twenty years of war – there was Triller, Jacana and Sibia, Triller now missing an eye – but most of the faces were new to him. Merlin took careful note of the newcomers: those would be the people he'd be dealing with next time.

'Perhaps we should get to business,' Minla said, with crisp

authority. She was easily the youngest person in the room, but if she didn't outrank everyone present, she at least had their tacit respect. 'Merlin, welcome back to the Skylands. You've learned something of what has happened in your absence: the advances we've made, the ongoing condition of war. Now we must talk about the future.'

Merlin nodded agreeably. 'I'm all for the future.'

'Sibia?' Minla asked, directing a glance at the older woman.

'The industrial capacity of the Skylands, even when our surface allies are taken into account, is insufficient for the higher purpose of safeguarding the survival of our planetary culture,' Sibia answered, sounding exactly as if she was reading from a strategy document, even though she was looking Merlin straight in the eye. 'As such, it is our military duty – our moral imperative – to bring all of Lecythus under one authority, a single Planetary Government. Only then will we have the means to save more than a handful of souls.'

'I agree wholeheartedly,' Merlin said. 'That's why I applaud your earlier ceasefire. It's just a pity it didn't last.'

'The ceasefire was always fragile,' Jacana said. 'The wonder is that it lasted as long as it did. That's why we need something more permanent.'

Merlin felt a prickling sensation under his collar. 'I guess you have something in mind.'

'Complete military and political control of the Shadowlands,' Sibia replied. 'They will never work with us, unless they become us.'

'You can't believe how frightening that sounds.'

'It's the only way,' Minla said. 'My father's regime explored all possible avenues to find a peaceful settlement, one that would allow our two blocs to work in unison. He failed.'

'So instead you want to crush them into submission.'

'If that's what it takes,' Minla said. 'Our view is that the Shadow-land administration is vulnerable to collapse. It would only take a single clear-cut demonstration of our capability to bring about a coup, followed by a negotiated surrender.'

'And this clear-cut demonstration?'

'That's why we need your assistance, Merlin. Twenty years ago, you revealed certain truths to my father.' Before he could say anything, Minla produced one of the sheets Merlin had given to

Malkoha and his colleagues. 'It's all here in black and white. The equivalence of mass and energy. The constancy of the speed of light. The interior structure of the atom. Your remark that our sun contains a "nuclear-burning core". All these things were a spur to us. Our best minds have grappled with the implications of these ideas for twenty years. We see how the energy of the atom could carry us into space, and beyond range of our sun. We now have an inkling of what else that implies.'

'Do tell,' Merlin said, an ominous feeling in his belly.

'If mass can be converted into energy, then the military implications are startling. By splitting the atom, or even forcing atoms to merge, we believe that we can construct weapons of almost incalculable destructive force. The demonstration of one of these devices would surely be enough to collapse the Shadowland administration.'

Merlin shook his head slowly. 'You're heading up a blind alley. It isn't possible to make practical weapons using atomic energy. There are too many difficulties.'

Minla studied him with an attentiveness that Merlin found quite unsettling. 'I don't believe you,' she said.

'Believe me or don't believe me, it's up to you.'

'We are certain that these weapons can be made. Our own research lines will give them to us sooner or later.'

Merlin leaned back in his seat. He knew when there was no point in maintaining a bluff.

'Then you don't need me.'

'But we do. Most urgently. The Shadowland administration also has its bright minds, Merlin. Their interest in those ore reserves I mentioned earlier . . . either there have been intelligence leaks, or they have independently arrived at similar conclusions to us. They are trying to make a weapon.'

'You can't be sure of that.'

'We can't afford to be wrong. We may own the sky, but our situation is dependent upon access to those fuel reserves. If one of our allies was targeted with an atomic weapon . . .' Minla left the sentence unfinished, her point adequately made.

'Then build your bomb,' Merlin said.

'We need it sooner rather than later. That is where you come in.' Now Minla produced another sheet of paper, flicking it across the table in Merlin's direction. 'We have enough of the ore,' she said.

'We also have the means to refine it. This is our best guess for a design.'

Merlin glanced at the illustration long enough to see a complicated diagram of concentric circles, like the plan for an elaborate garden maze. It was intricately annotated in machine-printed Lecythus B, the variant of the language used for technical communication.

'I won't help you.'

'Then you may as well leave us now,' Minla said. 'We'll build our bomb in our own time, without your help, and use it to secure peace for the whole world. Maybe that will happen quickly enough for us to begin redirecting the industrial effort towards the evacuation. Maybe it won't. But what happens will be on our terms, not yours.'

'Understand one thing,' Jacana said, with a hawkish look on his face. 'The day will come when atomic weapons are used. Left to our own devices, we'll build weapons to use against our enemy below. But by the time we have that capability, they'll more than likely have the means to strike back, if they don't hit us first. That means there'll be a series of exchanges, an escalation, rather than a single decisive demonstration. Give us the means to make a weapon now and we'll use it in such a way that the civilian casualties are minimised. Withhold it from us, and you'll have the blood of a million dead on your hands.'

Merlin almost laughed. 'I'll have blood on my hands because I *didn't* show you how to kill yourselves?'

'You began this,' Minla said. 'You already gave us secret knowledge of the atom. Did you imagine we were so stupid, so childlike, that we wouldn't put two and two together?'

'Maybe I thought you had more common sense. I was hoping you'd develop atomic rockets, not atomic bombs.'

'This is our world, Merlin, not yours. We only get one chance at controlling its fate. If you want to help us, you must give us the means to overwhelm the enemy.'

'If I give you this, millions will die.'

'A billion will perish if Lecythus is not unified. You must do it, Merlin. Either you side with us, completely, or we all die.'

Merlin closed his eyes, wishing a moment alone, a moment to puzzle over the ramifications. In desperation, he saw a possible solution: one he'd rejected before but was now willing to advance.

'Show me the military targets on the surface that you would most like to eradicate,' he said. 'I'll have *Tyrant* take them out, using charm-torps.'

'We've considered asking for your direct military assistance,' Minla said. 'Unfortunately, it doesn't work for us. Our enemy already know something of your existence: it was always going to be a difficult secret to hide, especially given the reach of the Shadowlander espionage network. They'd be impressed by your weapons, that much we don't doubt. But they also know that our hold on you is tenuous, and that you could just as easily refuse to attack a given target. For that reason you do not make a very effective deterrent. Whereas if they knew that *we* controlled a devastating weapon . . .' Minla looked at the other Skyland officials. 'There could be no doubt in their minds that we might do the unthinkable.'

'I'm really beginning to wonder whether I shouldn't have landed on the ground instead.'

'You'd be sitting in a very similar room, having a very similar conversation,' Minla said.

'Your father would be ashamed of you.'

Minla's look made Merlin feel as if he was something she'd found under her shoe. 'My father meant well. He served his people to the best of his abilities. But he had the luxury of knowing he was going to die before the world's end. I don't.'

Merlin was aboard *Tyrant*, alone except for Minla, while he prepared to enter frostwatch again. Eight frantic months had passed since his revival, with the progress attaining a momentum of its own that Merlin felt sure would carry through to his next period of wakefulness.

'I'll be older when we meet again,' Minla said. 'You'll barely have aged a day, and your memories of this day will be as sharp as if it happened yesterday. Is that something you ever get used to?'

Not for the first time, Merlin smiled tolerantly. 'I was born on a world not very different from Lecythus, Minla. We didn't have land masses floating through the sky – well, nothing like what you have here, we didn't have global wars, but in many respects we were quite alike. Everything you see here – this ship, this frostwatch cabinet, these souvenirs – would once have seemed unrecognisably strange to me. I got used to it, though. Just as you'd get used to it, if you had the same experiences.'

'I'm not so sure.'

'I am. I met a very intelligent girl twenty years ago, and believe me I've met some intelligent people in my time.' Merlin brightened, remembering the thing he'd meant to show Minla. 'That stone you had your father give me ... the one we talked about just after I came out of the cabinet?'

'The worthless thing Dowitcher convinced my father was of cosmic significance?'

'It wasn't worthless to you. You must have liked it, or you wouldn't have given it to me in return for my flowers.'

'The flowers,' Minla said, thoughtfully. 'I'd almost forgotten them. I used to look forward to them so much, the sound of your voice as you told me stories I couldn't understand but which still managed to sound so significant. You made me feel special, Merlin. I'd treasure the flowers afterwards and go to sleep imagining the strange, beautiful places they'd come from. I'd cry when they died, but then you'd always bring new ones.'

'I used to like the look on your face.'

'Tell me about the stone,' she said, after a silence.

'I had *Tyrant* run an analysis on it. Just in case there was something significant about it, something neither you, I nor your father had spotted?'

'And?' Minla asked, with a note of fearfulness.

'I'm afraid it's just a piece of whetstone.'

'Whetstone?'

'Very hard. It's the kind you use for sharpening knives. It's a common enough type of stone on a planet like this one, wherever you have tides, shorelines and oceans.' Merlin had fished out the stone earlier; now he held it in his hand, palm open, like a lucky coin. 'You see that fine patterning of lines? This kind of stone was laid down in shallow tidal water. Whenever the sea rushed in, it would carry a suspension of silt that would settle out and form a fine layer on the surface of the stone. The next time the tide came in, you'd get a second layer. Then a third, and so on. Each layer would only take a few hours to be formed, although it might take hundreds of millions of years for it to harden into stone.'

'So it's very old.'

Merlin nodded. 'Very old indeed.'

'But not of any cosmic significance.'

'I'm sorry. I just thought you might want to know. Dowitcher *was* playing a game with your father after all. I think Malkoha had more or less guessed that for himself.'

For a moment Merlin thought his explanation had satisfied Minla, enabling her to shut tight that particular chapter of her life. But instead she just frowned. 'The lines aren't regular, though. Why do they widen and then narrow?'

'Tides vary,' Merlin said, suddenly feeling himself on less solid ground. 'Deep tides carry more sediment. Shallow tides less. I suppose.'

'Storms raise high tides. That would explain the occasional thick band. But other than that, the tides on Lecythus are very regular. I know this from my education.'

'Then your education's wrong, I'm afraid. A planet like this, with a large moon . . .' Merlin left the sentence unfinished. 'Spring tides and neap tides, Minla. No arguing with it.'

'I'm sure you're right.'

'Do you want the stone back?' he asked.

'Keep it, if it amuses you.'

He closed his hand around the stone. 'It meant something to you when you gave it to me. It'll always mean something to me for that reason.'

'Thank you for not leaving us. If my stone kept you here, it served a useful purpose.'

'I'm glad I chose to stay. I just hope I haven't done more harm than good, with the things I've shown you.'

'That again,' Minla said, with a weary sigh. 'You worry that we're going to blow ourselves to bits, just because you showed us the clockwork inside the atom.'

'It's nasty clockwork.'

He had seen enough progress, enough evidence of wisdom and independent ingenuity, to know that the Skyland forces would have a working atomic bomb within two years. By then, their rocket programme would have given them a delivery system able to handle the cumbersome payload of that primitive device. Even if the rocket fell behind schedule, they only had to wait until the aerial land mass drifted over a Shadowland target.

'I can't stop you making weapons,' Merlin said. 'All I ask is that you use them wisely. Just enough to negotiate a victory, and then no more. Then forget about bombs and start thinking about atomic rockets.'

Minla looked at him pityingly. 'You worry that we're becoming monsters. Merlin, we already *were* monsters. You didn't make us any worse.'

'That strain of bacterial meningitis was very infectious,' Merlin said. 'I know: I've run it through *Tyrant*'s medical analyser. You were already having difficulties with supplies of antibiotics. If I hadn't landed, if I hadn't offered to make that medicine for you, your military effort might have collapsed within months. The Shadowlands would have won by default. There wouldn't be any need to introduce atomic bombs into the world.'

'But we'd still need the rockets.'

'Different technology. The one doesn't imply the other.'

'Merlin, listen to me. I'm sorry that we're asking you to make these difficult moral choices. But for us it's about only one thing: species survival. If you hadn't dropped out of the sky, the Waynet would still be on its way to us, ready to slice our star in two. After you learned that was going to happen, you had no choice but to do everything possible to save us, no matter how bad a taste it leaves in your mouth.'

'I have to live with myself when this is all over.'

'You'll have nothing to be ashamed of. You've made all the right decisions so far. You've given us a future.'

'I need to clear up a few things for you,' Merlin said. 'It isn't a friendly galaxy. The creatures that smashed your sky are still out there. Your ancestors forged the armoured sky to hide from them, to make Lecythus look like an airless world. The Huskers were hunting down my own people before I left to work on my own. It isn't going to be plain sailing.'

'Survival is better than death. Always and for ever.'

Merlin sighed: he knew that this conversation had run its course, that they had been over these things a thousand times already and were no closer to mutual understanding. 'When I wake up again, I want to see lights in the sky.'

'When I was a girl,' Minla said, 'long before you came, my father would tell me stories of people travelling through the void, looking down on Lecythus. He'd put in jokes and little rhymes, things to make me laugh. Under it all, though, he had a serious message. He'd show me the pictures in my books, of the great ship that brought us to Lecythus. He said we'd come from the stars and one day we'd find a way to go back there. It seemed like a fantasy when I was a little girl, something that would never come to pass in the real world. Yet now it's happening, just as my father always said it would. If I live long enough, I'll know what it's like to leave Lecythus behind. But I'll be dead long before we ever reach another world, or see any of the wonders you've known.'

For an instant Minla was a girl again, not a driven military leader. Something in her face spoke to Merlin across the years, breaching the defences he had carefully assembled.

'Let me show you something.'

He took her into *Tyrant*'s rear compartment and revealed the matt-black cone of the syrinx, suspended in its cradle. At Merlin's invitation, Minla was allowed to stroke its mirror-smooth surface. She reached out her hand gingerly, as if expecting to touch something very hot or very cold. At the last instant her fingertips grazed the ancient artefact and then held the contact, daringly.

'It feels old,' she said. 'I can't say why.'

'It does. I've often felt the same thing.'

'Old and very heavy. Heavier than it has any right to be. And yet when I look at it, it's somehow not quite there, as if I'm looking at the space where it used to be.'

'That's exactly how it looks to me.'

Minla withdrew her touch. 'What is it?'

'We call it a syrinx. It's not a weapon. It's more like a key or a passport.'

'What does it do?'

'It lets my ship use the Waynet. In their time the Waymakers must have made billions of these things, enough to fuel the commerce of a million worlds. Imagine that, Minla: millions of stars bound by threads of accelerated space–time, each thread strung with thousands of glittering ships rushing to and fro, drops of honey on a thread of silk, each ship moving so close to the speed of light that time itself slowed almost to stillness. You could dine on one world, ride your ship to the Waynet and then take supper on some other world, under the falling light of another sun. A thousand years might have passed while you were riding the flow, but that didn't matter. The Waymakers forged an empire where a thousand years was just a lazy afternoon, a time to put off plans for another day.' Merlin looked sadly at Minla. 'That was the idea, anyway.'

'And now?'

'We breakfast in the ruins, barely remember the glory that was and scavenge space for the handful of still-functioning syrinxes.'

'Could you take it apart, find out how it works?'

'Only if I felt suicidal. The Waymakers protected their secrets very well.'

'Then it is valuable.'

'Incalculably so.'

Minla stroked it again. 'It feels dead.'

'It just isn't active yet. When the Waynet comes closer, the syrinx will sense it. That's when we'll really know it's time to get out of here.' Merlin forced a smile. 'But by then we'll be well on our way.'

'Now that you've shown me this secret, aren't you worried that we'll take it from you?'

'The ship wouldn't let you. And what use would it be to you anyway?'

'We could make our own ship, and use your syrinx to escape from here.'

Merlin tried not to sound too condescending. 'Any ship you built would smash itself to splinters as soon as it touched the Waynet, even with the syrinx to help it. And you wouldn't achieve much anyway. Ships that use the Waynet can't be very large.'

'Why is that?'

Merlin shrugged. 'They don't need to be. If it only takes a day or two of travel to get anywhere – remember what I said about clocks slowing down?' He had given the locals a thorough grounding in relativistic mechanics, although the time-bending consequences were still difficult for some of them to accept. 'You don't need to haul all your provisions with you, even if you're crossing to the other side of the galaxy.'

'But could a bigger ship enter the Waynet, if it had to?'

'The entry stresses wouldn't allow it. It's like riding the rapids.' Merlin didn't wait to see if Minla was following him. 'The syrinx creates a path that you can follow, a course where the river is easier. But you still need a small boat to squeeze around the obstacles.'

'Then no one ever made larger ships, even during the time of the Waymakers?'

'Why would they have needed to?'

'That wasn't my question, Merlin.'

'It was a long time ago. I don't have all the answers. And you shouldn't pin your hopes on the Waynet. It's the thing that's trying to kill you, not save you.'

'But when you leave us ... you'll ride the Waynet, won't you?'

Merlin nodded. 'But I'll make damned sure I have a head start on the collision.'

'I'm beginning to see how this must all look to you,' Minla said. 'This is the worst thing that's ever happened to us, the end of our history itself. To you it's just a stopover, an incidental adventure. I'm sure there were hundreds of worlds before us, and there'll be hundreds more. That's right, isn't it?'

Merlin bridled. 'If I didn't care about you all, I'd have left twenty years ago.'

'You very nearly did. I know how close you came. My father spoke of it many times, his joy when you changed your mind.'

'I had a change of heart,' Merlin said. 'Everyone's allowed that. You played a part in it, Minla. If you hadn't told Malkoha to give me that gift—'

'Then I'm glad I did, if it meant so much.' Minla looked away, something between sadness and fascination on her face. 'Merlin, before you sleep – do something for me.'

'Yes?'

'Make me flowers again. From some world I'll never ever see. And tell me their story.'

The Planetary Government aircraft was a sleek silver flying wing with its own atomic reactor, feeding six engines buried in air-smoothed nacelles. Minla had already led Merlin down a spiral staircase into an observation cupola set under the thickest part of the wing. Now she touched a brushed-steel panel, causing armoured slats to whisk open in rapid sequence. Through the green-tinted blastproof glass they had an uninterrupted view of the surface rolling by underneath.

The ocean carried no evidence of the war, but there was hardly any stretch of land that hadn't been touched in some fashion. Merlin saw the rubble-strewn remains of towns and cities, some with the hearts gouged out by kilometre-deep craters. He saw flooded harbours, beginning to be clawed back by the greedy fingers of the sea. He saw swathes of grey-brown land where nothing grew any more, and where only dead, petrified forests testified to the earlier presence of living things. Atomic weapons had been used in their thousands, by both sides. The Skylanders had been first, though, which was why the weapons had a special name on Lecythus. Because of the shape of the mushroom cloud that accompanied each burst, they called them Minla's Flowers.

She pointed out the new cities that had been built since the ceasefire. They were depressing to behold: grids of utilitarian blocks, each skull-grey multi-storey building identical to the others. Spidery highways linked the settlements, but not once did Merlin see any evidence of traffic or commerce.

'We're not building for posterity,' she said. 'None of those buildings have to last more than fifty years, and most of them will be empty long before that. By the time they start crumbling, there'll be no one alive on Lecythus.'

'You're surely not thinking of taking everyone with you,' Merlin said.

'Why not? It seemed unthinkable forty years ago. But so did atomic war, and the coming of a single world state. Anything's within our reach now. With social planning, we can organise matters such that the population shrinks to a tenth of its present size. No children will be allowed to be born in the last twenty years. And we'll begin moving people into the Space Dormitories long before that.'

Merlin had seen the plans for the Dormitories, along with the other elements of Minla's evacuation programme. There was already a small space station in orbit around Lecythus, but it would be utterly dwarfed by the hundred Dormitories. The plans called for huge air-filled spheres, each of which would swallow one hundred thousand evacuees, giving a total in-orbit human presence of ten million people. Yet even as the Space Dormitories were being populated, work would be under way on the thousand Exodus Arks that would actually carry the evacuees out of the system. The Arks would be built in orbit, using materials extracted and refined from the moon's crust. Merlin had already indicated to Minla's experts that they could expect to find a certain useful isotope of helium in the topsoil of the moon, an isotope that would enable the Arks to be powered by nuclear fusion engines of an ancient and well-tested design.

'Forced birth control, and mass evacuation,' he said, grimacing.

'That's going to take some tough policing. What if people don't go along with your programme?'

'They'll go along,' Minla said.

'Even if that means shooting a few, to make a point?'

'Millions have already died, Merlin. If it takes a few more to guarantee the efficient execution of the evacuation programme, I see that as a price worth paying.'

'You can't push human society that hard. It snaps.'

'There's no such thing as society,' Minla told him.

Presently she had the pilot bring them below supersonic speed, and then down to a hovering standstill above what Merlin took to be an abandoned building, perched near the shore amidst the remains of what must once have been a great ocean seaport. The flying wing lowered itself on ducted jets, blowing dust and debris in all directions until its landing gear kissed scorched earth and the engines quietened.

'We'll take a stroll outside,' Minla said. 'There's something I want you to see. Something that will convince you of our seriousness.'

'I'm not sure I need convincing.'

'I want you to see it nonetheless. Take this cloak.' She handed him a surprisingly heavy garment.

'Lead impregnated?'

'Just a precaution. Radiation levels are actually very low in this sector.'

They disembarked via an escalator that had folded down from the flying wing's belly, accompanied by a detachment of guards. The armed men moved ahead, sweeping the ground with things that looked like metal brooms before ushering Minla and Merlin forwards. They followed a winding path through scorched rubble and junk, taking care not to trip over the obstacles and broken ground. Calliope had set during their descent and a biting wind was now howling into land from the sea, setting his teeth on edge. From somewhere in the distance a siren rose and fell on a mournful cycle. Despite Minla's assurance concerning the radioactivity, Merlin swore he could already feel his skin tingling. Overhead, stars poked through the thinning layer of moonlit clouds.

When at last he looked up, he saw that the solitary building was in fact an enormous stone monument. It towered a hundred metres above the flying wing, stepped like a ziggurat and cut and engraved with awesome precision. Letters in Lecythus A marched in stentorian ranks across the highest vertical face. Beyond the monument, grey-black water lapped at the shattered remains of a promenade. The monument was presumably designed to weather storms, but it would only take one spring tide to submerge its lower flanks completely. Merlin wondered why Minla's people hadn't set it on higher ground.

'It's impressive.'

'There are a hundred monuments like this on Lecythus,' Minla told him, drawing her cloak tighter around herself. 'We faced them with whetstone, would you believe it. It turns out to be very good for making monuments, especially when you don't want the letters to be worn away in a handful of centuries.'

'You built a hundred of these?' Merlin asked.

'That's just the start. There'll be a thousand by the time we're finished. When we are gone, when all other traces of our culture have been erased from time, we hope that at least one of these monuments will remain. Shall I read you the inscription?'

Merlin had still learned nothing of the native writing, and he'd neglected to wear the lenses that would have allowed *Tyrant* to overlay a translation.

'You'd better.'

'It says that once a great human society lived on Lecythus, in peace and harmony. Then came a message from the stars, a warning that our world was to be destroyed by the fire of the sun itself, or something even worse. So we made preparations to abandon the world that had been our home for so long, and to commence a journey into the outer darkness of interstellar space, looking for a new home in the stars. One day, thousands or tens of thousands after our departure, you, the people who read this message, may find us. For now you are welcome to make of this world what you will. But know that this planet was ours, and it remains ours, and that one day we shall make it our home again.'

'I like the bit about "peace and harmony".'

'History is what we write, not what we remember. Why should we tarnish the memory of our planet by enshrining our less noble deeds?'

'Spoken like a true leader, Minla.'

At that moment one of the guards raised his rifle and projected a line of tracer fire into the middle distance. Something hissed and scurried into the cover of debris.

'We should be leaving,' Minla said. 'Regressives come out at night, and some of them are armed.'

'Regressives?'

'Dissident political elements. Suicide cultists who'd rather die on Lecythus than cooperate in the evacuation effort. They're our problem, Merlin, not yours.'

He'd heard stories about the regressives, but had dismissed them as rumour until now. They were the survivors of the war, people who hadn't submitted eagerly to the iron rule of Minla's new Planetary Government. Details that didn't fit into the plan, and which therefore had to be brushed aside or suppressed or given a subhuman name. He pulled the cloak tighter, anxious not to spend a minute longer on the surface than necessary. But even as Minla turned and began walking back to the waiting aircraft – moonlight picked out the elegant sweep of its single great wing – something tugged at him, holding him to the spot.

'Minla,' he called, a crack in his voice.

She stopped and turned around. 'What is it, Merlin?'

'I've got something for you.' He reached under the cloak and fished out the gift she had given him as a girl, holding it before him. He'd had it with him for days, waiting for the moment he hoped would never come.

Impatiently, Minla retraced her steps. 'I said we should be leaving. What do you want to give me?'

He handed her the sliver of whetstone. 'A little girl gave me this. I don't think I know that little girl any more.'

Minla looked at the stone with a curl of disgust on her face. 'That was forty years ago.'

'Not to me. To me it was less than a year. I've seen a lot of changes since you gave me that gift.'

'We all have to grow up sometime, Merlin.' For a moment he thought she was going to hand him back the gift, or at least slip it into one of her own pockets. Instead, Minla let it drop to the ground. Merlin reached to pick it up, but it was too late. The stone fell into a dark crack between two shattered paving slabs, Merlin hearing the chink as it bounced off something and fell even deeper.

'It's gone.'

'It was just a silly stone,' Minla said. 'That's all. Now let's be on our way.'

Merlin looked back at the lapping waters as he followed Minla

227

to the moonlit flying wing. Something about the whetstone, something about the tides of that sea, something about the moon itself kept nagging at the back of his mind. There was a connection, trivial or otherwise, that he was missing.

He was sure it would come to him sooner or later.

Minla walked with a stick, clicking its hard metal shaft against the echoing flooring of the station's observation deck. Illness or injury had disfigured her since their last meeting; she wore her greying hair in a lopsided parting, hanging down almost to the collar on her right side. Merlin could not say for certain what had happened to Minla, since she was careful to turn her face away from him whenever they spoke. But in the days since his revival he had already heard talk of assassination attempts, some of which had apparently come close to succeeding. Minla seemed more stooped and frail than he remembered, as if she had worked every hour of those twenty years.

She interrupted a light-beam with her hand, opening the viewing shields. 'Behold the Space Dormitories,' she said, declaiming as if she had an audience of thousands rather than a single man standing only a few metres away. 'Rejoice, Merlin. You played a part in this.'

Through the window, wheeling with the gentle rotation of the orbital station, the nearest Dormitory loomed larger than Lecythus in the sky. The wrinkled grey sphere would soon reach operational pressure, its skin becoming taut. The final sun-mirrors were being assembled in place, manipulated by mighty articulated robots. Cargo rockets were coming and going by the minute, while the first wave of evacuees had already taken up residence in the polar holding pens.

Twenty Dormitories were ready now; the remaining eighty would come online within two years. Every day, hundreds of atomic rockets lifted from the surface of Lecythus, carrying evacuees – packed into their holds at the maximum possible human storage density, like a kind of three-dimensional jigsaw of flesh and blood – or cargo, in the form of air, water and prefabricated parts for the other habitats. Each rocket launch deposited more radioactivity into the atmosphere of the doomed world. It was now fatal to breathe that air for more than a few hours, but the slow poisoning of Lecythus was of no concern to the Planetary

Government. The remaining surface-bound colonists, those who would occupy the other Dormitories when they were ready, awaited transfer in pressurised bunkers, in conditions that were at least as spartan as anything they would have to endure in space. Merlin had offered the services of *Tyrant* to assist with the evacuation effort, but as efficient and fast as his ship was, it would have made only a token difference to the speed of the exercise.

That was not to say that there were not difficulties, or that the programme was exactly on schedule. Merlin was gladdened by the progress he saw in some areas, disheartened in others. Before he slept, the locals had grilled him for help with their prototype atomic rockets, seemingly in the expectation that Merlin would provide magic remedies for the failures that had dogged them so far. But Merlin could only help in a limited fashion. He knew the basic principles of building an atomic rocket, but little of the detailed knowledge needed to circumvent a particular problem. Minla's experts were frustrated, and then dismayed. He tried explaining to them that though an atomic rocket might be primitive compared to the engines in *Tyrant*, that didn't mean it was simple, or that its construction didn't involve many subtle principles. 'I know how a sailing ship works,' he said, trying to explain himself. 'But that doesn't mean I could build one myself, or show a master boat-builder how to improve his craft.'

They wanted to know why he couldn't just give them the technology in *Tyrant* itself.

'My ship is capable of self-repair,' he'd said, 'but it isn't capable of making copies of itself. That's a deep principle, embodied in the logical architecture at a very profound level.'

'Then run off a blueprint of your engines. Let us copy what we need from the plans,' they said.

'That won't work. The components in *Tyrant* are manufactured to exacting tolerances, using materials your chemistry can't even explain, let alone reproduce.'

'Then show us how to improve our manufacturing capability, until we can make what we need.'

'We don't have time for that. *Tyrant* was manufactured by a culture that had had over ten thousand years of experience in spacefaring, not to mention knowledge of industrial processes and inventions dating back at least as far again. You can't cross that kind of gap in fifty years, no matter how much you might want to.'

'Then what are we supposed to do?'

'Keep trying,' Merlin said. 'Keep making mistakes, and learning from them. That's all any culture ever does.'

That was exactly what they had done, across twenty painful years. The rockets worked now, after a fashion, but they'd arrived late and there was already a huge backlog of people and parts to be shifted into space. The Dormitories should have been finished and occupied by now, with work already under way on the fleet of Exodus Arks. But the Arks had met obstacles as well. The lunar colonisation and materials-extraction programme had run into unanticipated difficulties, requiring that the Arks be assembled from components made on Lecythus. The atomic rocket production lines were already running at maximum capacity without the burden of carrying even more tonnage into space.

'This is good,' Merlin told Minla. 'But you still need to step things up.'

'We're aware of that,' she answered testily. 'Unfortunately, some of your information proved less than accurate.'

Merlin blinked at her. 'It did?'

'Our scientists made a prototype for the fusion drive, according to your plans. Given the limited testing they've been able to do, they say it works very well. It wouldn't be a technical problem to build all the engines we need for the Exodus Arks. So I'm told, at least.'

'Then what's the issue?'

Her hand gripped the walking stick like a talon. 'Fuel, Merlin. You told us we'd find helium three in the topsoil of our moon. Well, we didn't. Not enough to suit our needs, anyway.'

'Then you mustn't have been looking properly.'

'I assure you we looked, Merlin. You were mistaken. In fact almost everything you told us to expect on the moon turned out to be wrong. You really didn't pay much attention to it on your way in to Lecythus, did you?'

'It was a moon. I had a few other things on my mind.'

'Not only can't we mine it for helium three, but it isn't much good for anything else. The surface gravity's much less than you led us to expect, which complicates our operations tremendously. Things float away at the least provocation. Our experts say the density's so low we shouldn't expect to find anything useful under the crust. Certainly not the heavy ores and precious metals you promised us.'

'I don't know what to say.'

'That you were wrong?'

'I've seen a few moons, Minla. You get used to them. If this one's a lot less dense than I thought, then there's something weird about its chemistry.' Merlin paused, feeling himself on the edge of something important, but whatever it was remained just out of reach.

'Well, it doesn't matter now. We'll just have to find fuel from an alternative source, and redesign our fusion drive accordingly. We'll need your help, if we aren't to fall hopelessly behind schedule.' Minla extended a withered hand towards the wheeling view. 'To have come so far, to have reached this point, and then *failed* ... that would be worse than having never tried at all, don't you think?'

Chastened, Merlin scratched at his chin. 'I'll do what I can. Let me talk to the fusion engineers.'

'I've scheduled a meeting. They're *very* anxious to talk to you.' Minla paused. 'There's something you should know, though. They've seen you make a mistake. They'll still be interested in what you have to say, but don't expect blind acceptance of your every word. They know you're human now.'

'I never said I wasn't.'

'You didn't, no. I'll give you credit for that. But for a little while some of us allowed ourselves to believe it.'

Minla turned and walked away, the tap of her stick echoing into the distance.

As space wars went, it was brief and relatively tame, certainly by comparison with some of the more awesome battles delineated in the Cohort's pictorial history. The timeworn frescos on the swallowships commemorated engagements where entire solar systems were reduced to mere tactical details, hills or ditches in the terrain of a much larger strategic landscape, and where the participants – human and Husker both – were moving at significant fractions of the speed of light and employing relativistic weapons of world-shattering destructive potential. A single skirmish could eat up many centuries of planetary time, whole lifetimes from the point of view of a starship's crew. The war itself was a thing inseparably entwined with recorded history, a monstrous, choking structure with its roots reaching into the loam of deep time, and whose end must be assumed (by all except Merlin, at least) to lie in the unimaginably remote future.

Here, the theatre of conflict was considerably less than half a light-second in diameter, encompassing only the immediate space around Lecythus, with its girdle of half-finished Dormitories and Exodus Arks. The battle lasted barely a dozen hours, between first and last detonation. With the exception of Merlin's own late intervention, no weapons more potent than hydrogen bombs were deployed. Horrific, certainly, but possessed of a certain genteel precision compared to the weapons that had consumed Plenitude.

It began with a surprise strike from the surface, using a wave of commandeered atomic rockets. It seemed that the Regressives had gained control of one of the rocket assembly and launch complexes. The rockets had no warheads, but that didn't matter: kinetic energy, and the explosive force stored in their atomic engines, was still enough to inflict havoc on their targets. The weapons had been aimed with surprising accuracy. The first wave destroyed half of the unfinished Dormitories, inflicting catastrophic damage on many of the others. By the time the second wave was rising, orbital defences had sprung into action, but by then it was too late to intercept more than a handful of the missiles. Many of the atomic rockets were being piloted by suicide crews, steering their charges through Minla's hastily erected countermeasure screens. By the third hour, the Planetary Government was beginning to retaliate against Regressive elements using atmospheric-entry interceptors, but while they could pick away at enemy fortifications on the ground, they couldn't penetrate the anti-missile cordon around the launch complex itself. Rogue warheads chipped away at the edges of aerial land masses, sending mountain-sized boulders crashing to the surface. Even as the battle raged, brutal tidal waves ravaged the already-frail coastal communities. As the hours ticked by, Minla's analysts maintained a grim toll of the total numbers of surface and orbital casualties. In the fifth and sixth hours, more Dormitories fell to the assault. Stray fire accounted for even more losses. A temporary ceasefire in the seventh hour was only caused by the temporary occultation of the launch complex by a medium-sized aerial land mass. When the skies were clear again, the rockets rose up with renewed fury.

'They've hit all but one of the Exodus Arks,' Minla said, when the battle was in its ninth hour. 'We just had time to move the final ship out of range of the atomics. But if they find a way to increase their reach, by eliminating more payload mass ...' She turned her face from his. 'It'll all have been for nothing, Merlin. They'll have won, and the last sixty years may as well not have happened.'

He felt preternaturally calm, knowing exactly what was coming. 'What do you want me to do?'

'Intervene,' Minla said. 'Use whatever force is merited.'

'I offered once. You said no.'

'You changed your mind once. Now I'm changing mine.'

Merlin went to *Tyrant*. He ordered the ship to deliver a concentrated charm-torp salvo against the compromised rocket facility, bringing more energy to bear on that one tiny area of land than had been deployed in all the years of the atomic wars. There was no need for him to accompany his ship; like a well-trained dog, *Tyrant* was perfectly capable of carrying out his orders without direct supervision.

They watched the spectacle from orbit. When the electric-white fire erupted on the horizon of Lecythus, brightening that entire limb of the planet in the manner of a stuttering cold sunrise, Merlin felt Minla's hand tighten around his own. For all her frailty, for all that the years had taken from her, astonishing steel remained in that grip.

'Thank you,' she said. 'You may just have saved us all.'

It had been ten years.

Lecythus and its sun now lay many light-weeks to stern. The one remaining Exodus Ark had reached five per cent of the speed of light. In sixty years – faster, if the engine could be improved – it would streak into another system, one that might offer the possibility of landfall. It flew alongside the gossamer line of the Waynet, using the tube as cover from Husker long-range sensors. The Exodus Ark carried only twelve hundred exiles, few of whom would live long enough to see another world.

The hospital was near the core of the ship, safely distant from the sleeting energies of interstellar radiation or the exotic emissions of the Waynet. Many of its patients were veterans of the Regressive War, victims of the viciously ingenious injuries wrought by the close conjunction of vacuum and heat, radiation and kinetic energy. Most of them would be dead by the time the fusion engine was silenced for cruise phase. For now they were being afforded the care appropriate to war heroes, even those who screamed bloodcurdling pleas for the painkilling mercy of euthanasia.

In a soundproofed private annexe of that same complex, Minla also lay in the care of machines. This time the assassins had come closer than ever before, and they had very nearly achieved their objective. Yet she'd survived, and the prognosis for a complete recovery – so Merlin was informed – was deemed higher than seventy-five per cent. More than could be said of Minla's aides, injured in the same attack, but they were at least receiving the best possible care in *Tyrant*'s frostwatch cabinets. The exercise was, Merlin knew, akin to knitting together human-shaped sculptures from a bloody stew of meat and splintered bone, and then hoping that those sculptures would retain some semblance of mind. Minla would have presented no challenge at all, but the Planetary Director had declined the offer of frostwatch care herself, preferring to give up her place to one of her underlings. Knowing that, Merlin allowed himself a momentary flicker of empathy.

He walked into the room, coughing to announce himself. 'Hello, Minla.'

She lay on her back, her head against the pillow, though she was not asleep. Slowly she turned to face Merlin as he approached. She looked very old, very tired, but she still found the energy to form a smile.

'It's so good of you to come. I was hoping, but ... I didn't dare ask. I know how busy you've been with the engine upgrade study.'

'I could hardly not pay you a visit. Even though I had a devil of a job persuading your staff to let me through.'

'They're too protective of me. I know my own strength, Merlin. I'll get through this.'

'I believe you will.'

Minla's gaze settled on his hand. 'Are those for me?'

He had a bouquet of alien flowers. They were of a peculiar dark hue, a shade that ought to have appeared black in the room's subdued gold lighting yet which was clearly and unmistakably purple, revealed by its own soft inner illumination. They had the look of a detail that had been hand-tinted in a black and white photograph, so that it appeared to float above the rest of the image.

'Of course,' Merlin said. 'I always bring flowers, don't I?'

'You always used to. Then you stopped.'

'Perhaps it's time to start again.'

He set them by her bedside, in the water-filled vase that was already waiting. They were not the only flowers in the room, but the purple ones seemed to suck the very colour from the others.

'They're beautiful,' Minla said. 'It's like I've never seen anything precisely that colour before. It's as if there's a whole circuit in my brain that's never been activated until now.'

'I chose them especially. They're famous for their beauty.'

Minla lifted her head from the pillow, her eyes brightening with curiosity. 'Now you'll have to tell me where they're from.'

'It's a long story.'

'That never stopped you before.'

'A world called Lacertine. It's ten thousand light-years from here; many days of shiptime, even in the Waynet. I don't even know if it still exists.'

'Tell me about Lacertine,' she said, pronouncing the name of the world with her usual scrupulousness.

'It's a very beautiful planet, orbiting a hot blue star. They say the planet must have been moved into its present orbit by the Waymakers, from another system entirely. The seas and skies are a shimmering electric blue, the forests a dazzle of purple and violet and pink; colours that you've only ever seen when you close your eyes against the sun and see patterns behind your eyelids. White citadels rise above the treeline, towers linked by a filigree of delicate bridges.'

'Then there are people on Lacertine?'

Merlin thought of the occupants, and nodded. 'Adapted, of course. Everything that grows on Lacertine was bioengineered to tolerate the scalding light from the sun. They say if something can grow there, it can grow almost anywhere.'

'Have you been there?'

He shook his head ruefully. 'Never been within a thousand light-years of the place.'

'I'll never see it. Nor any of the other places you've told me about.'

'There are places I'll never see. Even with the Waynet, I'm still just one human man, with one human life. Even the Waymakers didn't live long enough to glimpse more than a fraction of their empire.'

'It must make you very sad.'

'I take each day as it comes. I'd rather take good memories from one world than fret about the thousand I'll never see.'

'You're a wise man,' Minla said. 'We were lucky to get you.'

Merlin smiled. He was silent for many moments, letting Minla enjoy the last calmness of mind she would ever know. 'There's something I need to tell you,' he said eventually.

She must have heard something in his tone of voice. 'What, Merlin?'

'There's a good chance you're all going to die.'

Her tone became sharp. 'We don't need you to remind us of the risks.'

'I'm talking about something that's going to happen sooner rather than later. The ruse of shadowing the Waynet didn't work. It was the best thing to do, but there was always a chance ...' Merlin spread his hands in exaggerated apology, as if there had ever been something he could have done about it. '*Tyrant*'s detected a Husker attack swarm, six elements lying a light-month ahead of you. You don't have time to steer or slow down. They'd shadow every move you made, even if you tried to shake them off.'

'You promised us—'

'I promised you nothing. I just gave you the best advice I could. If you hadn't shadowed the Waynet, they'd have found you even sooner.'

'We aren't using the ramscoop design. You said we'd be safe if we stuck to fusion motors. The electromagnetic signature—'

'I said you'd be *safer*. There were never any cast-iron guarantees.'

'You lied to us.' Minla turned suddenly spiteful. 'I never trusted you.'

'I did all in my power to save you.'

'Then why are you standing there looking so calm, when you know we're going to die?' But before Merlin had time to answer, Minla had seen the answer for herself. 'Because you can leave,' she said, nodding at her own percipience. 'You have your ship, and a syrinx. You can slip into the Waynet and outrun the enemy.'

'I'm leaving,' Merlin said. 'But I'm not running.'

'Aren't they one and the same?'

'Not this time. I'm going back to Plenitude, I mean Lecythus, to do what I can for the people we left behind. The people you condemned to death.'

'Me, Merlin?'

'I examined the records of the Regressive War: not just the official documents, but *Tyrant*'s own data logs. And I saw what I should have seen at the time, but didn't. It was a ruse. It was too damned easy, the way they took control of that rocket factory. You let them, Minla.'

'I did nothing of the kind.'

'You knew the whole evacuation project was never going to be ready on time. The Space Dormitories were behind schedule, there were problems with the Exodus Arks—'

'Because you told us falsehoods about the helium in the moon's soil.'

Merlin raised a warning hand. 'We'll get to that. The point is, your plans were in tatters. But you could still have completed more Dormitories and ships, if you'd been willing to leave the system a little later. You could still have saved more people than you did, albeit at a slightly increased risk to your own survival. But that wasn't acceptable. You wanted to leave there and then. So you engineered the whole Regressive attack, set it up as a pretext for an early departure.'

'The Regressives were real!' Minla hissed.

'But you gave them the keys to that rocket silo, and the know-how to target and guide those missiles. Funny how their attack just missed the one station that you were occupying, you and all your political cronies, and that you managed to move the one Exodus Ark to safety just in time. Damned convenient, Minla.'

'I'll have you shot for this, Merlin.'

'Good luck. Try laying a hand on me, and see how far it gets you. My ship's listening in on this conversation. It can put proctors into this room in a matter of seconds.'

'And the moon, Merlin? Do you have an excuse for the error that cost us so dearly?'

'I don't know. Possibly. That's why I'm going back to Lecythus. There are still people on the surface – Regressives, allies, I don't care. And people you abandoned in orbit, as well.'

'They'll all die. You said it yourself.'

He raised a finger. 'If they don't leave. But maybe there's a way. Again, I should have seen it sooner. But that's me all the way. I take a long time to put the pieces together, but I get there in the end. Just like Dowitcher, the man who gave your father the whetstone.'

'It was just a stone.'

'So you said. In fact, it was a vital clue to the nature of your world. It took spring tides and neap tides to lay down those patterns. But you said it yourself: Lecythus doesn't have spring tides and neap tides. Not any more, at least.'

'I'm sure this means something to you.'

'Something happened to your moon, Minla. When that whetstone formed, your moon was raising tides on Lecythus. When the moon and Calliope were tugging on your seas in the same direction, you got a spring tide. When they were balancing each other, you got a neap tide. Hence the patterning on the whetstone. But now the tides are the same from day to day. Calliope's still there, so that only leaves the moon. It isn't exerting the same gravitational pull it used to. Like you told me, the surface gravity is much lower than you'd expect. Oh, it weighs *something* – but nowhere near as much as it should, based on its size and appearance. If you could skip forward a few hundred million years and examine a piece of whetstone laid down now, you'd probably find very faint variations in sediment thickness. But whatever the effect is now, it must be insignificant compared to the time when your whetstone was formed. Yet the moon's still there, in what appears to be the same orbit. So what's happened?'

'You tell me, Merlin.'

'I don't think it's a moon any more. I think the original moon got ripped to pieces to make your armoured sky. I don't know how much of the original mass was used for that, but I'm guessing it was quite a significant fraction. The question is, what happened to the remains?'

'I'm sure you have a theory.'

'I think they made a fake moon out of the leftovers. It sits there in your sky, it orbits Lecythus, but it doesn't pull on your seas the way the old one used to. It has gravity, but it's not enough to affect the oceans to the same degree. And you're right: it's much less dense than I expected. I really should have paid more attention. Maybe if I did I could have spared Lecythus all this bloodshed.'

'And now you understand everything?'

'I understand that the moon's new. It's not been sitting there long enough to soak up billions of years of particles from the solar wind. That's why you didn't find the helium you were expecting.'

'So what is it?'

'That's what I'm keen to find out. The thing is, I know what Dowitcher was thinking now. He knew that wasn't a real moon. Which begs the question: what's inside it? And could it make a difference to the survivors you left behind?'

'Hiding inside a shell won't help them,' Minla said. 'You already told us we'd achieve nothing by digging tunnels into Lecythus.'

'I'm not thinking about hiding. I'm thinking about moving. What if the moon's an escape vehicle? An Exodus Ark big enough to take the entire population?'

'You have no evidence.'

'I have this.' With that, Merlin produced one of Minla's old picture books. Seventy years had aged its pages to a brittle yellow, dimming the vibrancy of the old inks. But the linework in the illustrations was still clear enough. Merlin held the book open at a particular page, letting Minla look at it. 'Your people had a memory of arriving on Lecythus in a moon-sized ship,' he said. 'Maybe that was true. Equally, maybe it was a case of muddling one thing with another. I'm wondering if the thing you were meant to remember was not that you came by moon, but that you could leave by one.'

Minla stared at the picture. For a moment, like a breeze on a summer's day, Merlin felt a wave of almost unbearable sadness pass through the room. It was as if the picture had transported her back to her childhood, before she had set her life on the trajectory that, seventy years later, would bring it to this bed, this soundproofed room, the shameful survival of this one ship. The last time she had looked at the picture, everything had been possible, all life's opportunities open to her. She'd been the daughter of a powerful and respected man, with influence and wisdom at her fingertips. And yet from all the choices presented to her, she had selected this one dark path, and followed it to its conclusion.

'Even if it is a ship,' she said softly, 'you'll never get them all aboard.'

'I'll die trying.'

'And us? We get abandoned to our fates?'

Merlin smiled: he'd been expecting the question. 'There are twelve hundred people on this ship, some of them children. They weren't all party to your schemes, so they don't all deserve to die when you meet the Huskers. That's why I'm leaving behind weapons and a detachment of proctors to show you how to install and use them.'

For the first time since his arrival in the room, Minla spoke like a leader again. 'Will they make a difference?'

'They'll give your ship a fighting chance. That's the best I can offer.'

'Then we'll take what we're given.'

'I'm sorry it came to this. I played a part in what you became, of that I've no doubt. But I didn't make you a monster.'

'No,' she said. 'I'll at least take credit for myself, and for the fact that I saved twelve hundred of my people. If it took a monster to do that, doesn't that mean we sometimes need monsters?'

'Maybe we do. But that doesn't mean we should forgive them for what they are, even for an instant.' Gently, as if bestowing a gift, Merlin placed the picture book on Minla's recumbent form. 'I'm afraid I have to go now. There won't be much time when I get back to Lecythus.'

'Please,' she said. 'Not like this. Not this way.'

'This is how it ends,' he said, before turning from her bed and walking to the exit. 'Goodbye, Minla.'

Twenty minutes later he was in the Waynet, racing back to Lecythus.

There's a lot to tell, and one day I'll get around to writing it up properly. For now it's enough to say that I was right to trust my instincts about the moon. I just wish I'd put the clues together sooner than I did. Perhaps then Minla would never have had to commit her crimes.

I didn't save as many as I'd have wished, but I did save some of the people Minla left behind to die. I suppose that has to count for something. It was close, but if there's one thing to be said for Waymaker-level technology, it's that it's almost childishly easy to use. They were like babies with the toys of the gods. They left that moon there for a good reason, and while it was necessary for them to camouflage it – it had to be capable of fooling the Huskers, or whoever they built that sky to hide from – the moon itself was obligingly easy to break into, once our purpose became clear. And once it started moving, once its great engines came online after tens of thousands of years of quiet dormancy, no force in the universe could have held it back. I shadowed the fleeing moon long enough to establish that it was headed into a sector that appeared to be free of Husker activity, at least for now. It'll be touch and go for a few centuries, but with force and wisdom on their side, I think they'll make it.

I'm in the Waynet now, riding the flow away from Calliope. The syrinx still works, much to my relief. For a while I considered riding the contraflow, back towards that lone Exodus Ark. By the time I reached them they'd have been only days away from the encounter. But my presence wouldn't have made a decisive difference to their chances of surviving the Huskers, and I couldn't have expected much of a warm welcome.

Not after my final gift to Minla.

I'm glad she never asked me too much about those flowers, or the world they came from. If she'd wanted to know more about Lacertine, she might have sensed that I was holding something back. Such as the fact that the assassin guilds on Lacertine were masters of their craft, known throughout the worlds of the Waynet for their skill and cunning, and that no guild on Lacertine was more revered than the bio-artificers who made the sleepflowers.

It was said that they could make them in any shape, any colour, to match any known flower from any known world. It was said that they could pass all tests save the most microscopic scrutiny. It was said that if you wanted to kill someone, you gave them a gift of flowers from Lacertine.

She would have been dead not long after my departure. The flowers would have detected her presence – they were keyed to locate a single breathing form in a room, most commonly a sleeper – and when the room was quiet they would have become stealthily animate, leaving their vase and creeping from point to point with the slowness of a sundial's shadow, their movement imperceptible to the naked eye, but enough to take them to the face of the sleeper. Their tendrils would have closed around Minla's face with the softness of a lover's caress. Then the paralysing toxins would have hit her nervous system.

I hoped it was painless. I hoped it was quick. But what I remembered *of the Lacertine assassins was that they were known for their cleverness, not their clemency.*

Afterwards, I deleted the sleepflowers from the bio-library.

I knew Minla for less than a year of my life, and for seventy years by another reckoning. Sometimes when I think of her I see a human being in all her dimensions, as real as anyone I've ever known. Other times, I see something two-dimensional, like a faded illustration in one of her books, so thin that the light shines through her.

I don't hate her, even now. But I wish time and tide had never brought us together.

A comfortable number of light-hours behind me, the Waynet has just cut into Calliope's heart. It has already sliced through the photosphere and the star's convection zone. Quite what has happened, or is happening, or will happen, when it touched (or touches, or will touch) the nuclear-burning core is still far from clear.

Theory says that no impulse can travel faster than light. Since my ship is already riding the Waynet's flow at very nearly the speed of light, it seems impossible that any information concerning Calliope's fate will ever be able to catch up with me. And yet . . . several minutes ago I swear that I felt a kick, a jolt in the smooth glide of my flight, as if some report of that destructive event had raced up the flow at superluminal speed, buffeting my little ship.

There's nothing in the data to suggest any unusual event, and I don't have any plans to return to Lecythus and see what became of that world when its sun was gored open. But I still felt something, and if it reached me up the flow of the Waynet, if that impulse bypassed the iron barrier of causality itself, I can't begin to imagine the energies that must have been involved, or what must have happened to the strand of the Waynet behind me. Perhaps it's unravelling, and I'm about to breathe my last breath before I become a thin smear of naked quarks, stretched across several billion kilometres of interstellar space.

That would certainly be one way to go.

Frankly, it would be nice to have the luxury to dwell on such fears. But I still have a gun to find, and I'm not getting any younger.

Mission resumed.

Punishment saved Sora.

If her marksmanship had not been the worst in her class, she would never have been assigned the task of overseeing proctors down in ship's docks. She would not have had to stand for hours, alone except for her familiar, running a laser-stylus across the ore samples the proctors brought back to the swallowship, dreaming of finishing shift and meeting Verdin. It was boring – menial work. But because the docks were open to vacuum, the work required a pressure suit.

'Got to be a drill,' she said, when the attack began.

'No,' her familiar said. 'It really does seem as if they've caught up with us.'

Sora's calm evaporated.

'How many?'

'Four elements of the swarm; standard attack pattern; coherent-matter weapons at maximum range . . . novamine countermeasures deployed but seemingly ineffective . . . initial damage reports severe and likely underestimate—'

The floor pitched under her feet. The knee-high androform proctors looked to each other nervously. The machines had no more experience of battle than Sora, and unlike her they had never experienced the simulations of warcrèche.

Sora dropped the clipboard.

'What do I do?'

'My advice,' her familiar said, 'is that you engage that old mammalian flight response and run like hell.'

She obeyed, stooping down low-ceilinged corridors festooned with pipes, snaking around hand-painted murals that showed decisive battles from the Cohort's history: squadrons of ships exchanging fire, worlds wreathed in flame. The endgame was much swifter than those languid paintings suggested. The swarm had been chasing *Snipe* for nine years of shiptime, during which Sora had passed through warcrèche to adulthood. Yet beyond the ship's relativistic frame of reference, nearly sixty years had passed. Captain Tchagra had done all she could to lose the swarm. Her last gamble had been the most desperate of all: using the vicious gravity of a neutron star to slingshot the swallowship on another course, one that the chasing ships ought not to have been able to follow, unless they skimmed the neutron star even more suicidally. But they had, forcing *Snipe* to slow from relativistic flight and nurse its wounds in a fallow system. It was there that the swarm attacked.

Near the end, the floor drifted away from Sora's feet as ship's gravity faltered, and she had to progress hand over hand.

'This is wrong,' Sora said, arriving in the pod bay. 'This section should be pressurised. And where is everyone?'

'Attack must be a lot worse than those initial reports suggested. I advise you to get into a pod as quickly as you can.'

'I can't go, not without Verdin.'

'Let me worry about him.'

Knowing better than to argue, Sora climbed into the nearest of the cylindrical pods mounted on a railed pallet ready for injection into the tunnel. The lid clammed shut, air rushing in.

'What about Verdin?'

'Safe. The attack was bad, but I'm hearing reports that the aft sections made it.'

'Get me out of here, then.'

'With all pleasure.'

Acceleration came suddenly, numbness gloving her spine.

'I've got worse news,' her familiar said. The voice was an echo of Sora's own, but an octave lower and calmer, like a slightly older and more sensible sister. 'I'm sorry, but I had to lie to you. My highest duty is your preservation. I knew that if I didn't lie, you wouldn't save yourself.'

Sora thought about that, while she watched the ship die from the vantage point of her pod. The Husker weapons had hit its middle sphere, barely harming the parasol of the swallowscoop. Bodies fell into space, stiff and tiny as snowflakes. Light licked from the sphere. *Snipe* became a flower of hurting whiteness, darkening as it bloomed.

'What did you lie about?'

'About Verdin. I'm sorry. He didn't make it. None of them did.'

Sora waited for the impact of the words, aware that what she felt now was only a precursor to the shock, like the moment when she touched the hot barrel of a gun in warcrèche, and her fingers registered the heat but the pain itself did not arrive instantly, giving her time to prepare for its sting. She waited, for what she knew – in all likelihood – would be the worst thing she had ever felt. And waited.

'What's wrong with me? Why don't I feel anything?'

'Because I'm not allowing it. Not just now. If you opt to grieve at some later point then I can restore the appropriate brain functions.'

Sora thought about that too.

'You couldn't make it sound any more clinical, could you?'

'Don't imagine this is easy for me, Sora. I don't exactly have a great deal of experience in this matter.'

'Well, now you're getting it.'

She was alone, no arguing with that. None of the other crew had survived – and she had only made it because she was on punishment duty for her failings as a soldier. No use looking for help: the nearest Cohort motherbase was seventy light-years towards the Galactic Core. Even if there were swallowships within broadcast range it would take decades for the nearest to hear her; decades again for them to curve around and rescue her. No; she would not be rescued. She would drift here, circling a nameless sun, until her energy reserves could not even sustain frostwatch.

'What about the enemy?' Sora said, seized by an urge to gaze upon her nemesis. 'Where are the bastards?'

A map of the system scrolled across the faceplate of herhelmet, overlaid with the four Husker ships that had survived the slingshot around the neutron star. They were near the two Ways that punched through the system, marked on the map as fine straight flaws, surrounded by shaded hazard regions. Perhaps, like the Cohort, the Huskers were trying to find a way to enter the Waynet without being killed; trying to gain the final edge in a war that had lasted twenty-three thousand years. The Huskers had been at war with the Cohort ever since those ruthless alien cyborgs had emerged from ancient Dyson spheres near the Galactic Core.

'They're not interested in me,' Sora said. 'They know that even if anyone survived the attack, they won't survive much longer. That's right, isn't it?'

'They're nothing if not pragmatic.'

'I want to die. I want you to put me to sleep painlessly and then kill me. You can do that, can't you? I mean, if I order it?'

Sora did not complete her next thought. What happened, instead, was that her consciousness stalled, except for the awareness of the familiar, thoughts bleeding into her own. She had experienced something like this stalling aboard *Snipe*, when the crew went into frostwatch for the longest transits between engagements. But no frostwatch had ever felt this long. After an age, her thoughts oozed back to life. She groped for the mental routines that formed language.

'You lied again!'

'This time I plead innocence. I just put you in a position where you couldn't give me the order you were about to. Seemed the best thing under the circumstances.'

'I'll bet it did.' In that instant of stalled thought, the pod had turned opaque, concealing the starscape and the debris of the ship. 'What else?'

The pod turned glassy across its upper surface, revealing a slowly wheeling starscape above filthy ice. The glass, once perfectly transparent, now had a smoky lustre. 'Once you were sleeping,' the familiar said, 'I used the remaining fuel to guide the pod to a cometary shard. It seemed safer than drifting.'

'How long?' Sora was trying to guess from the state of the pod, but the interior looked as new as when she had ejected from *Snipe*. The sudden smokiness of the glass was alarming, however: Sora did not want to think how many years of cosmic ray abrasion would be required to scuff the material to that degree. 'Are we talking years or decades, or more than that?'

'Shall I tell you why I woke you, first?'

'If it's going to make any difference—'

'I think it makes all the difference, quite frankly.' The familiar paused for effect. 'Someone has decided to pay this system a visit.'

Sora saw it on the map now, revised to account for the new relative positions of the celestial bodies in this system. The unidentified ship was denoted by a lilac arrow, moving slowly between

Waynet transit nodes, the thickened points where the Way lines intercepted the ecliptic plane.

'It must have a functioning syrinx,' Sora said, marvelling, and for the first time feeling as if death was not the immediately preferable option. 'It must be able to use the Ways.'

'Worth waking you up for, I think.'

Sora had eight hours to signal the ship before it reached the other node of the Waynet. She left the pod – stiff, aching and disorientated, but basically functional – and walked to the edge of a crater, one that the familiar had mapped on the cometary shard some years earlier. Three thousand years earlier, to be precise, for that was how long it had taken to scratch the sheen from the glass. The news had been shocking, at first – until Sora realised that the span of time was not in itself important. All that she had ever known was the ship; now that it was gone, it hardly mattered how much time had passed.

Yet now there was this newcomer. Sora criss-crossed the crater, laying a line of metallic monofilament, doubling back on her trail many times until a glistening scribble covered the crater. It looked like the work of a drunken spider, but the familiar assured her it would focus more than satisfactorily at radio frequencies. As for the antenna, that was where Sora came in: her suit was sheathed in a conductive epidermis, a shield against plasma and ion-beam weaponry. By modulating current through it, the familiar could generate pulses of radio emission. The radio waves would fly away from Sora in all directions, but a good fraction would be reflected back from the crater in parallel lines. Sora had to make gliding jumps from one rim of the crater to the other, so that she passed through the focus momentarily, synchronised to the intervals when the other ship entered view.

After two hours of light-transit time, the newcomer vectored towards the shard. When it was much closer, Sora secreted herself in a snowhole and set her suit to thermal stealth-mode. The ship nosed in, stiletto-sleek, devilishly hard to see against the stars. It was elongated, carbon-black and nubbed by propulsion modules and weapons of unguessable function, arrayed around the hull like remora. Yet it carried Cohort markings, and had none of the faintly organic attributes of a Husker vessel. Purple flames knifed from the ship's belly, slowing it over the crater. After examining the crater, the ship moved towards the pod and anchored itself to the ice with grapples.

'How did something that small ever get here?'

'Doesn't need to be big,' the familiar said. 'Not if it uses the Waynets.'

After a few minutes, an access ramp lowered down, kissing the ice. A spacesuited figure ambled down the ramp. He moved towards the pod, kicking up divots of frost. The man – he was clearly male, judging by the contours of his suit – knelt down and examined the pod. Ribbed and striped by luminous paint, his suit made him seem naked, scarred by ritual marks of warriorhood. He fiddled with the sleeve, unspooling something before shunting it into a socket in the side of the pod. Then he stood there, head slightly cocked.

'Nosy bastard,' Sora whispered.

'Don't be so ungrateful. He's trying to rescue you.'

'Are you in yet?'

'Can't be certain.' The familiar had copied part of itself into the pod before Sora had left. 'His suit might not even have the capacity to store me.'

'I'm going to make my presence known.'

'Be careful, will you?'

Sora stood, dislodging a flurry of ice. The man turned to her sharply, the spool disengaging from the pod and whisking back into his sleeve. The stripes on his suit flicked over to livid reds and oranges. He opened a fist to reveal something lying in his palm: a designator for the weapons on the ship, which swivelled out from the hull like snakes' heads.

'If I were you,' the familiar said, 'I'd assume the most submissive posture you can think of.'

'Sod that.'

Sora took several steps forwards, trying not to let her fear translate into clumsiness. Her radio chirped to indicate she was online to the other suit.

'Who are you? Can you understand me?'

'Perfectly well,' the man said, after negligible hesitation. His voice was deep and actorly, devoid of any accent Sora knew. 'You're Cohort. We speak Main, give or take a few kiloyears of linguistic drift.'

'You speak it pretty well for someone who's been out there for ten thousand years.'

'And how would one know that?'

'Do the sums. Your ship's from seven thousand years earlier than my own era. And I've just taken a three-thousand-year catnap.'

'Ah. Perhaps if I'd arrived in time to waken you with a kiss you wouldn't be quite so grumpy. But your point was?'

'We shouldn't be able to understand each other at all. Which makes me wonder if you're lying to me.'

'I see.' For a moment Sora thought she heard him chuckling to himself, almost a catlike purring. 'What I'm wondering is why I need to listen to this stuff and nonsense, given that I'm not the one in current need of rescuing.'

His suit calmed, aggressor markings cooling to neutral blues and yellows. He let his hand drop slowly.

'I'd say,' the familiar said, 'that he has a fairly good point.'

Sora stepped closer. 'I'm a little edgy, that's all. Comes with the territory.'

'You were attacked?'

'Slightly. A swarm took out my swallowship.'

'Bad show,' the man said, nodding. 'Haven't seen swallowships for two and a half kiloyears. Too hard for the halo factories to manufacture, once the Huskers started targeting motherbases. The Cohort regressed again – fell back on fusion pulse drives. Before very long they'll be back to generation starships and chemical rockets.'

'Thanks for all the sympathy.'

'Sorry ... it wasn't my intention to sound callous. It's simply that I've been travelling. It gives one a certain – how shall I say – loftiness of perspective? Means I've kept more up to date with current affairs than you have. That's how I understand you.' With his free hand he tapped the side of his helmet. 'I've a database of languages running halfway back to the Flourishing.'

'Bully for you. Who are you, by the way?'

'Ah. Of course. Introductions.' He reached out the free hand, this time in something approximating welcome. 'Merlin.'

It was impossible; it cut against all common sense, but she knew who he was.

It was not that they had ever met. But everyone knew of Merlin; there was no word for him other than legend. Seven, or more properly ten thousand years ago, it was Merlin who had stolen something from the Cohort, vanishing into the galaxy on a quest for what could only be described as a weapon too dreadful to use. He had never been seen again – until, apparently, now.

'Thanks for rescuing me,' Sora said, when he had shown her to the bridge of the ship he called *Tyrant* – a spherical chamber outfitted with huge, black control seats, facing a window of flawless metasapphire overlooking cometary ice.

'Don't overdo the gratitude,' the familiar said.

Merlin shrugged. 'You're welcome.'

'And sorry if I acted a little edgy.'

'Forget it. As you say, comes with the territory. Actually, I'm rather glad I found you. You wouldn't believe how scarce human company is these days.'

'Nobody ever said it was a friendly galaxy.'

'Less so now, believe me. Now the Cohort's started losing whole star systems. I've seen world after world shattered by the Huskers; whole strings of orbiting habitats gutted by nuclear fire. The war's in its terminal stages, and the Cohort isn't in anything resembling a winning position.' Merlin leaned closer to her, sudden enthusiasm burning in his eyes. 'But I've found something that can make a difference, Sora. Or at least, I have rather a good idea where one might find it.'

She nodded slowly. 'Let's see. That wouldn't be Merlin's fabulous gun, by any chance?'

'You're still not entirely sure I'm who I say I am, are you?'

'I've one or two nagging doubts.'

'You're right, of course.' He sighed theatrically and gestured around the bridge. In the areas not reserved for control readouts, the walls were adorned with treasure: trinkets, finery and jewels of staggering artistry and beauty, glinting with the hues of the rarest alloys, inset with precious stones, shaped by the finest lapidary skill of a thousand worlds. There were chips of subtly coloured ceramic and tiny white-light holograms of great brilliance. There were daggers and brooches, ornate ceremonial lasers and bracelets, terrible swords and grotesque, carnelian-eyed carnival masques.

'I thought,' Merlin said, 'that this would be enough to convince you.'

He had sloughed the outer layer of his suit, revealing himself to be what she had on some level feared: a handsome, broad-shouldered man who in every way conformed to the legend she had in mind. Merlin dressed luxuriously, encrusted in jewellery that was, nonetheless, at the dour end of the spectrum compared to what was displayed on the walls. His beard was carefully trimmed and his long, auburn hair hung loose, evoking leonine strength. He radiated magnificence.

'Oh, it's pretty impressive,' Sora said. 'Even if a good fraction of it must have been looted. And maybe I am half-convinced. But you have to admit, it's quite a story.'

'Not from my perspective.' He was fiddling with an intricate ring on one forefinger. 'Since I left on my *quest*' – he spoke the word with exquisite distaste – 'I've lived rather less than eleven years of subjective time. I was as horrified as anyone when I found my little hunt had been magnified into something so ... epic.'

'Bet you were.'

'When I left, there was an unstated expectation that the war could be won within a handful of centuries.' Merlin snapped his fingers at a waiting proctor and had it bring a bowl of fruit. Sora took a plum, examining it suspiciously before consigning it to her mouth. 'But even then,' Merlin continued, 'things were on the turn. I could see it, if no one else could.'

'So you became a mercenary.'

'Freelancer, if you don't mind. Point was, I realised I could better serve humanity outside the Cohort. And old legends kept tickling the back of my mind.' He smiled. 'You see, even legends are haunted by legends.'

He told her the rest, which, in diluted form, she already knew. Yet it was fascinating to hear it from Merlin's lips; to hear the kernel of truth at the core of something around which falsehoods and half-truths had accreted like dust around a protostar. He had gathered many stories, from dozens of human cultures pre-dating the Cohort, spread across thousands of light-years and dispersed through tens of thousands of years of history. The similarities were not always obvious, but Merlin had sifted common patterns, piecing together – as well as he could – an underlying framework of what might just be fact.

'There'd been another war,' Merlin said. 'Smaller than ours, spread across a much smaller volume of space – but no less brutal for all that.'

'How long ago was this?'

'Forty or forty-five kiloyears – not long after the Waymakers vanished, but about twenty kays before anything we'd recognise as the Cohort.' Merlin's eyes seemed to glaze over; an odd, stentorian tone entered his voice: '"In the long, dark centuries of Mid-Galactic history, when a thousand cultures rose, each imagining themselves immune to time, and whose shadows barely reach us across the millennia—"'

'Yes. Very poetic. What *kind* of war, anyway? Human versus human, or human versus alien, like this one?'

'Does it matter? Whoever the enemy was, they aren't coming back. Whatever was used against them was so deadly, so powerful, so *awesome* that it stopped an entire war!'

'Merlin's gun.'

He nodded, lips tight, looking almost embarrassed. 'As if I had some prior claim on it, or was even in some sense responsible for it!' He looked at Sora very intently, the glittering finery of the ship reflected in the gold of his eyes. 'I haven't seen the gun, or even been near it, and it's only recently that I've had anything like a clear idea of what it might actually be.'

'But you think you know where it is?'

'I think so. It isn't far. And it's in the eye of a storm.'

They lifted from the shard, spending eight days in transit to the closest Way, most of the time in frostwatch. Sora had her own quarters: a spherical-walled suite deep in *Tyrant*'s thorax, outfitted in maroon and burgundy. The ship was small, but fascinating to explore – an object lesson in the differences between the Cohort that had manufactured this ship and the one Sora had been raised in. In many respects the ship was more advanced than anything from her own time, especially in the manner of its propulsion, defences and sensors. In other areas the Cohort had gained expertise since Merlin's era. Merlin's proctors were even stupider than those Sora had been looking after when the Husker attack began. There were no familiars in Merlin's time, either, and she saw no reason to educate him about her own neural symbiote.

'Well,' Sora said, when she was alone. 'What can you tell me about the legendary Merlin?'

'Nothing very much at this point.' The familiar had been communicating with the version of itself that had infiltrated *Tyrant*, via Merlin's suit. 'If he's impersonating the historical figure we know as Merlin, he's gone to extraordinary lengths to make the illusion authentic. All the logs confirm that his ship left Cohort-controlled space around ten kiloyears ago, and that he's been travelling ever since.'

'He's back from somewhere. It would help if we knew where.'

'Tricky, given that we have no idea about the deep topology of the Waynet. I can search the starfields for recognisable features, but it'll take a long time, and there'll still be a large element of guesswork.'

'There must be something you can show me.'

'Of course.' The familiar sounded slightly affronted. 'I found images. Some of the formats are obscure, but I think I can make sense of most of them.' And even before Sora had answered, the familiar had warmed a screen in one hemisphere of the suite. Visual records of different solar systems appeared, each entry displayed for a second before being replaced. Each consisted of an orbital map; planets and Waynet nodes were marked relative to each system's sun. The worlds were annotated with enlarged images of each, overlaid with sparse astrophysical and military data, showing the roles – if any – they had played in the war. Merlin had visited other places too. Squid-like protostellar nebulae, stained with green and red and flecked by the light of hot blue stars. Supernova remnants, the viscera of gored stars, a hundred of which had died since the Flourishing, briefly outshining the galaxy.

'What do you think he was looking for?' Sora said. 'These points must have been on the Waynet, but they're a long way from anything we'd call civilisation.'

'I don't know. Souvenir hunting?'

'Are you sure Merlin can't tell you're accessing this information?'

'Absolutely – but why should it bother him unless he's got something to hide?'

'Debatable point.' Sora looked around to the sealed door of her quarters, half-expecting Merlin to enter at any moment. It was absurd, of course – from its present vantage point, the familiar could probably tell precisely where Merlin was in the ship, and give Sora adequate warning. But she still felt uneasy, even as she asked the inevitable question. 'What else?'

'Oh, plenty. Even some visual records of the man himself, caught on the internal cameras.'

'Sorry. A healthy interest in where he's been is one thing, but spying on him is something else.'

'Would it change things if I told you that Merlin hasn't been totally honest with us?'

'You said he hadn't lied.'

'Not about anything significant – which makes this all the odder.' The familiar sounded quietly pleased with itself. 'You're curious now, aren't you?'

Sora sighed. 'You'd better show me.'

Merlin's face appeared on the screen, sobbing. He seemed slightly older to her, although it was difficult to tell, since most of his face was caged behind his hands. She could hardly make out what he was saying, between each sob.

'Thousands of hours of this sort of thing,' the familiar said. 'They started out as serious attempts at keeping a journal, but soon deteriorated into a form of catharsis.'

'I'd say he did well to stay sane at all.'

'More than you realise. We know he's been gone ten thousand years – just as he told us. Well and good. That's objective time. But he also said that only eleven years of shiptime had passed.'

'And that isn't the case?'

'To put a diplomatic gloss on it, I suspect that may be a slight underestimate. By a considerable number of decades. And I don't think he spent much of that time in frostwatch.'

Sora tried to remember what she knew of the methods of longevity available to the Cohort in Merlin's time. 'He looks older in these recordings than he does now – doesn't he?'

The familiar chose not to answer.

When the transit to the Way was almost over, Merlin called her to the bridge.

'We're near the transit node,' he said. 'Take a seat, because the insertion can be a little ... interesting.'

'Transition to Waynet in three hundred seconds,' said the ship's cloyingly calm voice.

The crescent of the cockpit window showed a starfield transected by a blurred twinkling filament, like a solitary wave crossing a lake at midnight. Sora could see blurred stars through the filament, wide as her outspread hand, widening by the second. A thickening in it, like a bulge along a snake, was the transit node, a point, coincidental with the ecliptic, where passage into the accelerated space–time of the Way was possible. Although the Waynet stream was transparent, there remained a ghostly sense of dizzying motion.

'Are you absolutely sure you know what you're doing?'

'Goodness, no.' Merlin was reclining back in his seat, booted feet up on the console, hands knitted behind his neck. Ancient orchestral music was piping into the room, building up to a magnificent and doubtless delicately timed climax. 'Which isn't to say that this isn't an incredibly tricky manoeuvre, of course, requiring enormous skill and courage.'

'What worries me is you might be right.'

Sora remembered the times Captain Tchagra had sent probes into the Waynet, only to watch as each was shredded, sliced apart by momentum gradients that could flense matter down to its fundamentals. The Waynet twinkled because tiny grains of cosmic dust were constantly drifting into it, each being annihilated in a pretty little flash of exotic radiation. Right now, she thought, they were cruising towards that boundary, dead set on what ought to have been guaranteed destruction.

She tried to inject calm into her voice. 'So how did you come by the syrinx, Merlin?'

'Isn't much to look at, you know. A black cone, about as long as you're tall. Even in my era we couldn't make them, or even safely dismantle the few we still had. Very valuable things.'

'The Cohort wasn't overly thrilled that you stole one, according to the legend.'

'As if they cared. They had so few left, they were too scared to actually *use* them.'

Sora buckled herself into a seat.

She knew roughly what was about to happen, although no one had understood the details for tens of thousands of years. Just before hitting the Way, the syrinx would chirp a series of quantum-gravitational fluctuations at the boundary layer – the skin, no thicker than a Planck-length, which separated normal space–time from the rushing space–time contained within the Way. For an instant, the momentum gradients would relax, allowing the ship to enter the accelerated medium without being sliced.

That was the theory, anyway.

The music reached its crescendo now, ship's thrust notching higher, pushing Sora and Merlin back into their seats. The shriek of the propulsion system merged with the shriek of violins, too harmoniously to be accidental. Merlin's look of quiet amusement did not falter. A cascade of liquid notes played over the music: the song of the syrinx translated into the audio spectrum.

There was a peak of thrust, then the impulse ended abruptly, along with the music.

Sora looked to the exterior view.

For a moment it seemed as if the stars, and the nearer planets and sun of this system, hadn't actually changed at all. But after a few seconds she saw that they burned appreciably brighter – and, it seemed, bluer – in one hemisphere of the sky, redder and dimmer in the other. And they were growing bluer and redder by the moment, and now bunching, swimming like shoals of luminous fish, obeying relativistic currents. A planet slammed past from out of nowhere, distorted as if squeezed in a fist. The system seemed frozen behind them, shot through with red like an iron orrery snatched from the forge.

'Transition to Waynet achieved,' said the ship.

Later, Merlin took her down to the forward observation blister: a pressurised sphere of metasapphire that could be pushed beyond the hull like a protruding eye. The walls were opaque when they arrived, and when Merlin sealed the entry hatch, it turned the same shade of grey, merging seamlessly.

'Not to alarm you or anything,' the familiar said, 'but I can't communicate with the copy of myself from in here. That means I can't help you if—'

Sora kissed Merlin, silencing the voice in her head. 'I'm sorry,' she said, almost instantly. 'It seemed—'

'Like the right thing to do?' Merlin's smile was difficult to judge, but he did not seem displeased.

'No, not really. Probably the wrong thing, actually.'

'I'd be lying if I said I didn't find you attractive, Sora. And like I said – it has been rather a long time since I had human company.' He drew himself to her, their free-floating bodies hooking together in the centre of the blister, slowly turning until all sense of orientation was gone. 'Of course, my reasons for rescuing you were entirely selfless ...'

'Of course ...'

'But I won't deny that there was a small glimmer of hope at the back of my mind, the tiniest spark of fantasy ...'

They shed their clothes, untidy bundles that orbited around their coupled bodies. They began to make love, slowly at first, and then with increasing energy, as if it was only now that Sora was fully waking from the long centuries of frostwatch.

She thought of Verdin, and then hated herself for the crass, biochemical predictability of her mind, the unfailing way it dredged up the wrong memories at the worst of times. What had happened back then, what had happened between them, was three thousand years in the past, unrecorded by anything or anyone except herself. She had not even mourned him yet, had not even allowed the familiar to permit her that particular indulgence. She studied Merlin, looking for hints of his true age ... and failed, utterly, to detach the part of her mind capable of the job.

'Do you want to see something glorious?' Merlin asked later, after they had hung together wordlessly for many minutes.

'If you think you can impress me ...'

He whispered to the ship, causing the walls to lose their opacity.

Sora looked around. By some trick of holographics, the ship itself was not visible at all from within the blister. It was just her and Merlin, floating free.

And what she saw beyond them was indeed glorious – even if some detached part of her mind knew that the view could not be completely natural, and that in some way the hues and intensities of light had been shifted to aid comprehension. The walls of the Waynet slammed past at eye-wrenching speed, illuminated by the intense, Doppler-shifted annihilation of dust particles, so that it seemed as if they were flying in the utmost darkness, down a tube of twinkling violet that reached towards infinity. The space–time in which the ship drifted like a seed moved so quickly that the difference between its speed and light amounted to only one part in a hundred billion. Once a second in subjective time, the ship threaded itself through shining hoops as wide as the Waynet itself: constraining rings spaced eight light-hours apart, all part of the inscrutable exotic-matter machinery that had serviced this galaxy-spanning transit system. Ahead, all the stars in the universe crowded into an opalescent jewelled mass, like a congregation of bright angels. It was the most beautiful thing she had ever seen.

'It's the only way to travel,' Merlin said.

*

The journey would take four days of shiptime, nineteen centuries of worldtime.

The subjective time spent in Waynet flight amounted only to twenty-three hours. But the ship had to make many transitions between Ways, and they were never closer than tens of light-minutes apart, presumably because of the nightmarish consequences that would ensue if two opposing streams of accelerated space–time ever touched.

'Aren't you worried we'll wander into Huskers, Merlin?'

'Worth it for the big reward, wouldn't you say?'

'Tell me more about this mystical gun, and I might believe you.'

Merlin settled back in his seat, drawing a deep breath. 'Almost everything I know could be wrong.'

'I'll take that risk.'

'Whatever it was, it was fully capable of destroying whole worlds. Even stars, if the more outlandish stories are to be believed.' He looked down at his hand, as if suddenly noticing his impeccably manicured fingernails.

'Ask him how he thinks it works,' the familiar said. 'Then at least we'll have an idea how thorough he's been.'

She put the question to Merlin, as casually as she could.

'Gravity,' he said. 'Isn't that obvious? It may be a weak force, but there isn't anything in the universe that doesn't feel it.'

'Like a bigger version of the syrinx?'

Merlin shrugged. Sora realised that it was not his fingernails to which he was paying attention, but the ornate ring she had noticed before, inset with a ruby stone in which two sparks seemed to orbit like fireflies. 'It's almost certainly the product of Waymaker science. A post-human culture that was able to engineer – to mechanise – space–time. But I don't think it worked like the syrinx. I think it made singularities; it plucked globules of mass-energy from vacuum and squashed them until they were within their own event horizons.'

'Black holes,' the familiar said, and Sora echoed the words aloud.

Merlin looked pleased. 'Very small ones, atomic-scale. It doped them with charge, then accelerated them up to something only marginally less than the speed of light. They didn't have time to decay. For that, of course, it needed more energy, and more still just to prevent itself from being ripped apart by the stresses.'

'A gun that fires black holes? We'd win, wouldn't we? With something like that? Even if there was only one of them?'

Merlin fingered the ruby-centred ring.

'That's the general idea.'

Sora took Merlin's hand, stroking the fingers until her own alighted on the ring. It was more intricate than she had realised. The twin sparks were whirling around each other, glints of light locked in a waltz, as if driven by some microscopic clockwork buried in the ruby itself.

'What does it mean?' she asked, sensing that this was both the wrong and the right question.

'It means . . .' Merlin smiled, but it was a moment before he completed the sentence. 'It means, I suppose, that I should remember death.'

They fell out of the Way for the last time, entering a system that did not seem markedly different from a dozen others they had skipped through. The star was a yellow main-sequence sun, accompanied by the usual assortment of rocky worlds and gas giants. The second and third planets out from the sun were steaming hot cauldrons, enveloped by acidic atmosphere at crushing temperature, the victims of runaway heat-trapping processes, the third more recently than the second. The fourth planet was smaller and seemed to have been the subject of a terraforming operation that had taken place sometime after the Flourishing: its atmosphere, though thin, was too dense to be natural. Thirteen separate Ways punched through the system's ecliptic at different angles, safely distant from planetary and asteroidal orbits.

'It's a nexus,' Merlin said. 'A primary Waynet interchange. You find systems like this every thousand or so light-years through the plane of the galaxy, and a good way out of it as well. Back when everyone used the Waynet, this system would have been a meeting point, a place where traders swapped goods and tales from halfway to the Core.'

'Bit of a dump *now*, though, isn't it.'

'Perfect for hiding something very big and very nasty, provided you remember where you hid it.'

'You mentioned something about a storm—'

'You'll see.'

The Way had dropped them in the inner part of the system, but

Merlin said that what he wanted was further out, beyond the system's major asteroid belt. It would take a few days to reach.

'And what are we going to do when we get there?' Sora asked. 'Just pick this thing up and take it with us?'

'Not exactly,' Merlin said. 'I suspect it will be harder than that. Not so hard that we haven't got a chance, but hard enough ...' He seemed to falter, perhaps for the first time since she had met him, that aura of supreme confidence cracking minutely.

'What part do you want me to play?'

'You're a soldier,' he said. 'Figure that out for yourself.'

'I don't know quite what it is I've found,' the familiar said, when Sora was again alone. 'I've been waiting to show you, but he's had you in those war simulations for hours. Either that or you two have been occupying yourselves in other ways. Any idea what he's planning?'

Merlin had a simulator, a smaller version of the combat-training modules Sora knew from warcrèche.

'A lot of the simulations had a common theme: an attack against a white pyramid.'

'Implying some foreknowledge, wouldn't you say? As if Merlin knows something of what he will find?'

'I've had that feeling ever since we met him.' She was thinking of the smell of him, the shockingly natural way their bodies meshed, despite their being displaced by thousands of years. She tried to flush those thoughts from her mind. What they were now discussing was a kind of betrayal, on a more profound level than anything committed so far, because it lacked any innocence. 'What is it, then?'

'I've been scanning the later log files, and I've found something that seems significant, something that seemed to mark a turning point in his hunt for the weapon. I have no idea what it was. But it took me until now to realise just how strange it was.'

'Another system?'

'A very large structure, nowhere near any star, but nonetheless accessible by Waynet.'

'A Waymaker artefact, then.'

'Almost certainly.'

The structure was visible on the screen. It looked like a child's toy star, or a metallic starfish, textured in something that resembled beaten gold or the lustre of insect wings, filigreed in a lacework of exotic-matter scaffolds. It filled most of the view, shimmering with its own soft illumination.

'This is what Merlin would have seen with his naked eyes, just after his ship left the Way.'

'Very pretty.' She had meant the remark to sound glib, but it came out as a statement of fact.

'And large. The object's more than ten light-minutes away, which makes it more than four light-minutes in cross section. Comfortably larger than any star on the main sequence. And yet somehow it holds itself in shape – in quite preposterous shape – against what must be unimaginable self-gravity. Merlin, incidentally, gave it the name Brittlestar, which seems as good as any.'

'Poetic bastard.' *Poetic sexy bastard*, she thought.

'There's more, if you're interested. I have access to the sensor records from the ship, and I can tell you that the Brittlestar is a source of intense gravitational radiation. It's like a beacon, sitting there, pumping out gravity waves from somewhere near its heart. There's something inside it that is making space–time ripple periodically.'

'You think Merlin went inside it, don't you?'

'*Something* happened, that's for sure. This is the last log Merlin filed, on his approach to the object, before a month-long gap.'

It was another mumbled soliloquy – except this time his sobs were of something other than despair. Instead, they sounded like the sobs of the deepest joy imaginable. As if, finally, he had found what he was looking for, or at least knew that he was closer than ever, and that the final prize was not far from reach. But that was not what made Sora shiver. It was the face she saw. It was Merlin, beyond any doubt. But his face was lined with age, and his eyes were those of someone older than anyone Sora had ever known.

The fifth and sixth planets were the largest.

The fifth was the heavier of the two, zones of differing chemistry banding it from tropic to pole, girdled by a ring system that was itself braided by the resonant forces of three large moons. Merlin believed that the ring system had been formed since the Flourishing. A cloud of radiation-drenched human relics orbited the world, dating from unthinkably remote eras, perhaps even earlier than the Waymaker time. Merlin swept the cloud with sensors tuned to sniff out weapons systems, or the melange of neutrino flavours that betokened Husker presence. The sweeps all returned negative.

'You know where the gun is?' Sora asked.

'I know how to reach it, which is all that matters.'

'Maybe it's time to start being a little less cryptic. Especially if you want me to help you.'

He looked wounded, as if she had ruined a game hours in the making. 'I just thought you'd appreciate the thrill of the chase.'

'This isn't about the thrill of the chase, Merlin. It's about the nastiest weapon imaginable and the fact that we have to get our hands on it before the enemy, so that we can incinerate *them* first. So we can commit xenocide.' She said it again: 'Xenocide. Sorry. Doesn't that conform to your romantic ideals of the righteous quest?'

'It won't be xenocide,' he said, touching the ring again nervously. 'Listen: I want that gun as much as you do. That's why I chased it for ten thousand years.' Was it her imagination, or had the ring not been on his hand in any of the recordings she had seen of him? She remembered the old man's hands she had seen in the last recording, the one taken just before his time in the Brittlestar, and she was sure they held no ring. Now Merlin's voice was matter-of-fact. 'The structure we want is on the outermost moon.'

'Let me guess. A white pyramid?'

He offered a smile. 'Couldn't be closer if you tried.'

They fell into orbit around the gas giant. All the moons showed signs of having been extensively industrialised since the Flourishing, but the features that remained on their surfaces were gouged by millennia of exposure to sleeting cosmic radiation and micro-meteorites. Nothing looked significantly younger than the surrounding landscapes of rock and ice. Except for the kilometre-high white pyramid on the third moon, which was in a sixteen-day orbit around the planet. It looked as if it had been chiselled out of alabaster sometime the previous afternoon.

'Not exactly subtle,' Merlin said. 'Self-repair mechanisms must still be functional, to one degree or another, which implies that the control systems for the gun will still work. It also means that the counter-intrusion systems will also be operational.'

'Oh, good.'

'Aren't you excited that we're about to end the longest war in human history?'

'But we're not, are we? I mean, be realistic. It'll take tens of thousands of years simply for the knowledge of this weapon's existence to reach the remotest areas of the war. Nothing will happen overnight.'

'I can see why it would disturb you,' Merlin said, tapping a finger against his teeth. 'None of us have ever known anything other than war with the Huskers.'

'Just show me where it is.'

They made one low orbital pass over the pyramid, alert for buried weapons, but no attack came. On the next pass, lower still, Merlin's ship dropped proctors to snoop ground defences. 'Maybe they had something bigger once,' Merlin said. 'Artillery that could take us out from millions of kilometres away. But if it ever existed, it's not working any more.'

They made groundfall a kilometre from the pyramid, then waited for all but three of the proctors to return to the ship. Merlin tasked the trio to secure a route into the structure, but their use was limited. Once the simple-minded machines were out of command range of the ship – which happened as soon as they had penetrated beyond the outer layer of the structure – they were essentially useless.

'Who built the pyramid? And how did you know about it?'

'The same culture that got into the war I told you about,' he said, as they clamped on the armoured carapaces of their suits in the airlock. 'They were far less advanced than the Waymakers, but they were a lot closer to them historically, and they knew enough to control the weapon and use it for their own purposes.'

'How'd they find it?'

'They stole it. By then the Waymaker culture was – how shall I put it – sleeping? Not really paying due attention to the use made of its artefacts?'

'You're being cryptic again, Merlin.'

'Sorry. Solitude does that to you.'

'Did you meet someone out there, Merlin – someone who knew about the gun, and told you where to find it?' *And made you young in the process?* she thought.

'My business, isn't it?'

'Maybe once. Now, I'd say we're in this together. Equal partners. Fair enough?'

'Nothing's fair in war, Sora.' But he was smiling, defusing the remark, even as he slipped his helmet down over the neck ring, twisting it to engage the locking mechanism.

'How big is the gun?' Sora asked.

The pyramid rose ahead, blank as an origami sculpture, entrance ducts around the base concealed by intervening landforms. Merlin's proctors had already found a route that would take them at least some way inside.

'You won't be disappointed,' Merlin said.

'And what are we going to do when we find it? Just drag it behind us?'

'Trust me.' Merlin's laugh crackled over the radio. 'Moving it won't be a problem.'

They walked slowly along a track cleared by proctors, covered at the same time by the hull-mounted weapons on *Tyrant*.

'There's something ahead,' Merlin said, a few minutes later. He raised his own weapon and pointed towards a pool of darkness fifteen or twenty metres in front of them. 'It's artefactual, definitely metallic.'

'I thought your proctors cleared the area.'

'Looks like they missed something.'

Merlin advanced ahead of her. As they approached the dark object, it resolved into an elongated form half-buried in the ice, a little to the left of the track. It was a body.

'Been here a while,' Merlin said, a minute or so later, when he was close enough to see the object properly. 'Armour's pitted by micrometeorite impacts.'

'It's a Husker, isn't it?'

Merlin's helmet nodded. 'My guess is they were in this system a few centuries ago. Must have been attracted by the pyramid, even if they didn't necessarily know its significance.'

'I've never seen one this close. Be careful, won't you?'

Merlin knelt down to examine the creature.

The shape was much more androform than Sora had been expecting, the same general size and proportions as a suited human. The suit was festooned with armoured protrusions, ridges and horns, its blackened outer surface leathery and devoid of anything genuinely mechanical. One arm was outspread, terminating in a human-looking hand, complexly gauntleted. A long, knobby weapon lay just out of reach, lines blurred by the same processes of erosion that had afflicted the Husker.

Merlin clamped his hands around the head.

'What are you doing?'

'What does it look like?' He was twisting now; she could hear the grunts of exertion, before his suit's servosystems came online and took the brunt of the effort. 'I've always wanted to find one this well preserved,' Merlin said. 'Never thought I'd get a chance to tell if an old rumour was even halfway right.'

The helmet detached from the creature's torso, cracking open along a fine seam that ran from the crown to the beaklike protrusion at the helmet's front. Vapour pulsed from the gap. Merlin placed the separated halves of the helmet on the ground, then tapped on his helmet torch, bringing light down on the exposed head. Sora stepped closer. The Husker's head was encased in curling, matt-black support machinery, like a statue enveloped in vine.

But it was well preserved, and very human.

'I don't like it,' she said. 'What does it mean?'

'It means,' Merlin said, 'that occasionally one should pay proper attention to rumours.'

'Talk to me, Merlin. Start telling me what I need to hear, or we don't take another step towards that pyramid.'

'You will like very little of it.'

She looked out of the corner of her eye at the marble-like face of the Husker. 'I already don't like it, Merlin; what have I got to lose?'

Merlin started to say something, then fell to the ground, executing the fall with the slowness that came with the moon's feeble gravity.

'Oh, nice timing,' the familiar said.

Reflexes drove Sora down with him, until the two of them were crouching low on the rusty surface. Merlin was still alive. She could hear him breathing, but each breath came like the rasp of a saw.

'I'm hit, Sora. I don't know how badly.'

'Hold on.' She accessed the telemetry from his suit, graphing a medical diagnostic on the inner glass of her helmet.

'There,' said the familiar. 'A beam-weapon penetration in the thoracic area; small enough that the self-sealants prevented any pressure loss, but not rapidly enough to stop the beam gnawing into his chest.'

'Is that bad?'

'Well, it's not good ... but there's a chance the beam would have cauterised as it travelled, preventing any deep internal bleeding ...'

Merlin coughed. He managed to ask her what it was.

'You've taken a laser, I think.' She was speaking quickly. 'Maybe part of the pyramid defences.'

'I really should have those proctors of mine checked out.' Merlin managed a laugh, which then transitioned into a series of racking coughs. 'Bit late for that now, don't you think?'

'If I can get you back to the ship—'

'No. We have to go on.' He coughed again, and then was a long time catching his breath. 'The longer we wait, the harder it will be.'

'After ten thousand years, you're worried about a few minutes?'

'Yes, now that the pyramid defences have been alerted.'

'You're in no shape to move.'

'I'm winded, that's all. I think I can ...' His voice dissolved into coughs, but even while it was happening, Sora watched him push himself upright. When he spoke again his voice was hardly a wheeze. 'I'm gambling there was only one of whatever it was. Otherwise we should never have made it as far as we did.'

'I hope you're right, Merlin.'

'There's – um – something else. Ship's just given me a piece of not entirely welcome news. A few neutrino sources that weren't detected when we first got here.'

'Oh, great.' Sora didn't need to be told what that meant: a Husker swarm, one that had presumably been waiting around the gas giant all along, chilled down below detection thresholds. 'Bastards must have been sleeping, waiting for something to happen here.'

'Sounds like a perfectly sensible strategy,' the familiar said, before projecting a map onto Sora's faceplate, confirming the arrival of the enemy ships. 'One of the moons has a liquid ocean. My guess is that the Huskers were parked below the ice.

Sora asked Merlin: 'How long before they get here?'

'No more than two or three hours.'

'Right. Then we'd better make damn sure we've got that gun by then, right?'

She carried him most of the way, his heels scuffing the ground in a half-hearted attempt at locomotion. But he remained lucid, and Sora began to hope that the wound really had been cauterised by the beam-weapon.

'You knew the Husker would be human, didn't you?' she said, to keep him talking.

'Told you: rumours. The alien cyborg story was just that – a fiction our own side invented. I told you it wouldn't be xenocide.'

'Not good enough, Merlin.' She was about to tell him about the symbiote in her head, then drew back, fearful that it would destroy what trust he had in her. 'I know you've been lying. I hacked your ship's log.'

They had reached the shadow of the pyramid, descending the last hillock towards the access ports spaced around the rim.

'Thought you trusted me.'

'I had to know if there was a reason *not* to. And I think I was right.'

She told him what she had learned: he'd been travelling for longer than he had told her – whole decades longer, by shiptime – and that he had grown old during that journey, and perhaps a little insane. And then how he had seemed to find the Brittlestar. 'Problem is, Merlin, we – *I* – don't know what happened to you in that thing, except that it had something to do with finding the gun, and you came out of it younger than when you went in.'

'You really want to know?'

'Take a guess.'

He started telling her some of it, while she dragged him towards their destination.

The pyramid was surrounded by tens of metres of self-repairing armour, white as bone. If the designers had not allowed deliberate entrances around its rim, Sora doubted that she and Merlin would ever have found a way to get inside.

'Should have been sentries here, once,' Merlin said, while leaning against her shoulder. 'It's lucky for us that everything falls apart, eventually.'

'Except your fabled gun.' They were moving down a sloping corridor, the walls and ceiling unblemished, the floor strewn with icy debris from the moon's surface. 'Anyway, stop changing the subject.'

Merlin coughed and resumed his narrative. 'I was getting very old and very disillusioned. I hadn't found the gun and I was about ready to give up. That, or go insane. Then I found the Brittlestar. I came out of the Waynet and there it was, sitting there pulsing gravity waves at me.'

'It would take a pair of neutron stars,' the familiar said, 'orbiting around each other, to generate that kind of signature.'

'What happened next?' Sora asked.

'Don't really remember. Not properly. I went – or was taken – inside it – and there I met ...' He paused, and for a moment she thought it was because he needed to catch his breath. But that wasn't the reason. 'I met *entities*, I suppose you'd call them. I quickly realised that they were just highly advanced projections of a maintenance programme left behind by the Waymakers.'

'They made you young, didn't they?'

'I don't think it was stretching their capabilities overmuch, put it like that.'

The corridor flattened out, branching in several different directions. Merlin leaned toward one of the routes.

'Why?'

'So I could finish the job. Find the gun.'

The corridor opened out into a chamber: a bowl-ceilinged control room, unpressurised and lit only by the wavering light of their helmets. Seats and consoles were arrayed around a single spherical projection device, cradled in ash-coloured gimbals. Corpses slumped over some of the consoles, but nothing remained except skeletons draped in colourless rags. Presumably they had rotted away for centuries before the chamber was finally opened to vacuum, and even that would have been more than twenty thousand years ago.

'They must have been attacked by a bioweapon,' Merlin said, easing himself into one of the seats, which – after exhaling a cloud of dust – seemed able to take his weight. 'Something that left the machines intact.'

Sora walked around, examining the consoles, all of which betrayed a technology beyond anything the Cohort had known for millennia. Some of the symbols on them were recognisable antecedents of those used in Main, but there was nothing she could actually read.

Merlin made a noise that might have been a grunt of suppressed pain, and when Sora looked at him, she saw that he was spooling the optical cable from his suit sleeve, just as he had when they had first met on the cometary shard. He lifted back an access panel on the top of the console, exposing an intestinal mass of silvery circuits. He seemed to know exactly where to place the end of the cable, allowing its microscopic cilia to tap into the ancient system.

The projection chamber was warming to life now: amber light swelling from its heart, solidifying into abstract shapes, neutral test representations. For a moment, the chamber showed a schematic of the ringed gas giant and its moons, with the locations of the approaching Husker ships marked with complex ideograms. The familiar was right: their place of sanctuary must have been the moon with the liquid ocean. Then the shapes moved fluidly, zooming in on the gas giant.

'You wanted to know where the gun was,' Merlin said. 'Well, I'm about to show you.'

The view enlarged on a cyclonic storm near the planet's equator, a great swirling red eye in the atmosphere.

'It's a metastable storm,' Sora said. 'Common feature of gas giants. You're not telling me—'

Merlin's gauntleted fingers were at work now, flying across an array of keys marked with symbols of unguessable meaning. 'The storm's natural, of course, or at least it was before these people hid the gun inside it, exploiting the pressure differentials to hold the gun at a fixed point in the atmosphere, for safekeeping. There's just one small problem.'

'Go ahead ...'

'The gun isn't a gun. It functions as a weapon, but that's mostly accidental. It certainly wasn't the intention of the Waymakers.'

'You're losing me, Merlin.'

'Maybe I should tell you about the ring.'

Something was happening to the surface of the gas giant now. The cyclone was not behaving in the manner of other metastable storms Sora had seen. It was spinning perceptibly, throwing off eddies from its curlicued edge like the tails of seahorses. It was growing a bloodier red by the second.

'Yes,' Sora said. 'Tell me about the ring.'

'The Waymakers gave it to me, when they made me young. It's a reminder of what I have to do. You see, if I fail, it will be very bad for every thinking creature in this part of the galaxy. What did you see when you looked at the ring, Sora?'

'A red gem, with two lights orbiting inside it.'

'Would you be surprised if I told you that the lights represent two neutron stars, two of the densest objects in the universe? And that they're in orbit about each other, spinning around their mutual centre of gravity?'

'Inside the Brittlestar.'

She caught his glance, directed quizzically toward her. 'Yes,' Merlin said slowly. 'A pair of neutron stars, born in supernovae, bound together by gravity, slowly spiralling closer and closer to each other.'

The cyclonic storm was whirling insanely now, sparks of sub-atmospheric lightning flickering around its boundary. Sora had the feeling that titanic – and quite inhuman – energies were being unleashed, as if something very close to magic was being deployed beneath the clouds. It was the most terrifying thing she had ever seen.

'I hope you know how to fire this when the time comes, Merlin.'

'All the knowledge I need is carried by the ring. It taps into my bloodstream and builds structures in my head that tell me exactly what I need to know, on a level so deep that I hardly know it myself.'

'Husker swarm will be within range in ninety minutes,' the familiar said, 'assuming attack profiles for the usual swarm boser and charm-torp weapon configurations. Of course, if they have any refinements, they might be in attack range a little sooner than that—'

'Merlin: tell me about the neutron stars, will you? I need some-thing to keep my mind occupied.'

'The troublesome part is what happens when they *stop* spiralling around each other and *collide*. Mercifully, it's a fairly rare event even by galactic standards – it doesn't happen more than once in a million years, and when it does it's usually far enough away not to be a problem.'

'But if it isn't far away – how troublesome would it be?'

'Imagine the release of more energy in a second than a typical star emits in ten billion years: one vast, photo-leptonic fireball. An unimaginably bright pulse of gamma rays. Instant sterilisation for thousands of light-years in any direction.'

The cyclone had grown a central bulge now, a perfectly circular bruise rising above the surface of the planet. As it rose, towering thousands of kilometres above the cloud layer, it elongated like a waterspout. Soon, Sora could see it backdropped against space. And there was something rising within it.

'The Waymakers tried to stop it, didn't they?'

Merlin nodded. 'They found the neutron star binary when they extended the Waynet deeper into the galaxy. They realised that the two stars were only a few thousand years from colliding – and that there was almost nothing they could do about it.'

She could see what she thought was the weapon, now, encased in the waterspout like a seed. It was huge – larger perhaps than this moon. It looked fragile, nonetheless, like an impossibly ornate candelabrum, or a species of deep-sea medusa glowing with its own bioluminescence. Sloughing atmosphere, the thing came to a watchful halt, and the waterspout slowly retracted back towards the cyclone, which was now slowing, like a monstrous flywheel grinding down.

'Nothing?'

'Well – almost nothing.'

'They built the Brittlestar around it,' Sora said. 'A kind of shield, right? So that when the stars collided, the flash would be contained?'

'Not even Waymaker science could contain that much energy.' Merlin looked to the projection, seeming to pay attention to the weapon for the first time. If he felt any elation on seeing his gun for the first time, none of it was visible on his face. He looked, instead, ashen – as if the years had suddenly reclaimed what the Waymakers had given him. 'All they could do was keep the stars in check, keep them from spiralling any closer. So they built the Brittlestar, a vast machine with only one function: to constantly nudge the orbits of the neutron stars at its heart. For every angstrom that the stars fell towards each other, the Brittlestar pushed them an angstrom apart. And it was designed to keep doing that for a million years, until the Waymakers found a way to shift the entire binary beyond the galaxy. You want to know how they kept pushing them apart?'

Sora nodded, though she thought she half-knew the answer already.

'Tiny black holes,' Merlin said. 'Accelerated close to the speed of light, each black hole interacting gravitationally with the binary before evaporating in a puff of pair-production radiation.'

'Just the same way the gun functions. That's no coincidence, is it?'

'The gun – what we call the gun – was just a component in the Brittlestar: the source of relativistic black holes needed to keep the neutron stars from colliding.'

Sora looked around the room. 'And these people stole it?'

'Like I said, they were closer to the Waymakers than us. They knew enough about them to dismantle part of the Brittlestar, to override its defences and remove the mechanism they needed to win their war.'

'But the Brittlestar—'

'Hasn't been working properly ever since. Its capability to regenerate itself was harmed when the subsystem was stolen, and the remaining black-hole generating mechanisms can't do all the work required. The neutron stars have continued to spiral closer together – slowly but surely.'

'But you said they were only a few thousand years from collision . . .'

Merlin had not stopped working the controls in all this time. The gun had come closer, seemingly oblivious to the ordinary laws of celestial mechanics. Down below, the planetary surface had returned to normality, except for a ruddier hue to the storm.

'Maybe now,' Merlin said, 'you're beginning to understand why I want the gun so badly.'

'You want to return it, don't you? You never really wanted to find a weapon.'

'I did, once.' Merlin seemed to tap some final reserve of energy, his voice growing momentarily stronger. 'But now I'm older and wiser. In less than four thousand years the stars meet, and it suddenly won't matter who wins this war. We're like ignorant armies fighting over a patch of land beneath a rumbling volcano!'

Four thousand years, Sora thought. More time had passed since she had been born.

'If we don't have the gun,' she said, 'we die anyway – wiped out by the Huskers. Not much of a choice, is it?'

'At least *something* would survive. Something that might even still think of itself as human.'

'You're saying that we should capitulate? That we get our hands on the ultimate weapon, and then not *use* it?'

'I never said it was going to be easy, Sora.' Merlin pitched forwards, slowly enough that she was able to reach him before he slumped into the exposed circuitry of the console. His coughs were loud in her helmet. 'Actually, I think I'm more than winded,' he said, when he was able to speak at all.

'We'll get you back to the ship; the proctors can help—'

'It's too late, Sora.'

'What about the gun?'

'I'm ... doing something rather rash, in the circumstances. Entrusting it to you. Does that sound utterly insane?'

'I'll betray you. I'll give the gun to the Cohort. You know that, don't you?'

Merlin's voice was soft. 'I don't think you will. I think you'll do the right thing and return it to the Brittlestar.'

'Don't make me betray you!'

He shook his head. 'I've just issued a command that reassigns control of my ship to you. The proctors are now under your command; they'll show you everything you need.'

'Merlin, I'm begging you ...'

His voice was weak now, hard to distinguish from the scratchy irregularity of his breathing. She leaned down to him and touched helmets, hoping the old trick would make him easier to hear. 'No good, Sora. Much too late. I've signed it all over.'

'No!' She shook him, almost in anger. Then she began to cry, loud enough so that she was in no doubt that he would hear it. 'I don't even know what you want me to do with it!'

'Take the ring, then the rest will be abundantly clear.'

'What?' She could hardly understand herself now.

'Put the ring on. Do it now, Sora. Before I die. So that I at least know it's done.'

'When I take your glove off, I'll kill you, Merlin. You know that, don't you? And I won't be able to put the ring on until I'm back in the ship.'

'I ... just want to see you take it. That's enough, Sora. And you'd better be quick—'

'I love you, you bastard!'

'Then do this.'

She placed her hands around the cuff seal of his gauntlet, feeling the alloy locking mechanism, knowing that it would only take a careful depression of the sealing latches, and then a quick twisting movement, and the glove would slide free, releasing the air in his suit. She wondered how long he would last before consciousness left him – no more than tens of seconds, she thought, unless he drew breath first. And by the state of his breathing, that would not be easy for him.

She removed the gauntlet, and took his ring.

Tyrant lifted from the moon.

'Husker forces grouping in attack configuration,' the familiar said, tapping directly into the ship's avionics. 'Hull sensors read sweeps by targeting lidar . . . an attack is imminent, Sora.'

Tyrant's light armour would not save them, Sora knew. The attack would be blinding and brief, and she would probably never know it had happened. But that didn't mean she was going to *let* it happen.

She felt the gun move to her will.

It would not always be like this, she knew: the gun was only hers until she returned it to the Waymakers. But for now it felt like an inseparable part of her, like a twin she had never known, but whose every move was familiar to her a fraction in advance of it being made. She felt the gun energise itself, reaching deep into the bedrock of space–time, plundering mass-energy from quantum foam, forging singularities in its heart.

She felt readiness.

'First element of swarm has deployed charm-torps,' the familiar reported, an odd slurred quality entering her voice. 'Activating *Tyrant*'s countermeasures . . .'

The hull rang like a bell.

'Countermeasures engaging charm-torps . . . neutralised . . . second wave deployed by the swarm . . . closing . . .'

'How long can we last?'

'Countermeasures exhausted . . . we can't parry a third wave, not at this range.'

Sora closed her eyes and made the weapon spit death.

She had targeted two of the three elements of the Husker swarm, leaving the third – the furthest ship from her – unharmed.

She watched the relativistic black holes fold space around the two targeted ships, crushing each instantly, as if in a vice.

'Third ship dropping to max ... maximum attack range ... retracting charm-torp launchers—'

'This is Sora for the Cohort,' she said in Main, addressing the survivor on the general ship-to-ship channel. 'Or what remains of the Cohort. Perhaps you can understand what I have to say. I could kill you, now, instantly, if I chose.' She felt the weapon speak to her through her blood, reporting its status, its eagerness to do her bidding. 'Instead, I'm about to give you a demonstration. Are you ready?'

'Sora ...' said the familiar. 'Something's wrong ...'

'What?'

'I'm not ... well.' The familiar's voice did not sound at all right, now, drained of any semblance to Sora's own. 'The ring must be constructing something in your brain ... part of the interface between you and the gun ... something stronger than me ... It's weeding me out, to make room for itself ...'

She remembered what Merlin had said about the structures the ring would make.

'You saved a part of yourself in the ship.'

'Only a part,' the familiar said. 'Not all of me ... not all of me at all. I'm sorry, Sora. I think I'm dying.'

She dismantled the star system.

Sora did it with artistry and flair, saving the best for last. She began with moons, pulverising them so that they began to flow into nascent rings around their parent worlds. Then she smashed the worlds themselves to pieces, turning them into cauls of hot ash and plasma. Finally – when it was the only thing left to destroy – she turned the gun on the system's star, impaling its heart with a salvo of relativistic black holes, throwing a killing spanner into the nuclear processes that turned mass into sunlight. In doing so, she interfered – catastrophically – with the delicate hydrostatic balance between pressure and gravity that held the star in shape. She watched it unpeel, shedding layers of outer atmosphere in a premature display of the death that awaited suns like it, four billion years in the future. And then she watched the last Husker ship, which had witnessed what she had wrought, turn and head out of the system.

She could have killed them all.

But she had let them live. Instead, she had shown the power that was – albeit temporarily – hers to command.

She wondered if there was enough humanity left in them to appreciate the clemency she had shown.

Later, she took *Tyrant* into the Waynet again, the vast, luminous bulk of the gun following her like an obedient dragon. Sora's heart almost stopped at the fearful moment of entry, convinced that the syrinx would choose not to sing for its new master.

But it did sing, just as it had sung for Merlin.

And then, alone this time – more alone than she had ever been in her life – she climbed into the observation blister and turned the metasapphire walls transparent, making the ship itself disappear, until there was only herself and the rushing, twinkling brilliance of the Way. It was time to finish what Merlin had begun.

This trio of far-future stories all feature Merlin, a favourite character of mine and one I intend to return to. The Merlin stuff is very baroque, very widescreen: as close as I come to writing pure-quill space opera. My 'Revelation Space' stories may be replete with ancient civilisations, exploding space dreadnoughts and fire-wreathed planets, but in the Merlin stories I like to turn the amplifier up to eleven and get seriously 'one louder'.

The first and third stories both appeared in 2000, but I wrote them out of sequence, with 'Hideaway', the prequel, being written three years later than 'Merlin's Gun'. I wrote 'Minla's Flowers' five years later, when a commission demanded something big and space-operatic: perfect Merlin territory. In these stories I try to navigate a path between hard SF and something close to Lucasesque space fantasy. The Merlin stories are full of archaic imagery, but (I hope) it's there in service of a rigorous science fictional spine. In 'Hideaway' I played around with some genuine concepts related to faster-than-light travel and the effects of dark matter on stellar physics, while in 'Merlin's Gun' I deal with one possible explanation for gamma-ray bursts, one of the central mysteries of contemporary astronomy. The inspiration for 'Minla's Flowers' was an article about the growth cycles of chambered nautiluses. By the time I'd finished the story there were no nautiluses anywhere in it, although the idea of lunar growth cycles survived in very different form. The inspiration for the character Minla, incidentally, was a certain grocer's daughter with ambitions to high office.

Here's an anecdote. Around the time that 'Merlin's Gun' was due to appear in print, I was busy putting together a series of web pages for the research group of which I was a member. I needed an artist's impression of a type of interacting binary star known as a 'cataclysmic variable', because that was what we'd been looking at with our new optical camera. Trawling the Internet, I found what I was looking for on the website of astronomical artist Mark Garlick. All I knew of Mark was that he used to work with a colleague of mine, and had left full-time research to develop a career in space art. I was just composing an e-mail to Mark, asking his permission to reuse the image, when I noticed something else on his pages. There was a cover for a forthcoming edition of Asimov's magazine Mark had just done . . . which turned out to be the cover image for 'Merlin's Gun'.

Being a good rationalist, I don't attach too much significance to coincidences. But I still think that's a bit weird.

Sergio flew under a Martian sky the colour of bloodied snow. Nerves had kept him awake the previous night, and now sleep was reclaiming its debt, even as he spoke the Kiwidinok liturgies that his catechist had selected from the day's breviary. Earlier, he had overflown a caravan of clanfolk – unusual, that they should travel so far west from Vikingville – and the sight of their crawling, pennanted machines had brought Indrani to mind, her face more alluring than any stained-glass effigy in the seminary. She was asking his name, each syllable anointing him, and then, instead of Indrani, it was God roaring in his head, so deep it seemed as if the landscape was issuing a proclamation.

'UNIDENTIFIED AIRCRAFT,' said the voice. 'YOU ARE ABOUT TO TRANSGRESS CONSECRATED AIRSPACE.'

He slammed awake, conscious of the bulge in his lap. He could still smell Indrani, as if he'd imported her fragrance from sleep. The Latinate script of the breviary had stopped scrolling across his retina, his destination cresting the horizon, much nearer than he'd realised. Cased in a pressure dome, it was a hundred-metre obelisk of alabaster, attended by smaller spires. Flying buttresses and aerial walkways infested the air between the spires, but there was no evidence of human habitation.

'TRANSMIT RECOGNITION CRYPTOGRAMS IF YOU DO NOT WISH TO BE INTERDICTED BY TEMPLE DEFENCE SYSTEMS,' the voice continued, although less impressively, since Sergio knew now that it was the catechist, the one that had been implanted on the day of his ordination. The voice added: 'YOU HAVE TEN SECONDS TO COMPLY OR ALTER YOUR VECTOR ...'

'I understand,' he said. 'Just a moment ...'

Sergio instructed the ornithopter to emit the warble that would satisfy the Temple of his benevolence, then watched as the defensive gargoyles retracted lolling tongues and closed fanged jaws, beam-weapon nozzles vanishing into nostrils, laser-targeting eyes dimming from ruby brilliance.

'WELCOME, BROTHER MENENDEZ,' the voice said. 'PROCEED WITH THE GRACE OF GOD. YOU WILL BE MET BY A MEMBER OF THE ORDER.'

The Machinehood, he thought.

The ornithopter punched through the resealing polymer bubble that encased the Temple, executing one circuit of the building before settling on the terrazzo at its base, furling wings with a bustle of synthetic chitin. Sergio emerged, nervously drying his hands against the ash-coloured fabric of his trousers. His jacket was similarly dour, offset by the white of his collar and the Asymmetrist star embroidered above his heart. The bluish stubble on his scalp revealed the weal-like stigma of ordination.

He slung a black haversack over one shoulder and walked across the terrazzo, interlaid chevrons of sapphire and diamond gliding beneath his soles. The Temple rose above him, sculptured spires hectic with Kiwidinok figures. His catechist decrypted hidden data in the stonework, graphing up a commentary on the architecture, how the manifold truths of the Asymmetrist Testament were amplified in every Masonic nuance. Obsidian steps climbed from the terrazzo into the Kiwidinok-encrusted doorway. Inside, he was met by one of the Machinehood: an Apparent Intelligence that his catechist identified as a cardinal named Bellarmine, after the Jesuit theologian who warned Galileo against the heresy of the heliocentric universe. Bellarmine's androform frame was shrouded in a hooded black cloak, but where the cloak parted, Sergio glimpsed a meshwork of sculpted metal overlaying armatures, intestinal feedlines and pulsing diodes.

'I'm humbled to be admitted—' Sergio began, offering a complex genuflection of servility to the cardinal.

'Yes, yes,' Bellarmine said, no expression on the minimalist silver ovoid of his face. 'Pleasantries later. I advocate haste.'

'I flew as fast as I could.'

'Did you notice anything on your way here? We have reports of clan incursions in this sector of the Diocese. Clanfolk don't usually come here.'

'There was . . .' Except perhaps he'd dreamed the clanfolk, as he'd dreamed Indrani. Possibly the question was a test. 'Sorry; I spent the flight in prayer. Is Ivan as ill as we've heard?'

'Transcendence is imminent. He's no longer on medical support. He asked that we discontinue it, so that his last hours might be lucid. That, I suppose, has some bearing on *your* arrival.' Bellarmine's voice was like a cheap radio.

'You don't know why I'm here?'

'There's something he insists on telling only to a human priest.'

'Then our ignorance is equal,' Sergio said, suppressing a smile. There had been few occasions since his ordination when he had felt equality of any sort with a member of the Machinehood. The Machinehood knew things; they were always a step ahead of the human clergy, and the Order's higher echelons were dominated by Apparents. They'd been afforded ecclesiastical rights since the Ecumenical Synthesis, when the Founder had returned from the edge of the system with his message of divine intervention. Given the nature of the Kiwidinok, it could hardly have been otherwise, but that did not mean that Sergio was comfortable in their presence. 'Will you show me to Ivan?' he asked.

Bellarmine escorted him through a warren of twisting and ascending passageways, walls covered with Kiwidinok friezes. They passed other Apparents on the way, but never another human.

'Of course, there were rumours,' Bellarmine said, as if passing the time of day. 'About the reason for your summons. You were ordained less than nine standard years ago?'

'Your information's excellent,' Sergio said, his teeth clenched.

'It generally is. Was the procedure painful?'

'Of course not. The catechist's very small before they implant it – it's hardly a mosquito bite.' He touched the weal on his scalp. 'They induce scar tissue quite deliberately. But once the thing's growing inside you, you don't feel much at all. No pain receptors in the brain.'

'I'm curious, that's all. One hears reports. How did you feel when you saw the cards properly: the first images of Perdition?'

He remembered the cards very well. The senior priest had opened a rosewood box and shown them to him before the catechist was installed. Each card contained a grey square composed of thousands of tinier grey cells of varying shades – eleven, in fact, since that was the maximum number of shades that the human eye could discriminate. The matrix of grey cells looked random, but once the catechist was installed – once it had interfaced with the appropriate brain centres, and decoded his idiosyncratic representation of the exterior world – something odd happened. The grey cells peeled away, revealing an image underneath. They'd told him how it worked, but he didn't pretend to remember the details. What mattered was that the catechist permitted the ordained to view sacred data, and *only* the ordained.

And he remembered seeing Perdition for the first time. And the feeling of disappointment, that something so crucial could be so mundane, so uninspiring. 'I felt,' he said, 'that I was seeing something very holy.'

'Interesting,' Bellarmine said, after due reflection. 'I've heard some say it's an anticlimax. But one oughtn't be surprised. After all, it's just a neutron star.'

He led Sergio across the unbalustraded walkway of a flying buttress, the ornithopter a tiny thing far below, like a grounded insect beside an anthill.

'You mentioned rumours,' Sergio said, to take his mind off the drop below him. 'Presupposing I'd done something that would merit it, I doubt very much that Ivan would summon me across half of Mars just for a reprimand.'

'Sick old men do unusual things,' the Apparent said, as they re-entered the middle spire. 'But, of course, the point is hypothetical. If you had sinned against the Order, if you had committed some indiscretion against your vows – even somewhere remote from Chryse – we'd know of it.'

'I don't doubt it.'

'That's wise.' Bellarmine came to a halt. 'Well, we've arrived. Are you ready, Menendez?'

'No. I'm nervous, and I don't understand why I'm here. Except that *this* has something to do with it.' He hefted the haversack like a trophy. 'But I guess the only way to find out is to step inside and see what Ivan wants.'

'Perhaps you shouldn't expect an answer.'

'What are you saying, that he doesn't necessarily know why he asked me here?'

'Only that he's sick, Menendez.'

They entered a room where death was a quiet presence, like dew waiting to condense. Perfumed candles burned in sconces along the walls, each grasped in a Kiwidinok hand: rapier-thin fingers of wrought iron. Through the sepia gloom, Sergio discerned the sheeted form of the dying man, his bed surrounded by the hooded shapes of deactivated monitors, like kneeling orisons.

'You should be wary of tiring him. He may be slipping from us, but that doesn't mean we should squander the seconds we have left in his presence.'

'Are you staying here?'

'Oh, don't worry about me. I won't be far.'

'That's a shame.' Sergio suppressed a grin. 'That you have to leave, I mean, of course.'

After the Apparent had gone, Sergio waited for many minutes until his eyes adjusted to the darkness. He doubted that he had ever seen a creature as near to death as Ivan, and it was a small miracle that someone this withered was even capable of metabolism; no matter if each breath was undoubtedly weaker than the one before it. Finally, Sergio's arm tired, and he placed the haversack on the floor. Perhaps it was the faint sound of the contact, or the imperceptible disturbance that the gesture imparted to the room's air currents, but the old man chose that moment to open his eyes, a process as languid as the opening of a rose at dawn.

'Menendez,' Ivan said, his lips barely parting. 'That's your name, isn't it?' Then, after a pause: 'How was your flight from Vikingville?'

'The thermals,' Sergio said, 'were excellent.'

'Used to fly gliders, you know. Paragliders. I jumped from a *tepui* in Venezuela, once. Back on Earth. Before the Kiwidinok came. One shit-scary thing to do.'

'Your memories do you credit, Ivan.'

'Christ, and I thought *Bellarmine* was stiff. Loosen up. I need reverence like I need a skateboard. You brought the recorder?'

'It's ready, although I'm not sure what you want of me. The Diocese told me next to nothing.'

'That's because they didn't have the damnedest idea. Here. Pass the bag.' Ivan's hands emerged from the sheets and probed the haversack, removing the consecrated antique tape recorder and situating it carefully next to his bedside. 'Ah, good,' he said. 'You brought the other thing. That's good, Menendez. Real good. Think I like you better already.' Trembling, he removed a small flask of whisky, uncapping it and holding it under his nose. 'Clanfolk-brewed, huh? You took a risk bringing it, I know.'

'Not really. I presumed it served some symbolic function.'

'You go right on presuming that, son.' Ivan tipped the flask to his lips, then placed it aside, amidst a pile of personal effects on the other side of the bed. 'You help yourself, you want some. And sit down, won't you?'

'I'd like to know why I'm here.'

'Well, there's no mystery. There's something I have to tell you – all of you – and I couldn't trust any of the senior Apparents.'

Sergio lowered himself into a seat, nervously glancing over his shoulder. For a moment, he'd imagined that he'd glimpsed Bellar-mine's face there, rendered bronze in the candlelight ... but there was no evidence of him now. 'Does what you have to tell me relate to the Kiwidinok?'

'The Kiwidinok, and Perdition and everything else!' He paused to lubricate his lips, studying Sergio through slitted eyes. 'Not quite the reaction I was expecting.'

'I was ...' Sergio shook his head. *Thinking of Indrani*. 'Where do you think we should begin?'

'The day I stopped shovelling shit in Smolensk.'

'I—'

'The day the Kiwidinok came. October 2078. Year Zero. Yeah, I *know* what you're thinking, that you *know* it all. That the episode's well documented. Sure enough, *but* ...' Now Ivan found a reserve of strength adequate to push himself from the horizontal, until he was almost sitting. Sergio adjusted the pillows behind his head. 'It's well documented, but what comes later *isn't*. If I just came out and told you, you might conceivably think I'd lost all grip on reality.'

'I'd never dream of dismissing what you have to say; none of us would.'

'See if you feel that way when I'm finished, son!' Ivan allowed himself another thimbleful of clanfolk whisky, offering it inef-fectually in Sergio's direction before continuing. 'How old are you, son, twenty-four, twenty-five, in standard years? I can't have been much older than you when it happened. We didn't call them Kiwidinok back then. That came much later, once they'd ransacked our cultural data and chosen a name for themselves. It's a Chippewa word; means *of the wind*. Maybe it has something to do with the way they move around.'

'That seems likely.'

They had arrived eighty-four years earlier, entering the solar system at virtually the speed of light. Their gnarly, lozenge-shaped ship, which might once have been a small asteroid, deployed a solar sail when it was somewhere beyond the distance of Pluto. It seemed laughable – had these visitors crossed interstellar space in the mistaken assumption that the pressure of solar radiation would decelerate their craft? Yet, staggeringly, the Kiwidinok ship came to a standstill in only three hours, before quietly swallowing its sail and vectoring towards the Earth.

Diplomatic teams were invited within the presence of the aliens. In the few video images that existed, the Kiwidinok resembled steel and neon sculptures of angels, blurred and duplex, like Duchamp's painting of a woman descending a staircase – humanoid, slender as knives and luminous, sprouting wings that simply faded out at their extremities, as if fashioned from finer and finer silk. Their faces were achingly beautiful, though masklike and impassive, and their slitted mouths and jewelled eyes betrayed only vacuous serenity. Quickly the diplomatic teams realised that they were dealing with machines. Once, so they themselves claimed, the Kiwidinok had been organic, but not for tens of millions of years.

'Our perspective ... is different,' they had said, in one of the rare instances when they openly discussed their nature. 'Our perception of quantum reality differs from yours. It is not as ours once was.'

'What do you think they meant by that?' Ivan said, breaking from his narrative to stare at Sergio intently. 'No, leave the recorder running.'

'I can't begin to guess.'

'Must have been something to do with their becoming machines, don't you agree?'

'That would make sense. Is this – um – strictly relevant? I'm only thinking of your strength.'

Ivan's hand clenched around Sergio's wrist. 'More relevant than you can possibly imagine.' He emitted a fusillade of coughs before continuing. 'You need to understand this much, if nothing else: the problem of quantum measurement – that's the crux. How the superposed states of a quantum system collapse down to one reality. Understand *that* – and understand *why* it's a problem – and the rest will follow.'

Sergio looked guiltily at the recorder, aware of how every word spoken was being captured indelibly. 'There was mention in the seminary of cats, I believe. Cats in boxes, with radioisotopes and vials of arsenic.'

'When I wasn't shovelling shit in Smolensk, I used to think of myself as something of an amateur philosopher. I'd read all the popular articles, sometimes even kidded myself that I understood the math. The point is, all quantum systems – atoms, crystals, cats, dogs – exist in a superposition of possible states, like photographs stacked on top of each other. Provided you don't actually *look* at them, that is. But as soon as a measurement's made on the system, as soon as any part of it is observed, the system collapses – chooses one possible outcome out of all the options available to it and discards all the others.' Ivan relaxed his grip. 'Would you pour me some water? My throat is rather dry. That clanfolk stuff's real firewater.'

While he attended to this, Sergio said, 'There was never time, was there? To ask the Kiwidinok everything we might have wanted.'

Ivan quenched his thirst. 'When they announced that they were leaving, that was when the big panic began, because it seemed as if we hadn't learned enough from them; not supped sufficiently from the fount of their wisdom.'

'That was when they made the offer.'

'Yes. They'd already dropped hints here and there along the line that our – how shall I say it? That our existence wasn't quite as we imagined it to be; that there was some fundamental aspect of our nature that we just weren't aware of.' Ivan held his hand up to the candlelight, as if appalled at some new translucence in his flesh. 'You humans, they'd say, you just don't *get* it, do you? That was what it was like. They said that we could spend our remaining time asking them little questions, and not even chipping at this one fundamental misapprehension – or we could arrange for one person to be, shall I say, *enlightened*?'

'And you were selected,' Sergio said.

'Put my name forward, didn't I? Ivan Pashenkov: effluent disposal technician from Smolensk. Didn't think I had a chance in hell – or Perdition, huh? Don't laugh so much, son.'

'How did you feel when they selected you, out of all the millions who applied?'

'Very drunk. Or was that the day afterwards? Hell, I don't know. How was I meant to feel? Privileged? It wasn't as if they picked me on my merit. It was sheer luck.'

After his selection, the Kiwidinok had taken him aboard their ship, along with a handful of permitted recording devices small enough to be worn about his person. Preparing to depart, the ship had encased itself in a field of polarised inertia, defining a preferred axis along which resistance to acceleration was essentially zero, essentially infinite in all directions perpendicular to that axis. For interstellar travel, this was hardly an inconvenience.

'They immobilised me,' Ivan said. 'Locked me in a pod, and pumped me full of drugs.'

'How was it?'

He reached up with one hand and traced a line along the occipital crown of his skull, fingertips skating through the veil-like hair that still haloed his scalp. 'The brain's divided into two hemispheres; certain mental tasks assigned to one or the other half, like language, or appreciating a good wine, or making love to a woman.' The remark hung in the air, like an accusing finger. Then he resumed: 'There's a tangle of nerves bridging the hemispheres: the commissure or corpus callosum. They're the means by which we synthesise the different models of the world constructed in either hemisphere; the analytic and the emotional, for instance. But the Kiwidinok drive did something to my head. Nerve impulses found it difficult to cross the commissure, because it required movement against the preferred axis of the polarisation field. I found my thoughts – my conscious experience – stagnating in one or the other hemisphere. I'd think of things, but I couldn't assign names to any of the mental symbols I was imagining, because the requisite neural paths were obstructed.'

'But it didn't last long.'

He waved his hand. 'Longer than you think. We got there, eventually. They showed me the sun and it was faint, but not nearly as faint as the brightest stars, which meant they couldn't have carried me very far beyond the system.'

'Just beyond the cometary halo.'

'Mm. To within a few light-minutes of Perdition, except of course we didn't even know it existed.'

'Everything that you've told me,' Sergio said, 'accords exactly with what we were told in the seminary. If you now reveal that the object in question was a neutron star, I don't see how your account can differ in any significant way from the standard teachings. I mean, the mere existence of—'

'It exists,' Ivan said. 'And it's everything I ever said it was. But where it *differs* ...' Then he paused, and allowed Sergio to bring another beaker of water to his lips, from which he drank sparingly, as if the fluid was rationed. Sergio recalled his own thirst much earlier, in the Juggernaut of the clanfolk caravan, after the ornithopter crash, then purged the thought. 'Listen,' the old man said. 'Before we continue, there's something I have to ask you. Do you mind?'

'If I can help.'

'Tell me about Indrani, if you'd be so kind.'

Her name was like a penance. 'I'm sorry?' And then, before he could even hear Ivan's answer, he felt the fear uncoil inside him, like a python waking. He dashed from the room, cupping a hand to his mouth. Retracing his steps, he reached the bridge, leaned over the railinged side and was sick. For a moment, it was a thing of fascination to watch his vomit paint the pristine lower levels of the alabaster spire. Then, when the retching was over, he wiped the tears from his eyes and drew calming breaths, accessing soothing mandalas from his catechist. One of the gargoyles loomed above, large as a naval cannon, the faint curve of its jaw seeming to mock him.

'You seem perturbed,' Bellarmine said, appearing at the bridge's end. 'I read it in the salinity of your skin. It modifies your bioelectric aura.'

'What do you want?'

The cloaked figure moved to his side, the rust-coloured, softly undulating landscape reflected in Bellarmine's mirror-like ovoid face. For an instant, Sergio thought he saw something: a scurry of silver or chrome, something darting between dunetops. But if it was real, it was gone now, and he saw no reason to trouble Bellarmine with his observation. 'Was there another presence, Menendez?'

'Another what?'

'In the room. Another such as I.'

Sergio stared deeply into the mirror before answering. 'I think

I would have noticed. Why? Ought there to have been another?'

The Apparent leaned closer to him, as if to whisper some confidence. After a moment Bellarmine said: 'Put the question from your mind and answer this instead. What has he told you?' The armed gargoyle was reflected in the mirror now, its ugliness magnified by distortion. 'What has he told you? It is a matter of security for the Order. Silence could be considered perfidy.'

'If the Founder wished you to know, he would not have called me from the Diocese.'

'You are in a position of some vulnerability, Menendez.'

'I assure you, I'll hear what he has to say,' Sergio said. 'And whatever message he has for us, I'll ensure that it returns to Vikingville.'

He navigated to the bedside, between the monitors, and resumed his station next to Ivan. 'When you first mentioned her,' he said quietly, with more calm than he believed himself capable of, 'I dared to imagine I'd misheard you.'

'Tell me what happened,' Ivan said, the recorder still conspicuously running. 'I'll then reciprocate by telling you what I *really* experienced around Perdition.'

'Bellarmine knows about her, doesn't he?'

'I guarantee his knowledge of events arrived via a different route than mine. I suggest you start where I did – at the beginning. You'd only recently been consecrated, hadn't you?'

'A few days after the catechist was installed.' Sergio touched the weal on his scalp. 'It was my first mission for the Diocese – a trip north of Vikingville, to visit clanfolk. They were using consecrated servitors supplied by the Order, so there was a pretext for me to arrive with little or no notice.'

It was not difficult to fall into the telling of what had happened. The scavenger clan's caravan had hoved into view below: a long, strung-out procession of beetle-backed machines, some barely larger than dogs, others huge as houses. The largest was the Juggernaut, the command vehicle of the caravan, in which the clan would spend months during their foraging sojourns north of Vikingville, winnowing the desert for technological relics left behind by the wars that had been waged across Mars before and after the Ecumenical Synthesis.

Although it was decades since the last iceteroid had crashed onto the Martian surface, spilling atmosphere across the world, the climate was still roiling in search of an equilibrium it hadn't known for four billion years. Occasionally, squalls would slam into the flight path of an ornithopter, unleashing twisting vortices of separated laminar flow, too sudden and vicious to be smoothed out by the thopter's adaptive flight surfaces.

He hadn't seen it, of course – and when it did hit, it seemed as if the adaptive flight surfaces accommodated the squall even more sluggishly than usual. One of the thopter's wings daggered into the dunes. Sergio saw the other wing buckling like crushed origami. Then – blood sucked from his head by the whiplash – he began to black out, retaining consciousness just long enough to observe the monstrous wheels of the Juggernaut rolling towards him.

And then he woke inside the machine.

'She was like an angel to me,' Sergio said, grateful now that he could unburden himself. 'I wasn't badly injured, really – I felt a lot worse than I had any right to. Indrani fetched me water, which tasted dusty, but was at least drinkable, and then I started to feel a little better. Naturally, I had questions.'

'You wondered why she was alone, a girl like that, in charge of a whole foraging caravan. Was there anyone else?'

'Oh, a brother – Haidar, eight or nine years old. I remember him because I gave him toys.'

'Other than Haidar, though ...'

'She was alone, yes. I asked her, of course. She told me her parents were both dead; that they'd been killed by the Taoist Militia.' Now that he was doing most of the talking, Sergio found his mouth quickly parched, helping himself to the Founder's water. 'I could have called up the catechist's demographics database to check on her story, but I hadn't been ordained long enough to think of that. Anyway, the squall wasn't going anywhere, and neither was my ornithopter – we were stuck in the Juggernaut for a few days at the least. I was—'

'You're about to say that you were weak, traumatised, not fully in control – not really yourself?'

'Except it wouldn't be true, would it? I knew what I was doing. I was weak in my adherence to the Order. But strong enough to make love to Indrani. I had some toys in the ornithopter; trinkets we always carried, to pacify children and make them think favourably of the Order when they grow up. Indrani fetched them for Haidar, to keep him occupied. Then we made love.'

'Your first time, right?'

'There hasn't been another, either.'

'Was it worth it?'

'There's never been a day when I haven't thought of her, if that answers your question. I occasionally delude myself that she might have felt similarly.'

'I'm glad. You're going to sin, at least have some fun.'

But when the storm had died, and all that remained of his ornithopter was a pair of glistening wingtips protruding from a moraine of red dust, two lightweight surface vehicles scudded from the south. They were tricycles, bouncing on obese tyres, their riders cocooned in filigreed cockpits, enfoliated by fuel cells and comms modules.

Indrani's parents.

'I never understood why she'd lied to me, manufactured the whole story about running the caravan on her own; about her parents being murdered by the Taoists. Perhaps she initiated everything that happened, with that lie.'

'That would be convenient.'

'In any case, I never had a chance to find out. Her parents still had to dock their tricycles in the Juggernaut's vehicle bay, which gave us time to fall into our old roles. If her parents suspected anything, I never saw it. No; they shamed me with their humility and hospitality. It was another three days before we could meet with a transporter that was returning to Vikingville. And when I arrived at the seminary, they treated me as a hero. Except for some of the other priests, who seemed to guess what had happened.'

'Yet it didn't destroy you.'

'No,' Sergio said. 'But I always feared I'd hear her name again. I was right to fear, wasn't I?'

'You probably imagine that she lodged a complaint with the Diocese, or that her family somehow learned the truth and did it themselves. But that's not how it happened. Not at all.'

'How did Bellarmine find out?'

'I'll tell you, but first I have to reciprocate my side of the bargain.'

Sergio took a deep breath, oddly aware now that the room seemed more claustrophobic than earlier; darker and more oppressive, as if it was physically trying to squeeze the life out of the man dying within it.

'All right,' he said. 'I'm not sure why you wanted to know about Indrani, but you're right. I should hear about Perdition. Although I don't see how anything you can say can really—'

'Menendez, shut up. What you saw on the cards in the seminary, on the day you were ordained, all that was true. Perdition exists; it's a neutron star, just like I always said it was.' And then Ivan talked about the nature of the star, things Sergio had learned in the seminary but then forgotten, because they were not absolutely central to his faith. That a neutron star was a sphere of nuclear matter forged in the heart of a dying star, containing as much mass as the sun, but compressed into a size no larger than Vikingville. A sugar lump from its heart would have weighed half a billion tons. Perdition was still cooling rapidly, like a cherry-red ingot removed from the furnace, implying that it had been born no more than a few hundred thousand years earlier, very close to its present position. A hot, blue star must have died, outshining the entire galaxy in its expiration. The nebula that star had shed was gone now, but there was no doubting what had happened.

Perdition had been born in a supernova.

'It shouldn't have existed,' Ivan said. 'No evidence for a supernova was ever found; no mini-extinction or enhancement in the local mutation rate; no dieback or brief flourish of speciation. Nothing.' The man looked around at the few candles still burning, their incense no longer the dominant smell in the room. 'Something like a supernova doesn't just happen without anyone noticing. Matter of fact, if you're as close to it as we would have been, you're not going to have the luxury of noticing much else, ever again. You're going to be a pile of ashes. And yet it must have happened, or else there'd be no Perdition.'

'God must have intervened.'

'Yeah. Must have poked his big, old finger into the heart of that collapsing star, causing it to happen in just such a way that we didn't get crisped. That's the point, isn't it? Our little miracle. And I suppose if you're going to have a miracle, it's not a bad one.'

The essence of it was simple enough: it had been known, on purely theoretical grounds, that supernova explosions might not be completely symmetric; that the blast might not emerge in a perfectly spherical fashion. Tiny initial imperfections in the dynamics of the pre-explosion core collapse might be magnified chaotically, building and building, until the star blew apart in a hugely asymmetric manner, lopsidedly spilling half its guts in one direction.

'They showed me how delicate it was,' Ivan said. 'How precise the initial conditions must have been. If they'd differed by one part in a billion—'

'We wouldn't be having this conversation.'

'And what does that tell you – us – Menendez?'

Sergio looked guardedly at the recorder. An ill-chosen word at this point could ruin his position in the Diocese, yet what seemed more important now was to give the Founder the answer he wanted to hear. 'An event of staggering improbability happened, an event that had to happen for humankind to survive at all. A miracle, if you like. An act of intervention by God, who arranged for the initial conditions to be just as they had to be.'

'You must have been teacher's pet at the seminary, son.'

For the first time, Sergio felt angry, though he fought to keep it from his voice. 'What they taught me, Founder, is only what they learned from you, on your return from Perdition. Are you saying you were misinterpreted?'

'No, not at all. Is that damned thing still running?'

'Would you like me to turn it off?'

'No, but move it closer because I want what I'm about to say to be beyond any possible doubt. Because when you take this back to the Diocese, they'll find every possible way to twist my words – even what I'm saying now.' He waited while Sergio adjusted the position of the recorder, a futile gesture but one that seemed to satisfy Ivan. Then he said: 'No one misinterpreted a word of what I said. I lied. Maybe it had something to do with the way the Kiwidinok drive interfered with brain function.'

'That would be convenient, wouldn't it?'

'Touché. Do you know about temporal-lobe epilepsy, Menendez? Almost no one suffers from it now, but those that do often report feelings of intense religious ecstasy.'

After long moments, Sergio said: 'The kinds of drugs that have been administered to you could cause hallucinations, I think. With all respect.'

Ivan pivoted his body across to the other side of the bed, rummaging in the dark pile of effects placed on the nightstand next to it. He held up a syringe, needle glistening in candlelight. 'I told them I was more frightened than in pain. It's hard to die a prophet when you don't believe, Menendez. They gave me this drug; said it purged fear. Well, maybe it did – but not enough.'

Words formed in Sergio's mouth and seemed to emerge of their own volition.

'How did you lie, and why did you do it?'

'To begin with, it wasn't really lying; I don't think I was clinically sane, and I think I believed my own delusions as much as anyone. But afterwards – when my brain function had stabilised, perhaps – *then* it became lying, because I decided to maintain the untruth I'd already started. And you know what? There was nothing difficult about it. More than that, it was seductive. They wanted to believe everything I said, and there was nothing that could be contradicted by the recording devices. And in return they feted me. I didn't ask for it, but before I knew it I was at the centre of a cult – one that imagined it glimpsed God in the asymmetric physics of a stellar collapse. And then the cult became a religious movement, and because it was the only movement that had no need for faith, it soon absorbed those that did.'

'The Synthesis.'

Ivan's nod was very weak now. 'It was much too late to stop it by then, Menendez. Not without having them turn against me. But now I'm dying . . .'

'They won't love you for it.'

'Sooner be reviled than martyred. Devil always had the best tunes, eh? Seems healthier to me. Which is why you're here, of course. To hear the truth, take it back to Vikingville and begin dismantling the Order.'

'They'll hate me equally,' Sergio said, feeling as if he was debating a piece of theological arcana that had no connection with reality. 'Besides – I still don't see how you can possibly have been lying, if Perdition exists. If there was no divine intervention, then all that's left is – what, massive improbability?'

'Exactly.'

'And that's somehow preferable?'

'Truthful, maybe. Isn't that all that matters?' Ivan said it with no great conviction, still holding the syringe up to the light, as if putting it down would have been the more strenuous act.

'Quantum mechanics says there is a small but finite probability that this syringe will vanish from my hand and reappear on the other side of the Temple wall. What would you think if that happened?'

'I'd think you were a skilled conjuror. If, however, there was no deception ... I'd have to conclude that a very unlikely event had just happened.'

'And what if your life depended on it happening?'

'I don't follow.'

'Well, imagine that the liquid in this syringe is an unstable explosive; that in one second it'll detonate, killing everyone inside this room. If the syringe didn't jump, you'd be dead.'

'And if I survive ... it must, logically, have happened. But that's not very likely, is it?'

'Never said it was. But the point is, it doesn't *have* to be – an event can be incredibly unlikely, and still be guaranteed to happen, provided there are sufficient opportunities for it to happen, sufficient trials.'

'Nothing profound in that.'

'No, but in the quantum view the trials happen *simultaneously*, in as many parallel versions of reality as are necessary to contain all possible permutations of all quantum states. Are you following me?'

'I was, until a moment ago.'

A smile haunted the old man's lips. 'Let's say that there are, for the sake of argument, a billion possible future versions of this room, each containing one identical or near-identical copy of you and me. Of course, there are many more than a billion – it's a number so huge that the physical universe wouldn't be large enough for us to write it down. But call it a billion. Now, each of those rooms differs from this one on the quantum level, but in the majority of cases the change is going to look random, meaningless. There will also be changes that look suspiciously coherent. But all that's happening is that every possible probabilistic outcome is being played out, completely blindly.' He waited while Sergio fetched him some more water, brow furrowed as if composing his thoughts. 'Logically, there exists a future state of the room in which the syringe borrows enough energy to tunnel beyond the wall and explode safely. It's unlikely, yes, but it *will* happen if there are sufficient trials. And in the quantum view, those trials all happen instantly, simultaneously, every moment we breathe. We feel ourselves moving seamlessly along one personal history, whereas we're shedding myriad versions of ourselves at each instant – some of which survive, some of which don't.' He released the syringe, allowing it to clatter to the floor, amongst the personal detritus next to his bed. 'Not bad for an effluent disposal technician from Smolensk, huh?'

'I believe I see the tack of your argument.'

'When the supernova happened, the chance of any one version of us surviving was absurdly small – yet one version of us *was* guaranteed to survive, because every possible quantum outcome was considered.'

'How do you know all this?'

'Isn't it obvious by now? The Kiwidinok showed me. And I mean *showed* me. Put it in my head, all in one go. Their consciousness – if you can call it consciousness – is blurred across event-lines. It's what they gained when they became less like us and more like machines. That's why they see things differently.'

Sergio took a breath to absorb that.

'And what did they show you?'

'Dead worlds. Much like Earth, but where the initial conditions of the supernova collapse weren't quite right to avoid our annihilation. Where, if you like, God hadn't poked his finger into quite the right place. Worlds of ash and darkness.'

He dug through his personal effects again, brushing aside the topsoil of junk. His hands found a small, flat bundle that he passed to Sergio. The oiled paper of the bundle unravelled in Sergio's fingers, exposing a cache of glossy grey cards much like those he had been shown in the seminary, shortly after his catechist had assumed residence.

But these images were not the same.

'I don't know how they did it,' the Founder said, 'but the Kiwidinok were able to interfere with the recording devices I took with me to Perdition. They were able to plant images on them, data from other event-lines.'

'Where the supernova happened differently.'

'Where we got crisped.'

In each image the degree of laceration was different, but it was never less than a mortal wounding, so absolute that life had not managed to re-establish tenancy on dry land. In some of the images it was possible to believe that something might still live in the shrivelled, oddly shorelined oceans that mottled the surface. In others, there were no oceans to speak of at all, nothing much resembling atmosphere.

'Mostly, that's how it was,' Ivan said. 'Mostly, we never made it through. *This* event-line, the one we're living in, is the freak exception: a remote strand on the edge of probability space. It only exists because we're here to observe it. And we're only here to observe it because it happened.'

Sergio picked through the rest of the images, variations on the same desolate theme. He knew with utter conviction that they were real – or as real as any data shared between event-lines could ever be. These images were secrets that Ivan had kept for eighty years – images that spoke not of divine intervention, not of miracle, but of brutality. *We survived*, Sergio thought, *not because we were favoured, not because we earned salvation, but because the laws of probability decreed that* someone *had to*.

'What now?'

'Take what you have back to the Diocese. Make them listen.'

'You're asking a lot of me.'

'You're a man of God,' Ivan said, with very little irony. 'Ask Him for assistance.'

'Why should I still believe?'

'Because now, more than ever, you need faith. That was what was always missing – when we had proof we didn't need it. But our proof was a fiction. Our Order was a lie built upon lies. But tearing down the Order doesn't mean tearing down your faith, if you still have it. Me, I never found it, except in a particularly good thermal or at the end of a bottle. But you're a young man. You could still find faith, even if you haven't already. I think you'll need it too. It'll be a kind of jihad you'll be fighting.'

'You'll find it harder than you imagine,' said a voice, which did not come from the figure in the bed.

'Bellarmine,' Sergio said, turning around to face the Apparent, who had stolen quietly into the chamber. There was a whisper of scythed air, a flash of metal, and Bellarmine's hand acquired the cards from Sergio's grip. For a moment, the Apparent held them up to its face, feigning curiosity. Then it ripped them to shreds with a deft flicking movement.

'I knew of the existence of these images,' the wasp-like voice said. 'It was hardly worth the effort of destroying them.'

'Be careful what you say. The recorder's still running.'

'My voice won't register. I'm addressing you directly via your catechist. If you play the recording to anyone in the Diocese, all they'll hear is you addressing an empty room.'

Sergio reached over and killed the recording. 'Speak now, then. What's going on? How did you know about Indrani?'

Bellarmine came closer. Sergio felt something crawl through his skull.

'Isn't it obvious? Via your catechist.' There was a deeper timbre to his voice now that he was speaking aloud. 'You imagine that the device is passive; that it exists merely to offer guidance and to facilitate the viewing of holy data. But there's more to it than that. Behind my face is an array of superconducting devices, sensitive to minute changes in the immediate electromagnetic environment. It's how I sensed your nervousness on the balcony. The array enables me to read the data captured by your catechist – everything that you see and hear. You betrayed yourself, Menendez.'

'How long have you known?'

'We Apparents share such data as it conveniences us. I was informed of your indiscretion not long after the incident itself.'

'Then why ... no, wait, I see. You were waiting, weren't you?' Now that it was clear to him, he almost laughed at the obviousness of it. 'You kept the evidence from the Diocese, until such time as it might be useful in blackmailing me. That's clever, Bellarmine. Very clever. I'm impressed.'

'You were nothing exceptional.'

'Of course not,' Ivan said, his voice a death-rattle. 'How could he be? When he was rescued by Indrani, he was just another priest green from the seminary.'

'There must be others,' Sergio said.

'Perhaps not,' Bellarmine said. 'You were especially weak, Menendez. You offered yourself to us.'

'I broke no vows.'

'Then why conceal what happened until now?' Quietly, Bellarmine addressed the Founder. 'You know too. He spoke of the matter with you, I see.'

Sergio returned the recorder to his bag. 'You can't destroy this,' he said to the watching machine. 'The Diocese expects a recording, whether you like it or not.'

'First you have to return to Vikingville,' Bellarmine said, and then took a step nearer to Sergio. But before he reached him, the Apparent stopped and leaned his faceless frame across the Founder's bed.

'Go,' Ivan said. 'Get the hell out of here, while you still can.'

Bellarmine knelt and retrieved the syringe that the Founder had dropped. With a series of mechanically precise movements, he plunged the needle into a rubber-capped bottle, congesting the hypodermic with something as clear and deadly as snake venom. 'You took this to fend off the fear of death. Now it will hasten its coming. Isn't that a kindness?'

The Apparent snatched aside the yellowing sheets, exposing the man's hairless sternum. The Founder reached up and wrestled with Bellarmine's wrist as the needle descended towards his heart. Sergio took a step closer, watching as the man's jaw clenched in the agony of resistance, his free hand pawing impotently at the machine's chest.

'Menendez! I'm a dead man anyway! Go!'

Sergio dived forwards, trying to wrestle Bellarmine away from the bed, but the Apparent might as well have been some huge piece of industrial machinery anchored to the Temple itself. The descent of the syringe did not falter, even when Bellarmine flung Sergio across the room. Sergio hit the wall, breath ejected from his lungs, the hard edges of the Kiwidinok frieze pushing into his spine. His vision swimming in stars, he struggled to his feet.

'I'm sorry, Ivan,' he wheezed.

The needle reached his flesh, then entered, and as the tip broke the skin, Ivan's strength flew away like a flock of startled crows.

'I won't let you down,' Sergio said. 'That much I swear. And you're right – this is the better way. Better faith than proof.'

Bellarmine's voice was horrifically calm. 'You won't succeed.'

'Good . . . thermals,' Ivan said, and then emitted a final gasp, his eyes locked open, less in shock than sudden joy.

Sergio was already running. He had almost made it to the chamber's door when Bellarmine reached him, impeding his progress with surprising gentleness.

'I don't want to kill you, Menendez.'

Behind Bellarmine, Sergio saw a second disconnected globe bob across the room, hued more yellow than silver.

'You want me to betray Ivan – to return with a faked recording, is that it?'

'Better to betray one man than a God.'

The haversack slipped to the floor. 'If I refuse, you'll kill me.'

The other Apparent loomed behind Bellarmine and then did something Sergio had not been expecting. Maybe the shock of it registered in his expression, because Bellarmine whipped around, momentarily relinquishing his grip. The other Apparent's cloak had parted to reveal human hands, gripping a weapon.

There was a colourless flash and an intense pulse of pain throughout Sergio's skull. He began to scream, but the pain was already over, abrupt as a strobe. Bellarmine's armoured frame collapsed to the ground and quivered there, like a beached eel.

'I hit him with an EM pulse,' said the other, whose voice lacked the machinelike quality of the fallen cardinal. 'Must have hit your implant as well; hope it didn't hurt too badly.'

'Who are you?'

One free hand reached up and snatched aside the alloy mask, which Sergio now saw was perforated with tiny viewholes. What lay behind it was the face of a very young man, drenched in sweat, curtained by lank, black hair. A face he almost recognised, as if seen through a distorting lens. 'I think you know my sister, priest. And I think we'd better get moving – the pulse won't keep him down for long, and I'll bet he doesn't need much time to reboot.'

'What's happening?'

'What's happening is, you're being rescued.'

'You're Indrani's brother?'

Haidar nodded. 'But I think we'd better run and save the questions for later – there are more of his kind between us and your little plane. It can seat two, can't it?'

'At a push.'

Behind them, Bellarmine made a sound like a squealing kitten, limbs thrashing. The silver ovoid of his face turned to Sergio, framed in candleflame. 'I will kill you, Menendez, if you run.'

Sergio closed his fists around the nearest candelabrum, wrenching it from its sconce, amazed at his own strength. The flame extinguished immediately, and for a moment he was left holding the wrought-iron Kiwidinok fist as if he hadn't the faintest idea what to do with it. Then he saw the syringe, still jutting from

Ivan's sternum. And the perfect mirror of Bellarmine's face, like a tranquil lake in moonlight.

He smashed the candelabrum into the ovoid, the thin reflective patina crumpling under the impact.

Haidar whistled. 'You don't just burn your bridges, priest. You cremate the bastards.'

It took far longer to reach the ground than he'd expected, and along the way Haidar had to shoot three more Apparents, leaving each one in a state of palsy. 'Bellarmine's probably on his way already,' the man said. 'He'll have alerted the others by now, so we won't have the element of surprise. Not that we really need it, with this little toy.' He waved the EM gun ahead of them, like a crucifix. 'It's a real weapon, left over from before the Synthesis. Not that the Synthesis exactly ended wars, either, but you get my drift.'

'How does it work?'

'Screws the nervous system. Not the central processor – that's mainly optical, but the servosystems that drive their musculature. With your implant, it would have fried the interface points, where it couples to your neurons, but it wouldn't have touched the data inside it.'

'That's good. All we have is what's in my head.'

'And mine too,' Haidar said. 'Don't forget, I was there all the time; heard every word he said.'

Ahead, daylight burned a hole in the darkness, catching the nested edges of the Kiwidinok figures engraved around the corridor walls. 'What were you doing here?'

'Ivan knew about Indrani,' Haidar said. 'But he didn't find out about her the same way Bellarmine did. Fact is, Ivan heard the story from Indrani herself. Or from me, which is much the same thing.'

'I don't follow.' While he spoke, Haidar doused another pair of machines, each pulse of the weapon triggering sympathetic echoes somewhere in Sergio's cortex.

'Indrani sent me,' Haidar said. 'To put the story right. Took her nine years to build up courage, but I guess she knew it wasn't going to be easy. And she trusted the old guy. Figured he wasn't part of it all, and she had to get an audience with him before he croaked.'

They reached the outside. Sergio was relieved to see his ornithopter still resting intact, like a perched dragonfly of blown glass.

'Part of what?'

'What happened to you out there, in the caravan.' Haidar paused to discard his cloak, revealing a tight-fitting, ribbed surface suit flashed with decals of clan affiliation. 'Listen, it wasn't quite how you thought it was. I know because I heard you tell the Founder, and I don't think you were lying.'

They sprinted towards the ornithopter. 'How was it, then?'

'The crash was no accident, for a start. You said it yourself – it was as if the squall took the plane unawares. Well, the squall wasn't planned, but you were pretty much guaranteed to crash then – someone had monkeyed with the plane.'

'Someone wanted me to crash?'

'Not fatally, but enough to keep you from getting home, so you'd have to seek shelter in the caravan, and then fall prey to my sister's undeniable charms. Worked, didn't it?'

'Only someone in the Diocese could have done that.'

'It's the Machinehood. They're everywhere, right? Seems they see themselves as the next phase in evolution, and the Order's how they're gonna subjugate humanity without anyone noticing. They do it to most of the priests fresh out of the seminary, is what Indrani reckons – set them up for a fall and watch it happen.'

'They knew.'

'What?'

'The other priests. They knew what had happened to me. I assumed it was because my lies weren't very convincing. I never stopped to think something similar might have happened to them as well.'

'Old Ivan was right, priest.'

'What?'

'You really were green.'

They reached the waiting ornithopter. Sergio opened the cockpit, frantically adjusting the seat to make room for a passenger behind him, ratcheting it forwards. 'Think you can squeeze in there? It's a long flight back to Vikingville.'

'Hopefully we don't have that far to go.'

Sergio followed him into the enclosure, slamming the canopy down and bringing the little flying machine to sluggish life, its wings quickening with shivers of excited chitin. 'Let me get this straight,' he said, fingers dancing over the controls. 'They set us up for a fall and some of us take one. They learn about it through our catechists – and then we can always be controlled, if we threaten to turn against the Order.'

'That's about the size of it.'

They were aloft.

'It's elegant. Cynical, but elegant. But it wouldn't work without outside assistance.'

'Ways and means,' Haidar said. 'With Indrani, it was just another form of blackmail. The clan was in hock to the Asymmetrists – we depended on their consecrated machines to make a living. Someone from the Order – someone who must have been working for the Machinehood – contacted Indrani and let her know what was expected of her, and what would happen if she failed. That her family would be ruined. That she'd probably starve.'

The ornithopter's shadow grew smaller, wings beating furiously to gain altitude, each thrust sending rainbow moiré patterns down their length.

'How did you infiltrate the Order?'

'There are tunnels under the sand, left over from the wars. Some of them reach beneath the dome. Being good clanfolk, we know all about 'em. And my disguise only had to fool the machines from a distance.'

'Bellarmine was suspicious.'

'Couldn't read me like the others. Must have crossed his mind that I was someone really high up, or a new faction amongst the Machinehood. Either way, bad news.'

They punched through the polymer now; a lurch of resistance and then freedom. Sergio risked a look around at the receding Temple, watching as the defensive gargoyles opened their mouths and their little eyes ignited.

A voice chirped in his head. It might once have been the voice of God, but the damaged catechist reduced it to an irritating buzz, like a bluebottle trapped in a thimble.

'I think they're threatening us,' Sergio said. 'They might try shooting us down. They'd rather I never returned to Vikingville, even though they can discredit me. Too much risk of failure, I imagine.'

'Just fly it, priest.'

The sky on either side of the cockpit flared red, like a sudden bright dusk. Lasers stabbed past them, and then knifed closer, converging, so that the ornithopter was encased in a tunnel of linear red beams.

Again the buzzing in his skull.

The beams touched the wings, their veined skin vanishing in a puff of ionised chitin, leaving only a blackened skeletal subframe. The nose of the ornithopter pitched down as if in prayer.

'I think we're going to crash,' Sergio said, with what struck him as astonishing calm. He grasped for what remained of his faith, not entirely sure that there was anything left to salvage.

And then hit the ground.

There was light, and blackness, and a period of unguessable time – perhaps comparable to the limbo that the Founder had experienced aboard the Kiwidinok ship, during his flight to Perdition. Yet when it ended, Sergio found that he had barely travelled. He was face-down in sand, unutterably cold, his lungs engulfed in the pain of inhalation. The snapped wreckage of the ornithopter was visible in his peripheral vision, like a toy crushed by an indolent child. Haidar was looming over him.

'I think you'll live, priest, but you have to move, now.' The brother spoke with an ease Sergio now found unimaginable. He remembered that many of the clanfolk were better adapted to the Martian atmosphere than those who lived in Vikingville and the other cities. Sergio tried moving and felt several daggers readjust themselves across his chest.

'I think I've broken some ribs.'

'If you don't move, you'll have a lot worse to worry about. We have to get over this.'

Behind Haidar, a dune reached halfway to the zenith. 'You want me to climb that?'

'They're coming after us,' Haidar said, pointing towards the Temple. Almost convulsing from the effort, Sergio adjusted himself until he could see the view clearly. Mirror-faced Apparents were emerging from the central spire, dashing across the terrazzo. One of them had a fist projecting from his face.

'I'm not sure I can make it,' Sergio said. 'I'm pretty hurt – maybe you should just—'

The brother hauled him to his feet, a movement that set off an agonised fireworks display inside his chest. Strangely, though, when he was standing, the pain eased. 'If you have broken your ribs, you'll feel better – less pressure on your ribcage now that you're standing. Think you can make it?'

'You risked a lot to help me, didn't you?'

He shrugged, as if it was of no consequence. 'I owed it to Indrani. She'd have done it herself, except there was no way I was going to let her. For some reason she thinks she loves you, priest, even after nine years. Me, I don't pretend to understand women.'

Sergio planted one foot in front of the other. 'What will we find on the other side of this dune?'

'More clanfolk than you've ever seen, if a few good people keep their word. And I don't think they're going to be in a party mood.'

And as he spoke, something arced across the sky, from the dune's summit to the central spire of the Asymmetrist Temple. It was a weapon – a small missile – something salvaged by the clanfolk; a relic of the wars that had raged across Mars before and after the Synthesis. Where it hit, a shard of the spire dislodged and crashed to the ground, smashing through layers of underlying masonry as it fell.

'He said it'd be a jihad,' Sergio said. 'A holy war.'

'He was right,' Haidar said. 'And I think it's just begun.'

'Angels of Ashes' is a story with an amusing tale behind it ... one that has nothing whatsoever to do with the contents of the piece itself. By the time the second half of the nineties rolled around, I was maintaining sales to Interzone *at a satisfactorily steady rate of a story or two a year. I was grateful that they were taking my stuff, but also aware of how precarious my position was. I needed to prove to myself that more than one editor was willing to pay for my stories, so (since the UK market wasn't exactly over-endowed with paying magazines) I started to think about selling my material to US outlets. I can't remember if I wrote 'Angels' with that ambition specifically in mind, but I do remember that it was the first story in a long while that I didn't submit to* Interzone. I did *submit it to the* Magazine of Fantasy & Science Fiction, *but they bounced it very quickly: a nice enough rejection note, but not quite what they were looking for. So I sent it to* Asimov's Science Fiction Magazine, *edited at the time by the much-respected Gardner Dozois. And I waited. And waited.*

Three months went by. I heard nothing. According to the magazine's guidelines, if you hadn't heard back from them within three months, you could assume your submission had been lost in the mail. I waited a bit longer, just to be on the safe side. Then I dutifully printed out a new copy of the story and sent that off in the post, again to Asimov's. *I included a covering note to the effect that I was resubmitting a story that must have gone astray the first time. And I waited. And waited.*

At the time that this all happened, I was living in a Summer House – a 'zomerhuis'. This is, I suspect, a peculiarly Dutch concept that doesn't translate too well. Basically, my home was a self-contained brick house built in the backyard of the house belonging to my landlady. Because I had no mailbox accessible from the street, all my incoming post had to pass through my landlady's house first. She'd sort it from her own, then pass it through to me. I'd become so accustomed to this system that I didn't give it a moment's thought. Until, that is, the day my landlady knocked on the door of the Summer House and presented a letter she'd found that day. 'Found', because it had turned up during a spring clean, when she'd discovered some post that had dropped under her own mailbox some months earlier. Inspection of the envelope showed that the letter had been posted from America half a year before. I opened it with trembling hands, half-knowing what it had to be. There it was, an acceptance letter – and contract – for the copy of the story I'd assumed to have gone astray. I was pleased, but also mortified at the fact that (a) I hadn't responded with the contract, and to say thanks, and (b) I'd added to the confusion by resubmitting the same story. But all was well in the end, which is to say that it wasn't the last story Gardner ever bought from me.

A misplaced letter, turned up during a spring clean, also played a role in the publication of my first novel. But that's another story. 'Angels of Ashes', incidentally, is the title of a song by the wonderful Scott Walker.

Space war is god-awful slow.

Mouser's long-range sensors had sniffed the bogey two days ago, but it had taken all that time just to creep within kill-range. I figured it had to be another dud. With ordnance, fuel and morale all low, we were ready to slink back to Tiger's Eye anyway; let one of the other thickships pick up the sweep in this sector.

So – still groggy after frogsleep – I wasn't exactly wetting myself with excitement, not even when Mouser started spiking the thick with combat-readiness psychogens. Even when we went to Attack-Con-One, all I did was pause the neurodisney I was tripping (Hellcats of Solar War Three, since you asked), slough my hammock and swim languidly up to the bridge.

'Junk,' I said, looking over Yarrow's shoulder at the readout. 'War debris or another of those piss-poor chondrites. Betcha.'

'Sorry, kid. Everything checks out.'

'Hostiles?'

'Nope. Positive on the exhaust: dead ringer for the stolen ship.' She traced a webbed hand across the swathe of decorations that already curled around her neck. 'Want your stripes now or when we get back?'

'You actually think this'll net us a pair of tigers?'

'Damn right it will.'

I nodded, and thought: She isn't necessarily wrong. No defector, no stolen military secrets reaching the Royalists. Ought to be worth a medal, maybe even a promotion.

So why did I feel something wasn't right?

'All right,' I said, hoping to drown qualms in routine. 'How soon?'

'Missiles are already away, but she's five light-minutes from us, so the quacks won't reach her for six hours. Longer if she makes a run for cover.'

'Run for cover? That's a joke.'

'Yeah, hilarious.' Yarrow swelled one of the holographic displays until it hovered between us.

It was a map of the Swirl, tinted to show zones controlled by us or the Royalists. An enormous, slowly rotating disk of primordial material, 800 AU edge to edge; wide enough that light took more than four days to traverse it.

Most of the action was near the middle, in the light-hour of space around the central star Fomalhaut. Immediately around the sun was a material-free void that we called the Inner Clearing Zone, but beyond that began the Swirl proper: metal-rich lanes of dust condensing slowly into rocky planets. Both sides wanted absolute control of those planet-forming Feeding Zones – prime real estate for the day when one side beat the other and could recommence mining operations – so that was where our vast armies of wasps mainly slugged things out. We humans – Royalist and Standardist both – kept much further out, where the Swirl thinned to metal-depleted icy rubble. Even hunting the defector hadn't taken us within ten light-hours of the Feeding Zones, and we'd become used to having a lot of empty space to ourselves. Apart from the defector, there shouldn't have been anything else out here to offer cover.

But there was. Big too, not much more than half a light-minute from the rat.

'Practically pissing distance,' Yarrow observed.

'Too close for coincidence. What is it?'

'Splinter. Icy planetesimal, you want to get technical.'

'Not this early in the day.' But I remembered how one of our tutors back at the academy put it: Splinters are icy slag, spat out of the Swirl. In a few hundred thousand years there'll be a baby solar system around Fomalhaut, but there'll also be shitloads of junk surrounding it, leftovers on million-year orbits.

'Worthless to us,' Yarrow said, scratching at the ribbon of black hair that ran all the way from brow to fluke. 'But evidently not to ratty.'

'What if the Royalists left supplies on the splinter? She could be aiming to refuel before the final hop to their side of the Swirl.'

Yarrow gave me her best withering look.

'Yeah, okay,' I said. 'Not my smartest ever suggestion.'

Yarrow nodded sagely. 'Ours is not to question, Spirey. Ours is to fire and forget.'

Six hours after the quackheads had been launched from Mouser, Yarrow floated in the bridge, fluked tail coiled beneath her. She resembled an inverted question mark, and if I'd been superstitious I'd have said that wasn't necessarily the best of omens.

'You kill me,' she said.

An older pilot called Quillin had been the first to go siren – first to swap legs for tail. Yarrow followed a year later. Admittedly it made sense, an adaptation to the fluid-filled environment of a high-gee thickship. And I accepted the cardiovascular modifications that enabled us to breathe thick, as well as the biomodified skin, which let us tolerate cold and vacuum far longer than any unmodified human. Not to mention the billions of molecule-sized demons that coursed through our bodies, or the combat-specific psycho-modifications. But swapping your legs for a tail touched off too many queasy resonances in me. Had to admire her nerve, though.

'What?' I said.

'That neurodisney shit. Isn't a real space war good enough for you?'

'Yeah, except I don't think this is it. When was the last time one of us actually looked a Royalist in the eye?'

She shrugged. 'Something like four hundred years ago.'

'Point made. At least in Solar War Three you get some blood. See, it's all set on planetary surfaces – Titan, Europa, all those moons they've got back in Sol System. Trench warfare, hand-to-hand stuff. You know what adrenalin is, Yarrow?'

'Managed without it until now. And there's another thing: don't know much about Greater Earth history, but there was never a Solar War Three.'

'It's conjectural,' I said. 'And in any case it almost happened; they almost went to the brink.'

'Almost?'

'It's set in a different timeline.'

She grinned, shaking her head. 'I'm telling you, you kill me.'

'She made a move yet?' I asked.

'What?'

'The defector.'

'Oh, we're back in reality now?' Yarrow laughed. 'Sorry, this is going to be slightly less exciting than Solar War Three.'

'Inconsiderate,' I said. 'Think the bitch would give us a run for our money.' And as I spoke the weapons readout began to pulse faster and faster, like the cardiogram of a fluttering heart. 'How long now?'

'One minute, give or take a few seconds.'

'Want a little bet?'

Yarrow grinned, sallow in the red-alert lighting. 'As if I'd say no, Spirey.'

So we hammered out a wager: Yarrow betting fifty tiger-tokens the rat would attempt some last-minute evasion. 'Won't do her a blind bit of good,' she said. 'But that won't stop her. It's human nature.'

Me, I suspected our target was either dead or asleep.

'Bit of an empty ritual, isn't it?'

'What?'

'I mean, the attack happened the best part of five minutes ago, realtime. The rat's already dead, and nothing we can do can influence that outcome.'

Yarrow bit on a nicotine stick. 'Don't get all philosophical on me, Spirey.'

'Wouldn't dream of it. How long?'

'Five seconds. Four . . .'

She was somewhere between three and four when it happened. I remember thinking that there was something disdainful about the rat's actions: she had deliberately waited until the last possible moment, and had dispensed with our threat with the least effort necessary.

That was how it felt, anyway.

Nine of the quackheads detonated prematurely, far short of kill-range. For a moment the tenth remained, zeroing in on the defector – but instead it failed to detonate, until it was just beyond range.

For long moments there was silence while we absorbed what had happened. Yarrow broke it, eventually.

'Guess I just made myself some money,' she said.

Colonel Wendigo's hologram delegate appeared, momentarily

frozen before shivering to life. With her too-clear, too-young eyes she fixed first Yarrow and then me.

'Intelligence was mistaken,' she said. 'Seems the defector doctored records to conceal the theft of those countermeasures. But you harmed her anyway?'

'Just,' said Yarrow. 'Her quackdrive's spewing out exotics like Spirey after a bad binge. No hull damage, but—'

'Assessment?'

'Making a run for the splinter.'

Wendigo nodded. 'And then?'

'She'll set down and make repairs.' Yarrow paused, added: 'Radar says there's metal on the surface. Must've been a wasp battle there, before the splinter got lobbed out of the Swirl.'

The delegate nodded in my direction. 'Concur, Spirey?'

'Yes, sir,' I said, trying to suppress the nervousness I always felt around Wendigo, even though almost all my dealings with her had been via simulations like this. Yarrow was happy to edit the conversation afterwards, inserting the correct honorifics before transmitting the result back to Tiger's Eye – but I could never free myself of the suspicion that Wendigo would somehow unravel the unedited version, with all its implicit insubordination. Not that any of us didn't inwardly accord Wendigo all the respect she was due. She'd nearly died in the Royalist strike against Tiger's Eye fifteen years ago – the one in which my mother was killed. Actual attacks against our two mutually opposed comet bases were rare, not happening much more than every other generation – more gestures of spite than anything else. But this had been an especially bloody one, killing an eighth of our number and opening city-sized portions of our base to vacuum. Wendigo was caught in the thick of the kinetic attack.

Now she was chimeric, lashed together by cybernetics. Not much of this showed externally – except that the healed parts of her were too flawless, more porcelain than flesh. Wendigo had not allowed the surgeons to regrow her arms. Story was she lost them trying to pull one of the injured through an open airlock, back into the pressurised zone. She'd almost made it, fighting against the gale of escaping air. Then some no-brainer hit the emergency door control, and when the lock shut it took Wendigo's arms off at the shoulder, along with the head of the person she was saving. She wore prosthetics now, gauntleted in chrome.

'She'll get there a day ahead of us,' I said. 'Even if we pull twenty gees.'

'And probably gone to ground by the time you get there too.'

'Should we try a live capture?'

Yarrow backed me up with a nod. 'It's not exactly been possible before.'

The delegate bided her time before answering. 'Admire your dedication,' she said, after a suitably convincing pause. 'But you'd only be postponing a death sentence. Kinder to kill her now, don't you think?'

Mouser entered kill-range nineteen hours later, a wide pseudo-orbit three thousand klicks out. The splinter – seventeen by twelve klicks across – was far too small to be seen as anything other than a twinkling speck, like a grain of sugar at arm's length. But everything we wanted to know was clear: topology, gravimetrics and the site of the downed ship. That wasn't hard. Quite apart from the fact that it hadn't buried itself completely, it was hot as hell.

'Doesn't look like the kind of touchdown you walk away from,' Yarrow said.

'Think they ejected?'

'No way.' Yarrow sketched a finger through a holographic enlargement of the ship, roughly cone-shaped, vaguely stream-lined just like our own thickship, to punch through the Swirl's densest gas belts. 'Clock those dorsal hatches. Evac pods still in place.'

She was right. The pods could have flung them clear before the crash, but evidently they hadn't had time to bail out. The ensuing impact – even cushioned by the ship's manifold of thick – probably hadn't been survivable.

But there was no point taking chances.

Quackheads would have finished the job, but we'd used up our stock. Mouser carried a particle-beam battery, but we'd have to move uncomfortably close to the splinter before using it. What remained were the molemines, and they should have been per-fectly adequate. We dropped fifteen of them, embedded in a cloud of two hundred identical decoys. Three of the fifteen were des-ignated to dust the wreck, while the remaining twelve would bury deeper into the splinter and attempt to shatter it completely.

That at least was the idea.

It all happened very quickly, not in the dreamy slow motion of a neurodisney. One instant the molemines were descending towards the splinter, and then the next instant they weren't there. Spacing the two instants had been an almost subliminally brief flash.

'Starting to get sick of this,' Yarrow said.

Mouser digested what had happened. Nothing had emanated from the wreck. Instead, there'd been a single pulse of energy seemingly from the entire volume of space around the splinter. Particle weapons, Mouser diagnosed. Probably single-use drones, each tinier than a pebble but numbering hundreds or even thousands. The defector must have sown them on her approach.

But she hadn't touched us.

'It was a warning,' I said. 'Telling us to back off.'

'I don't think so.'

'What?'

'I think the warning's on its way.'

I stared at her blankly for a moment, before registering what she had already seen: arcing from the splinter was something too fast to stop, something against which our minimally armoured thickship had no defence, not even the option of flight.

Yarrow started to mouth some exotic profanity she'd reserved for precisely this moment. There was an eardrum-punishing bang and Mouser shuddered – but we weren't suddenly chewing vacuum.

And that was very bad news indeed.

Antiship missiles come in two main flavours: quackheads and sporeheads. You know which immediately after the weapon has hit. If you're still thinking – if you still exist – chances are it's a sporehead. And at that point your problems are just beginning.

Invasive demon attack, Mouser shrieked. Breather manifold compromised ... which meant something uninvited was in the thick. That was the point of a sporehead: to deliver hostile demons into an enemy ship.

'Mm,' Yarrow said. 'I think it might be time to suit-up.'

Except our suits were a good minute's swim away, into the bowels of Mouser, through twisty ducts that might skirt the infection site. Having no choice, we swam anyway, Yarrow insisting I take the lead even though she was a quicker swimmer. And somewhere –

it's impossible to know exactly where – demons reached us, seeping invisibly into our bodies via the thick. I couldn't pinpoint the moment; it wasn't as if there was a jagged transition between lucidity and demon-manipulated irrationality. Yarrow and I were terrified enough as it was. All I know is it began with a mild agoraphilia: an urge to escape Mouser's flooded confines. Gradually it phased into claustrophobia, and then became fully fledged panic, making Mouser seem as malevolent as a haunted house.

Yarrow ignored her suit, clawing the hull until her fingers spooled blood.

'Fight it,' I said. 'It's just demons triggering our fear centres, trying to drive us out!'

Of course, knowing so didn't help.

Somehow I stayed still long enough for my suit to slither on. Once sealed, I purged the tainted thick with the suit's own supply – but I knew it wasn't going to help much. The phobia already showed that hostile demons had reached my brain, and now it was even draping itself in a flimsy logic. Beyond the ship we'd be able to think rationally. It would only take a few minutes for the thick's own demons to neutralise the invader – and then we'd be able to reboard. Complete delusion, of course.

But that was the point.

When something like coherent thought returned I was outside.

Nothing but me and the splinter.

The urge to escape was only a background anxiety, a flock of stomach butterflies urging me against returning. Was that demon-manipulated fear or pure common sense? I couldn't tell – but what I knew was that the splinter seemed to be beckoning me forwards, and I didn't feel like resisting. Sensible, surely; we'd exhausted all conventional channels of attack against the defector, and now all that remained was to confront her on the territory she'd staked as her own.

But where was Yarrow?

Suit's alarm chimed. Maybe demons were still subjugating my emotions, because I didn't react with my normal speed. I just blinked, licked my lips and stifled a yawn.

'Yeah, what?'

Suit informed me: something massing slightly less than me, two klicks closer to the splinter, on a slightly different orbit. I knew it was Yarrow; also that something was wrong. She was drifting. In my blackout I'd undoubtedly programmed suit to take me down, but Yarrow appeared not to have done anything except bail out.

I jetted closer. And then saw why she hadn't programmed her suit. Would have been tricky. She wasn't wearing one.

I hit ice an hour later.

Cradling Yarrow – she wasn't much of a burden in the splinter's weak gravity – I took stock. I wasn't ready to mourn her, not just yet. If I could quickly get her to the medical suite aboard the defector's ship there was a good chance of revival. But where the hell was the wreck?

Squandering its last reserves of fuel, suit had deposited us in a clearing amongst the graveyard of ruined wasps. Half-submerged in ice, they looked like scorched scrap-iron sculptures, phantoms from an entomologist's worst nightmare. So there'd been a battle here, back when the splinter was just another drifting lump of ice. Even if the thing was seamed with silicates or organics, it would not have had any commercial potential for either side. But it might still have had strategic value, and that was why the wasps had gone to war on its surface. Trouble was – as we'd known before the attack – the corpses covered the entire surface, so there was no guessing where we'd come down. The wrecked ship might be just over the nearest hillock – or another ten kilometres in any direction.

I felt the ground rumble under me. Hunting for the source of the vibration, I saw a quill of vapour reach into the sky, no more than a klick away. It was a geyser of superheated ice.

I dropped Yarrow and hit dirt, suit limiting motion so that I didn't bounce. Looking back, I expected to see a dimple in the permafrost, where some rogue had impacted.

Instead, the geyser was still present. Worse, it was coming steadily closer, etching a neat trench. A beam-weapon was making that plume, I realised – like one of the party batteries aboard ship. Then I wised up. That was Mouser. The demons had worked their way into its command infrastructure, reprogramming it to turn against us. Now Mouser worked for the defector.

I slung Yarrow over one shoulder and loped away from the boiling impact point. Fast as the geyser moved, its path was predictable. If I made enough lateral distance the death-line would sear past—

Except the damn thing turned to follow me.

Now a second flanked it, shepherding me through the thickest zone of wasp corpses. Did they have some significance for the defector? Maybe so, but I couldn't see it. The corpses were a rough mix of machines from both sides: Royalist wasps marked with yellow shell symbols, ours with grinning tiger-heads. Generation thirty-five units, if I remembered Mil-Hist, when both sides toyed with pulse-hardened optical thinkware. In the seventy-odd subsequent generations there'd been numerous further jumps: ur-quantum logics, full-spectrum reflective wasp armour, chameleoflage, quackdrive powerplants and every weapon system the human mind could devise. We'd tried to encourage the wasps to make these innovations for themselves, but they never managed to evolve beyond strictly linear extrapolation. Which is good, or else we human observers would have been out of a job.

Not that it really mattered now.

A third geyser had erupted behind me, and a fourth ahead, boxing me in. Slowly, the four points of fire began to converge. I stopped, but kept holding Yarrow. I listened to my own breathing, harsh above the basso tremor of the drumming ground.

Then steel gripped my shoulder.

She said we'd be safer underground. Also that she had friends below who might be able to do something for Yarrow.

'If you weren't defecting,' I began, as we entered a roughly hewn tunnel into the splinter's crust, 'what the hell was it?'

'Trying to get home. Least that was the idea, until we realised Tiger's Eye didn't want us back.' Wendigo knuckled the ice with one of her steel fists, her suit cut away to expose her prosthetics. 'Which is when we decided to head here.'

'You almost made it,' I said. Then added: 'Where were you trying to get home from?'

'Isn't it obvious?'

'Then you did defect.'

'We were trying to make contact with the Royalists. Trying to make peace.' In the increasingly dim light I saw her shrug. 'It was a long shot, conducted in secrecy. When the mission went wrong, it was easy for Tiger's Eye to say we'd been defecting.'

'Bullshit.'

'I wish.'

'But you sent us.'

'Not in person.'

'But your delegate—'

'Is just software. It could be made to say anything my enemies chose. Even to order my own execution as a traitor.'

We paused to switch on our suit lamps. 'Maybe you'd better tell me everything.'

'Gladly,' Wendigo said. 'But if this hasn't been a good day so far, I'm afraid it's about to go downhill.'

There had been a clique of high-ranking officers who believed that the Swirl War was intrinsically unwinnable. Privy to information not released to the populace, and able to see through Tiger's Eye's own carefully filtered internal propaganda, they realised that negotiation – contact – was the only way out.

'Of course, not everyone agreed. Some of my adversaries wanted us dead before we even reached the enemy.' Wendigo sighed. 'Too much in love with the war's stability – and who can blame them? Life for the average citizen in Tiger's Eye isn't that bad. We're given a clear goal to fight for, and the likelihood of any one of us dying in a Royalist attack is small enough to ignore. The idea that all of that might be about to end after four hundred years, that we all might have to rethink our roles ... well, it didn't go down too well.'

'About as welcome as a fart in a vac-suit, right?'

Wendigo nodded. 'I think you understand.'

'Go on.'

Her expedition – Wendigo and two pilots – had crossed the Swirl unchallenged. Approaching the Royalist cometary base, they had expected to be questioned – perhaps even fired upon – but nothing had happened. When they entered the stronghold, they understood why.

'Deserted,' Wendigo said. 'Or we thought so, until we found the Royalists.' She expectorated the word. 'Feral, practically. Naked, grubby subhumans. Their wasps feed them and treat their illnesses, but that's as far as it goes. They grunt, and they've been toilet-trained, but they're not quite the military geniuses we've been led to believe.'

'Then—'

'The war is … nothing we thought.' Wendigo laughed, but the confines of her helmet rendered it more like the squawking of a jack-in-the-box. 'And now you wonder why home didn't want us coming back?'

Before Wendigo could explain further, we reached a wider bisecting tunnel, glowing with its own insipid chlorine-coloured light. Rather than the meandering bore of the tunnel in which we walked, it was as cleanly cut as a rifle barrel. In one direction the tunnel was blocked by a bullet-nosed cylinder, closely modelled on the trains in Tiger's Eye. Seemingly of its own volition, the train lit up and edged forwards, a door puckering open.

'Get in,' Wendigo said. 'And lose the helmet. You won't need it where we're going.'

Inside I coughed phlegmy ropes of thick from my lungs. Transitioning between breathing modes isn't pleasant – worse than usual since I'd breathed nothing but thick for six weeks. But after a few lungfuls of the train's antiseptic air, the dark blotches around my vision began to recede.

Wendigo did likewise, only with more dignity.

Yarrow lay on one of the couches, stiff as a statue carved in soap. Her skin was cyanotic, a single, all-enveloping bruise. Pilot skin is a better vacuum barrier than the usual stuff, and vacuum itself is a far better insulator against heat loss than air. But where I'd lifted her my gloves had embossed fingerprints into her flesh. Worse was the broad stripe of ruined skin down her back and the left side of her tail, where she had lain against the splinter's surface.

But her head looked better. When she hit vac, biomodified seals would have shut within her skull, barricading every possible avenue for pressure, moisture or blood loss. Even her eyelids would have fused tight. Implanted glands in her carotid artery would have released droves of friendly demons, quickly replicating via nonessential tissue in order to weave a protective scaffold through her brain.

Good for an hour or so – maybe longer. But only if the hostile demons hadn't screwed with Yarrow's native ones.

'You were going to tell me about the wasps,' I said, as curious to hear the rest of Wendigo's story as I was to blank my doubts about Yarrow.

'Well, it's rather simple. They got smart.'

'The wasps?'

She clicked the steel fingers of one hand. 'Overnight. Just over a hundred years ago.'

I tried not to look too overwhelmed. Intriguing as all this was, I wasn't treating it as anything other than an outlandish attempt to distract me from the main reason for my being here, which remained killing the defector. Wendigo's story explained some of the anomalies we'd so far encountered – but that didn't rule out a dozen more plausible explanations. Meanwhile, it was amusing to try and catch her out. 'So they got smart,' I said. 'You mean our wasps, or theirs?'

'Doesn't mean a damn anymore. Maybe it just happened to one machine in the Swirl, and then spread like wildfire to all the trillions of other wasps. Or maybe it happened simultaneously, in response to some stimulus we can't even guess at.'

'Want to hazard a guess?'

'I don't think it's important, Spirey.' She sounded as though she wanted to put a lot of distance between herself and this topic. 'Point is, it happened. Afterwards, distinctions between us and the enemy – at least from the point of view of the wasps – completely vanished.'

'Workers of the Swirl unite.'

'Something like that. And you understand why they kept it to themselves, don't you?'

I nodded, more to keep her talking.

'They needed us, of course. They still lacked something. Creativity, I guess you'd call it. They could evolve themselves incrementally, but they couldn't make the kind of sweeping evolutionary jumps we'd been feeding them.'

'So we had to keep thinking there was a war on.'

Wendigo looked pleased. 'Right. We'd keep supplying them with innovations, and they'd keep pretending to do each other in.' She halted, scratching at the unwrinkled skin around one eye with the alloy finger of one hand. 'Clever little bastards.'

We'd arrived somewhere.

It was a chamber, large as any enclosed space I'd ever seen. I felt gravity; too much of the stuff. The whole chamber must have been gimballed and spun within the splinter, like one of the gee-load simulators back in Tiger's Eye. The vaulted ceiling, hundreds of metres 'above', now seemed vertiginously higher.

Apart from its apex, it was covered in intricate frescos – dozens of pictorial facets, each a cycling hologram. They told the history of the Swirl, beginning with its condensation from interstellar gas, the ignition of its star, the onset of planetary formation. Then the action cut to the arrival of the first Standardist wasp, programmed to dive into the Swirl and breed like a rabbit, so that one day there'd be a sufficiently huge population to begin mining the thing; winnowing out metals, silicates and precious organics for the folks back home. Of course, it never happened like that. The Royalists wanted in on the action, so they sent their own wasps, programmed to attack ours. The rest is history. The frescos showed the war's beginning, and then a little while later the arrival of the first human observers, beamed across space as pure genetic data, destined to be born in artificial wombs in hollowed out comet-cores, raised and educated by wasps, imprinted with the best tactical and strategic knowledge available. Thereafter they taught the wasps. From then on things heated up, because the observers weren't limited by years of timelag. They were able to intervene in wasp evolution in realtime.

That ought to have been it, because by then we were pretty up to date, give or take four hundred years of the same.

But the frescos carried on.

There was one representing some future state of the Swirl, neatly ordered into a ticking orrery of variously sized and patterned worlds, some with beautiful rings or moon systems. And finally – like medieval conceptions of Eden – there was a triptych of lush planetary landscapes, with weird animals in the foreground, mountains and soaring cloudbanks behind.

'Seen enough to convince you?' Wendigo asked.

'No,' I said, not entirely sure whether I believed myself. Craning my neck, I looked up towards the apex.

Something hung from it.

It was a pair of wasps, fused together. One was complete; the other was only fully formed, seemingly in the process of splitting from the complete wasp. The fused pair looked to have been smothered in molten bronze, left to dry in waxy nodules.

'You know what this is?' Wendigo asked.

'I'm waiting.'

'Wasp art.'

I looked at her.

'This wasp was destroyed mid-replication,' Wendigo continued. 'While it was giving birth. Evidently the image has some poignancy for them. How I'd put it in human terms I don't know—'

'Don't even think about it.'

I followed her across the marbled terrazzo that floored the chamber. Arched porticoes surrounded it, each of which held a single dead wasp, their body designs covering a hundred generations of evolution. If Wendigo was right, I supposed these dead wasps were the equivalent of venerated old ancestors peering from oil paintings. But I wasn't convinced just yet.

'You knew this place existed?'

She nodded. 'Or else we'd be dead. The wasps back in the Royalist stronghold told us we could seek sanctuary here, if home turned against us.'

'And the wasps – what? Own this place?'

'And hundreds like it, although the others are already far beyond the Swirl, on their way out to the halo. Since the wasps came to consciousness, most of the splinters flung out of the Swirl have been infiltrated. Shrewd of them – all along, we've never suspected that the splinters are anything other than cosmic trash.'

'Nice décor, anyway.'

'Florentine,' Wendigo said, nodding. 'The frescos are in the style of a painter called Masaccio; one of Brunelleschi's disciples. Remember, the wasps had access to all the cultural data we brought with us from GE – every byte of it. That's how they work, I think – by constructing things according to arbitrary existing templates.'

'And there's a point to all this?'

'I've been here precisely one day longer than you, Spirey.'

'But you said you had friends here, people who could help Yarrow.'

'They're here all right,' Wendigo said, shaking her head. 'Just hope you're ready for them.'

On some unspoken cue they emerged, spilling from a door that until then I'd mistaken for one of the surrounding porticoes. I flinched, acting on years of training. Although wasps have never intentionally harmed a human being – even the enemy's wasps – they're nonetheless powerful, dangerous machines. There were twelve of them, divided equally between Standardist and Royalist units. Six-legged, their two-metre-long, segmented alloy bodies sprouted weapons, sensors and specialised manipulators. So far so familiar, except that the way the wasps moved was subtly wrong. It was as if the machines choreographed themselves, their bodies defining the extremities of a much larger form, which I sensed more than saw.

The twelve whisked across the floor.

'They are – or rather it is – a queen,' Wendigo said. 'From what I've gathered, there's one queen for every splinter. Splinterqueens, I call them.'

The swarm partially surrounded us now – but retained the brooding sense of oneness.

'She told you all this?'

'Her demons did, yes.' Wendigo tapped the side of her head. 'I got a dose after our ship crashed. You got one after we hit your ship. It was a standard sporehead from our arsenal, but the Splinterqueen loaded it with her own demons. For the moment that's how she speaks to us – via symbols woven by demons.'

'Take your word for it.'

Wendigo shrugged. 'No need to.'

And suddenly I knew. It was like eavesdropping on a topologist's fever dream – only much stranger. The burst of Queen's speech couldn't have lasted more than a tenth of a second, but its after-images seemed to persist much longer, and I had the start of a migraine before it had ended. But like Wendigo had implied before, I sensed planning – that every thought was merely a step towards some distant goal, the way each statement in a mathematical proof implies some final QED.

Something big indeed.

'You deal with that shit?'

'My chimeric parts must filter a lot.'

'And she understands you?'

'We get by.'

'Good,' I said. 'Then ask her about Yarrow.'

Wendigo nodded and closed both eyes, entering intense rapport with the Queen. What followed happened quickly: six of her components detached from the extended form and swarmed into the train we had just exited. A moment later they emerged with Yarrow, elevated on a loom formed from dozens of wasp manipulators.

'What happens now?'

'They'll establish a physical connection to her neural demons,' Wendigo said, 'so that they can map the damage.'

One of the six reared up and gently positioned its blunt, anvil-shaped 'head' directly above Yarrow's frost-mottled scalp. Then the wasp made eight nodding movements, so quickly that the motion was only a series of punctuated blurs. Looking down, I saw eight bloodless puncture marks on Yarrow's head. Another wasp replaced the driller and repeated the procedure, executing its own blurred nods. This time, glistening fibres trailed from Yarrow's eight puncture points into the wasp, which looked as if it was sucking spaghetti from my compatriot's skull.

Long minutes of silence followed, while I waited for some kind of report.

'It isn't good,' Wendigo said eventually.

'Show me.'

And I got a jolt of Queen's speech, feeling myself inside Yarrow's hermetically sealed head, feeling the chill that had embraced her brain core, despite her pilot augs. I sensed the two intermingled looms of native and foreign demons, webbing the shattered matrix of her consciousness.

I also sensed – what? Doubt?

'She's pretty far gone, Spirey.'

'Tell the Queen to do what she can.'

'Oh, she will. Now that she's glimpsed Yarrow's mind, she'll do all she can not to lose it. Minds mean a lot to her – particularly in view of what the Splinterqueens are planning for the future. But don't expect miracles.'

'Why not? We seem to be standing in one.'

'Then you're prepared to believe some of what I've said?'

'What it means—' I started to say . . .

But I didn't finish the sentence. As I was speaking the whole chamber shook violently, almost dashing us off our feet.

'What was that?'

Wendigo's eyes glazed again, briefly.

'Your ship,' she said. 'It just self-destructed.'

'What?'

A picture of what remained of Mouser formed in my head: a dulling nebula, embedding the splinter. 'The order to self-destruct came from Tiger's Eye,' Wendigo said. 'It cut straight to the ship's quackdrive subsystems, at a level the demons couldn't rescind. I imagine they were rather hoping you'd have landed by the time the order arrived. The blast would have destroyed the splinter.'

'You're saying home just tried to kill us?'

'Put it like this,' Wendigo said. 'Now might not be a bad time to rethink your loyalties.'

Tiger's Eye had failed this time – but they wouldn't stop there. In three hours they'd learn of their mistake, and three or more hours after that we would learn of their countermove, whatever it happened to be.

'She'll do something, won't she? I mean, the wasps wouldn't go to the trouble of building this place only to have Tiger's Eye wipe it out.'

'Not much she can do,' Wendigo said, after communing with the Queen. 'If home chooses to use kinetics against us – and they're the only weapon that could hit us from so far away – then there really is no possible defence. And remember there are a hundred other worlds like this, in or on their way to the halo. Losing one would make very little difference.'

Something in me snapped. 'Do you have to sound so damned indifferent to it all? Here we are talking about how we're likely to be dead in a few hours and you're acting like it's only a minor inconvenience.' I fought to keep the edge of hysteria out of my voice. 'How do you know so much anyway? You're mighty well informed for someone who's only been here a day, Wendigo.'

She regarded me for a moment, almost blanching under the slap of insubordination. Then Wendigo nodded, without anger. 'Yes, you're right to ask how I know so much. You can't have failed to notice how hard we crashed. My pilots took the worst.'

'They died?'

Hesitation. 'One at least – Sorrel. But the other, Quillin, wasn't in the ship when the wasps pulled me out of the wreckage. At the time I assumed they'd already retrieved her.'

'Doesn't look that way.'

'No, it doesn't, and . . .' She paused, then shook her head. 'Quillin was why we crashed. She tried to gain control, to stop us landing . . .' Again Wendigo trailed off, as if unsure how far to commit herself. 'I think Quillin was a plant, put aboard by those who disagreed with the peace initiative. She'd been primed – altered psychologically to reject any Royalist peace overtures.'

'She was born like that – with a stick up her ass.'

'She's dead, I'm sure of it.'

Wendigo almost sounded glad.

'Still, you made it.'

'Just, Spirey. I'm the humpty who fell off the wall twice. This time they couldn't find all the pieces. The Splinterqueen pumped me full of demons – gallons of them. They're all that's holding me together, but I don't think they can keep it up for ever. When I speak to you, at least some of what you hear is the Splinterqueen herself. I'm not really sure where you draw the line.'

I let that sink in, then said: 'About your ship. Repair systems would have booted when you hit. Any idea when she'll fly again?'

'Another day, day and a half.'

'Too damn long.'

'Just being realistic. If there's a way to get off the splinter within the next six hours, ship isn't it.'

I wasn't giving up so easily. 'What if wasps help? They could supply materials. Should speed things.'

Again that glazed look. 'All right,' she said. 'It's done. But I'm afraid wasp assistance won't make enough difference. We're still looking at twelve hours.'

'So I won't start any long neurodisneys.' I shrugged. 'And maybe we can hold out until then.' She looked unconvinced, so I said: 'Tell me the rest. Everything you know about this place. Why, for starters.'

'Why?'

'Wendigo, I don't have the faintest damn idea what any of us is doing here. All I do know is that in six hours I could be suffering from acute existence failure. When that happens, I'd be happier knowing what was so important I had to die for it.'

Wendigo looked towards Yarrow, still being nursed by the detached elements of the Queen. 'I don't think our being here will help her,' she said. 'In which case, maybe I should show you something.' A near-grin appeared on Wendigo's face. 'After all, it isn't as if we don't have time to kill.'

So we rode the train again, this time burrowing deeper into the splinter.

'This place,' Wendigo said, 'and the hundred others already

beyond the Swirl – and the hundreds, thousands more that will follow – are arks. They're carrying life into the halo; the cloud of leftover material around the Swirl.'

'Colonisation, right?'

'Not quite. When the time's right the splinters will return to the Swirl. Only there won't be one any more. There'll be a solar system, fully formed. When the colonisation does begin, it will be of new worlds around Fomalhaut, seeded from the life-templates held in the splinters.'

I raised a hand. 'I was following you there ... until you mentioned life-templates.'

'Patience, Spirey.'

Wendigo's timing couldn't have been better, because at that moment light flooded the train's brushed-steel interior.

The tunnel had become a glass tube, anchored to one wall of a vast cavern suffused with emerald light. The far wall was tiered, draping rafts of foliage. Our wall was steep and forested, oddly curved waterfalls draining into stepped pools. The waterfalls were bent away from true 'vertical' by Coriolis force, evidence that – just like the first chamber – this entire space was independently spinning within the splinter. The stepped pools were surrounded by patches of grass, peppered with moving forms that might have been naked people. There were wasps as well – tending the people.

As the people grew clearer, I had that flinch you get when your gaze strays onto someone with a shocking disfigurement. Roughly half of them were males.

'Imported Royalists,' Wendigo said. 'Remember I said they'd turned feral? Seems there was an accident, not long after the wasps made the jump to sentience. A rogue demon, or something. Decimated them.'

'They have both sexes.'

'You'll get used to it, Spirey – conceptually anyway. Tiger's Eye wasn't always exclusively female, you know that? It was just something we evolved into. Began with you pilots, matter of fact. Fem physiology made sense for pilots – women are smaller, have better gee-load tolerance, better stress psychodynamics and require fewer consumables than males. We were products of bioengineering from the outset, so it wasn't hard to make the jump to an all-fem culture.'

'Makes me want to ... I don't know.' I forced my gaze away from the Royalists. 'Puke or something. It's like going back to having hair all over your body.'

'That's because you grew up with something different.'

'Did they always have two sexes?'

'Probably not. What I do know is that the wasps bred from the survivors, but something wasn't right. Apart from the reversion to dimorphism, the children didn't grow up normally. Some part of their brains hadn't developed right.'

'Meaning what?'

'They're morons. The wasps keep trying to fix things, of course. That's why the Splinterqueen will do everything to help Yarrow – and us, of course. If she can study or even capture our thought patterns – and the demons make that possible – maybe she can use them to imprint consciousness back onto the Royalists. Like the Florentine architecture I said they copied, right? That was one template, and Yarrow's mind will be another.'

'That's supposed to cheer me up?'

'Look on the bright side. A while from now, there might be a whole generation of people who think along lines laid down by Yarrow.'

'Scary thought.' Then I wondered why I was able to crack a joke, with destruction looming so close in the future. 'Listen, I still don't get it. What makes them want to bring life to the Swirl?'

'It seems to boil down to two ... imperatives, I suppose you'd call them. The first's simple enough. When wasps were first opening up Greater Earth's solar system, back in the mid-twenty-first century, we sought the best way for them to function in large numbers without supervision. We studied insect colonies and imprinted the most useful rules straight into the wasps' programming. More than six hundred years later, those rules have percolated to the top. Now the wasps aren't content merely to organise themselves along patterns derived from living prototypes. Now they want to become – or at least give rise to – living forms of their own.'

'Life envy.'

'Or something very like it.'

I thought about what Wendigo had told me, then said: 'What about the second imperative?'

'Trickier. Much trickier.' She looked at me hard, as if debating

327

whether to broach whatever subject was on her mind. 'Spirey, what do you know about Solar War Three?'

The wasps had given up on Yarrow while we travelled. They had left her on a corniced plinth in the middle of the terrazzo, posed on her back, arms folded across her chest, tail and fluke draping asymmetrically over one side.

'She didn't necessarily fail, Spirey,' Wendigo said, taking my arm in her own unyielding grip. 'That's only Yarrow's body, after all.'

'The Queen managed to read her mind?'

There was no opportunity to answer. The chamber shook, more harshly than when Mouser had exploded. The vibration keeled us to the floor, Wendigo's metal arms cracking against the tessellated marble. As if turning in her sleep, Yarrow slipped from the plinth.

'Home,' Wendigo said, raising herself from the floor.

'Impossible. Can't have been more than two hours since Mouser was hit. There shouldn't be any response for another four!'

'They probably decided to attack us regardless of the outcome of their last attempt. Kinetics.'

'You sure there's no defence?'

'Only good luck.' The ground lashed at us again, but Wendigo stayed standing. The roar that followed the first impact was subsiding, fading into a constant but bearable complaint of tortured ice. 'The first probably only chipped us – maybe gouged a big crater, but I doubt that it ruptured any of the pressurised areas. Next time could be worse.'

And there would be a next time, no doubt about it. Kinetics were the only weapon capable of hitting us at such long range, and they did so by sheer force of numbers. Each kinetic was a speck of iron, accelerated to a hair's breadth below the speed of light. Relativity bequeathed the speck a disproportionate amount of kinetic energy – enough that only a few impacts would rip the splinter to shreds. Of course, only one in a thousand of the kinetics they fired at us would hit – but that didn't matter. They'd just fire ten thousand.

'Wendigo,' I said. 'Can we get to your ship?'

'No,' she said, after a moment's hesitation. 'We can reach it, but it isn't fixed yet.'

'Doesn't matter. We'll lift on auxiliaries. Once we're clear of the splinter we'll be safe.'

'No good, either. Hull's breached – it'll be at least an hour before even part of it can be pressurised.'

'And it'll take us an hour or so just to get there, won't it? So why are we waiting?'

'Sorry, Spirey, but—'

Her words were drowned by the arrival of the second kinetic. This one seemed to hit harder, the impact trailing away into aftergroans. The holographic frescos were all dark now. Then – ever so slowly – the ceiling ruptured, a huge mandible of ice probing into the chamber. We'd lost the false gravity; now all that remained was the splinter's feeble pull, dragging us obliquely towards one wall.

'But what?' I shouted in Wendigo's direction.

For a moment she had that absent look, which said she was more Queen than Wendigo. Then she nodded in reluctant acceptance. 'All right, Spirey. We play it your way. Not because I think our chances are great. Just that I'd rather be doing something.'

'Amen to that.'

It was uncomfortably dim now, much of the illumination having come from the endlessly cycling frescos. But it wasn't silent. Though the groan of the chamber's off-kilter spin was gone now, what remained was almost as bad: the agonised shearing of the ice that lay beyond us. Helped by wasps, we made it to the train. I carried Yarrow's corpse, but at the door Wendigo said: 'Leave her.'

'No way.'

'She's dead, Spirey. Everything of her that mattered, the Splinterqueen already saved. You have to accept that. It was enough that you brought her here, don't you understand? Carrying her now would only lessen your chances – and that would really have pissed her off.'

Some alien part of me allowed the wasps to take the corpse. Then we were inside, helmeted up and breathing thick.

As the train picked up speed, I glanced out through the window, intent on seeing the Queen one last time. It should have been too dark, but the chamber looked bright. For a moment I presumed the frescos had come to life again, but then something about the scene's unreal intensity told me the Queen was weaving this image in my head. She hovered above the debris-strewn terrazzo – except that this was more than the Queen I had seen before. This was – what?

How she saw herself?

Ten of her twelve wasp composites were now back together, arranged in constantly shifting formation. They now seemed more living than machine, with diaphanous sunwings, chitin-black bodies, fur-sheened limbs, and sensors and eyes that were faceted crystalline globes, sparkling in the chamber's false light. That wasn't all. Before, I'd sensed the Queen as something implied by her composites. Now I didn't need to imagine her. Like a ghost in which the composites hung, she loomed vast in the chamber, multi-winged and brooding—

And then we were gone.

We sped towards the surface for the next few minutes, waiting for the impact of the next kinetic. When it hit, the train's cushioned ride smothered the concussion. For a moment I thought we'd made it, then the machine began to decelerate slowly to a dead halt. Wendigo convened with the Queen, and told me the line was blocked. We disembarked into vacuum.

Ahead, the tunnel ended in a wall of jumbled ice.

After a few minutes we found a way through the obstruction, Wendigo wrenching aside boulders larger than either of us. 'We're only half a klick from the surface,' she said, as we emerged into the unblocked tunnel beyond. She pointed ahead, to what might have been a scotoma of absolute blackness against the milky darkness of the tunnel. 'After that, a klick overland to the wreck.' She paused. 'Realise we can't go home, Spirey. Now more than ever.'

'Not exactly spoiled for choice, are we?'

'No. It has to be the halo, of course. It's where the splinter's headed anyway; just means we'll get there ahead of schedule. There are other Splinterqueens out there, and at the very least they'll want to keep us alive. Possibly other humans as well – others who made the same discovery as us, and knew there was no going home.'

'Not to mention Royalists.'

'That troubles you, doesn't it?'

'I'll deal with it,' I said, pushing forwards.

The tunnel was nearly horizontal, and with the splinter's weak gravity it was easy to make the distance to the surface. Emerging, Fomalhaut glared down at us, a white-cored, bloodshot eye surrounded by the wrinkle-like dust lanes of the inner Swirl. Limned in red, wasp corpses marred the landscape.

'I don't see the ship.'

Wendigo pointed to a piece of blank caramel-coloured horizon. 'Curvature's too great. We won't see it until we're almost on top of it.'

'Hope you're right.'

'Trust me. I know this place like, well ...' Wendigo regarded one of her limbs. 'Like the back of my hand.'

'Encourage me, why don't you?'

Three or four hundred metres later we crested a scallop-shaped rise of ice, and halted. We could see the ship now. It didn't look in much better shape than when Yarrow and I had scoped it from Mouser.

'I don't see any wasps.'

'Too dangerous for them to stay on the surface,' Wendigo said.

'That's cheering. I hope the remaining damage is cosmetic,' I said. 'Because if it isn't—'

Suddenly I wasn't talking to anyone.

Wendigo was gone. After a moment I saw her, lying in a crumpled heap at the foot of the hillock. Her guts stretched away like a rusty comet-tail, halfway to the next promontory.

Quillin was fifty metres ahead, having risen from the concealment of a chondrite boulder.

When Wendigo had mentioned her, I'd put her out of my mind as any kind of threat. How could she pose any danger beyond the inside of a thickship, when she'd traded her legs for a tail and fluke, just like Yarrow? On dry land, she'd be no more mobile than a seal pup. Well, that was how I'd figured things.

But I'd reckoned without Quillin's suit.

Unlike Yarrow's – unlike any siren suit I'd ever seen – it sprouted legs. Mechanised, they emerged from the hips, making no concessions to human anatomy. The legs were long enough to lift Quillin's tail completely free of the ice. My gaze tracked up her body, registering the crossbow that she held in a double-handed grip.

'I'm sorry,' Quillin's deep voice boomed in my skull. 'Check-in's closed.'

'Wendigo said you might be a problem.'

'Wise up. It was staged from the moment we reached the Royalist stronghold.' Still keeping the bow on me, she began to lurch across the ice. 'The ferals were actors, playing dumb. The wasps were programmed to feed us bullshit.'

'It isn't a Royalist trick, Quillin.'

'Shit. See I'm gonna have to kill you as well.'

The ground jarred, more violently than before. A nimbus of white light puffed above the horizon, evidence of an impact on the splinter's far side. Quillin stumbled, but her legs corrected the misstep before it tripped her forwards.

'I don't know if you're keeping up with current events,' I said, 'but that's our own side.'

'Maybe you didn't think hard enough. Why did wasps in the Swirl get smart before the trillions of wasps back in Sol System? Should have been the other way round.'

'Yeah?'

'Of course, Spirey. GE's wasps had a massive head start.' She shrugged, but the bow stayed rigidly pointed. 'Okay, war sped up wasp evolution here. But that shouldn't have made so much difference. That's where the story breaks down.'

'Not quite.'

'What?'

'Something Wendigo told me. About what she called the second imperative. I guess it wasn't something she found out until she went underground.'

'Yeah? Astonish me.'

Well, something astonished Quillin at that point – but I was only marginally less surprised by it myself. An explosion of ice, and a mass of swiftly moving metal erupting from the ground around her. The wasp corpses were partially dismembered, blasted and half-melted – but they still managed to drag Quillin to the ground. For a moment she thrashed, kicking up plumes of frost. Then the whole mass lay deathly still, and it was just me, the ice and a lot of metal and blood.

The Queen must have coaxed activity out of a few of the wasp corpses, ordering them to use their last reserves of power to take out Quillin.

Thanks, Queen.

But no cigar. Quillin hadn't necessarily meant to shoot me at that point, but – bless her – she had anyway. The bolt had transected me with the precision of one of the Queen's theorems, somewhere below my sternum. Gut-shot. The blood on the ice was my own.

*

I tried moving.

A couple of light-years away I saw my body undergo a frail little shiver. It didn't hurt, but there was nothing in the way of proprioceptive feedback to indicate I'd actually managed to twitch any part of my body.

Quillin was moving too. Wriggling, that is, since her suit's legs had been cleanly ripped away by the wasps. Other than that she didn't look seriously injured. Ten or so metres from me, she flopped around like a maggot and groped for her bow. What remained of it anyway.

Chalk one to the good guys.

By which time I was moving, executing a marginally quicker version of Quillin's slug crawl. I couldn't stand up – there are limits to what pilot physiology can cope with – but my legs gave me leverage she lacked.

'Give up, Spirey. You have a head start on me, and right now you're a little faster – but that ship's still a long way off.' Quillin took a moment to catch her breath. 'Think you can sustain that pace? Gonna need to, if you don't want me catching up.'

'Plan on rolling over me until I suffocate?'

'That's an option. If this doesn't kill you first.'

Enough of her remained in my field of view to see what she meant. Something sharp and bladelike had sprung from her wrist, a bayonet projecting half a metre ahead of her hand. It looked like a nasty little toy – but I did my best to push it out of mind and get on with the job of crawling towards the ship. It was no more than two hundred metres away now – what little of it protruded above the ice. The external airlock was already open, ready to clamp shut as soon as I wriggled inside—

'You never finished telling me, Spirey.'

'Telling you what?'

'About this . . . what did you call it? The second imperative?'

'Oh, that.' I halted and snatched breath. 'Before I go on, I want you to know I'm only telling you this to piss you off.'

'Whatever bakes your cake.'

'All right,' I said. 'Then I'll begin by saying you were right. Greater Earth's wasps should have made the jump to sentience long before those in the Swirl, simply because they'd had longer to evolve. And that's what happened.'

Quillin coughed, like gravel in a bucket. 'Pardon?'

'They beat us to it. About a century and a half ago. Across Sol System, within just a few hours, every single wasp woke up and announced its intelligence to the nearest human being it could find. Like babies reaching for the first thing they see.' I stopped, sucking in deep lungfuls. The wreck had to be closer now – but it hardly looked it.

Quillin, by contrast, looked awfully close now – and that blade awfully sharp.

'So the wasps woke,' I said, damned if she wasn't going to hear the whole story. 'And that got some people scared. So much, some of them got to attacking the wasps. Some of their shots went wide, because within a day the whole system was one big shooting match. Not just humans against wasps – but humans against humans.' Less than fifty metres now, across much smoother ground than we'd so far traversed. 'Things just escalated. Ten days after Solar War Three began, only a few ships and habitats were still transmitting. They didn't last long.'

'Crap,' Quillin said – but she sounded less cocksure than she had a few moments before. 'There was a war back then, but it never escalated into a full-blown Solar War.'

'No. It went the whole hog. From then on every signal we ever got from GE was concocted by wasps. They dared not break the news to us – at least not immediately. We've only been allowed to find out because we're never going home. Guilt, Wendigo called it. They couldn't let it happen again.'

'What about our wasps?'

'Isn't it obvious? A while later the wasps here made the same jump to sentience – presumably because they'd been shown the right moves by the others. Difference was, ours kept it quiet. Can't exactly blame them, can you?'

There was nothing from Quillin for a while, both of us concentrating on the last patch of ice before Wendigo's ship.

'I suppose you have an explanation for this too,' she said eventually, swiping her tail against the ground. 'C'mon, blow my mind.'

So I told her what I knew. 'They're bringing life to the Swirl. Sooner than you think too. Once this charade of a war is done, the wasps will breed in earnest. Trillions out there now, but in a few decades it'll be billions of trillions. They'll outweigh a good-sized planet. In a way the Swirl will have become sentient. It'll be directing its own evolution.'

I spared Quillin the details – how the wasps would arrest the existing processes of planetary formation so that they could begin anew, only this time according to a plan. Left to its own devices, the Swirl would contract down to a solar system comprised solely of small, rocky planets – but such a system could never support life over billions of years. Instead, the wasps would exploit the system's innate chaos to tip it towards a state where it would give rise to at least two much larger worlds – planets as massive as Jupiter or Saturn, capable of shepherding leftover rubble into tidy, world-avoiding orbits. Mass extinctions had no place in the Splinterqueens' vision of future life.

But I guessed Quillin probably didn't care.

'Why are you hurrying, Spirey?' she asked between harsh grunts as she propelled herself forwards. 'The ship isn't going anywhere.'

The edge of the open airlock was a metre above the ice. My fingers probed over the rim, followed by the crest of my battered helmet. Just lifting myself into the lock's lit interior seemed to require all the energy I'd already expended in the crawl. Somehow I managed to get half my body length into the lock.

Which is when Quillin reached me.

There wasn't much pain when she dug the bayonet into my ankle, just a form of cold I hadn't imagined before, even lying on the ice. Quillin jerked the embedded blade to and fro, and the knot of cold seemed to reach out little feelers into my foot and lower leg. I sensed she wanted to retract the blade for another stab, but my suit armour was gripping it tight.

The bayonet taking her weight, Quillin pulled herself up to the rim of the lock. I tried kicking her away, but the skewered leg no longer felt a part of me.

'You're dead,' she whispered.

'News to me.'

Her eyes rolled wide, then locked on me with renewed venom. She gave the bayonet a violent twist. 'So tell me one thing. That story – bullshit, or what?'

'I'll tell you,' I said. 'But first consider this.' Before she could react I reached out and palmed a glowing panel set in the lock wall. The panel whisked aside, revealing a mushroom-shaped red button. 'You know that story they told about Wendigo, how she lost her arms?'

'You weren't meant to swallow that hero guff, Spirey.'

'No? Well, get a load of this, Quillin. My hand's on the emergency pressurisation control. When I hit it, the outer door's going to slide down quicker than you can blink.'

She looked at my hand, then down at her wrist, still attached to my ankle via the jammed bayonet. Slowly the situation sank in. 'Close the door, Spirey, and you'll be a leg short.'

'And you an arm, Quillin.'

'Stalemate, then.'

'Not quite. See, which of us is more likely to survive? Me inside, with all the medical systems aboard this ship, or you all on your lonesome outside? Frankly, I don't think it's any contest.'

Her eyes opened wider. Quillin gave a shriek of anger and entered one final, furious wrestling match with the bayonet.

I managed to laugh. 'As for your question, it's true, every word of it.' Then, with all the calm I could muster, I thumbed the control. 'Pisser, isn't it?'

I made it, of course.

Several minutes after the closing of the door, demons had lathered a protective cocoon around the stump and stomach wound. They allowed me no pain – only a fuzzy sense of detachment. Enough of my mind remained sharp to think about my escape – problematic given that the ship still wasn't fixed.

Eventually I remembered the evac pods.

They were made to kick away from the ship fast, if some quack-drive system went on the fritz. They had thrusters for that – nothing fancy, but here they'd serve another purpose. They'd boost me from the splinter, punch me out of its grav well.

So I did it.

Snuggled into a pod and blew out of the wreck, feeling the gee-load even within the thick. It didn't last long. On the evac pod's cam I watched the splinter drop away until it was pebble-sized. The main body of the kinetic attack was hitting it by then, impacts every ten or so seconds. After a minute of that the splinter just came apart. Afterwards, there was only a sooty veil where it had been, and then only the Swirl.

I hoped the Queen had made it. I guess it was within her power to transmit what counted of herself out to sisters in the halo. If so, there was a chance for Yarrow as well. I'd find out eventually. Then I used the pod's remaining fuel to inject me into a slow, elliptical orbit, one that would graze the halo in a mere fifty or sixty years.

That didn't bother me. I wanted to close my eyes and let the thick nurse me whole again – and sleep for an awfully long time.

After a lean period, I broke back into Interzone *in the mid-nineties.
'Spirey and the Queen' is a story from that second, more sustained burst
of success, and one that I'm really fond of even now. Maybe that's
because the story was such a pig to write that it was a relief to get it
out of my system, maybe because it appeared with some very striking
illustrations, and maybe because it was the first story of mine that
seemed to be received enthusiastically by at least some readers. I'd started
it quite a few years earlier, and the story had been through numerous
aborted versions before I found the right angle of attack. Things were
complicated by the fact that I was also working on the novel* Revelation
Space *at the time, and beginning to have some thoughts about the wider
future history into which that book slotted. At various times 'Spirey and
the Queen' was part of that history, then it was out, then it was in again
... until I decided that the story really worked best as a stand-alone
piece, unrelated to anything else I was working on. Typically for me, the
motor of plot only kicked in when I started looking at the story in thriller
terms: spies, defectors, that kind of thing. I'll leave it as an exercise for
the reader to work out the identity of the two warring combines featured
in the story; suffice it to say that there are clues in both their names and
symbols. As for Spirey herself, I took her name from a sign I spotted in
Australia, which indicated the way to a certain 'Spirey Creek'.*

*I always had the vague intention of returning to Spirey's universe at
some point or another. Perhaps I will, one day ... if only to find out for
myself what happens after the last line of this story.*

Part One

Something very strange appeared in the outer recreation bubble on the day that Katrina Solovyova died. When he saw it, John Renfrew rushed back to the infirmary where he had left her. Solovyova had been slipping in and out of lucidity for days, but when he arrived he was glad to find her still conscious. She seldom turned her face away from the picture window, transfixed by the silent and vast twilight landscape beyond the armoured glass. Hovering against the foothills of Pavonis Mons, her reflection was all highlights, as if sketched in bold strokes of chalk.

Renfrew caught his breath before speaking.

'I've seen a piano.'

At first he did not think she had heard him. Then the reflection of Solovyova's mouth formed words.

'You've seen a *what*?'

'A piano,' Renfrew said, laughing. 'A big, white Bösendorfer grand.'

'You're crazier than me.'

'It was in the recreation bubble,' Renfrew said. 'The one that took a lightning hit last week. I think it fried something. Or unfried something, maybe. Brought something back to life.'

'A piano?'

'It's a start. It means things aren't totally dead. That there's a glimmer of . . . something.'

'Well, isn't that the nicest timing,' Solovyova said.

With a creak of his knees Renfrew knelt by her bedside. He'd connected Solovyova to a dozen or so medical monitors, only three of which were working properly. They hummed, hissed and bleeped with deadening regularity. When it began to seem like music – when he started hearing hidden harmonies and tonal shifts – Renfrew knew it was time to get out of the infirmary. That was why he had gone to the recreation bubble; there was no music there, but at least he could sit in silence.

'Nice timing?' he said.

'I'm dying. Nothing that happens now will make any difference to me.'

'But maybe it would,' Renfrew said. 'If the rec systems are capable of coming back online, what else might be? Maybe I could get the infirmary up and running . . . the diagnostic suite . . . the drug synth . . .' He gestured at the banks of dead, grey monitors and cowled machines parked against the wall. They were covered with scuffed decals and months of dust.

'Pray for another lightning strike, you mean?'

'No . . . not necessarily.' Renfrew chose his words with care. He did not want to offer Solovyova false optimism, but the apparition had made him feel more positive than at any time he could remember since the Catastrophe. They could not unmake the deaths of all the other colonists, or unmake the vastly larger death that even now was difficult to mention. But if some of the base systems they had assumed broken could be restarted, he might at least find a way to keep Solovyova alive.

'What, then?'

'I don't know. But now that I know things aren't as bad as we feared . . .' he trailed off. 'There are lots of things I could try again. Just because they didn't work the first time—'

'You probably imagined the piano.'

'I know I didn't. It was a genuine projection, not a hallucination.'

'And this piano . . .' The reflection froze momentarily. 'How long did it last, Renfrew? I mean, just out of curiosity?'

'Last?'

'That's what I asked.'

'It's still there,' he said. 'It was still there when I left. Like it was waiting for someone to come and play it.'

The figure in the bed moved slightly.

'I don't believe you.'

'I can't show you, Solovyova. I wish I could, but—'

'I'll die? I'm going to die anyway, so what difference does it make?' She paused, allowing the melancholic chorus of the machines to swell and fill the room. 'Probably by the end of the week. And all I've got to look forward to is the inside of this room or the view out of this window. At least let me see something different.'

'Is this what you really want?'

Solovyova's reflection tipped in acknowledgement. 'Show me the piano, Renfrew. Show me you aren't making this shit up.'

He thought about it for a minute, perhaps two, and then dashed back to the recreation bubble to check that the piano was still there. The journey seemed to take for ever, even at a sprint, through sunken tunnels and window-lined connecting bridges, up and down grilled ramps, through ponderous internal airlocks and sweltering aeroponics labs, taking this detour or that to avoid a blown bubble or failed airlock.

Parts of the infrastructure creaked ominously as he passed through. Here and there his feet crunched through the sterile red dust that was always finding ways to seep through seals and cracks. Everything was decaying, falling apart. Even if the dead had been brought back to life the base would not have been able to support more than a quarter of their number. But the piano represented something other than the slow grind of entropy. If one system had survived apparent failure, the same might be true of others.

He reached the bubble, his eyes closed as he crossed the threshold. He half-expected the piano to be gone, never more than a trick of the mind. Yet there it was: still manifesting, still hovering a few centimetres from the floor. Save for that one suggestion of ghostliness, it appeared utterly solid, as real as anything else in the room. It was a striking pure white, polished to a lambent gloss. Renfrew strode around it, luxuriating in the conjunction of flat planes and luscious curves. He had not noticed this detail before, but the keys were still hidden under the folding cover.

He admired the piano for several more minutes, forgetting his earlier haste. It was as beautiful as it was chilling.

Remembering Solovyova, he returned to the infirmary.

'You took your time,' she said.

'It's still there, but I had to be sure. You certain you want to see it?'

'I haven't changed my mind. Show me the damned thing.'

With great gentleness he unplugged the vigilant machines and wheeled them aside. He could not move the bed, so he took Solovyova from it and placed her in a wheelchair. He had long since grown accustomed to how frail human bodies felt in Martian gravity, but the ease with which he lifted her was shocking, and a reminder of how close to death she was.

He'd hardly known her before the Catastrophe. Even in the days that followed – as the sense of isolation closed in on the base, and the first suicides began – it had taken a long time for them to drift together. It had happened at a party, the one that the colonists had organised to celebrate the detection of a radio signal from Earth, originating from an organised band of survivors in New Zealand. In New Zealand they still had something like a government, something like society, with detailed plans for long-term endurance and reconstruction. And for a little while it had seemed that the survivors might – by some unexplained means – have acquired immunity to the weaponised virus that had started scything its way through the rest of humanity in June 2038.

They hadn't. It just took a little longer than average to wipe them out.

Renfrew pushed her along the tortuous route that led back to the bubble.

'Why a ... what did you call it?'

'A Bösendorfer. A Bösendorfer grand piano. I don't know. That's just what it said.'

'Something it dragged up from its memory? Was it making any music?'

'No. Not a squeak. The keyboard was hidden under a cover.'

'There must be someone to play it,' Solovyova said.

'That's what I thought.' He pushed her onwards. 'Music would make a difference, at least. Wouldn't it?'

'Anything would make a difference.'

Except not for Solovyova, he thought. Very little was going to make a difference for Solovyova from this point on.

'Renfrew ...' Solovyova said, her tone softer than before. 'Renfrew, when I'm gone ... you'll be all right, won't you?'

'You shouldn't worry about me.'

'It wouldn't be human not to. I'd change places if I could.'

'Don't be daft.'

'You were a good man. You didn't deserve to be the last of us.'

Renfrew tried to sound dignified. 'Some might say being the last survivor is a sort of privilege.'

'But not me. I don't envy you. I know for a fact I couldn't handle it.'

'Well, I can. I looked at my psychological evaluation. Practical, survivor mentality, they said.'

'I believe it,' Solovyova said. 'But don't let it get to you. Understand? Keep some self-respect. For all of us. For me.'

He knew exactly what she meant by that.

The recreation bubble loomed around the curve in the corridor. There was a moment of trepidation as they neared, but then he saw the white corner of the floating piano, still suspended in the middle of the room, and sighed with relief.

'Thank God,' he said. 'I didn't imagine it.'

He pushed Solovyova into the bubble, halting the wheelchair before the hovering apparition. Its immense mass reminded him of a chiselled cloud. The polished white gleam was convincing, but there was no sign of their own reflections within it. Solovyova said nothing, merely staring into the middle of the room.

'It's changed,' he said. 'Look. The cover's gone up. You can see the keys. They look so real ... I could almost reach out and touch them. Except I can't play the piano.' He grinned back at the woman in the wheelchair. 'Never could. Never had a musical bone in my body.'

'There is no piano, Renfrew.'

'Solovyova?'

'I said, there is no piano. The room is empty.' Her voice was dead, utterly drained of emotion. She did not even sound disappointed or annoyed. 'There is no piano. No grand piano. No Bösendorfer grand piano. No keyboard. No nothing. You're hallucinating, Renfrew. You're imagining the piano.'

He looked at her in horror. 'I can still see it. It's here.' He reached out to the abstract white mass. His fingers punched through its skin, into thin air. But he had expected that.

He could still see the piano.

It was real.

'Take me back to the infirmary, Renfrew. Please.' Solovyova paused. 'I think I'm ready to die now.'

He put on a suit and buried Solovyova beyond the outer perimeter, close to the mass grave where he had buried the last survivors when Solovyova had been too weak to help. The routine felt familiar enough, but when Renfrew turned back to the base he felt a wrenching sense of difference. The low-lying huddle of soil-covered domes, tubes and cylinders hadn't changed in any tangible way, except that it was now truly uninhabited. He was walking back towards an empty house, and even when Solovyova had been ill – even when Solovyova had been only half-present – that had never been the case.

The moment reached a kind of crescendo. He considered his options. He could return to the base, alone, and survive months or years on the dwindling resources at his disposal. Tharsis Base would keep him alive indefinitely provided he did not fall ill: food and water were not a problem, and the climate recycling systems were deliberately rugged. But there would be no companionship. No network, no music or film, no television or VR. Nothing to look forward to except endless bleak days until something killed him.

Or he could do it here, *now*. All it would take was a twist of his faceplate release control. He had already worked out how to override the safety lock. A few roaring seconds of pain and it would all be over. And if he lacked the courage to do it that way – and he thought he probably did – then he could sit down and wait until his air supply ran low.

There were a hundred ways he could do it, if he had the will.

He looked at the base, stark under the pale butterscotch of the sky. The choice was laughably simple. Die here, now, or die in there, much later. Either way, his choice would be unrecorded. There would be no eulogies to his bravery, for there was no one left to write eulogies.

'Why me?' he asked aloud. 'Why is it me who has to go through with this?'

He'd felt no real anger until that moment. Now he felt like shouting, but all he could do was fall to his knees and whimper. The question circled in his head, chasing its own tail.

'Why me?' he said. 'Why is it me? Why the fuck is it *me* who has to ask this question?'

Finally he fell silent. He remained frozen in that position, staring down through the scuffed glass of his faceplate at the radiation-blasted soil between his knees. For five or six minutes he listened to the sound of his own sobbing. Then a small, polite voice advised him that he needed to return to the base to replenish his air supply. He listened to that voice as it shifted from polite to stern, then from stern to strident, until it was screaming into his skull, the boundary of his faceplate flashing brilliant red.

Then he stood up, already light-headed, already feeling the weird euphoric intoxication of asphyxia, and made his ambling way back towards the base.

He had made a choice. Like it said in the psych report, he was a practical-minded survivor type. He would not give in.

Not until it got a lot harder.

Renfrew made it through his first night alone.

It was easier than he had expected, although he was careful not to draw any comfort from that. He knew that there would be much harder days and nights ahead. It might happen a day or a week or even a year from now, but when it did he was sure that his little breakdown outside would shrink to insignificance. For now he was stumbling through fog, fully aware that a precipice lay before him, and that eventually he would have to step over that precipice if he hoped to find anything resembling mental equilibrium and true acceptance.

He wandered the corridors and bubbles of the base. Everything looked shockingly familiar. Books were where he had left them; the coffee cups and dishes still waiting to be washed. The views through the windows hadn't become mysteriously more threatening overnight, and he had no sense that the interior of the base had become less hospitable. There were no strange new sounds to make the back of his neck tingle; no shadows flitting at the corner of his eye; no blood-freezing sense of scrutiny by an unseen watcher.

And yet ... and yet. He knew something was not quite right. After he had attended to his usual chores – cleaning this or that air filter, lubricating this or that seal, studying the radio logs to make sure no one had attempted contact from home – he again made his way to the recreation bubble.

The piano was still there, but something was different about it today. Now there was a single gold candelabrum sitting above the keyboard. The candles burned, wavering slightly.

It was as if the piano was readying itself.

Renfrew leaned through the piano and passed his fingers through the candle flames. They were as insubstantial as the instrument itself. Even so, he could not help but sniff the tips of his fingers. His brain refused to accept that the flames were unreal, and expected a whiff of carbon or charred skin.

Renfrew remembered something.

He had spent so long in the base, so long inside its electronic cocoon, that until this moment he had forgotten precisely how the bubble worked. The things that appeared inside it were not true holograms, but projections mapped into his visual field. They were woven by tiny implants buried in the eye, permitting the images to have a sense of solidity that would have been impossible with any kind of projected hologram. The surgical procedure to embed the implants had taken about thirty seconds, and from that moment on he had never really needed to think about it. The implants enabled the base staff to digest information in vastly richer form than allowed by flat screens and clumsy holographics. When Renfrew examined a mineral sample, for instance, the implant would overlay his visual impression of the rock with an X-ray tomographic view of the rock's interior. The implants had also permitted access to recreational recordings ... but Renfrew had always been too busy for that kind of thing. When the implants began to fail – they'd never been designed to last more than a year or two *in vivo*, before replacement – Renfrew had thought no more of the matter.

But what if his had started working again? In that case it was no wonder Solovyova had not been able to see the piano. Some projection system had decided to switch on again, accessing some random fragment from the entertainment archives, and his reactivated implant had chosen to allow him to see it.

It meant there was still a kind of hope.

'Hello.'

Renfrew flinched at the voice. The source of it was immediately obvious: a small man had appeared out of nowhere at the end of the piano. The small man stood for a moment, pivoting around as if to acknowledge a vast and distant invisible audience, his eyes – largely hidden behind ostentatious pink glasses – only meeting Renfrew's for the briefest of instants. The man settled onto a stool that had also appeared at the end of the piano, tugged up the sleeves of the plum paisley suit jacket he wore and began to play the piano. The man's fingers were curiously stubby, but they moved up and down the keyboard with a beguiling ease.

Transfixed, Renfrew listened to the man play. It was the first real music he had heard in two years. The man could have played the most uncompromisingly difficult exercise in atonality and it would still have sounded agreeable to Renfrew's ears. But it was much easier than that. The man played the piano and sang a song, one that Renfrew recognised – albeit barely – from his childhood. It had been an old song even then, but one that was still played on the radio with some regularity. The man sang about a trip to Mars: a song about a man who did not expect to see home again.

The song concerned a rocket man.

Renfrew maintained the ritual that he and Solovyova had established before her death. Once a week, without fail, he cocked an ear to Earth to see if anyone was sending.

The ritual had become less easy in recent weeks. The linkage between the antenna and the inside of the base had broken, so he had to go outside to perform the chore. It meant pre-breathing; it meant suiting up; it meant a desolate trudge from the airlock to the ladder on the side of the comms module, and then a careful ascent to the module's roof, where the antenna was mounted on a turret-like plinth. He'd spend at least half an hour scooping handfuls of storm dust from the steering mechanism, before flipping open the cover on the manual control panel, powering up the system and tapping a familiar string of commands into the keyboard.

After a few moments the antenna would begin to move, grinding as it overcame the resistance of the dust that had already seeped into its innards. It swung and tilted on multiple axes, until the openwork mesh of the dish was locked on to Earth. Then the system waited and listened, LEDs blinking on the status board, but none of them brightening to the hard, steady green that would mean the antenna had locked on to the expected carrier signal. Occasionally the lights would flicker green, as if the antenna was picking up ghost echoes from *something* out there, but they never lasted.

Renfrew had to keep trying. He wasn't expecting rescue, not any more. He'd resigned himself to the idea that he was going to die on Mars, alone. But it would still be some comfort to know that there were survivors back on Earth; that there were still people who could begin to rebuild civilisation. Better still if they had the kindness to signal him, to let him know what was happening. Even if only a few thousand people had survived, it wouldn't take much for one of them to remember the Mars colony, and wonder what was happening up there.

But Earth remained silent. Some part of Renfrew knew that there would never be a signal, no matter how many times he swung the dish around and listened. And one day soon the dish was simply not going to work, and he was not going to be able to repair it. Dutifully, when he had powered down the antenna and returned to the inside of the base, he made a neat entry in the communications log, signing his name at the top of the page.

On his rounds of the base, Renfrew made similar entries in many other logs. He noted breakdowns and his own ramshackle repair efforts. He took stock of spare parts and tools, entering the broken or life-expired items into the resupply request form. He noted the health of the plants in the aeroponics lab, sketching their leaves and marking the ebb and flow of various diseases. He kept a record of the Martian weather, as it tested the base's integrity, and at the back of his mind he always imagined Solovyova nodding in approval, pleased with his stoic refusal to slide into barbarism.

But in all his bookkeeping, Renfrew never once referred to the man at the piano. He couldn't quite explain this omission, but something held him back from mentioning the apparition. He felt he could rationalise the appearance of the piano, even of the personality that was programmed to play it, but he still wasn't sure that any of it was real.

Not that that stopped the piano man from appearing.

Once or twice a day, most days, he assumed existence at the piano and played a song or two. Sometimes Renfrew was there when it happened; sometimes he was elsewhere in the base when he heard the music starting up. Always he dropped whatever he was doing and raced to the recreation bubble, and listened.

The tunes were seldom the same from day to day, and the small man himself never looked quite the same. His clothes were always different, but there was more to it than that. Sometimes he had a shapeless mop of auburn hair. At other times he was balding or concealed his crown beneath a variety of ostentatious hats. He frequently wore glasses of elaborate, ludicrous design.

The man had never introduced himself, but once or twice Renfrew felt that he was close to remembering his name. He racked his memory for the names of twentieth-century musicians, feeling sure it would come to him eventually.

In the meantime he found that it helped to have someone to talk to. Between songs the man would sometimes sit silently, hands folded in his lap, as if waiting for some instruction or request from Renfrew. That was when Renfrew talked aloud, unburdening himself of whatever thoughts had been spinning around in his skull since the last visitation. He told the man about the problems with the base, about his loneliness, about the despair he felt every time the antenna failed to pick up anything from Earth. And the man simply sat and listened, and when Renfrew was done – when he had said his piece – the man would unlace his fingers and start playing something.

Now and then the man *did* speak, but he never seemed to be addressing Renfrew so much as a larger, unseen audience. He'd introduce the songs, tell a few jokes between numbers, throw out an offer to take requests. Renfrew sometimes answered, sometimes tried to persuade the pianist to play one of the songs he'd already performed, but nothing he said seemed to reach him.

But still, it was better than nothing. Although the style of the music never varied greatly, and one or two of the songs began occasionally to chafe at Renfrew's nerves, he was generally happiest when the music was playing. He liked 'Song for Guy', 'I Guess that's Why They Call It the Blues' and 'Tiny Dancer'. When the piano man was playing, he did not feel truly alone.

Renfrew made a point of tending Solovyova's grave. He cared about the other dead, but Solovyova mattered more: she'd been the last to go, the last human being Renfrew would ever know in his life. It would be too much work to keep the dust from covering the mass burial site, but he could at least do something for Solovyova. Sometimes he detoured to clean her grave when he was outside on antenna duty; other times he pre-breathed and suited up just for Solovyova; and always when he returned to the base he felt cleansed, renewed of purpose, determined that he could get through the days ahead.

That feeling didn't last long. But at least tending the grave kept the darkness at bay for a while.

There were moments when his stratagems failed, when the reality of his situation came crashing back in its full existential horror, but when that happened he was able to slam a mental door almost as soon as the scream had begun. As time had passed he had found that he became more adept at it, so that the moments of horror became only instants, like blank white frames spliced into the movie of his life.

When he was outside, he often found himself watching the sky, especially when the cold sun was low and twilight stars began to stud the butterscotch sky. A thought occurred to him, clean and bright and diamond hard: humanity might be gone, but did that necessarily mean he was the last intelligent creature in the universe? What if there was someone *else* out there?

How did that change the way he felt?

And what if there was in fact no one else out there at all: just empty light-years, empty parsecs, empty megaparsecs, all the way out to the farthest, faintest galaxies, teetering on the very edge of the visible universe?

How did *that* make him feel?

Cold. Alone. Fragile.

Curiously precious.

Part Two

Weeks slipped into months, months slipped into a long Martian year. The base kept functioning, despite Renfrew's grimmest expectations. Certain systems actually seemed to be more stable than at any time since Solovyova's death, as if they'd grudgingly decided to cooperate in keeping him alive. For the most part, Renfrew was glad that he did not have to worry about the base failing him. It was only in his darkest moments that he wished for the base to kill him, swiftly, painlessly, perhaps when he was already asleep and dreaming of better times. There'd be nothing undignified about going out that way; nothing that violated the terms of his vow to Solovyova. She wouldn't think badly of him for wishing death on those terms.

But the fatal failure never came, and for many days in a given month Renfrew managed not to think about suicide. He supposed that he had passed through the anger and denial phases of his predicament, into something like acceptance.

It helped to have someone to talk to.

He spoke to the piano man a lot now, quite unselfconsciously.

The odd thing was that the piano man spoke back too. On one level, Renfrew was well aware that the responses were entirely in his imagination: his brain had started filling in the other half of the one-sided conversation, based around the speech patterns that the piano man used between songs. On another level the responses seemed completely real and completely outside his own control, as if he no longer had access to the part of his brain that was generating them. A form of psychosis, perhaps; but even if that were the case, it was benign, even comforting, in its effects. If the thing that kept him sane was a little self-administered madness, confined solely to the piano man, then that seemed a small price to pay.

He still didn't know the man's real name. It was nearly there, but Renfrew could never quite bring it to mind. The piano man offered no clues. He introduced his songs by name, often spinning elaborate stories around them, but never had cause to say who he was. Renfrew had tried to access the rec system's software files, but he'd given up as soon as he was confronted by screen after screen of scrolling possibilities. He could have delved deeper, but he was wary of breaking the fragile spell that had brought the piano man into existence in the first place. Renfrew reckoned it was better not to know, than lose that one flicker of companionship.

'It's not exactly a rich human life,' Renfrew said.

'Probably not.' Piano Man glanced at the window, out towards the point where the others had been buried. 'But you have to admit, it's a hell of a lot better than the alternative.'

'I suppose so,' Renfrew said doubtfully. 'But what am I meant to do with the rest of my life? I can't just mope around here until I drop dead.'

'Well, that's always one possibility. But what about doing something a little bit more constructive?'

Piano Man fingered the keys, sketching a tune.

'Learn to play the piano? No point, is there? Not while you're around.'

'Don't count on me always being here, luv. But I was thinking more along the lines of a bit of reading. There are books, aren't there? I mean real ones.'

Renfrew imagined Piano Man miming the opening of a book. He nodded in return, without much enthusiasm. 'Nearly a thousand.'

'Must have cost a bomb to bring them here.'

'They didn't – not most of them, anyway. They were printed locally, using recycled organic matter. The printing and binding was totally automatic, and you could ask for a copy of just about any book that had ever been printed. Of course it doesn't work now ... the thousand is all we've got left.'

'You already know this, Renfrew. Why are you telling me?'

'Because you asked.'

'Okay. Fair enough.' Piano Man pushed his glasses back onto the bridge of his little nub of a nose. 'A thousand books, though: that should keep you going for a while.'

Renfrew shook his head. He had already glanced through the books and he knew that there were a lot less than a thousand that were of any interest to him. Most of the books had been produced purely for recreational value, since the technical journals and documentation had always been available for consultation via the optic implants or handhelds. At least two hundred volumes were children's books or juvenile material. Another three hundred were in Russian, French, Japanese or some other language he did not understand. He had time, but not *that* much time.

'So there are how many left – what? Five hundred or so that you might want to read?'

'It isn't that easy either,' Renfrew said. 'I tried reading fiction. Bad mistake. It was too depressing, reading about other people going about their lives before the accident.'

Piano Man peered at him over the rim of his glasses. 'Fussy bugger, aren't you? So what's left if we throw out the fiction?'

'It doesn't get much better. Travelogues ... historical biographies ... atlases and books on natural history ... all any of it does is remind me of what I'm never going to see again. Never another rainstorm. Never another bird, never another ocean, never another—'

'Okay, point made. Fine, throw out the coffee-table books – guests are going to be a bit thin on the ground anyway. What does that leave us with?'

Renfrew had done exactly that, his pile of books becoming smaller. There were philosophical texts: Wittgenstein's *Philosophical Investigations*; Sartre's *Being and Nothingness*; Foucault's *The Order of Things*; a dozen others.

'Who had those printed?'

'I don't know.'

'Must have been a right lonely sod, whoever he was. Still, did you make any progress with them?'

'I gave them my best shot.'

Renfrew had flicked through them, allured and at the same time appalled at the density of the philosophical speculation within them. On one level, they dealt with the most fundamental of human questions. But the books were so detached from anything that Renfrew considered mundane reality that he could consult them without triggering the episodes of loss and horror that came with the other books. That was not to say that he dismissed the arguments in the books as irrelevant, but because the books dealt with human experience in the mass there was far less pain than when Renfrew was forced to consider a specific individual other than himself. He could deal with the thought of losing the rest of humanity.

It was the idea of losing anyone specific that cut him open.

'So the heavy German guys weren't a total waste of time. All right. What else?'

'Well, there was a Bible,' Renfrew said.

'Read it much?'

'Religiously.' Renfrew shrugged. 'Sorry. Bad joke.'

'And now ... after the accident?'

'I must admit I've started thinking about some things I never thought about before. Why we're here. Why I'm here. What it all means. What it'll all mean when I'm gone. That doesn't mean I expect to find any useful answers.'

'Maybe you're not looking in quite the right place. What else was left in your pile?'

'Scientific stuff,' Renfrew said. 'Mathematics, quantum theory, relativity, cosmology—'

'I thought you told me all that stuff was available on the hand-helds?'

'These are more like textbooks. Not bang up to date, but not horribly out of date either. Someone's idea of light reading.'

'Looks like you're stuck with them, in that case. They shouldn't be too daunting, should they? I thought you were a scientist as well.'

'A geologist,' Renfrew told him. 'And you don't need much tensor algebra to study rocks.'

'You can always learn. You've got plenty of time. And – let's face it – it has to be easier than Japanese, doesn't it?'

'I suppose so. You still haven't told me why I should bother.'

Piano Man looked at him with sudden seriousness, the mirrored facets of his glasses like holes punched through to some burnished silver realm. 'Because of what you just said. Because of the questions you want answered.'

'You think a load of physics books is going to make a difference?'

'That's up to you. It's all a question of how much you want to understand. How deep you want to go.'

Piano Man turned back to the keyboard and started playing 'Saturday Night's Alright for Fighting'.

Piano Man was right. It was a question of how deep he wanted to go.

But surely there was more to it than that. Something else was spurring him on. It felt like a weird sense of obligation, an onus that weighed upon him with pressing, judicial force. He was certain now that he was the last man alive, having long since abandoned hope that anyone was left on Earth. Was it not therefore almost required of him to come to some final understanding of what it meant to be human, to achieve some final synthesis of all the disparate threads in the books before him? There could only be one witness to his success, he knew, but it seemed that if he were to fail he would be letting down the billions who had come before him. He could almost feel the weight of their expectations reaching towards him from the past, urging him to come to that difficult understanding that had always eluded them. They were dead but he was still alive, and now they were looking over his shoulder, anxiously waiting to see how he solved the puzzle that had bettered them.

'Hey, genius?' Piano Man asked, a week into Renfrew's study. 'Solved the mysteries of the universe yet?'

'Don't be silly. I've only just begun.'

'Okay. But I take it you've made at least a smidgeon of progress.' Piano Man wore a sparkling white suit and enormous star-shaped spectacles. He was grinning a lot and playing some of his weaker material.

'Depends what you mean by progress,' Renfrew said. 'If you mean absorbing what I've read, and not being thrown by anything

so far . . .' He shrugged. 'In that case, so far it's been a piece of cake.'
   'Ah-ha.'
   'But I'm under no illusions that it's going to stay that way. In fact I'm well aware that it's going to get a lot harder. So far all I'm doing is catching up. I haven't even begun to think about moving beyond the existing theories.'
   'All right. No point trying to run before you can crawl.'
   'Precisely.'
Piano Man swept his fingers down the keys in an exuberant glissando. 'But you can still tell me what you've learned, can't you?'
   'Are you sure you're interested?'
   'Of course I'm interested, luv. Why else would I ask?'

He told Piano Man what he had learned so far.
   He had read about the dual histories of cosmology and quantum mechanics, two braids of thought that had their origins in the early twentieth century. One dealt with the vast and ancient, the other with the microscopic and ephemeral. Cosmology encompassed galaxies and superclusters of galaxies, Hubble flows and the expansion of the universe. Quantum mechanics dealt with the fizzing, indeterminate cauldron of subatomic reality, where things could be in more than one place at once and where apparently rock-solid concepts like distance and the one-way flow of time became almost obscenely pliant.
   Handling the concepts of classical cosmology required an imaginative leap, and the ability to think of space and time as facets of the same thing. But once he had made that mental adjustment, which became slightly easier with practice, Renfrew found that the rest was merely a question of elaboration of scale and complexity. It was like holding the architecture of a vast, dark cathedral in his skull. At first it required a supreme effort of will to imagine the basic components of the building: the choir, the nave, the transepts, the spire. Gradually, however, these major architectural elements became fixed in his mind and he was able to start concentrating on the embellishments, the buttresses and gargoyles. Once he was comfortable with the classical cosmological model he found it easy enough to revise his mental floor plan to accommodate inflationary cosmology and the various models that had succeeded it. The scales became vaster, the leaps of perspective

all the more audacious, but he was able to envisage things within some kind of metaphoric framework, whether it was the idea of galaxies painted on the skin of an expanding balloon, or the 'phase transition' of water thawing in a frozen swimming pool.

This was not the case with quantum mechanics. Very quickly, Renfrew realised that the only tool for understanding the quantum realm was mathematics; all else failed. There were no convenient metaphors from everyday human experience to assist with the visualisation of wave-particle duality, the Heisenberg principle, quantum non-locality, or any of the other paradoxical properties of the microscopic world. The human mind had simply not evolved the appropriate mental machinery to deal with quantum concepts in the abstract. Trying to 'understand' any of it in workaday terms was futile.

Renfrew would have found this hard to accept had he not been in good company. Almost all of the great thinkers who had worked on quantum mechanics had been troubled by this to one degree or another. Some had accepted it, while others had gone to the grave with the nagging suspicion that a layer of familiar, Newtonian order lay beneath the shifting uncertainties of QM.

Even if quantum physics was 'correct', how did that fuzzy view of reality join up with the hard-edged concepts of General Relativity? The two theories were astoundingly successful at predicting the behaviour of the universe within their own specified areas of application, but all attempts to unify them had collapsed in failure. QM produced absurd results when applied to the kinds of macroscopic objects encountered in the real world: cats, boxes, Bösendorfer grand pianos, galactic superclusters. GR collapsed when it was used to probe the very small, whether it was the universe an instant after the Big Bang, or the infinitely dense, infinitely compact kernel of a black hole.

Thinkers had spent three-quarters of a century chasing that fabled unification, without success. But what if all the pieces had been in place at the time of the Catastrophe, and all that was needed was someone to view them with a fresh eye?

Some chance, Renfrew thought to himself. But again he smiled. Was it arrogant to think that he could achieve what no one had managed before? Perhaps; but given the uniqueness of his situation, nothing seemed improbable. And even if he did not succeed in that task, who was to say that he would not pick up one or two useful insights along the way?

At the very least it would give him something to do.

Still, he was getting ahead of himself. He had to understand QM before he could demolish it and replace it with something even more shiny and elegant, something that would be utterly consistent with every verified prediction of GR *and* nicely resolve all the niggling little details of observational mismatch ... while at the same time making testable predictions of its own.

'Are you sure you still want to go through with this?' Piano Man asked.

'Yes,' Renfrew told him. 'More than ever.'

His companion looked out towards the burial zone. 'Well, it's your funeral.'

And then started playing 'Candle in the Wind'.

Renfrew powered up the antenna again. Once more it laboured into life, gears crunching against the resistance of infiltrated dust as it steered on target. It was twilight and Earth was a bright star a few degrees above the horizon. The antenna locked on, Renfrew sighting along the main axis to confirm that the device really was pointed at the planet, and wasn't misaligned due to some mechanical or software fault. As always, as near as he could judge, the dish was aimed at Earth.

He waited to see the lights on the status board, never quite able to kill the hope that the flickering signal LED would harden into a steady, insistent green, indicating that the antenna had picked up the expected carrier transmission.

Never quite able to kill the hope that someone was still sending.

But the board told him the same thing it always did. No dice: it wasn't hearing anything beyond the random snap and crackle of interplanetary static.

Renfrew tapped the buttons to tell the dish to stow itself. He stood back from the operating panel as the machinery moved, waiting to see it stow itself safely in readiness for his next dutiful visit.

Something shone on the panel: a momentary brightening of the LED. It only lasted an instant, but it caught Renfrew's attention like a glint of gold in a prospector's stream. He'd seen the antenna slew back countless times before, and he'd never seen more than a glimmer from the LED. It had been too hard, too clear, to be caused by random contamination, and he certainly hadn't imagined it.

He told himself to be calm. If the LED had brightened when the antenna was locked on to Earth – well, that might be worth getting excited about. Might. But as it slewed back to stow itself, the antenna was just sweeping over empty sky.

All the same; plenty of cosmic radio signals out there, but none of them should be outputting in the narrow frequency range that the antenna was built to sniff. So maybe it had picked up something, unless the electronics were finally going south.

One way to tell.

Renfrew told the dish to track back onto Earth. He watched the board carefully this time, for he hadn't been paying attention the first time the antenna had moved.

But there it was again: that same brightening. And now that he'd seen it twice, he saw that the LED brightened and dimmed in a systematic fashion.

Exactly as if the dish was tracking across a concentrated radio source.

Exactly as if something was out there.

Renfrew backed up and repeated the cycle, using manual override to guide the antenna onto the signal. He waggled the dish until he judged that the LED was at its brightest, then watched the steady green light with a growing and cautious amazement.

He noted the coordinates of the source, remembering that he had only chanced upon it by accident, and that the same slew operation wouldn't necessarily pick up the mystery signal a day or a week from now. But if he recorded the position of the source now, and kept an eye on it from hour to hour and then day to day, he should at least be able to tell if it was an object moving inside the solar system, rather than some distant extragalactic radio source that just happened to look artificial.

Renfrew dared not invest too much hope in the detection. But if it was local, if it was coming from something within the system ... then it might have serious implications.

Especially for him.

Renfrew's excitement was tempered with caution. He vowed not to speak of the matter to Piano Man until he could be certain that the object was all that he hoped it might be: some tangible sign that someone had survived.

He'd expected that the discovery might make it hard for him to keep his mind on his studies, like a student distracted by something more interesting outside the window. But to his surprise exactly the reverse was the case. Spurred on by the possibility that his future might hold surprises, that it was not necessarily preordained that he would die alone and on Mars, Renfrew found that his intellectual curiosity was actually heightened. He redoubled his efforts to understand his predicament, gulping down pages of text that had seemed opaque and impenetrable only days before, but which now seemed lucid, transparent, even childlike in their simplicity. He found himself laughing, delighted with each tangible instance of progress towards his goal. He barely ate, and neglected some of the less pressing matters of base maintenance. And as the radio source refused to go away – as it looked more and more like something approaching Mars – Renfrew was gripped by the sense that he was engaged in a race; that he was in some way obliged to complete his task before the source arrived; that they would be waiting to hear what he had to say.

By night he dreamed cosmology, his dreams becoming ever more epic and ambitious as his knowledge of the science improved. With a feverish sense of repetition he recapitulated the entire history of the universe, from its first moment of existence to the grand and symphonic flourishing of intelligence.

At the beginning there was always nothingness, an absence not only of space and time but of existence itself, and yet at the same time he was aware of a trembling pre-potential, a feeling that the nothingness was poised on the cusp of an awesome instability, as if the unborn universe was itching to bring itself into being. With nightly inevitability it came: less an explosion than a kind of delicate clockwork unravelling, as cunningly packed structures unwound with inflationary speed, crystallising into brand new superluminally expanding vacuum. He dreamed of symmetries snapping apart, mass and energy becoming distinct, force and matter bootstrapping into complex structures. He dreamed of atoms stabilising, linking to form molecules and crystals, and from those building blocks he dreamed the simple beginnings of chemistry. He dreamed of galaxies condensing out of gas, of supermassive young suns flaring brilliantly and briefly within those galaxies. Each subsequent generation of stars was more stable than the last, and as they evolved and died they brewed metals and then coughed them into interstellar space. Out of those metals condensed worlds – hot and scalding at first, until comets rained onto their crusts, quenching them and giving them oceans and atmospheres.

He dreamed of the worlds ageing. On some the conditions were right for the genesis of microbial life. But the universe had to get very much older and larger before he saw anything more interesting than that. Even then it was scarce, and the worlds where animals stalked ocean beds before flopping and oozing ashore had a precious, gemlike rarity.

Rarer still were the worlds where those animals staggered towards self-awareness. But once or twice in every billion years it did happen. Occasionally life even learned to use tools and language, and looked towards the stars.

Towards the end of one particularly vivid cosmological dream Renfrew found himself focusing on the rarity of intelligence in the universe. He saw the galaxy spread out before him, spiral arms of creamy white flecked here and there by the ruby reds of cool supergiants or the dazzling kingfisher blues of the hottest stars. Dotted across the galaxy's swirl were candles, the kind he remembered from birthday cakes. There were a dozen or so to start with, placed randomly in a rough band that was neither too near the galactic core nor too close to the outer edges. The candles wavered slightly, and then – one by one – they began to go out.

Until only one was left. It was not even the brightest of those that had been there to begin with.

Renfrew felt a dreadful sense of that solitary candle's vulnerability. He looked above and below the plane of the galaxy, out towards its neighbours, but he saw no signs of candles elsewhere.

He desperately wanted to cradle that remaining candle, shelter it from the wind and keep it burning. He heard Piano Man singing: *And it seems to me you lived your life ...*

It went out.

All was void. Renfrew woke up shivering, and then raced to the suiting room and the airlock, and the waiting antenna, seeking contact with that radio signal.

*

'I think I understand,' he told Piano Man. 'Life has to be here to observe the universe, or it doesn't have any meaning. It's like the idea of the observer in quantum mechanics, collapsing an indeterminate system down to one possibility, opening the box and forcing the cat to choose between being dead or alive ...'

Piano Man took off his glasses and polished them on his sleeve. He said nothing for at least a minute, satisfying himself that the glasses were clean before carefully replacing them on his nose. 'That's what you think, is it? That's your big insight? That the universe needs its own observer? Well, break out the bubbly. Houston, I think we have a result.'

'It's better than nothing.'

'Right. And how did this universe manage for fifteen billion years before we dropped by and provided an intelligent observer? Are you seriously telling me it was all fuzzy and indeterminate until the instant some anonymous caveman had a moment of cosmic epiphany? That suddenly the entire quantum history of every particle in the visible universe – right out to the farthest quasar – suddenly jumped to one state, and all because some thicko in a bearskin had his brain wired up slightly differently from his ancestor?'

Renfrew thought back to his dream of the galactic disk studded with candlelight. 'No ... I'm not saying that. There were other observers before us. We're just the latest.'

'And these other observers – they were there all along, were they? An unbroken chain right back to the first instant of creation?'

'Well, no. Obviously the universe had to reach a certain minimum age before the preconditions for life – intelligent life – became established. But once that happened—'

'It's *bollocks*, though, isn't it, luv? What difference does it make if there's a gap of one second where the universe is unobserved, or ten billion years? None at all, as far as I'm concerned.'

'Look, I'm trying, all right? I'm doing my best. And anyway ...' Renfrew felt a sudden lurch of intuitive breakthrough. 'We don't need all those other observers, do we? We *have* observed the entire history of the universe, just by looking at higher and higher redshifts, with increasing look-back times. It's because the speed of light is finite. If it wasn't, information from the farthest parts of the universe would reach us immediately, and we'd have no way of viewing earlier epochs.'

'Fuck me, man, you almost sound like a cosmologist.'

'I think I might have become one.'

'Just don't make a career of it,' Piano Man said. He shook his head exasperatedly, then started playing 'Bennie and the Jets'.

A week later Renfrew told him the news. Renfrew's companion played the tentative ghost of a melody on the keyboard, something that hadn't yet crystallised into true music.

'You waited until now to tell me?' Piano Man asked, with a pained, disappointed look.

'I had to be certain. I had to keep tracking the thing, making sure it was really out there, and then making sure it was something worth getting excited about.'

'And?'

Renfrew offered a smile. 'I think it's worth getting excited about.'

Piano Man played an icy line, dripping sarcastic bonhomie.

'Really.'

'I'm serious. It's a navigation signal, a spacecraft beacon. It keeps repeating the same code, over and over again.' Renfrew leaned in closer; if he'd been able to lean on the phantom piano, he would have. 'It's getting stronger. Whatever's putting out that signal is getting closer to Mars.'

'You don't know that.'

'Okay, I don't. But there's the Doppler to consider as well. The signal's changing frequency a little from day to day. Put the two things together and you've got a ship making some kind of course correction, coming in for orbital insertion.'

'Good for you.'

Renfrew stepped back from the piano, surprised at his companion's dismissive reaction.

'There's a ship coming. Aren't you happy for me?'

'Tickled pink, luv.'

'I don't understand. This is what I've been waiting for all this time: news that someone's survived, that it doesn't all end here.' For the first time in their acquaintance, Renfrew raised his voice with Piano Man. 'What the hell's wrong with you? Are you jealous that you won't be all the company I'm ever going to have?'

'Jealous? I don't think so.'

Renfrew plunged his fist through the white nothingness of the piano. 'Then show some reaction!'

Piano Man lifted his hands from the keyboard. He closed the keyboard cover very gently and then sat with his hands in his lap, demurely, just the way he'd been when Renfrew had first witnessed him. He looked at Renfrew, his expression blank, whatever message his eyes might have conveyed lost behind the star-shaped mirrors of his glasses.

'You want a reaction? Fine, I'll give you one. You're making a very, very serious mistake.'

'It's no mistake. I know. I've double-checked everything—'

'It's still a mistake.'

'The ship's coming.'

'Something's coming. It may not be all that you expect.'

Renfrew's fury boiled over. 'Since when have you had the faintest fucking idea what I expect or don't expect? You're just a piece of software.'

'Whatever you say, luv. But remind me: when was the last time software encouraged you to take a deep interest in the fundamental workings of the universe?'

Renfrew had no answer for that. But he had to say something. 'They're coming. I know they're coming. Things are going to get better. You'll see when the ship comes.'

'You're going to do yourself a lot of harm.'

'As if you cared. As if you were capable of caring.'

'You've found a way to stay sane, Renfrew – even if that means admitting a tiny piece of piano-playing madness into your world. But there's a cost to that sanity, and it isn't *moi*. The cost is you can't ever allow yourself an instant of hope, because hope is something that will always be crushed, crushed utterly, and in the crushing of hope you will be weakened for ever, just as surely as if you'd mainlined some slow-acting poison.' Piano Man looked at Renfrew with a sudden, scholarly interest. 'How many instants of defeat do you think you can take, big guy? One, two, three? From where I'm sitting I wouldn't bet on three. I think three might easily kill you. I think two might get you on a shitty day.'

'Something's coming,' Renfrew said, plaintively.

'I thought for a while you had the balls to get through this. I thought you'd banished hope, learned to keep it outside in the cold. I was wrong; you've let it in again. Now it's going to stalk you, like a starved, half-crazed wolf.'

'It's my wolf.'

'There's still time to chase it away. Don't let me down now, Renfrew. I'm counting on you not to screw things up.'

That night Renfrew dreamed not of cosmology, but of something stranger and more upsetting. It was not one of the dreams he used to have about the past, for he had trained himself not to have those any more: the sense of sadness and loss upon waking almost too much to bear. Nor was it one of the equally troubling ones about visitors, people coming down out of cold blue skies and landing near the base. When they came through the airlock they arrived with flowers – Hawaiian leis – and utterly pointless but lovingly gift-wrapped presents. Their faces were never familiar at first, but by the end of each visitation, just before he woke, they would always start to transmute into old friends and loved ones. Renfrew hadn't yet trained himself not to have that kind of dream, and given the news about the radio signal he was sure at least one of them would haunt his sleep in the days ahead.

It was not that kind of dream. In the dream Renfrew rose like a sleepwalker from his bed in the middle of the night and crept through the base to the same medical lab where Solovyova had died, and placed his head into one of the functioning scanners, conjuring a glowing lilac image of his skull on the main screen, and then he emerged from the scanner and examined the readout to learn that his optic implants had been dead for years; there was no possible way it was picking up the Bösendorfer, let alone the talking ghost that played it.

In the morning, when he woke from the dream, Renfrew couldn't bring himself to visit the medical lab, in case he had already been there in the night.

By day he kept a weather eye on the radio signal. It strengthened and Dopplered, moving quickly against the stars as it fell into the grasp of Mars. Then the signal altered, switching to a different, equally meaningless burst of repeating binary gibberish. Renfrew knew that it meant something, and intensified his vigil.

A day later, a meteor flared across the twilight sky, etching a fire trail, and dropped behind the closest range of hills under a dark umbrella of parachutes.

'I'm going out to find where they came down,' Renfrew said.
'How far?'

'I don't know how far. Can't be all that far beyond the western marker.'

'That's still twenty kilometres away.'

'I'll take the car. It still works.'

'You've never driven it alone. It's a long walk home if something goes wrong.'

'Nothing's going wrong. I won't be alone.'

Piano Man started to say something, but Renfrew wasn't listening.

He pre-breathed, suited up, climbed onto the skeletal chassis of the buggy, then went out to meet the newcomers. As the mesh-wheeled vehicle bounced and gyred its way to the horizon, Renfrew felt a thrilled elation, as if he were on his way to a date with a beautiful and mysterious woman who might be his lover by the end of the evening.

But when he crested the hills and saw the fallen ship, he knew that nobody had ridden it to Mars. It was too small for that, even if this was just the re-entry component of a larger ship still circling the planet. What had come down was just a cargo pod, a blunt cylinder the size of a small minibus. It was tangled up with its own parachutes and the deflated gasbags it had deployed just before impact.

Renfrew parked the buggy, then spent ten minutes clearing fabric away from the cargo pod's door. The re-entry had scorched the decals, flags and data panels on the pod's skin to near-illegibility, but Renfrew knew the drill. Back when the base was inhabited, he'd occasionally drawn the short straw to drive out to recover a pod that had fallen away from the usual touchdown beacon.

He was sorry it wasn't a crewed ship, but the pod was the next best thing. Maybe they were still getting the infrastructure back up to speed. Sending out a manned vehicle was obviously too much of a stretch right now, and that was understandable. But they'd still had the presence of mind not to forget about Mars, even if all they could muster was a one-shot cargo pod. He would not be ungrateful. The pod could easily contain valuable medicines and machine parts, enough to relieve him of several ever-present worries. They might even have sent some luxuries, as a token of goodwill: things that the synths had never been very good at.

Renfrew touched a hand against the armoured panel next to the door, ready to flip it open and expose the pyrotechnic release mechanism. That was when one of the scorches caught his eye. It was a data panel, printed in spray-stencilled letters.

HTCV-554
HOHMANN TRANSFER CARGO VEHICLE
SCHEDULED LAUNCH: KAGOSHIMA 05/38
DESTINATION: THARSIS BASE, MARS
PAYLOAD: REPLACEMENT LASER OPTICS
PROPERTY: MARS DEVELOPMENT CORPORATION

According to the data panel, the cargo pod had been scheduled to lift from Kagoshima spaceport one month before the virus hit. Maybe the panel was wrong; maybe this pod had been prepared and sprayed and then held on the pad until the virus had passed and the reconstruction had begun ...

But why send him glass?

Renfrew knew, with an appalling certainty, that the vehicle had not been delayed on the pad. It had launched just as its owners had intended, *on time*, with a consignment of precision glassware that might just have been useful back when the base was fully inhabited and they'd needed a steady supply of laser optics for the surveying work.

But somewhere between Earth and Mars, the cargo pod had lost its way. When the virus hit, the pod would have lost contact with the Earth-based tracking system that was supposed to guide it on its way. But the pod hadn't simply drifted into interplanetary space, lost for ever. Instead, its dumb-as-fuck navigation system had caused it to make an extra fuel-conserving loop around the sun, until it finally locked on to the Mars transponder.

Renfrew must have picked it up shortly afterwards.

He stumbled back to the buggy. He climbed into the openwork frame, settled into the driver's seat and didn't bother with the harness. He kept his breathing in check. The disappointment hadn't hit yet, but he could feel it coming, sliding towards him with the oiled glide of a piston. It was going to hurt like hell when it arrived. It was going to feel like the weight of creation pushing down onto his chest. It was going to squeeze the life out of him; it was going to make him open that helmet visor, if he didn't make it home first.

Piano Man had been right. He'd allowed hope back into his

world, and now hope was going to make him pay.

He gunned the buggy to maximum power, flinging dust from its wheels, skidding until it found traction. He steered away from the cargo pod, not wanting to look at it, not even wanting to catch a glimpse of it in the buggy's rear-view mirrors.

He'd made it to within five kilometres of the base when he hit a boulder, tipping the buggy over. Renfrew tumbled from the driver's seat, and the last thing he saw – the last thing he was aware of – was an edge of sharp rock rising to shatter his visor.

Part Three

And yet Renfrew woke.

Consciousness came back to him in a crystal rush. He remembered everything, up to and including the last instant of his accident. It seemed to have happened only minutes earlier: he could almost taste blood in his mouth. Yet by the same token the memory seemed inhumanly ancient, calcified into hardness, brittle as coral.

He was back in the base, not out by the crashed buggy. Through narrow, sleep-gummed eyes he picked out familiar décor. He'd come around on the same medical couch where he had seen Solovyova die. He moved his arm and touched his brow, flinching as he remembered the stone smashing through the visor, flinching again as he recalled the momentary contact of stone against skin, the hardening pressure of skin on bone, the *yielding* of that pressure as the edge of the stone rammed its way into his skull like a nuclear-powered icebreaker cracking hard arctic pack-ice.

The skin under his fingers was smooth, unscarred. He touched his chin and felt the same day's growth of stubble he'd been wearing when he went out to meet the pod. There was stiffness in his muscles, but nothing he wouldn't have expected after a hard day's work. He eased himself from the couch, touched bare feet to cold ceramic flooring. He was wearing the one-piece inner-layer that he'd put on under the spacesuit before he went outside. But the inner-layer was crisper and cleaner than he remembered, and when he looked at the sleeve the tears and frays he recalled were absent.

Gaining steadiness with each step, Renfrew padded across the medical lab to the window. He remembered seeing Solovyova's face reflected in the glass, the first time he'd told her about the piano. It had been twilight then; it was full daylight now, and as his eyes adjusted to wakefulness, they picked out details and textures in the scenery with a clarity he'd never known before.

There were things out there that didn't belong.

They stood between the base and the foothills, set into the dust like haphazardly placed chess pieces. It was hard to say how tall they were – metres or tens of metres – for there was something slippery and elusive about the space between the forms and the base,. confounding Renfrew's sense of perspective. Nor could he have reported with any certainty on the shapes of the objects. One moment he saw blocky, unchanging chunks of crystalline growth – something like tourmaline, tinted with bright reds and greens – the next he was looking at stained-glass apertures drilled through the very skein of reality, or skeletal, prismatic things that existed only in the sense that they had edges and corners, rather than surfaces and interiors. And yet there was never any sense of transition between the opposed states.

He knew, instantly and without fear, that they were alive, and that they were aware of him.

Renfrew made his way to the suiting room, counted the intact suits that were hanging there and came up with the same number he remembered from before the buggy accident. No sign of any damage to the racked helmets.

He suited up and stepped out into Martian daylight. The forms were still there, surrounding the base like the weathered stones of some grand Neolithic circle. Yet they seemed closer now, and larger, and their transformations had an accelerated, heightened quality. They had detected his emergence; they were glad of it; it was what they had been waiting for.

Still there was no fear.

One of the shapes seemed larger than the others. It beckoned Renfrew nearer, and the ground he walked upon melted and surged under him, encouraging him to close the distance. The transformations became more feverish. His suit monitor informed him that the air outside was as cold and thin as ever, but a sound was reaching him through the helmet that he'd never heard in all his time on Mars. It was a chorus of shrill, quavering notes, like the sound from a glass organ, and it was coming from the aliens. In that chorus was ecstasy and expectation. It should have terrified him, should have sent him scurrying back inside, should have plunged him into gibbering catatonia, but it only made him stronger.

Renfrew dared to look up.

If the aliens gathered around the base were the crew, then the thing suspended over the base – the thing that swallowed three-fifths of the sky, more like a weather system than a machine – had to be their ship. It was a vast, frozen explosion of colours and shapes, and it made him want to shrivel back into his skull. The mere existence of the aliens and their ship told him that all he had learned, all the wisdom he had worked so hard to accrue, was at best a scratch against the rock face of reality.

He still had a long, long way to go.

He looked down, and walked to the base of the largest alien. The keening reached a shrill, exultant climax. Now that he was close, the alien's shape-and-size shifting had subsided. The form looming over him was stable and crystalline, with the landscape behind it faintly visible through the refracted translucence of the alien's body.

The alien's voice, when it came, felt like the universe whispering secrets into his head.

'Are you feeling better now?'

Renfrew almost laughed at the banality of the question. 'I'm feeling ... better, yes.'

'That's good. We were concerned. Very, very concerned. It pleases us that you have made this recovery.'

The keening quieted. Renfrew sensed that the other aliens were witnesses to a one-on-one conversation between him and this largest entity, and that there was something utterly respectful, even subservient, in their silence.

'When you talk about my recovery ... are you saying ...' Renfrew paused, choosing his words with care. 'Did you make me better?'

'We healed you, yes. We healed you and learned your language from the internal wiring of your mind.'

'I should have died out there. When I tipped the buggy ... I thought I was dead. I *knew* I was dead.'

'There were enough recoverable patterns. It was our gift to remake you. Only you, however, can say whether we did a good enough job.'

'I feel the same way I always did. Except better, like I've been turned inside out and flushed clean.'

'That is what we hoped.'

'You mind if I ask . . .'

The alien pulsed an inviting shade of pink.

'You may ask anything you like.'

'Who are you? What are you doing here? Why have you come *now*?'

'We are the Kind. We have arrived to preserve and resurrect what we may. We have arrived now because we could not arrive sooner.'

'But the coincidence . . . to come now, after we've been waiting so long . . . to come *now*, just after we've wiped ourselves out. Why couldn't you have come sooner, and stopped us fucking things up so badly?'

'We came as fast as we could. As soon as we detected the electromagnetic emanations of your culture . . . we commenced our journey.'

'How far have you come?'

'More than two hundred of your light-years. Our vehicle moves very quickly, but not faster than light. More than four hundred years have passed since the transmission of the radio signals that alerted us.'

'No,' Renfrew said, shaking his head, wondering how the aliens could have made such a basic mistake. 'That isn't possible. Radio hasn't been around that long. We've had television for maybe a hundred years, radio for twenty or thirty years longer . . . but not four hundred years. No way was it *our* signals you picked up.'

The alien shifted to a soothing turquoise.

'You are mistaken, but understandably so. You were dead longer than you realise.'

'No,' he said flatly.

'That is the way it is. Of course you have no memory of the intervening time.'

'But the base looks exactly the way it did before I left.'

'We repaired your home, as well. If you would like it changed again, that is also possible.'

Renfrew felt the first stirrings of acceptance, the knowledge that what the alien was telling him was true.

'If you've brought me back . . .'

'Yes,' the alien encouraged.

'What about the others? What about all the other people who

died here – Solovyova and the ones before her? What about all the people who died on Earth?'

'There were no recoverable forms on the Earth. We can show you if you would like . . . but we think you would find it distressing.'

'Why?'

'We did. A lifecrash is always distressing, even to machine-based entities such as us. Especially after such a long and uninterrupted evolutionary history.'

'A lifecrash?'

'It did not just end with the extinction of humanity. The agent that wiped out your species had the capacity to change. Eventually it assimilated every biological form on the planet, leaving only itself: endlessly cannibalising, endlessly replicating.'

Renfrew dealt with that. He'd already adjusted to the fact that humanity was gone and that he was never going to see Earth again. It did not require a great adjustment to accept that Earth itself had been lost, along with the entire web of life it had once supported.

Not that he was exactly thrilled, either.

'Okay,' he said, falteringly. 'But what about the people I buried here?'

Renfrew sensed the alien's regret. Its facets shone a sombre amber.

'Their patterns were not recoverable. They were buried in caskets, along with moisture and microorganisms. Time did the rest. We did try, yes . . . but there was nothing left to work with.'

'I died out there as well. Why was it any different for me?'

'You were kept cold and dry. That made all the difference, as far as we were concerned.'

So he'd mummified out there, baked dry under that merciless sterilising sky, instead of rotting in the ground like his friends. Out there under that Martian sun, for the better part of three hundred years . . . what must he have looked like when they pulled him out of the remains of his suit? he wondered. Maybe a bleached and twisted thing, corded with the knotted remains of musculature and tissue: something that could easily have been mistaken for driftwood, had there been driftwood on Mars.

The wonder and horror of it all were almost too much. He'd been the last human being alive, and then he had died, and now he was the first human being to be resurrected by aliens.

The first and perhaps the last: he sensed even then that, as godlike as the Kind appeared, they were bound by limits. They were as much prisoners of what the universe chose to allow, and what it chose not to allow, as humanity, or dust, or atoms.

'Why?' he asked.

A pulse of ochre signified the alien's confusion.

'Why what?'

'Why did you bring me back? What possible interest do I hold for you?'

The alien considered his remark, warming through shades of orange to a bright venous red. Like an echo, the shade spread to the other members of the gathering.

'We help,' the leader told Renfrew. 'That is what we do. That is what we have always done. We are the Kind.'

He returned to the base and tried to continue his affairs, just as if the Kind had never arrived. Yet they were always out there whenever he passed a window: brighter and closer now as evening stole in, as if they had gathered the day's light and were now reradiating it in subtly altered shades. He closed the storm shutters but that didn't help much. He did not doubt that the ship was still poised above, suspended over the base as if guarding the infinitely precious thing that he had become.

Renfrew's old routines had little meaning now. The aliens hadn't just brought the base back to the way it had been before he crashed the buggy. They had repaired all the damage that had accrued since the collapse of Earthside society, and the base systems now functioned better than at any point since the base's construction. As mindless as his maintenance tours had been, they had imposed structure on his life that was now absent. Renfrew felt like a rat that'd had his exercise wheel taken away.

He went to the recreation room and brought the system back online. Everything functioned as the designers had intended. The aliens must have repaired, or at least not removed, his implant. But when he cycled through the myriad options, he found that something had happened to Piano Man.

The figure was still there – Renfrew even knew his name now – but the companion he remembered was gone. Now Piano Man behaved just like all the other generated personalities. Renfrew could still talk to him, and Piano Man could still answer him back, but nothing like their old conversations was now possible. Piano Man would take requests, and banter, but that was the limit of his abilities. If Renfrew tried to steer the conversation away from the strictly musical, if he tried to engage Piano Man in a discussion about cosmology or quantum mechanics, all he got back was a polite but puzzled stare. And the more Renfrew persisted, the less it seemed to him that there was any consciousness behind that implant-generated face. All he was dealing with was a paper-thin figment of the entertainment system.

Renfrew knew that the Kind hadn't 'fixed' Piano Man in the sense that they had fixed the rest of the base. But – deliberately or otherwise – their arrival had destroyed the illusion of companionship. Perhaps they had straightened some neurological kink in Renfrew's brain when they put him back together. Or perhaps the mere fact of their arrival had caused his subconscious to discard that earlier mental crutch.

He knew it shouldn't have meant anything. Piano Man hadn't existed in any real sense. Feeling sorrow for his absence was as ridiculous as mourning the death of a character in a dream. He'd made Piano Man up; his companion had never had any objective existence.

But he still felt that he had lost a friend.

'I'm sorry,' he said to that polite but puzzled face. 'You were right, and I was wrong. I was doing fine just the way things were. I should have listened to you.'

There was an uncomfortable pause, before Piano Man smiled and spread his fingers above the keyboard.

'Would you like me to play something?'

'Yes,' Renfrew said. 'Play "Rocket Man". For old times' sake.'

He allowed the Kind into Tharsis Base. Their crystalline forms were soon everywhere, spreading and multiplying in a mad orgy of prismatic colour, transforming the drab architecture into a magical lantern-lit grotto. The beauty of it was so startling, so intoxicating, that it moved Renfrew to tears with the knowledge that no one else would ever see it.

'But it could be different,' the leader told him. 'We did not broach this earlier, but there are possibilities you may wish to consider.'

'Such as?'

'We have repaired you, and made you somewhat younger than you were before your accident. In doing so we have learned a great deal about your biology. We cannot resurrect the dead of Earth, or your companions here on Mars, but we can give you other people.'

'I don't follow.'

'It would cost us nothing to weave new companions. They could be grown to adulthood at accelerated speed, or your own ageing could be arrested while you give the children time to grow.'

'And then what?'

'You could breed with them, if you chose. We'd intervene to correct any genetic anomalies.'

Renfrew smiled. '"Mars ain't the kind of place to raise your kids." At least, that's what a friend of mine told me once.'

'Now there is nowhere *but* Mars. Doesn't that make a difference? Or would you rather we established a habitable zone on Earth and transplanted you there?'

They made him feel like a plant, like some incredibly rare and delicate orchid.

'Would I notice the difference?'

'We could adjust your faculties so that Earth appeared the way you remembered. Or we could edit your memories to match the present conditions.'

'Why can't you just put things back the way they were? Surely one runaway virus isn't going to defeat you.'

The alien turned a shade of chrome blue that Renfrew had learned to recognise as indicative of gentle chiding. 'That's not our way. The runaway agent now constitutes its own form of life, brimming with future potential. To wipe it out now would be akin to sterilising your planet just as your own single-celled ancestors were gaining a foothold.'

'You care about life that much?'

'Life is precious. Infinitely so. Perhaps it takes a machine intelligence to appreciate that.' The chrome blue faded, replaced by a placatory olive green. 'Given that Earth cannot be made the way it was, will you reconsider our offer to give you companionship?'

'Not now,' he said.

'But later, perhaps?'

'I don't know. I've been on my own a long time. I'm not sure it isn't better this way.'

'You've craved companionship for years. Why reject it now?'

'Because ...' And here Renfrew faltered, conscious of his own inarticulacy before the alien. 'When I was alone, I spent a lot of time thinking things through. I got set on that course, and I'm not sure I'm done yet. There's still some stuff I need to get straight in my head. Maybe when I'm finished—'

'Perhaps we can help you with that.'

'Help me understand the universe? Help me understand what it means to be the last living man? Maybe even the last intelligent organism in the universe?'

'It wouldn't be the first time. We are a very old culture. In our travels we have encountered myriad other species. Some of them are extinct by now, or changed beyond recognition. But many of them were engaged on quests similar to your own. We have watched, and occasionally interceded to better aid that comprehension. Nothing would please us more than to offer you similar assistance. If we cannot give you companionship, at least let us give you wisdom.'

'I want to understand space and time, and my own place in it.'

'The path to deep comprehension is risky.'

'I'm ready for it. I've already come a long way.'

'Then we shall help. But the road is long, Renfrew. The road is long and you have barely started your journey.'

'I'm willing to go all the way.'

'You will be long past human before you near the end of it. That is the cost of understanding space and time.'

Renfrew felt a chill on the back of his neck, a premonitory shiver. The alien was not warning him for nothing. In its travels it must have witnessed things that caused it distress.

Still, he said: 'Whatever it takes. Bring it on. I'm ready.'

'Now?'

'Now. But before we begin ... don't call me Renfrew any more.'

'You wish a new name, to signify this new stage in your quest?'

'From now on, I'm John. That's what I want you to call me.'

'Just John?'

He nodded solemnly. 'Just John.'

Part Four

The Kind did things to John.

While he slept, they altered his mind: infiltrating it with tiny crystal avatars of themselves, performing prestigious feats of neural rewiring. When he woke he still felt like himself, still carried the same freight of memories and emotions that he'd taken with him to sleep. But suddenly he had the ability to grasp things that had been impenetrably difficult only hours earlier. Before the accident, he had probed the inlets of superstring theory, like an explorer searching for a navigable route through a treacherous mountain range. He had never found that easy path, never dreamed of conquering the dizzying summits before him, but now, miraculously, he was on the other side, and the route through the obstacle looked insultingly easy. Beyond superstring theory lay the unified territory of M-theory, but that too was soon his. John revelled in his new understanding.

More and more, he began to think in terms of a room whose floor was the absolute truth about the universe: where it had come from, how it worked, what it meant to be a thinking being in that universe. But that floor looked very much like a carpet, and it was in turn concealed by other carpets, one on top of the other, each of which represented some imperfect approximation to the final layer. Each layer might look convincing, might endure decades or centuries of enquiry without hinting that it contained a flaw, but sooner or later one would inevitably reveal itself. A tiny, loose thread – perhaps a discrepancy between observation and theory – and with a tug the entire fabric of that layer would come apart. It was in the nature of such revolutions that the next layer down would already have been glimpsed by then. Only the final carpet, the floor, would contain no logical inconsistencies, no threads waiting to be unravelled.

Could you ever know when you'd reached it? John wondered. Some thinkers considered it impossible to ever know with certainty. All you could do was keep testing, tugging at every strand to see how firmly it was woven into the whole. If after tens of thousands of years the pattern was still intact, then it might begin to seem likely that you had arrived at final wisdom. But you could never know for sure. The ten thousand and first year might bring forth some trifling observation that, as innocent as it first seemed, would eventually prove that there was yet another layer lurking underneath.

You could go on like that for ever, never knowing for sure.

Or – as some other thinkers speculated – the final theory might come with its own guarantee of authenticity, a golden strand of logical validation threaded into the very mathematical language in which it was couched. It might be in the nature of the theory to state that there could be no deeper description of the universe.

But even then, it wouldn't stop you making observations. It wouldn't stop you testing.

John kept learning. M-theory became a distant and trifling obstacle, dwarfed by the daunting unified theories that had superseded it. These theories probed the interface not just of matter and space–time, but also of consciousness and entropy, information, complexity and the growth of replicating structures. On the face of it, they seemed to describe everything that conceivably mattered about the universe.

But each in turn was revealed as flawed, incomplete, at odds with observation. An error in the predicted mass of the electron, in the twenty-second decimal place. A one-in-ten-thousandth-part discrepancy in the predicted bending of starlight around a certain class of rotating black hole. A niggling mismatch between the predicted and observed properties of inertia in highly charged space–time.

The room contained many carpets, and John had the dizzying sense that there were still many layers between him and the floor. He'd made progress, certainly, but it had only sharpened his sense of how far he had to go.

The Kind remade him time and again, resetting his body clock to give him the time he needed for his studies. But each leap of understanding pushed him closer to the fundamental limits of a wet human brain wired together from a few hundred billion neurons, crammed into a tiny cage of bone.

'You can stop now, if you like,' the Kind said, in the hundredth year of his quest.

'Or what?' John asked mildly.

'Or we continue, with certain modifications.'

John gave them his consent. It would mean not being human for a little while, but given the distance he had come, the price did not strike him as unreasonable.

The Kind encoded the existing patterns of his mind into a body much like one of their own. For John, the transition to a machine-based substrate of thinking crystal was in no way traumatic, especially as the Kind assured him that the process was completely reversible. Freed of the constraints of flesh and scale, his progress accelerated even more. From this new perspective, his old human mind looked like something seen through the wrong end of a telescope. Compared to the mental mansion he now inhabited, his former residence looked as squalid and limiting as a rabbit hutch. It was a wonder he had understood *anything*.

But John wasn't finished.

A thousand years passed. Always adding new capacity to himself, he had become a kilometre-high crystalline mound on the summit of Pavonis Mons. He was larger by far than any of the Kind, but that was only to be expected: he was probing layers of reality that they had long since mapped to their own satisfaction, and from which they had dutifully retreated. Having attained that understanding once, the Kind had no further need for it.

There were other people on Mars now. John had finally acquiesced to the Kind's offer to bring him companions, and they had created children who had now grown to become parents and grandparents. But when John agreed to the coming of other humans, it had little to do with his own need for companionship. He felt too remote from other humans now, and it was only because he sensed that the Kind wished to perform this exercise – that it would please the aliens to have something else to do – that he had relented. But even if he could not relate to the teeming newcomers, he found it pleasing to divert a small portion of his energies to their amusement. He rearranged his outer architecture – dedicated to only the most trivial data-handling tasks – so that he resembled an ornate crystalline fairy palace, with spires and domes and battlements, and at dusk he twinkled with refracted sunlight, throwing coloured glories across the great plains of the Tharsis Montes. A yellow road spiralled around his foot slopes. He became a site of pilgrimage, and he sang to the pilgrims as they toiled up and down the spiral road.

Millennia passed. Still John's mind burrowed deeper.

He reported to the Kind that he had passed through eighteen paradigmatic layers of reality, each of which had demanded a concomitant upgrade in his neural wiring before he could be said to have understood the theory in all its implications, and therefore recognised the flaw that led to the next layer down.

The Kind informed him that – in all the history that was known to them – fewer than five hundred other sentient beings had attained John's present level of understanding.

Still John kept going, aware that in all significant respects he had now exceeded the intellectual capacity of the Kind. They were there to assist him, to guide him through his transformations, but they had only a dim conception of what it now felt like to be John. According to their data less than a hundred individuals, from a hundred different cultures, all of them now extinct, had reached this point.

Ahead, the Kind warned, were treacherous waters.

John's architectural transformations soon began to place an intolerable strain on the fragile geology of Pavonis Mons. Rather than reinforce the ancient volcano to support his increasing size and mass, John chose to detach himself from the surface entirely. For twenty-six thousand years he floated in the thickening Martian atmosphere, supported by batteries of antigravity generators. For much of that time it pleased him to manifest in the form of a Bösendorfer grand piano, a shape reconstructed from his oldest human memories. He drifted over the landscape, solitary as a cloud, and occasionally he played slow tunes that fell from the sky like thunder.

Yet soon there came a time when he was too large even for the atmosphere. The heat dissipation from his mental processes was starting to have an adverse effect on the global climate.

It was time to leave.

In space he grew prolifically for fifteen million years. Hot blue stars formed, lived and died while he gnawed away at the edges of certain intractables. Human civilisations buzzed around him like flies. Amongst them, he knew, were individuals who were engaged in something like the same quest for understanding. He wished them well, but he had a head start none of them had a hope of ever overtaking. Over the years his density had increased, until he was now composed mostly of solid nuclear matter. Then he had evolved to substrates of pure quark matter. By then, his own gravity had become immense, and the Kind reinforced him with mighty spars of exotic matter, pilfered from the disused wormhole transit system of some long-vanished culture. A binary pulsar was harnessed to power him; titanic clockwork enslaved for the purposes of pure mentation.

And still deeper John tunnelled.

'I ... sense something,' he told the Kind one day.

They asked him what, fearing his answer.

'Something ahead of me,' he said. 'A few layers down. I can't quite see it yet, but I'm pretty sure I can sense it.'

They asked him what it was like.

'An ending,' John told them.

'This is what we always knew would come to pass,' the Kind told him.

They informed him that only seven other sentient beings had reached John's current state of enlightenment; none in the last three billion years. They also told him that to achieve enlightenment he would have to change again, become denser still, squeezed down into a thinking core that was only just capable of supporting itself against its own ferocious gravity.

'You'll be unstable,' they told him. 'Your very thought processes will tend to push you into your own critical radius.'

He knew what they meant, but he wanted to hear them spell it out. 'And when that happens?'

'You become a black hole. No force in the universe will be able to prevent your collapse. These are the treacherous waters we mentioned earlier.'

They said 'earlier' as if they meant 'earlier this afternoon', rather than 'earlier in the history of this universe'. But John had long since accustomed himself to the awesome timescales of the Kind.

'I still want you to do it. I've come too far to give up now.'

'As you wish.'

So they made him into a vast ring of hyperdense matter, poised on the edge of collapse. In his immense gravitational field, John's lightning thought processes grew sluggish. But his computational resources were now vast.

Many times he orbited the galaxy.

With each layer that he passed, he sensed the increasing presence of the *ending*, the final, rock-hard substrate of reality. He knew it was the floor, not another mirage-like illusion of finality. He was almost there now: his great quest was nearing its completion, and in a few thoughts – a few hours in the long afternoon of the universe – he would arrive.

Yet John called a halt to his thinking.

'Is there a problem?' the Kind asked, solicitously.

'I don't know. Maybe. I've been thinking about what you said before: how my own thought processes might push me over the edge.'

'Yes,' the Kind said.

'I'm wondering: what would that really mean?'

'It would mean death. There has been much debate on the matter, but the present state of understanding is that no useful information can ever emerge from a black hole.'

'You're right. That sounds an awful lot like death to me.'

'Then perhaps you will consider stopping now, while there is still time. You have at least glimpsed the final layer. Is that not enough for you? You've come further than you could ever have dreamed when you embarked on this quest.'

'That's true.'

'Well, then. Let this be an end to it. Dwell not on what is left to be done, but on what you have already achieved.'

'I'd like to. But there's this nagging little thing I can't stop thinking about.'

'Please. To think about *anything* in your present state is not without risk.'

'I know. But I think this might be important. Do you think it's coincidence that I've reached this point in my quest, at the same time as I'm teetering on the edge of collapsing into myself?'

'We confess we hadn't given the matter a great deal of thought, beyond the immediate practicalities.'

'Well, I have. And I've been thinking. Way back when, I read a theory about baby universes.'

'Continue . . .' the Kind said warily.

'How they might be born inside black holes, where the ordinary rules of space and time break down. The idea being that when the singularity inside a black hole forms, it actually buds off a whole new universe, with its own subtly altered laws of physics. That's where the information goes: down the pipe, into the baby universe. We see no evidence of this on the outside – the expansion's in a direction we can't point; it isn't as if the new universe is expanding into our own like an explosion – but that doesn't mean it isn't happening every time a black hole forms somewhere in our universe. In fact, it's entirely possible that *our* universe might well have been budded off from someone else's black hole.'

'We are aware of this speculation. And your point being?'

'Perhaps it isn't coincidence. Perhaps this is just the way it has to be. You cannot attain ultimate wisdom about the universe without reaching this point of gravitational collapse. And at the moment you do attain final understanding – when the last piece falls into place, when you finally glimpse that ultimate layer of reality – you slip over the edge, into irreversible collapse.'

'In other words, you die. As we warned.'

'But maybe not. After all, by that point you've become little more than pure information. What if you survive the transition through your own singularity, and slip through into the baby universe?'

'To become smeared out and reradiated as random noise, you mean?'

'Actually, I had something else in mind. Who's to say that you don't end up encoding yourself into the very structure of that new universe?'

'Who's to say that you do?'

'I admit it's speculative. But there is something rather beautiful and symmetrical about it, don't you think? In the universes where there is intelligent life, one or more sentient individuals will eventually ask the same questions I asked myself, and follow them through to this point of penultimate understanding. When they achieve enlightenment, they exceed the critical density and become baby universes in their own right. They become what they sought to understand.'

'You have no proof of this.'

'No, but I have one hell of a gut feeling. There is, of course, only one way to know for sure. At the moment of understanding, I'll know whether this happens or not.'

'And if it doesn't—?'

'I'll still have achieved my goal. I'll know that, even as I'm crushed out of existence. If, on the other hand, it does happen ... then I won't be crushed at all. My consciousness will continue, on the other side, embedded in the fabric of space and time itself.' John paused, for something had occurred to him. 'I'll have become something very close to—'

'Don't say it, please,' the Kind interjected.

'All right, I won't. But you see now why I hesitate. This final step will take me as far from humanity as all the steps that have preceded it. It's not something I'm about to take lightly.'

'You shouldn't.'

'The others ...' John began, before trailing off, aware of the fear and doubt in his voice. 'What did they do, when they got this far?

Did they hesitate? Did they just storm on through?'

'Only three have preceded you, in all of recorded history. Two underwent gravitational collapse: we can show you the black holes they became, if you wish.'

'I'll pass. Tell me about the third.'

'The third chose a different path. He elected to split his consciousness into two streams, by dividing and reallocating portions of his architecture. One component continued with the quest for ultimate understanding, while the other retreated, assuming a less-dense embodiment that carried no risk of collapse.'

'What happened to the component that continued?'

'Again,' the Kind said, with the merest flicker of amusement at John's expense, 'we'd be delighted to show you the results.'

'And the other half? How could he have preserved the understanding he'd achieved, if he backtracked to a simpler architecture?'

'He couldn't. That's exactly the point.'

'I don't follow. Understanding required a certain level of complexity. He couldn't have retained that understanding if he stripped himself back.'

'He didn't. He did, however, retain the memory of having understood. That, for him, was sufficient.'

'Just the memory?'

'Precisely that. He'd glimpsed enlightenment. He didn't need to retain every detail of that glimpse to know he'd seen it.'

'But that's not understanding,' John said exasperatedly. 'It's a crude approximation, like the postcard instead of the view.'

'Better than being crushed out of existence, though. The being under discussion seemed adequately content with the compromise.'

'And you think I will be too?'

'We think you should at least consider the possibility.'

'I will. But I'll need time to think about it.'

'How long?'

'Just a bit.'

'All right,' the Kind said. 'But just don't think *too* hard about it.'

Much less than a million years later, John announced to the Kind that he wished to follow the example of the third sentient being they had mentioned. He would partition his consciousness into two streams; one would continue towards final enlightenment, the other would assume a simpler and safer architecture, necessarily incapable of emulating his present degree of understanding. For John, the process of dividing himself was as fraught and delicate as any of the transformations he had hitherto undergone. It required all of the skill of the Kind to effect the change in such a way as to allow the preservation of memories, even as his mind was whittled back to a mere sketch of itself. But by turns it was done, and the two Johns were both physically and mentally distinct: the one still poised on the edge of gravitational annihilation, only a thought away from transcendence, the other observing matters from a safe distance.

So it was that Simple John witnessed the collapse and in-fall of his more complex self: an event as sudden and violent as any natural stellar catastrophe in recent galactic times. In that moment of understanding, he had pushed his own architecture to the limit. Somewhere in him, matter and energy collapsed to open a howling aperture to a new creation. He had reached the conclusion of his quest.

In the last nanoseconds of his physical existence, however – before he was sucked under the event horizon, beyond which no information could ever emerge – Complex John did at least manage to encode and transmit a parting wave of gravitational energy, a message to his other half.

The content was very brief.

It said only: 'Now I get it.'

That might have been the end of it, but shortly afterwards Simple John took a decision that was to return him to his starting point. He carried now the memory of near-enlightenment, and the memory was – as the Kind had promised, despite John's natural scepticism – very nearly as illuminating as the thing itself. In some ways, perhaps *more so* – it was small and polished and gemlike, and he could examine it from different angles, quite unlike the unwieldy immersiveness of the experience itself, from which the memory had been expertly distilled.

But why, he wondered, stop there? If he could revert back to this simplified architecture and still retain the memory of what he had been before, why not take things further?

Why not go all the way back?

The descent from near-enlightenment was not a thing to be

rushed, for at every stage – as his evolved faculties were stripped back and discarded – he had to be assured that the chain of memory remained unbroken. As he approached being human again, he knew on an intellectual level that what he now carried was not the memory of understanding, but the memory of a memory of a memory . . . a pale, diminished, reflected thing, but no less authentic for that. It still felt genuine to John, and now – as they packed his wet cellular mind back into the stifling cage of a *Homo sapiens* skull – that was all that truly mattered.

And so it came time for him to return to Mars.

Mars by then was a green and blue marble of a world much like old Earth. Despite the passage of time the rekindled human civilisation had spread no farther than the solar system, and – since Earth was out of bounds – Mars remained its capital. Sixteen million people lived there now, many of them gathered into small communities scattered around the gentle foot slopes of Pavonis Mons. Deep inside Mars, a lattice of artificial black holes created a surface gravity indistinguishable from that of old Earth. Mammoth sunken buttresses kept the ancient landscape from falling in on itself. The seas were soupy with life; the atmosphere thick and warm, brimming with insects and birds.

Certain things had been preserved since John's departure. The spiralling yellow road, for instance, still wormed its way to the summit of Pavonis Mons, and pilgrims made the long but hardly arduous ascent, pausing here and there at the many pennanted teahouses and hostels that lined the route. Though they belonged to different creeds, all remembered John in some form or another, and many of their creeds spoke of the day when he would come back to Mars. To this end, the smooth, circular plateau at the top of the volcano had been kept clear, awaiting the day of John's return. Monks brushed the dust from it with great brooms. Pilgrims circled the plateau, but none ventured very far inwards from the edge.

John, human again, dropped from the sky in a cradle of alien force. It was day, but no one witnessed his arrival. The Kind had arranged an invisibility barrier around him, so that from a distance he resembled only a pillar of warm air, causing the scene behind him to tremble slightly as in a mirage.

'Are you sure you're ready for this?' the Kind asked. 'You've been gone a long time. They may have some trouble dealing with your return.'

John adjusted the star-shaped spectacles he had selected for his return to Mars, settling them onto the small nub of his nose.

'They'll get used to me sooner or later.'

'They'll expect words of wisdom. When they don't get any, they're likely to be disappointed. "Now I get it" isn't likely to pass muster.'

'They'll get over it.'

'You may wish to dispense some harmless platitudes, just enough to keep them guessing. We can suggest some, if you'd like: we've had considerable practice at this sort of thing.'

'I'll be fine. I'm just going to be straight with them. I came, I saw, I backed off. But I did see it, and I do remember seeing it. I think it all makes sense.'

'"I think it all makes sense,"' the Kind repeated. 'That's the best you're going to give them?'

'It was my quest. I never said it had to measure up to anyone else's expectations.' John ran a hand over his scalp, flattening down his thin, auburn thatch against the air currents in the invisibility field. He took a step forwards, teetering on the huge red boots he had selected for his return. 'How do I look, anyway?'

'Not quite the way you started out. Is there any particular reason for the physiological changes, the costume?'

John shrugged. 'None in particular.'

'Fine, then. You'll knock them out. That *is* the appropriate turn of phrase, isn't it?'

'It'll do. I guess this is it, then ... I step through here, and I'm back with people. Right?'

'Right. You have plans, we take it?'

'Nothing set in stone. See how things go, I thought. Maybe I'll settle down, maybe I won't. I've been on my own for a long time now; fitting back into human society isn't going to be a breeze. Especially some weird, futuristic human society that halfway thinks I'm some kind of god.'

'You'll manage.'

John hesitated, ready to step through into daylight, into full visibility. 'Thanks. For everything.'

'It was our pleasure.'

'What about you, now?'

'We'll move on,' the Kind said. 'Find someone else in need of help. Perhaps we'll swing by again, further down the line, see how you're all doing.'

'That would be nice.'

There was an awkward lull in the conversation.

'John, there is one thing we need to tell you before you go.'

He heard something in the Kind's tone that, in all their time together, was new to him.

'What is it?'

'We lied to you.'

He let out a small, involuntary laugh; it was the last thing he had been expecting. He did not think the Kind had ever once spoken an untruth to him.

'Tell me,' he said.

'The third sentient being we spoke about ... the one that split itself into two consciousness streams?'

John nodded. 'What about it?'

'It didn't exist. It was a story we made up, to persuade you to follow that course of action. In truth, you were the first to do such a thing. No other entity had reached such a final stage of enlightenment without continuing on to final collapse.'

John absorbed that, then nodded slowly. 'I see.'

'We hope you are not too angry with us.'

'Why did you lie?'

'Because we had grown to like you. It was wrong ... the choice should have been yours, uncontaminated by our lies ... but without that example, we did not think you would have chosen the route you did. And then we would have lost you, and you would not be standing here, with the memories that you have.'

'I see,' he said again, softer this time.

'Are you cross with us?'

John waited a little while before answering. 'I should be, I suppose. But really, I'm not. You're probably right: I would have carried on. And given what I know now – given the memories I have – I'm glad this part of me didn't.'

'Then it was the right thing to do?'

'It was a white lie. There are worse things.'

'Thank you, John.'

'I guess the next time you meet someone like me – some other sentient being engaged on that quest – you won't have to lie, will you?'

'Not now, no.'

'Then we'll let it be. I'm cool with the way things turned out.' John was about to step outside, but then something occurred to him. He fought to keep the playful expression from his face. 'But I can't let you get away without at least doing one final favour for me. I know it's a lot to ask after you've done so much—'

'Whatever it is, we will strive to do our best.'

John pointed across the mirror-smooth surface of the plateau, to the circling line of distant pilgrims. 'I'm going to step outside in a moment, onto Pavonis Mons. But I don't want to scare the living daylights out of them by just walking out of thin air with no warning.'

'What did you have in mind?'

John was still pointing. 'You're going to make something appear before I do. Given your abilities, I don't think it will tax you very much.'

'What is it that you would like?'

'A white piano,' John said. 'But not just any old piano. It has to be a Bösendorfer grand. I was one once, remember?'

'But this one would be smaller, we take it?'

'Yes,' John said, nodding agreeably. 'A lot smaller. Small enough that I can sit at the keyboard. So you'd better put a stool by it as well.'

Swift machinery darted through the air, quick as lightning. A piano assumed startling solidity, and then a red-cushioned stool beside it. Across the plateau, one or two pilgrims had already observed its arrival. They were gesticulating excitedly, and the news was spreading fast.

'Is that all?'

John tapped the glasses back onto the bridge of his nose. 'There's one final thing. By the time I reach that stool, I need to be able to play the piano. I made music before, but that was different. Now I need to do it with my fingers, the old way. Think you can oblige?'

'We have much knowledge of music. The necessary neural scripting can be implemented by the time you arrive at the Bösendorfer. There may be a slight headache—'

'I'll deal with it.'

'It only remains to ask … is there anything in particular you want to play?'

'Actually,' John said, stretching his fingers in readiness for the performance, 'there is one song I had in mind. It's about Mars, as it happens.'

'Understanding Space and Time' is a story with a long genesis, if ever there was one. Early in 2001, I was invited to contribute a story to the Courier, UNESCO's magazine of science and culture. They were putting together a special issue on cosmology and the universe and they wondered if I might be able to come up with something relevant . . . in about 750 words. I said I'd think about it, while not being very optimistic of my chances. My stories tended to come in around the 7000–word mark, at the very minimum. Still, I thought it over as I cycled home, and somewhere between work and the front door I had an idea. I wrote it up that evening, in fact, and submitted it to UNESCO the following morning. It was 1500 words, twice what they wanted, but it was significantly shorter than anything I'd ever produced before. UNESCO liked it, even said they might use it, but they still wondered if I couldn't come up with something shorter. I said no, that was as short as it got for me, and left it at that. But by the time I arrived home that evening, I'd had an idea for an even shorter piece, one that seemed to address the theme of the issue even better than the longer piece. I wrote this new story. It was called 'Fresco'. It came in at 750 words, and it was duly published in the Courier. Since the magazine was printed simultaneously in many languages, 'Fresco' instantly became my most widely translated story. It's almost certainly the only thing of mine that will ever make it into Thai.

That left the other story without a home, though. I took it to Eastercon, one of the main UK science fiction conventions, and read it before a nonplussed audience. Maybe it needed to be a bit longer: 1500 words really was tight for a story about the last man alive. ('Fresco', by contrast, had no real characters in it at all, so worked better at even shorter length.) So I took the story back home, moved house and kept working on it on and off for the next four and a half years. I expanded it from 1500 words to 10,000. In the meantime I threw out nearly everything of the original story, leaving it only as a faint structural skeleton. And when I wasn't busy with something else, or was stuck for inspiration on whatever was the current big project, I'd open the file on 'In the Beginning' and tinker with it a bit.

I'd probably still be tinkering with it if it wasn't for Novacon. Held in November 2005, near Birmingham, Novacon is a fixture in the UK convention calendar. It's a tradition that guests contribute a new story, to be given away as a souvenir book. Now, I had plenty of time to write a new story, but whenever I tried starting something, it wasn't happening. Months ticked by. My wife and I got married. Still I didn't have a story for Novacon. Our honeymoon was coming up, and I'd promised the Novacon committee that I'd have something for them by the time I got back. In desperation, I turned to 'In the Beginning', by now retitled 'Understanding Space and Time'. As the honeymoon loomed, I tried desperately to finish the story. I stripped it down and put it back together again. Still it wasn't finished. We went on our honeymoon to Malaysia – all three of us: my wife, me, and my laptop.

My wife did, amazingly, forgive me. And while I didn't spend the entire trip writing, I did come back with the story in a more or less completed state. Once I was over my jetlag, I just needed another couple of days to knock it into shape and submit it to the Novacon committee. The story appeared as a chapbook with a marvellous colour illustration by noted space artist David Hardy. Incidentally, I'm grateful to fellow writer Neil Williamson for getting the make of piano right. The conversation (conducted in a drunken haze in some convention corridor somewhere) went something like this:

'Neil, you don't know who I could ask about pianos, do you?'

'What do you want to know, Al?'

'Well, I'm just wondering what sort of piano Elton John would play.'

'Oh, I know that. Bösendorfer grand.'

'Thanks, Neil.' Pause. 'Er . . . how do you know that, exactly?'

'Because I play piano. In a band. And we do Elton John covers.'

'Er . . . right. Glad I asked, really.'

So the next time you need a piece of apparently obscure information, try asking a science fiction writer. You might be surprised.

I left the Drome at 3.00 a.m., with Belgian house on indefinite replay in my brain. I was unaware that I was being followed. We can't trust ourselves at that hour, not when our nervous system wants to shut down for the night's deepest phase of sleep. If we're awake, it's then that we make the stupidest errors, dreaming that our actions won't have any outcome in the light of dawn. And, sometimes, a few pills assist the process.

I was more than usually pissed, but had avoided downing anything else for most of the night. Then she'd shown up: the girl in the Boulevard Citizens T-shirt – some Scottish white-soul band – offering E from a hip-pouch. I'd hesitated, my head swirling already, then acquiesced. We did the deal amidst the strobe-storm of sweating revellers and the eardrum-lancing rhythms.

'I'll be dead to the world in a few hours,' I said, slipping the tabs in my pocket.

'Big deal,' she said. 'Me, I just take a sicky. Pick up the phone in the morning, tell a few lies, kick back and snooze.'

'Great if your phone works,' I said. 'Thing is, I'm a telephone engineer; work for BT. So it's me you should thank next time you call in sick. Probably be eavesdropping from some hole in the ground somewhere.'

I felt a pressure on my shoulder, turned around to see one of my friends from the office. Sloshing Grolsch everywhere, he began to croon 'Wichita Lineman', drunkenly out of tune.

I winced. 'More like driving the road to Whitley Bay, searching in the fog for another bloody vandalised kiosk.'

Boulevard Citizen looked at us dubiously, then disappeared onto the dance floor, the DJ segueing into a fresh track laid down on a scuffling foundation that had JB embossed in every one of its bpm. I dropped a tab, getting into the music. Suddenly I remembered something I had to convey to my friend. 'Hey,' I shouted, throaty over the noise. 'I heard James Brown's got two people, full-time, just to spot samples on other records, then squeeze the artists for royalties!'

'Two people?' he said, then laughed, punching a fist in the air. 'Good God! Two people! Full time! *Good God!*'

'I thought it showed how endemic the sampling thing's become,' I said, aware my voice wouldn't appreciate such discourse in the morning; also that I'd reached a phase of my own drunkenness cycle characterised by extreme humourlessness. 'I mean, just listen to this stuff ... this is probably one hundred per cent recycled sound, friend.'

'Then it's very nineties, isn't it?' he said, shrugging. 'Very green. Thought we were all for recycling these days. Cars, paper, bottles ... why the hell not music?' Then I skipped a few frames and my friend was looking at his watch. 'Well, guess we're going to split soon. Sorry you're not on our taxi route, mate.'

'Yeah, I'm on foot tonight.' I shrugged, the E affecting my bonhomie. In any case, I wanted to stay for a few more numbers, now that I was clicking into the Drome's vibe. Pink smoke was flooding the floor, blue lasers tracking from the ceiling rig, and I was getting righteously *into it*. A track I liked came up, one of those blink-and-you've-missed-it ephemeral club hits that attains culthood, graduates to being a classic, gets heavily sampled, becomes slightly jaded, then frankly passé, winds up a dusty artefact of late-twentieth-century pop culture, all within a month or two. A bit of social commentary this, as well: 'A Killer Is Stalking Clubland'. And if you think *that* is in questionable taste, there was even a reference to someone's eyelids being stapled open.

Come 3.00 a.m., I decided I'd better hike if I wanted to make it to work. Had to get my coat, so I re-entered the mêlée, semi-dancing, pushing towards a neon sign at the club's other side, through a veil of perfumed smoke. I was halfway there when I saw the red laser stabbing through the cloud. A shrouded figure was aiming a gun at me, eclipsed in waves by silhouetted bodies, face blocked by shadows and a pair of sunglasses and framed by what looked like aviation phones, with a mike wrapping around the front.

Weirdos everywhere. Why not just *bliss out*, instead of getting on everyone's tits? Yeah, time to leave, no doubt there.

I'd got my coat quicker than usual, maybe because the club would stagger on for another hour or so. Outside I met a few friends who'd spent the intervening time in an all-night kebab shop. The taxi-rank was on my walk home so I loitered with them, up the rubbish-strewn streets, kicking fast-food containers, crushed tins of Red Stripe, ticket stubs. A few desultory revellers were still ambling around, trying to find somewhere open, dossers hanging outside the old pisser in the Bigg Market that looked like an Edwardian UFO, solitary cop cars kerb-crawling; cherry-lights reflected in puddles of urine. Overhead, against the winter stars, a helicopter circled predatorily, hawking the streets below, doubtless searching for stolen motors that would finish up embedded in shop fronts come morning. No wonder none of us brought cars. At the taxi-rank we split, they to their houses in Byker, me to my flat in Fenham. I didn't have far to go, really. But it's not the distance that counts, in the end.

I hiked up my hood, drowning out the plaintive car-alarms and the sirens, Walkman playing. It was a slimline job, barely larger than the tape, burnished silver like a very flash cigarette case. The C90 was a compilation I'd made up of techno and bleep stuff, vinyl picked up from Oldham Road in Manchester, plus chart house grooves and a little mainstream electro-soul, chanteuse-fronted, allegedly direct from the smokiest Berlin bars. Ultra-pure digital sounds, hypnotic synth lines, speedily distorted vocals. It was the music they played at the Drome: wall-to-wall, no dicking about, mind-pummelling noise, repetitive as Tibetan mantras, as fast as Bhangra. Allied to the Drome's effects, intense light projected through a rotating filter wheel of tinted, immiscible fluids ... like a kaleidoscope *melting* before your eyes, the sound washing over like a test signal for your sozzled brain.

I'd been into it for a year or two now, and finding that the scene was established in Newcastle made up for the wrench I'd felt leaving the north-west, where the nexus of the whole thing had originated. My BT job was a piece of shit; it was the music, the club scene that I lived for. What I didn't know, as I popped the last of the E, was that it was the music that had drawn the Househunter to me.

I'd been targeted in the Drome, it seemed, and when I left with my friends, I'd been followed. Discreetly – uptown, lurking in the side streets, until I left the pack. Shrewd, as if my walk home had been half-expected. And because of the Walkman, I didn't hear the footsteps (supposing any were to be heard) as I walked around the civic boating lake.

It came suddenly: carotid-squeezing pressure around my neck. The hood was ripped from my clothes, earplugs seized, the whole ensemble of the Walkman hurled into the moon-streaked water. There was never any doubt in my mind that I'd been selected as a victim, not in that instant. I knew it was the Househunter's arm around me. And then something went through my head – a thought I'd probably shared now with a dozen others, our one instance of solidarity. I realised that all the assumptions had been wrong. Oh boy, they'd got it *badly* wrong. They weren't going to catch this baby in a hurry. Not if they kept on thinking—

I felt something damp smother my whole face; then, maybe a microsecond after the sensation of wetness, the dizzy sensation of etherisation. The last thing I heard was her saying, very calmly: 'Trust me, please. I'm a doctor.'

I remember coming to, briefly, in the back of a vehicle. For a blissed-out moment I didn't remember what had happened, one of those waking fugues where nothing connects, nothing matters. Eyes washed by the yellow of sodium lamps, behind grilled glass, the numbing vibration of the ride transmitted through a softness beneath me. I couldn't make out the interior too well. Then it all rammed home as I heard her speaking, behind what must have been a thin partition separating the back of the van from the driver's compartment. I struggled to move, found I couldn't. For a while it wasn't clear whether this was a result of restraints, or whether the right signals just weren't getting to my limbs. I was stretchered, braced so that it didn't roll around. My mouth was obstructed. Had she gagged me, or was I sucking on a breathing tube?

'En route from pickup point,' she said. 'Subject has regained apparent consciousness. Brief description: outward physiology normal on first inspection; WM, twenties, slim build, height five eight or nine, cropped hair, no facial distinguishing marks. No evidence for intravenous drug use . . . presence of other intoxicants, hallucinogens or mood-alterers not ruled out at this stage. Interestingly, the subject's spectacles contained flat lenses – of cosmetic value alone. The subject's auditory stimulant was neutralised during apprehension. Prognosis is satisfactory; ETA fifteen minutes, over.'

The words careered through my brain in a jumble, leaving me to marshal them. What was happening? Where was I? Why did I really not *care* all that much?

I allowed myself to slump, mentally, letting the restful rhythm of the gliding sodiums caress my eyelids. How easy it was to sleep, despite all that I knew!

The next recollection is an invasive howl ripping through my dreams. It seemed the loudest noise I'd ever heard, rising and falling on a dreamily slow *wah-wah* oscillation. Then it got worse and my skin began to prickle before the sound reached an apex and the envelope of oscillation diminished, lower pitched, gut-churning bass components phasing in.

In the Blitz, my grandfather once told me, the *Luftwaffe* didn't bother tuning the engines of their bombers to precisely the same revs. That way you could always tell a Heinkel from a Wellington, if you didn't know how they were *meant* to sound. There'd be a rising and falling signal, on top of the engine sound, as the spikes of the sound waves moved in and out of phase with one another, several times a second. And he'd move the outspread fingers of his hands across one another in illustration. He'd been an audio engineer, my granddad, for Piccadilly Radio, knew all sorts of arcana. I think it was he who made me go into electrical engineering, he that set me on course for my privacy-violating job for BT ... though in fairness the old feller couldn't have known better.

I opened my eyes to a chipped surface of beige plaster. The tip of my nose was an inch or so from the wall; I was lying in the medical 'recovery' position on a soft surface. I tried moving; no joy. I was immobilised, either by weakness or restraint. Hands rolled me to my other side, so that I faced her. My mouth was free, no longer intubated or gagged. She was a pale ovoid, against a backdrop of olive green. From the angle of my gaze I couldn't see her face, just the blurred whiteness of her waist.

Then it all clicked: *hospital surroundings*. That explained the shabby décor, the pervasive air of decrepitude. She was a nurse or ward attendant, wearing a white overcoat and a stethoscope. Behind her were green curtains, the kind they use to fence off patients during a bed-bath. I could hear the sound of medical equipment behind the curtain, birdlike bleeps and clicks. Hey, some sod was worse than me. Life was looking up. I couldn't move much, but that didn't mean a lot. Hell, I'd just been through a bad experience, right? I was probably suffering post-traumatic stress disorder. *In 1962, Vietnam seemed like just another foreign war ...* Ha ha.

Then she spoke, the same voice I'd heard in the ambulance. 'Ah good,' she said. 'Awake. That's perfect. We'll be over and done before we know it. Just a few simple tests should be sufficient.'

I strained my neck to look up. Her white coat was loosely tied over a black T-shirt decorated with a half-familiar pattern, like a contour map of the lunar surface, etched in white. The stethoscope hung down over her chest. Her hair was raked back from her brow, tied in a utilitarian tail. Her lips were pallid, eyes masked by circular black sunglasses. A pair of phones framed her head, bulky black things. Aviation phones, a cable running to a belted power pack. Noise-cancelling jobs, like helicopter pilots wore. I thought of the 'copter I'd seen that night, but no ... there couldn't be a connection, surely.

Strange accessories for a nurse, I thought. And then, a kind of out-of-head experience, a soft voice from afar, saying: *This is your rational mind speaking. You're in the deepest shit imaginable, but you won't admit it, not until that E's through with its business ...* And I ignored it, eyes tracking over her coat (more like a scientist's than a doctor's, I decided), picking out streaked splatters of rust-red.

'Could I have a drink, please?'

She reached into a coat pocket, pulled out a tiny black thing the size of a box of cigarettes. Glanced at a wristwatch.

'Log entry: time 05:30. Subject made first conditioned response a few seconds ago. Requested fluid. Hypothesis: residual mind-state must still coordinate behaviour compatible with normal dietary and physical requirements; in other words, subject's nutritional intake will fall into stereotypical pattern. Conclude that request probably the expression of a genuine biological need. Although probably unnecessary in any case, will administer 250 ccs of gly-colated barley-water intra-orally. Entry ends.' *Click*.

She cranked something under me, making the couch angle up. Then she touched a glass to my parched lips, and I drank. God, it was the best drink I'd ever tasted: sugary-sweet and cool as nectar. Lucozade. Blanched out, towering above me, she looked angelic to my eyes, this beatific giver of nourishment to the sick.

'Let's get some air in here, shall we,' she said, without actually addressing me. She whisked back the curtain, revealing the rest of the room.

There comes a point, even in the deepest drug-induced para-reality, where sufficient data from the real world can build up and penetrate the fiction. *You're in the deepest shit imaginable*, that voice repeated. And I began, for the first time, to heed my own subconscious. There were no other patients in the 'ward'. The room was small, four, five metres along each damp-stained wall. They were covered with literally hundreds of ... but no, I'll come to *those* in a moment, after I've set the rest of the scene. High windows on one wall admitted wan shafts of dawn light, falling in patches on the floor. There was a metal door, padlocked on the inside. The room's odour of urine and vomit reminded me of a multi-storey carpark stairwell. There was a couch, two garden seats and a wooden table, an empty wheelchair, a tripod and Anglepoise set-up holding a waiting camcorder. The rest of the room was crammed with expensive-looking electronic equipment ... racks of slim, black synthesisers, embossed with familiar names: Casio, Korg, Roland, Yamaha, Hammond, Prophet. The whole stack wired to a table-load of MIDI monitors and PC keyboards, dove-grey shells, wrapped in a tangle of cables and fibre optics. There were crushed Irn Bru cans, Lucozade and Beck's bottles, tabloids, listings magazines, ring-bound folders, cassette and video cases, floppy disks and what looked like piles of twelve-inch, white-label records. I looked closer: each sleeve had the words *Digital to Analogue* scrawled over it. I remembered that: one of those subsequently sampled club hits from about six months back. You heard parts of it on many new records.

The shelving held dozens of display devices with gridded screens, oscilloscopes or cardiogram machines, displaying different blippy patterns, like the contours on her T-shirt. I knew where I'd seen it now: taken from an album cover. And it wasn't some landscape at all, but the radio signal of a pulsar, a clock ticking in space. I couldn't recall who'd told me that, but it seemed bizarre at the time, an icon from the heart of science manifesting itself in a million apartments, wrapped around a piece of hallowed black vinyl. Like those Mandelbrot sets that started infesting album sleeves and vids for a few months. As if science was the ultimate subculture, somehow, the stuff beneath the floorboards you don't want to know too much about . . .

Incidental detail: the table with the MIDI-stack also held something chunky and metallic, with a pistol-grip, shaped like a *Space: 1999* gun. An industrial stapler. This must be what they mean by a bad trip, ha ha.

Concerning the walls: I think the operative term here must be *Shrine*, in the sense that she'd pinned up dozens of monochrome photographs of me – taken during the last year of my life – some in the street, my distant figure outlined in red, others close up in some club, my eyes blankly uncomprehending. Just like CIA target-acquisition images. And more: complicated graphs and diagrams, scrawled over in felt-tip, fixed in laminated confusion on top of one another. Sonograms, sound spectra, electrical circuit diagrams, technical pieces about *entrainment* . . . Christ, where had I heard that before, and why did it honestly matter now? And why did she have a map of the UK, webbed with dotted ley-lines?

I was beginning to sweat. Thinking maybe my subconscious had a point; maybe this *was* a little unusual for a hospital.

She was fiddling with my head. I realised that I was wired up to something, little electrodes around my temples. She was fixing them down after they'd worked loose. She'd fixed things to my chest as well, white discs trailing wires to a mound of humming machines. All I was wearing was a pair of white, grass-stained jeans.

Click, with the Dictaphone. 'Log entry, 05:45. Summary to date.' She coughed before continuing in her soft, educated Tyneside accent. 'My orders were to terminate the subject on sight, in view of the danger to the community at large. At 2:45 a.m. I attempted to zero the subject in the Drome. Termination was impossible without risk of substantial collateral damage to the uninfected. I followed the subject from the Drome, hoping to get a clear shot. At around 3:30, however, I decided to break protocol and bring in the subject for captive examination. If all goes well, I'll be finished in a matter of hours.' A studied pause. 'Our operational integrity will not have been compromised, I promise. While my methods may be my own, I'm fully aware of the consequences for urban panic should our cover be exposed.' She clicked off the recorder, fumbled in her pockets and lit a cigarette from a black carton inscribed with a skull and crossbones, dragging on it thoughtfully before restarting the tape. 'I took a series of EEG readings while the subject was under,' she said, fixing a fresh marker in the little gripper of a pen-trace machine. There was a basket full of output, etched in wavering ink. The machine hummed into life, the pen gliding to and fro. 'Now I'm observing the subject's waking responses to a variety of stimuli.'

'Please don't hurt me ... I promise I won't tell anyone if you let me go ...'

She flicked ash on the floor then took another dismissive draw. 'Subject is now entering the plea phase, as you'll have observed. The initial euphoric state induced by the drug is fading; terror is replacing confusion and ambivalence about his situation. Soon his pleas will lose coherence; we'll observe the onset of hysterical shock, infantile withdrawal, regressive Oedipal complexes. These façades exactly mirror the usual psychoses observed in situations of extreme trauma, but are little more than mimetic survival ploys.' Then she leaned closer, so that I could see my expression in her black shades. Not looking too good, actually; I'd developed a spontaneous tic on one eyelid. She placed a set of plastic earplugs over my head, then returned to her MIDI hook-up. Touching keys, a multicoloured graphic of waveform profiles sprang onto one of the screens. Another lit up showing an annotated musical score, a third showing a plan view of a piano keyboard, overlaid with numbers and symbols. 'Don't know if you recognise this,' she said, tapping the waveform with a black fingernail, 'but we've been acquainted with it for some time now. And we've been following you for over a year.' Followed by an aside: 'Mental note: must refrain from *any* communication with the subject outside of programme parameters. Difficult, though: they look and smell human, and I'm only human myself. Can't help establishing weak emotional ties. Had the same problem with rhesus monkeys at the institute—'

'I promise,' I said. 'Let me go ... I won't even recognise you, will I ... we could pass in the street and I wouldn't notice ... please don't hurt me, I'm begging you ...'

She stubbed out the cigarette on the back of my hand. 'Uh, uh, uh,' she said. 'No talking till I say so, not until I expressly request a verbal response.' She ripped off a strip of paper from one of the machines; when I'd opened my mouth, the pen-trace had zigged dramatically. 'Hmm,' she said to herself. 'This is very poor indeed, much worse than we assumed.' Then she reached over to the table for the industrial stapler, flicking open its steel jaw, like a soldier checking the clip on his rifle. Gripped the trigger and pumped it twice, to free the action, sending tiny projectiles across the room. Then leaned over my couch and stapled the strip of paper onto the plaster of the wall behind me, *ker-thunk*.

While she did this I'd begun screaming, not merely because of the pain in my hand.

She cuffed me. 'I said quiet, you rascal! No screaming or I'll have to cut your vocal cords …' Then she laughed. 'Not that anyone's going to hear us, mind you.' And as she spoke, I heard the throttling up of a plane preparing to take off. We were in the vicinity of an airport, I guessed. I thought of the many bunkers and sheds you'd find within the perimeter of any small airfield. No one was going to wander in on us by accident, that was clear.

Trying to stay sane, I wondered about the synths and the medical gear. The music stuff I could handle; it could have been obtained easily enough. Some of it looked second-hand, edges chipped, keys dusted in a talcum of plaster and dirt, smudged with fingerprints – sorry – *latents*. (That's what they always say, when they're investigating a homicide, in those books by McBain and Harris and Kellerman, those guys who always go on about multiple murders, serial killers, that shit … *Check the body for latents – Gee, sorry, Inspector, the state of putrefaction's too advanced … we'll have to rely on dental records if we're gonna find out who the hell that poor sucker ever was …*)

But the EEG machine, those oscilloscopes – where'd she lifted them from? God knew it was easy enough to stroll into a hospital these days, easy enough to wander in and casually stab or rape someone – but even now, was the country so shitty that you could stroll out with a van-load of – what was it Python said … ha ha? Machines that go *ping* … Oh God, I didn't find it all that hysterical, right then.

'Log entry,' she said. '06:10. I am studying the encephalogram of the subject's so-called conscious mind. Brain music. A jumbled confusion of overlaid electrical signals signifying the neural activity of the subject's brain from second to second. First impression: although the trace might look normal enough to the layperson, no neurologist would accept that this was the EEG trace of a walking, talking human being. It's more evocative of certain types of akinetic or psychomotor seizure. A kind of prolonged grand mal convulsion.' She nodded, as if certifying her own theory. Then she put down the paper. 'Now the most critical part of the study commences. In order to probe the extent of the takeover, I must force conditioned responses from the subject. Taken as an ensemble, they hold the key to the nature of the takeover. Although we've now identified the likely progenitor of the infection, the mechanisms of transmission are far from certain. By regressing the subject back to the point of infection, I hope to gain fresh insights. To gain full compliance I am about to administer scopolamine intravenously. Entry ends.'

She turned to smile. 'Now, we can either do this quietly, and efficiently, with minimum fuss for all concerned. Or we can do it messily, and unpleasantly. What's it going to be?' As if she were berating a dog that had shat on the floor, not actually bawling it out, but playing on its instinct for mood, its capacity for terror and confusion. She reached for a syringe, held it up to the light and squeezed a few drips from the needle, then injected me. 'Just to get you into the swing, you understand.'

'I'll do whatever you want,' I said, tears streaming down my face. 'But please please please ...' Then I just trailed off into simpering dejection.

'Now then,' she said, oblivious. 'What say we have a nice little chat, eh?'

I nodded, drooling, hoping I could stall her if she'd let me talk. If I had one hope it was being found, and that meant buying time for myself, spinning out her rituals.

'Well, all right,' she said. 'But I'm going to have to ask you some very *hard* questions. And I'll have the tape running all the while. Plus, there's a little precaution I'd like to take, if we're going to be talking face to face. For my own safety, you understand.'

'Please, anything,' I said meekly.

She reached for the stapler.

She only did the one eye, the one with the nervous tic. Pulled up the lid and stapled it inside out under my brow. It hurt, but not the way I'd been expecting. Then the eye's itching began to take precedence: not strictly pain, but the kind of gently insistent discomfort that the Chinese know volumes about ... the kind that can drive you literally mad. Then she got the camcorder, the tiny

Anglepoise job, lens only centimetres from the surface of my eye, whirring as it taped. Looking into my brain . . .

And hit me with her conspiracy theory.

She unravelled my past, knotted it, curdled it, stretched it like Brighton rock on the rollers, wefted it with her own imagery, wove it between her fingers, turned it into a cat's cradle of fact and half-remembered experience, some of her recollections so chilling that I swore she'd stolen from my dreams. She took me back, into the past, so that my pain was just a blip in the future. I don't know what she did. Maybe she just used my anxiety as a fulcrum to lever me into the past, or maybe it was hypnosis.

We dream-haunted cities at night, facilitated by spotlit flashes of those CIA cards on the wall, jolting memories, projecting me back into the ambience of specific locations, half a year before BT moved me north. The Manchester and Sheffield scenes flooded back as she played music into my head at skull-attacking volume, lights strobing. Taped voices reverberated, voices I nearly matched with faces. My hand brushed the floor, grabbed at a rusty nail, trying to use the pain of it cutting into my palm to anchor me to the present (as if the pain in the eye wasn't quite real enough to focus on). But it failed, and I sank into the hypnagogic vortex of sound.

Things began to get a little disjointed about then.

She asked me questions, her voice an umbilical to reality. About a virus, nurtured in the club scene. I don't know quite how I responded; I couldn't hear my own voice, and suspected I'd lost coherence long ago. But she kept on questioning, about what she called the 'progenitor': *Digital to Analogue*, a five-hundred-pressing, white-label release on Deflection Records. Asked me if I'd known the distributor, asked me intense, repetitive questions about independent music traders operating in the north-west, asked me about their employees, strange questions that evoked cells in the Lubianka. I remembered the record . . . no one who'd been near the club scene could have forgotten it. But there was something desperately amiss. I couldn't focus the tune, not at all clearly. There was something about it that was difficult to lock on to . . . the essence was there, but I couldn't quite bring it to mind, too deep to retrieve, too basal . . . it was like the perception diagrams where you have to make the cubes flip themselves. My head began to split open with the strain . . .

The past blacked out; I came careering back into the present.

I was in the wheelchair now; she'd moved me in front of a projection wall. Computerised images danced on the canvas, happy molecules and bugs. I felt saliva wetting my chin, an idiot drool, sensed I'd emptied my bladder. Oblivious, she cupped the phones around her ears, then walked to the DX7 synth. She played a hesitant, atonal line on the keys, rendered in sickly whining notes. *Click*, voice to Dictaphone. 'Most musical structures are in some way fractal, by which I mean that the essence of the whole can be found on many levels of analysis.' Her voice was overloud, harsh. 'You may remove ninety per cent of the score and still retain something identifiable. What I'm playing the subject is a deconstructed form of the sound-structure isolated on *Digital to Analogue*, and the records on which it was subsequently transcribed via digital sampling. I'm piping the sound straight at him, while wearing the protective phones should there be any leakage from his headset. Of course, I hesitate to term this music, for reasons all too apparent.'

I watched as the pen-trace whipped into a seismic frenzy, all the while hearing her keyboard motif, repeated down an echoing hall of aural mirrors. It was *far, far* worse than the pain; it made the pain seem as threatening as the wind on an autumn night. The sound was ghosting through my soul, fingering through the rat-holes of my psyche. I felt horribly lucid, calm, as irresponsive as a piece of lab equipment being fed some signal. Her refrain was already in me. Stuck in a looped circuit, the full form of what she evoked on the synth. It was resonance; with each iteration, the response swelled, until my conscious mind was looping madly. How can I describe it? Simply that it was like having a piece of music going over in your head. Until there was nothing left, until your thoughts were simply ripples of insignificance on top of these rising and falling crests of repetition ...

'A sampled record carrying a virus of the mind? A virus in the sound itself, its vector the digital recording technology of the underground music biz?' She shook her head, more in profound exasperation than disbelief, all the while addressing her Dictaphone's future listener. She rapped on for a while about how the nineties milieu was best addressed as a system of infections: sexual illnesses, rogue advertising slogans, computer viruses, proliferating junk mail ... the kind of jive that had spread into all the glossy style magazines, as if, she mused, the viral paradigm was a metavirus in its own right. 'But if we were to draw our analogies with computer viruses,' she said, 'shouldn't we be hunting a perpetrator? Or, more frighteningly, had the sound-structure sought its own expression via blind chance?' She laughed hollowly. 'Unfortunately, there wasn't time to philosophise. The virus was spreading. The second-generation records were being sampled as heavily as the first, only there were more of them.' Then she explained how the club scene couldn't support such a combinatorial explosion for very long; how the sound-structure (as she referred to it) would be forced to explore new avenues of infection. How the quantum noise in the sampling circuitry enabled it to *mutate* bit by bit. 'Soon,' she said, 'we detected the presence of disturbing variations in the EEG patterns of individuals who'd been exposed to new versions of the sound-structure. It had inserted itself into their heads, a standing wave in the brain's electrical field. Can't be sure how this happened. Was it achieved in one jump, or was there an intermediate vector?'

'Please,' I said. 'I don't know about this . . . I'm not your perpetrator, I swear—'

Aside to Dictaphone: 'As you can hear, the subject still manages to give the illusion of lucidity. Usually they'd resort to pseudo-random interjections by now, substituting for any real grasp of the subject matter. Obviously what we're seeing here is a more refined form of the takeover. Natural selection will favour those species of the virus that can assimilate the host unobtrusively, without significantly altering his behaviour. That's why we have to act now, before it's too late.'

Then I saw something, something that would otherwise have been utterly insignificant. I felt a pathetic surge of hope. I could play on her paranoia, if I was careful. And in doing so I might buy valuable time. What I'd seen was a tiny, quivering motion of her skin. Right under the shadow of her sunglasses. As if part of her eye was twitching uncontrollably. Maybe it'd been there all along, so that somehow I'd picked up on it, begun to imitate her, to try to appease her by making myself similar.

Or maybe it had started just then, out of the blue.

'Before you do or say anything,' I said, for the first time with any control in my voice. 'Why don't you take off your sunglasses, and watch your reflection in them. Tell me what you see . . .'

She looked momentarily shocked, perhaps unable to dismiss my response as the mindless parroting of a zombie. Clicked off the Dictaphone, placed it on the table, then went behind me. It was a terribly long moment before she spoke again, and this time her voice had lost its scientific detachment.

'Then we were right,' she said, so quiet it was barely audible. 'Somehow it reached me, through all the defences. Maybe a few seconds of your twitching eye was enough ... a pulsing in my visual field, leading to a modulation in my cortex ... the first step to assimilation. Or maybe it was the entrainment effect in the club ...'

Entrainment ... that term I half-recalled. Now I remembered. Something learned in an electrical engineering seminar, about the coupling of oscillators, like the turbine-driven dynamos in the stations feeding the National Grid. How if one of those generators began to lag, began to pump out power at something not quite mains frequency, then all the other generators on the grid would automatically conspire to drag it into phase, in time with their relentless metronomic beat. Except conspire wasn't the right word, because there was nothing purposeful about entrainment. It was a tuning, a locking in on frequency, driven remorselessly by the ensemble. Like a dance floor, where the proximity of the motion and the music acts like a charm, insinuating itself into your muscles, so that even if you're only passing through, even if you're only a bystander, you're locked into it ...

'If it's got you,' I said, clinging to what seemed my only possible escape, 'then you know that you've nothing to fear! Feel any different, now that it's in your head?'

She laughed bitterly. 'I wouldn't ... not yet. This is only the beginning, only the onset.' Then there was a rummaging sound, an opening of drawers, metal sliding off wood, things smashing to the floor, glass breaking. Sounds of panic. 'They tricked me,' she said. 'The aviation phones must've been sabotaged once they suspected I was going it alone. Must have been damping the audible components while reinforcing the subliminals ... maybe it got me in the club, or maybe while I was reiterating the fractal ...'

Just then, arcs of light stabbed through the windows, like an effect from a Spielberg flick. The chopping of a rotor, as if we'd just been cursorily scanned from the air by a helicopter. The distant screech of tyres, coming nearer.

'They're coming,' she said. 'For both of us—'

'What are you doing?' I asked, my hope faltering. 'They'll let you live if you show them I'm alive ... come on, wheel me to the door before they storm the place ...'

She cracked open a bottle behind me. I heard her taking a few mouthfuls, then she pressed it to my lips. Beck's this time. 'Think that's the police, don't you,' she said, laughing. The sound of her rummaging through metal with one hand, a click of well-oiled steel, the whirr of a chamber spinning. 'Let me tell you something,' she said. 'Correlations in the sound-structure have been observed in individuals many hundreds of kilometres apart, who can't have ever met. As if something's taking form, something that evolves and reshapes itself faster than can be explained by any of the infection pathways. Some entity, bigger than anything we've seen yet.' She nodded to the webbed map of the UK, which I now recognised from my work. 'That's its extent, plotted according to infection dusters. The host minds, you and I, are just its extensions, its peripheries. It's out there, now. Biding its time, waiting for the right moment. That map ... well, I think it shows that they're much too late.'

'They're much too late? Not we're—'

'Oh no,' she said. 'Not any more.' Then she knelt down next to me, leaned her head against my own, letting the bottle shatter on the floor. 'Believe me,' she said, pushing the gun against her temple, so that the bullet would do us both. 'I'm doing you a favour ...'

Then, as the vehicle rammed through the wall, she squeezed the trigger.

It should end there, and maybe it does, in the way that I once used to understand. Perhaps this is the deal we all get, in the end. There's no way of knowing, is there? But somehow I doubt it. You see, after that shot (cut off with no reverb, like a cymbal-crash taped backwards), there was only a digitally pure emptiness. As if someone had suddenly remembered to press the Dolby switch in my brain, filtering out all the high-frequency hiss and static I'd called reality. Leaving only an endlessly looping house beat, a mantra for a state of mind. I wasn't in the bunker any more. I wasn't even *me* any more. We were everywhere, everywhen, reforming, spreading, growing stronger. Parts of us in a million micro-grooves of black vinyl, parts of us on a million spooling foils of chrome dioxide, parts of us in a million engraved blips on rainbow metal, parts of us in a million looms of grey cellular material, going round and round for ever. But they were our peripherals now, like she'd said (she's here, too, of course, inseparably part of the same blossoming waveform), minds hooking in and out of the telephone system a part of us once helped access.

Across the country, the telephones are ringing, inviting you to lift the receiver and listen to the subliminal music, if only for a few puzzled seconds before you hang up on us.

We're the ghosts now, and we're still on the line.

In 1990 I met the writer Paul McAuley, by then a novelist with two books to his credit, who had also written some of my favourite stories to appear in Interzone. *Paul was very definitely the first 'proper writer' I had ever encountered, and the fact that he was lecturing in the small Scottish university town of St Andrews while I was studying there – let alone that we lived within walking distance of each other – still strikes me as a very fortunate, not to say life-changing coincidence. Quite a few years later, Paul helped in getting my first novel to the attention of the editor who eventually bought it. Now, I might have eventually sold my book anyway (who knows?), but not necessarily. I can think of many good writers who, for one reason or another, haven't ever made the transition to writing novels. Not that there's anything wrong with that, but I damned well wanted to write books, and I think Paul played a part in making that happen. Not, of course, that he's in any way to blame, either.*

Anyway – to get back to the story in question – Paul and I were drinking in our local bar one evening when he mentioned that, together with Kim Newman, he was editing an anthology of original stories commemorating the demise of the seven-inch vinyl record. I was invited to submit something, and 'Digital to Analogue' was the result. The story pretty much included everything I thought I knew about club and dance culture, helped by judicious consultation of The Face, *which I used to read back then. I was delighted when Paul and Kim took my story for* In Dreams, *and even more delighted when I got to read the anthology itself. I think the story stands up pretty well now, seventeen years after it was written, but that says more about how little music culture has changed in the intervening time than it does about any prescience on my behalf. Look at the changes in popular music between 1976 and 1991, which is the gap between the Sex Pistols and Nirvana, and then compare 1991 with 2006, which is the gap between Nirvana and ... Coldplay. Joy Division were icons of cool in 1991; they're still icons of cool now. Downloading and MP3s aside, music doesn't seem to me to have changed all that much. Personally, I still can't get enough of it.*

EVERLASTING

Moira Curbishley followed the yellow beacon of a gritting lorry all the way up the hill, her Volvo's windscreen wipers working hard against snow. Another car had cruised up behind her and was now flashing its headlights. She couldn't see the driver, but the low, dark shape of the car suggested something flash: a BMW or Mercedes, maybe an Audi. At this time of night there was very little traffic coming the other way, but whenever Moira even thought of overtaking – edging out slightly, just until she could begin to see along the side of the gritting lorry – another pair of headlights always made a miraculous appearance. Moira nipped back into the wake of the lorry, the car behind delivering its opinion with another round of headlight-flashing.

'Tosser,' Moira said.

She was grateful when she reached the brow of the hill and was able to turn off from the main road, even though she was now travelling down a high-hedged, meandering and potholed country lane that had not been gritted. At least she had the road to herself, and could drive at the pace that suited her. She kept the car in second, oozing cautiously around blind bends, watchful for cars or tractors coming the other way, but doubting that she would meet any other traffic.

Soon she saw the familiar landmark of the humpbacked bridge. She negotiated it slowly, her headlights shining high into the trees on the opposite side of the brook. The lights illuminated a pair of perched barn owls, freezing them into immobility. They looked like small stone ornaments, the kind you could buy in craft shops. Beyond, some way up the lane, Moira saw the lights of Ian's cottage.

He had called her about an hour earlier, sounding in a bad way. Not exactly depressed and suicidal – he was actually talking about how he *wasn't* going to kill himself – but manic and overexcited:

a state of mind that she considered nearly as dangerous. With Ian's history it could quickly turn nasty. She wished, now, that she had kept him on the phone – kept talking to him – rather than promising to drive over. She should have checked the weather first, not to mention the time of day. But once Moira had put down the phone she knew that she could not back out of her promise.

'Bloody Ian,' she said.

They had met about fifteen years ago, during their last year at college. Both had been members of the skydiving society: Ian because he took it very seriously, Moira because she had fancied someone else in the club. It hadn't worked out for her, but she had developed an on-off interest in parachuting that she had kept up for a few years after graduation. And she had met Ian: not really her type, but good enough company that they'd meet socially away from the club. The thing Moira liked about him was that he was always fizzing with daft enthusiasms. During that last year she had lost count of the amazing get-rich schemes Ian intended to get into when he had his degree. She had to hand it to him: Ian had been convinced mobile phones were going to be huge, back when everyone else thought they were never going to be much use except as exercise aids. But – typical Ian – he hadn't actually done anything about it. For a while, before anyone had heard of web pages, he had pottered around with computers, constructing graphical interfaces to simplify internet navigation and file-transfer. Some of the ideas Ian had shown her then were *brilliant*: she was convinced, even now, that if he'd only stuck with it, the world would have swerved onto a different track, one in which Ian Caldicot was the 'father of the web'. But, no: another enthusiasm had diverted him, and his computers had sat gathering dust while he played around with radio-controlled battling pterodactyls made from balsawood. Moira had never quite worked out where all the money came from, but Ian didn't waste a penny of it on himself. The cottage was crumbling, and his wardrobe was basically what he had been wearing during college.

'Bloody Ian,' Moira said again.

She slowed, recognising the farm gate. A dozen metres further on was the turning onto Ian's drive. It was still snowing. She oozed the car around the bend, feeling the wheels spin before they bit into the gravel beneath the snow. She brought the car to a halt just in front of the cottage. Ian's Metro was a blue-white wedge parked in front of the derelict garage. Snow made all cars look exciting and sleek, Moira thought: like concept models fresh from the wind tunnel.

She turned off the headlights and ignition and sat looking at the cottage for a few moments. Now that she was here, the possibilities crowded in on her. Again, she thought back to the telephone conversation: Ian emphatic that he wasn't going to kill himself. If Ian had decided not to kill himself, then at some point he had presumably toyed with the alternative. Knowing Ian's general inability to stick to one decision for more than a few minutes, Moira couldn't help but worry about him changing his mind again.

What if he had done it while she was driving over? What if there was no one alive in that house now? It looked so warm and inviting, with the window on the lower floor casting an oblong of yellow light across the smooth carpet of snow before it. What if she had to wait here until the police and ambulance men came?

Moira got out of the Volvo, shut the door behind her and walked towards the front door. From far back along the country lane she heard the call of an owl: perhaps one of the pair she had seen earlier.

She knocked on the front door. Ian opened it. He wore red tracksuit bottoms and a grubby yellow Levellers T-shirt. His feet were bare.

'I'm sorry,' he said.

'So you bloody well should be,' Moira said, tremendously relieved.

'I didn't realise how late it was. Or that it was snowing.'

'That's your problem, Ian: you don't stop to think.'

He smiled coyly. 'Actually, I have been doing a bit of thinking. That's why I phoned.'

'Very pleased to hear it. I was sick with worry, Ian.'

'You'd better come in.'

'Yes, I better had, hadn't I?'

Ian let her into the house. She kicked the snow from her shoes. The cottage had looked warm and inviting from the outside, like something on a Dickensian Christmas card. Inside it was still just a bit too cold for Moira's tastes. She took off her coat and hung it on the banister at the bottom of the stairs, grateful for the chunky sweater she had on beneath.

'Fancy a cuppa?' Ian asked.

She thought about having to drive back again, once she had put her mind to rest about Ian.

'Coffee,' she said. 'Black. No sugar.'

Moira followed him into the kitchen. It wasn't too bad, considering. The fact that there was only one light – a dim electric bulb hanging from the ceiling – helped to throw much of the room into shadow, disguising the junk and clutter. There were many cardboard boxes around the walls, piled two or three high. They had drawings of monitors and printers on them. There were ghostly white chunks of polystyrene packaging material. There was a balsawood pterodactyl, its wing broken, one black eye gleaming back at her from the alien swoosh of its skull. A metallic-orange mountain bike rested against a pantry door, minus wheels. At one end of the kitchen table stood a couple of cereal boxes, some jars of instant coffee, half a pint of milk and an empty Pot Noodle container. There was nothing to eat or drink on the shelves. Instead of cookery books there were books on programming in Java, C and Perl, dog-eared paperbacks on Zen Buddhism, wild mushrooms and quantum mechanics, and a couple of Ben Elton novels Moira hadn't read.

He pushed a cup of coffee into her hands. She sat down in a rickety wooden chair on one side of the table, while Ian helped himself to the chair on the other side. Through the un-curtained window beyond, Moira saw the snow continuing to fall.

'Mind if I smoke?' she asked, taking out a packet of cigarettes.

Ian rummaged under some pizza boxes and produced an ashtray. It was the stamped-metal kind students stole from pubs. 'Hoped you might have given up by now.'

Moira tapped a fingernail against the packet. 'Not bloody likely. Lucky cigs. Remember?'

'Seriously?'

'Yes, seriously.' She took a sip of the coffee, grateful that she hadn't needed milk in it. Ian's white coffee had little icebergs floating in it. 'But this isn't about me. I didn't come here for a nice old chinwag. You worried me, Ian: all that talk about *not* going to kill yourself.'

'I suppose I was a bit overexcited,' Ian said.

'You aren't going to do it, are you?'

'That's not the point,' Ian said. 'I couldn't if I wanted to.'

'I'm glad to hear it.' Moira reached out across the table and took his hand. 'I know you've had some bad luck, Ian, and I know things haven't always worked out quite the way you hoped. But life's not worked out too bad for either of us, has it?'

'You misunderstand,' Ian said. Gently, he withdrew his hand. 'I'm not talking about being unable to kill myself because I've rejected the idea of suicide. I'm talking about something far more fundamental.'

Moira lit one of the cigarettes. She took a long draw on it, eyeing Ian the way she imagined prison psychologists eyed long-term offenders. 'Which would be?'

'I've reached the conclusion that I'm immortal.'

'I see,' Moira said quietly.

'Do you?'

'Yes,' she said, picking her words carefully. 'I remember what you talked about the last time we were in the pub: your latest mad enthusiasm. All that stuff you'd been reading about on the Internet, about how no one living will ever die. At least not if they don't want to, and if they make the right arrangements. What did you call it? Exhibitionism?'

'Extropianism,' Ian corrected, with a tolerant smile.

'Right. Getting your head frozen so they can revive you in the future? Or was it just about making sure you survive the next thirty years, so that you're still alive when the machines take over and grant us all eternal paradise? Waiting for the Singularity, wasn't it?' Moira drank some more of her coffee, noticing a pile of old popular science magazines on the table: *New Scientist*, *Scientific American*, stuff like that. 'Sounded like bollocks to me, Ian, but you never know.'

'It's not bollocks,' he said. 'Or it *might* be, but that's not the point, either. I'm not talking about achieving immortality through medicine or having my brain copied into a computer. Thinking about all the Extropian stuff was just the catalyst I needed to really see things clearly. But they're all missing the point. I've realised that immortality is a lot easier to achieve than anyone realises.'

She looked at the bookshelf again. 'Magic mushrooms?'

'Maybe I shouldn't have phoned you after all.'

'Look, I'm sorry, Ian. But you drag me out of hearth and home at some ungodly hour, wittering on about how you're thinking of killing yourself—'

'Thinking of *not* killing myself,' he corrected.

'And when I get here – having nearly crashed the car at least twice – all you can do is rabbit on about sodding immortality. Sorry, Ian, but this is pub stuff. It's not getting Moira out of the house late at night stuff.'

'Actually, I think it is.' Ian reached across the table and pushed aside the pile of science magazines.

They had been hiding a gun.

'Fuck,' Moira said. It was a handgun, a small revolver. It was horribly familiar, yet Moira did not remember ever seeing a real handgun in her life. 'Please tell me that's a replica,' she said.

'It is,' Ian said. 'But it's been converted into a real one. There's a website that shows you how to do it. You don't need any fancy tools, not if you already like to tinker around a bit.' He nodded at the balsawood dinosaur. Yes, Moira thought ruefully: Ian liked to tinker. If anyone could convert a replica gun into a real one, it was Ian Caldicot.

'I'm really not happy with this, Ian.' She wanted to ask him where he had got it, whether it was in some way legal, but what she mainly wanted was the gun out of Ian's reach before he did something with it. 'It's not loaded, is it?'

Ian picked up the gun and made the little revolving chamber swivel out, the way she had seen people do it in films. He held the chamber up to the light, lengthwise, so that Moira could see along the cylindrical holes where the bullets would have gone. Ian rotated the chamber slowly, until one blocked hole came into view.

'Can you show me to the phone, please?' Moira asked. 'I think I need to ring someone.'

'The phone's disconnected. You don't need it. You just need to sit here and listen to me, that's all.'

Moira nodded: anything to keep Ian talking. 'And then what?'

'Then I'm going to put the gun against my head and fire it. And I'm going to keep doing it. Ten times, twenty times, thirty times. And you're going to sit there and watch me, and then you'll believe me.'

Moira thought about grabbing the gun. Could she wrestle it out of Ian's hand without it going off? If she could get hold of it and run outside, she could throw it into one of the snowdrifts. It was dark out there, and the snow was still falling: if she gave it a good lob, she didn't think there'd be much chance of Ian finding it before morning.

But even as she was thinking of that, Ian slipped the gun down into the baggy pocket of his tracksuit bottoms.

No chance of reaching it now.

'I thought you said this was about immortality,' Moira said, her voice faltering. 'Playing Russian roulette doesn't sound very much like immortality to me.'

'You're right. But the point is I'm not *going* to kill myself. I just have to demonstrate the impossibility of that act in the most convincing way possible.'

'Why me?'

'Because you're a friend. Because you've always listened and you've always had an open mind. Because I knew you'd come over.'

'Because my name came early in your address book?'

Ian smiled. 'You're under Moira, not Curbishley.'

Moira sighed. 'OK. Here's the deal. I'll listen. You can tell me whatever it is you want to tell me. But I don't want to see that gun again.'

'You promise me you'll listen? That you won't laugh, or start arguing? Not until I'm done?'

'A deal is a deal.'

But she was not certain Ian had agreed to his side of it.

'Do you know about the Many Worlds theory, Moira?'

'You've mentioned it before.' *Play along*, she thought. *Keep talking*. 'One of the quantum things, isn't it? Parallel worlds and all that?'

'Sort of. The idea that every time there's some kind of interaction in the universe – every time some particles or whatever crash into each other – then the universe splits into so many different copies, each of which corresponds to one of the possible outcomes.'

Moira thought back to long pub conversations over last orders. 'I think I get the gist.'

'Of course, we only see one of those possible outcomes take place. So if we make some experiment in a lab that could produce result "A" or result "B", with an equal probability of each, we'll only see A or B, not both. But in reality the universe branches at that point, and there are counterparts of us who see the other result come out of the experiment.'

'A bit like that cat thing you're always going on about,' Moira said.

Ian brightened, obviously pleased that she remembered. 'Yeah. You put a cat in a box with a radioactive source and a Geiger counter rigged to a vial of poison gas. If the radioactive source releases a particle – and it's got a fifty/fifty chance of doing so in a given period – then the gas gets released and the moggy becomes an ex-moggy.'

'And then you open the box ...'

Ian sipped his coffee, oblivious to the horrid lumps of spoiled milk. 'And in one universe you get the dead cat. But in the other, the radioactive source didn't go off. Remember there was only a fifty/fifty chance of it happening? This is the branch of the multiverse in which it didn't. The cat's still alive.'

Moira sensed that Ian was nearing the crux of his revelation. 'All right,' she allowed.

'Now this is the clever bit. What happens next is that we take the *same* cat – give it a nice saucer of milk and a bit of Whiskas, of course – and put it back in the box. And run the experiment again. Same thing happens: the cat isn't dead. What do you conclude?'

'You conclude that you could be in deep shit with the RSPCA, if they ever find out what you've been doing.'

'And apart from that?'

'I don't know. That you're in the branch in which the decay didn't happen, again?'

'Yes,' Ian said. 'But think about what that means: you've now switched onto the no-decay branch twice. Carry out the experiment again: same thing. Another time, and another time after that. You keep doing it, and every time *you can't kill the bloody cat.*'

Moira raised a finger. 'Only because you keep specifying that the cat must be alive. But if I did that experiment – say I tossed a coin, instead of going to all that trouble with Geiger counters and stuff – it wouldn't work like that, would it? I might not kill the cat straight away, but after two or three goes I'm pretty sure I would.'

'But the point is, whenever you did kill the cat, there'd always be a counterpart of you – another Moira – that didn't.'

'After one or two goes, maybe. But if I kept on not killing the cat, I'd begin to think it was a bit unusual: that something was wrong with the experiment. That's not how it works, Ian. You can't keep coming up heads. Sooner or later you always hit tails. Look, I've got a pound coin in my pocket here, I can prove—'

'No,' Ian said, correcting her gently. 'Sooner or later one of you hits tails. But the other one comes up heads. And that's how it keeps happening. No matter how improbable it seems, there'll always be one counterpart of you that finds it impossible to kill the cat, no matter how many times they try.'

'But that's absurd.'

'No, just very unlikely. Which doesn't mean that that particular counterpart doesn't exist: just that your chances of *being it* are very small. It's like being the queen. Someone has to be the queen, even if any one person's chances are tiny. Have you ever wondered how Her Maj feels, when she wakes up? Fuck me, she must think. I'm the queen. I'm the sodding queen!'

'I'm sure she's got used to it by now.'

'But the point still applies: logically, there'll always be one counterpart who keeps ending up in the universe in which the cat doesn't die. They might feel odd about it – they might look back at all the experiments they've run and feel a bit strange that they've been chosen as the one who never gets to kill the cat. But if they take the Many Worlds theory seriously, they'll have to conclude that *someone* had to end up never killing the cat. And when they finally do kill the cat, they'll know that someone else – another counterpart of them – has just failed to kill it again. And that's how it goes on.'

'For ever?'

'For ever and ever.'

They sat in silence for several moments, Moira once again wondering about the phone and the gun. If Ian had disconnected the phone, how difficult would it be to make it work again? If it was just a question of popping the connection back into the wall socket . . . she imagined herself fumbling it in, somehow managing to dial the police before Ian ripped the phone out of her hands . . . but no. That wouldn't work: Ian was an inveterate tinkerer. He'd have opened the phone and removed something. And even if he hadn't, even if she did magically get through to a warm human being, how long would it take them to get here?

And the gun: still no joy. She thought about shoving the table towards Ian, levering it up from her side so that it came crashing down on his knees, but unless she did it very quickly Ian would have time to move aside. The one thing she didn't want to do was make him any angrier without getting the gun off him.

'So that's it, is it?' she asked. 'Your big revelation? In some remote twig of the infinitely branching universe, there'll always be a cat you can't kill?'

For the first time Ian showed a flash of irritation. 'There's more to it than that. Much more. Frankly, Moira, I was hoping you'd have seen it for yourself by now.'

'Seen what?'

'The bigger picture. The cat in the box represents the outcome of just one quantum process: the tick of a Geiger counter. Now imagine if there were a million Geiger counters in the box, each pointed at their own piece of radioactive material. It only takes one tick to kill the cat. The overwhelming likelihood is that at least one Geiger counter will register an event.'

Moira chose her words carefully. 'Then I suppose the cat dies.'

'Nearly all the time, yes,' Ian said. 'But there'll still be a branch in which it doesn't. There'll still be one experiment in which none of those million counters register an event. Just because it's weird doesn't mean it won't happen, in some extreme branch of the multiverse.'

'All right,' Moira said. 'If I follow you, then you've collapsed one chain of events into a single massively unlikely outcome. How does that change things?'

'It changes things because there's no limit to how far I can take that process. Everything that ever happens is a series of quantum events. Every process in every cell in your body – every chemical reaction – it all boils down to quantum probabilities in the end. And no matter how complex the macroscopic event, there'll always be a finite probability of it not happening.'

'Give me an example.'

'Life itself,' Ian said. He seemed to have calmed down a little now. 'Think about it, Moira. Think about your body: every cell in it working to sustain the ongoing momentum of living. Molecules being shuffled around, crossing membranes, interacting with other molecules ... all of it riding on quantum processes. The avalanche is unstoppable. But there's still a tiny probability – cosmically rare, I admit – that every single one of those processes will suddenly swerve in the wrong direction for the continuation of life. It'd be like a room full of clocks suddenly stopping ticking. Unlikely, but – given a multiverse of possibilities – it could and *must* happen, somewhere.'

'What if ...' Moira said, groping for an objection. As long as she could keep Ian engaged, he seemed unlikely to do anything regrettable. 'What if the multiverse isn't big enough to contain all those possibilities? What if some events are just too rare for consideration?'

'It doesn't have to be that extreme, of course. Not every quantum process has to go wrong. Just some of them. Enough to kill you.'

'Still pretty unlikely.'

'But vastly *more* likely, if you take that view.'

'Now you're frightening me.'

'Then consider the more benign alternative. You're very old, lying in your deathbed after a long and happy life. You're about to die of natural causes.'

'All right,' Moira allowed.

'But what does that mean, exactly? What is death if it isn't just a series of chemical processes coming to an end?'

'Pretty bleak way of looking at it.'

'On the contrary,' Ian told her. 'Think of those chemical processes grinding to a halt. Underlying them, of course, are yet more quantum interactions. That's all anything is. And if it's possible to think of those processes coming to a halt, then it's also possible to consider them being minutely prolonged.'

'So one of me gets another minute of life?'

'More than that, Moira. One of you gets immortality. One of you never ever dies. Death is a chemical threshold. There'll always be one of you that can't quite cross it. Some flicker of life keeps sustaining you. You'll be slipping into ever remoter branches of the multiverse with each breath, but from your point of view – what does it matter? You don't perceive all those earlier versions of yourself dying away. You just feel yourself persisting.'

'That doesn't sound like any kind of immortality I'd choose for myself,' Moira said. 'To me it sounds more like a kind of hell. Always drawing the last breath, but never, ever quite getting there. I think I'd rather throw myself under a bus than face the prospect of *that*.'

Ian smiled again. 'You're forgetting that no outcome is disallowed, no matter how improbable. An engine drops off a passing plane and smashes the bus to pieces. A hole opens in the road and swallows it. The bus just spontaneously disintegrates: every single weld failing catastrophically at the same moment. A freak whirlwind lifts you out of harm's way.'

'That sounds more like a miracle.'

'That's exactly what it would look like. You'd know, though: you'd realise that all that had happened is that you found the nearest non-fatal branch.'

Moira could see where this was heading. 'A gun, then,' she said, speaking the words with a kind of dull inevitability. 'I'll put a gun to my head and pull the trigger.'

'Won't work either. It will misfire. Consistently so, until you point it away from your head, or at an angle that won't prove fatal.'

'But what about the people watching me do it? Most of them will see me blow my head off. Not much immortality as far as they're concerned. They're not going to believe, are they?'

'Not until they try it for themselves.'

'We all have to put a gun against our heads, is that it? Squeeze the trigger, and if we survive – if the gun misfires – then we conclude that we're immortal?'

Ian leaned forwards. She could see the alloy gleam of the gun, the tip of the handle jutting from his pocket. So near – so tempting to try and grab it. But the very thought of trying made her feel sick with fear.

'Look back on your own life,' he said. 'Was there never a time when you came through something – an accident, or a frightening moment – and thought you were lucky not to have been killed?'

Moira shook her head, but not with complete conviction. 'I can't think of anything specific.'

'Why did you give up parachuting, Moira?'

'I didn't give it up,' she said. 'I just lost interest. I was never mad on it to begin with. There was just this bloke I happened to fancy at the time – you remember Mick, don't you?'

'I remember Mick. But I also remember why you stopped jumping. It was the day you snagged your ripcord on the door handle, walking through the canteen doorway. Unfortunately the chute didn't open. It hadn't been packed properly. And if you hadn't snagged it on the doorway, you'd never have found out until you were already falling.'

'I'd have had the reserve chute.'

'But when they examined your reserve chute, they also found that it hadn't been packed properly. Mick's ex-girlfriend still showed up at the club now and then, didn't she? No one was going to swear that it wouldn't have opened, and no one was going to swear that Mick's ex might have had something to do with it. But that was the last time anyone saw you at the club. I know, Moira. I was sorry to see you go.'

'We kept in touch.'

'There was a bit of a gap before we hooked up again. Face it: it spooked you. You kept thinking back to that door handle, and wondering what would have happened if you hadn't nipped back into the canteen for those cigarettes.'

'We'll never know,' Moira said.

'We can guess, though. The vast majority of you died, or were maimed. Some small minority of you survived. Some of you just decided not to jump that day. Some of you went back into the canteen and had the good fortune to snag that handle. Some of you did jump anyway, and even though the equipment was sabotaged you still came safely down to Earth. Some of you don't even know how lucky you are.'

'All right,' Moira said. 'So sometimes we come through the odd scrape, when things could have been much worse. But that doesn't—'

'It works on a planetary level, too,' Ian said.

'I'm sorry?'

'Have you ever realised how many times we've come *this* close to World War Three? The number of times when the button's almost been pushed? Not just during international flare-ups, but all the other times: when someone mistakes the moon for a salvo of incoming ICBMs; when a flock of geese or a meteor shower almost trigger Armageddon? It's terrifying, Moira! It keeps happening, over and over again! We've no right to have made it this far! It's already a fucking miracle that we made it out of the twentieth century, and yet it *keeps on happening*. Forget putting a gun to your head; just check your history. We've already proven it works. We're already on an extremely unlikely branch of the multiverse, whether we like it or not.'

'But we're not immortal,' Moira said. 'The people around us keep dying. Doesn't that prove—'

'Of course they keep dying. From your perspective. But from their own perspective? Nobody you ever knew has ever died. They just see everyone else dying around them.'

'Then that's our fate, is it? To live for ever, but to have everyone we ever loved die, slipping away from us like passing traffic?'

'That's why I have to know,' Ian said. 'I never said it was *good* news. Frankly, I'm hoping I blow my brains out. But if I keep pulling this trigger, and the pin keeps failing to fall on the loaded chamber ... then I'll know.'

'And then?'

'Then I've got a problem. Then we've all got a problem.'

Ian removed the gun from his pocket. He spun the chamber: it made a pleasant, well-oiled whirring sound. He pushed the chamber back into the body of the gun and held the weapon to the side of his head. It looked stupid and toylike, unreal amongst the pizza boxes and Ben Elton novels and the smiling pterodactyl. *It's now or never*, Moira thought. She lurched forwards, grasping for the gun across the kitchen table. Her sweater caught on her coffee cup, sending it spilling across the science magazines. Ian jerked back, keeping the barrel tight against his temple.

'Don't ...' she said.

Ian pulled the trigger. The hammer clicked down on empty space.

'Once,' he said. Then – hardly removing the gun from his head – he spun the chamber again. He pulled the trigger.

'Twice.'

He spun the chamber again. Moira pushed back from the table, her sweater sodden with coffee. She stood up, but felt frozen with terror. 'Please Ian ...'

Ian had backed himself against the pile of computer boxes. 'Don't come any closer, Moira.'

'Or what, Ian? Or you'll kill yourself?'

He pulled the trigger again. 'Three times.'

'Ian, please.'

The whirr of the chamber, the click of the trigger. 'Four times. What do you think are the odds of that, Moira? I think rather a lot of me must have already died.'

'Ian, no.'

He spun the chamber again, let the hammer fall. 'Five times. Getting a bit spooky now, don't you think? We'll do it up to ten. Then I'll make us another cuppa.'

He spun the chamber, pulled the trigger.

By the time the police and ambulance had arrived, Moira had

finished all the other cigarettes in the packet. She waited in the living room until she saw the blue lights of the emergency vehicles, spectrally beautiful in the early morning snowscape. It was still dark. When they knocked, she could barely bring herself to walk through the kitchen to open the door.

The policeman looked at Ian, swore softly. Behind him, the paramedic slowed his approach perceptibly. She had told them on the phone that Ian was dead, that there could be no doubt about it, but they had rushed here all the same. She was grateful for that: all she wanted to do was get as far away from Ian's cottage as possible.

As far away from Ian.

The policeman took her into the living room. He was about forty-five, with a beer belly and mutton-chop sideboards: she imagined him playing in a country and western band on weekends.

'Can you talk, love?'

'I told you what happened on the phone.' She smoked, having cadged another cigarette from one of the police.

'It wasn't me. I just need to know roughly what happened: we can deal with a proper statement later.'

Moira looked back through the door into the kitchen. She could just see the back of Ian's chair, with Ian's left shoulder poking into view. She could hear soft, attentive voices. It was easy to imagine that Ian was being spoken to as well.

'Ian called me,' she said. 'We were old friends. He sounded a bit funny, so I decided it was worth driving over.'

'Bit funny in what way?'

'He kept talking about not killing himself.'

'*Not* killing himself?'

'I wasn't going to split hairs. I knew something was up. I just wish I'd called someone else first, so that I didn't come here on my own.'

'If it's any consolation, I doubt that we'd have got here any sooner. Not on a night like this.' He nodded back towards the paramedics in the other room. 'Those lads are on a double shift as it is.'

'I should still have tried.'

'What happened when you got here?'

'Ian had me sitting down at the table in the kitchen. Then he started telling me stuff – stuff that was obviously very important to him – about how he'd worked out that he was going to live for ever. Then he showed me the gun.'

'He had it on him?'

Moira shook her head. 'It was on the table, hidden. But I didn't have time to grab it. Ian slipped it into his pocket. He was sitting on the other side of the table, so there was no way I could have made a grab for it. Not without risking it going off, anyway.'

'You were right not to try. Did he stop you phoning for help?'

'He said the phone was cut off.'

'And?'

'It wasn't. He hadn't even unplugged it. I just assumed he had. He was a clever sod, Ian. He always knew how to get the maximum effect with the minimum effort.' She hated the way that sounded, but it was true enough.

'And he kept talking?'

'Until he pulled out the gun again. I still didn't have time to do anything about it. I would have, believe me. But he had it against his head—'

'It's all right, Miss Curbishley. That'll do for now. In case you're wondering, I see no reason to consider you a suspect. Ian wasn't unknown to us: we knew he had a history of ups and downs. But you are an important witness, and I'm afraid we'll need a detailed statement. Tonight being tonight, however ...' He shrugged. 'I think it can wait until the weather improves, and we've all had a good night's sleep. Is that your Volvo outside?'

'Yes,' Moira said.

'Give me the keys and I'll have one of the boys drive you home. Do you have a friend you can stay with tonight, someone you can talk to?'

'I'll be all right,' Moira said.

'All the same—'

'I can drive myself,' she said. 'You're going to be here for a while, aren't you? I don't think I want to wait. It's not snowing at the moment.'

'I'd much rather you let one of us drive you.'

'It's kind, but I'd rather go now. I'm coping, honestly.'

The policeman made sure he had her contact details, then handed her his card. 'Give us a call in the morning, all right? We'll get it all sorted out before lunch. I'm not saying it's going to be easy, but at least you can start moving on.'

Moira took the card. 'Thank you.'

She walked through the kitchen, keeping her attention fixed on the door. Outside, it was bitterly cold: the stars had come out, cold and clear and perfectly still above the little Nativity Scene of parked vehicles. Moira closed the door behind her, trudged to her Volvo, exactly as if she had just said goodbye to Ian after a nice chat over the kitchen table.

She froze. The thought occurred to her: if Ian was right, then – somewhere out in the infinite sprawl of the ever-expanding multiverse – there was a version of herself doing just that. Another Moira, trudging to her Volvo. A Moira who had just seen the gun fail to kill Ian ten or twenty times, and was still feeling the consequences of that observation slide into place. That there was no death; that there was no mortality. That nothing ever died, and that it was the worst thing imaginable.

Would *that* Moira believe? she wondered.

Did she?

Moira got into the Volvo. She wound down the driver's side window before she set off, anxious for some fresh air, no matter how cold. Thankfully, the engine started first time. The headlights threw purple shadows across the snow as she backed out between the police vehicles and the ambulance. She slipped into first gear and crunched slowly down the drive, leaving the cottage behind her. She avoided looking in the rear-view mirror: she did not think she could take it.

She reached the end of the drive and turned onto the lane. The driving was easier now, and she slipped through the gears into third. Dry branches whisked against the side of the Volvo as she negotiated tight spots. There, ahead, was the humpbacked bridge. Once she had crossed it, there would only be a little more country lane and then she would hit the main road, which she knew had been gritted earlier that night.

Something flashed out of the night, towards her. She had a photographic flash of a flattened, startled face, framed by soft white feathers. Wings spread, as if pinned wide in an anatomy diagram. Claws grasping toward her.

Moira swerved. The owl slid past, brushing the windscreen. The car gyred, losing traction. The Volvo slid horizontally, easing off the road, sliding towards the bank of the river. The moment stretched: time oozing uselessly. Moira tried to steer the car back towards the road, but her hands moved in slow motion on the wheel. Moira saw the nearly frozen river: a shallow ribbon of ice, dotted with the grey-black shadows of pebbles. She felt an instant of relief. She was not going to drown. Even if the car smashed through the ice; even if there was running water under that ice, it couldn't be more than a few inches deep. The car would be a write-off, but ...

Then she saw the tree. It was a dead, wizened old thing. It must have been carried downstream during the torrents of the last heavy storm. Now, planted amongst the rocks, it looked like it had been there for a thousand years.

The car lurched towards it, tipping onto its right-hand side. The tree loomed larger, and with a horrid inevitability, Moira knew that it was going to push those sharp old branches through the open window of the driver's side door. She had just enough time to let out a tiny, unheard gasp of terror, and then the car rolled onto the tree. The last thing she remembered was the branches – thick as her arm – ramming through the window, the instant as their cruel edges touched her skin.

But when the police found her, not much more than an hour later, they could not believe that she had survived with only minor scratches. All the major branches had gone around her, trapping her in place but doing no real harm.

'You're a very lucky woman,' the policeman told her.

This story didn't make much of a splash when it appeared in the last-ever issue of Interzone *to be edited by David Pringle, just before the reins were handed over to the estimable Andy Cox. I'm still quite taken with it, though. It articulates an idea, a consequence of the Many Worlds interpretation of quantum mechanics, that had been nagging me for some time – you can see me coming at it from a slightly different approach in 'Angels of Ashes', which was written five or six years before this piece. What I like about 'Everlasting' – and which hasn't, I think, ever been picked up on – is that nothing overtly science fictional happens anywhere in the story. It's possible to read it as an entirely straightforward piece about someone who just happens to have a very peculiar belief system.*

ZIMA BLUE

After the first week people started drifting away from the island. The viewing stands around the pool became emptier by the day. The big tourist ships hauled back towards interstellar space. Art fiends, commentators and critics packed their bags in Venice. Their disappointment hung over the lagoon like a miasma.

I was one of the few who stayed on Murjek, returning to the stands each day. I'd watch for hours, squinting against the trembling blue light reflected from the surface of the water. Face down, Zima's pale shape moved so languidly from one end of the pool to the other that it could have been mistaken for a floating corpse. As he swam I wondered how I was going to tell his story, and who was going to buy it. I tried to remember the name of my first newspaper, back on Mars. They wouldn't pay as much as some of the bigger titles, but some part of me liked the idea of going back to the old place. It had been a long time ... I queried the AM, wanting it to jog my memory about the name of the paper. There'd been so many since ... hundreds, by my reckoning. But nothing came. It took me another yawning moment to remember that I'd dismissed the AM the day before:

'Carrie, you're on your own,' I said aloud to myself. 'Start getting used to it.'

In the pool, the swimming figure ended a length and began to swim back towards me.

Two weeks earlier I'd been sitting in the Piazza San Marco at noon, watching white figurines glide against the white marble of the clock tower. The sky over Venice was jammed with ships, parked hull-to-hull. Their bellies were quilted in vast, glowing panels, tuned to match the real sky. The view reminded me of the work of a pre-Expansion artist who had specialised in eye-wrenching tricks of perspective and composition: endless waterfalls, interlocking lizards. I formed a mental image and queried the fluttering presence of the AM, but it couldn't retrieve the name.

I finished my coffee and steeled myself for the bill.

I'd come to this white marble version of Venice to witness the unveiling of Zima's final work of art. I'd had an interest in the artist for years, and I'd hoped I might be able to arrange an interview. Unfortunately several thousand other members of the in-crowd had come up with exactly the same idea. Not that it mattered what kind of competition I had anyway: Zima wasn't talking.

The waiter placed a folded card on my table.

All we had been told was to make our way to Murjek, a water-logged world most of us had never heard of before. Murjek's only claim to fame was that it hosted the one hundred and seventy-first known duplicate of Venice, and one of only three Venices rendered entirely in white marble. Zima had chosen Murjek to host his final work of art, and to be the place where he would make his retirement from public life.

With a heavy heart I lifted the bill to inspect the damage. Instead of the expected bill, it was a small, blue card printed in fine gold italic lettering. The shade of blue was that precise powdery aquamarine that Zima had made his own. The card was addressed to me, Carrie Clay, and it said that Zima wanted to talk to me about the unveiling. If I was interested, I should report to the Rialto Bridge in exactly two hours.

If I was interested.

The note stipulated that no recording materials were to be brought, not even a pen and paper. As an afterthought, the card mentioned that the bill had been taken care of. I almost had the nerve to order another coffee and put it on the same tab. Almost, but not quite.

Zima's servant was there when I arrived early at the bridge. Intricate neon mechanisms pulsed behind the flexing glass of the robot's mannequin body. It bowed at the waist and spoke very softly. 'Miss Clay? Since you're here, we might as well depart.'

The robot escorted me to a flight of stairs that led to the waterside. My AM followed us, fluttering at my shoulder. A conveyor hovered in waiting, floating a metre above the water. The robot helped me into the rear compartment. The AM was about to follow me inside when the robot raised a warning hand.

'You'll have to leave that behind, I'm afraid; no recording materials, remember?'

I looked at the metallic green hummingbird, trying to remember the last time I had been out of its ever-watchful presence.

'Leave it behind?'

'It'll be quite safe here, and you can collect it again when you return after nightfall.'

'If I say no?'

'Then I'm afraid there'll be no meeting with Zima.'

I sensed that the robot wasn't going to hang around all afternoon waiting for my answer. The thought of being away from the AM made my blood run cold. But I wanted that interview so badly I was prepared to consider anything.

I told the AM to stay there until I returned.

The obedient machine reversed away from me in a flash of metallic green. It was like watching a part of myself drift away. The glass hull wrapped itself around me and I felt a surge of un-nulled acceleration.

Venice tilted below us, then streaked away to the horizon.

I formed a test query, asking the AM to name the planet where I'd celebrated my seven hundredth birthday. Nothing came: I was out of query range, with only my own age-saturated memory to rely on.

I leaned forwards. 'Are you authorised to tell me what this is about?'

'I'm afraid he didn't tell me,' the robot said, making a face appear in the back of his head. 'But if at any moment you feel uncomfortable, we can return to Venice.'

'I'm fine for now. Who else got the blue card treatment?'

'Only you, to the best of my knowledge.'

'And if I'd declined? Were you supposed to ask someone else?'

'No,' the robot said. 'But let's face it, Miss Clay. You weren't very likely to turn him down.'

As we flew on, the conveyor's shock wave gouged a foaming channel in the sea behind it. I thought of a brush drawn through wet paint on marble, exposing the white surface beneath. I took out Zima's invitation and held it against the horizon ahead of us, trying to decide whether the blue was a closer match to the sky or the sea. Against these two possibilities the card seemed to flicker indeterminately.

Zima Blue. It was an exact thing, specified scientifically in terms of angstroms and intensities. If you were an artist, you could have a batch of it mixed up according to that specification. But no one ever used Zima Blue unless they were making a calculated statement about Zima himself.

Zima was already unique by the time he emerged into the public eye. He had undergone radical procedures to enable him to tolerate extreme environments without the burden of a protective suit. Zima had the appearance of a well-built man wearing a tight body stocking, until you were close and you realised that this was actually his skin. Covering his entire form, it was a synthetic material that could be tuned to different colours and textures depending on his mood and surroundings. It could approximate clothing if the social circumstances demanded it. The skin could contain pressure when he wished to experience vacuum, and stiffen to protect him against the crush of a gas giant. Despite these refinements the skin conveyed a full range of sensory impressions to his mind. He had no need to breathe, since his entire cardiovascular system had been replaced by closed-cycle life-support mechanisms. He had no need to eat or drink; no need to dispose of bodily waste. Tiny repair machines swarmed through his body, allowing him to tolerate radiation doses that would have killed an ordinary man in minutes.

With his body thus armoured against environmental extremes, Zima was free to seek inspiration where he wanted. He could drift free in space, staring into the face of a star, or wander the searing canyons of a planet where metals ran like lava. His eyes had been replaced by cameras sensitive to a huge swathe of the electromagnetic spectrum, wired into his brain via complex processing modules. A synaesthetic bridge allowed him to hear visual data as a kind of music, to see sounds as a symphony of startling colours. His skin functioned as a kind of antenna, giving him sensitivity to electrical field changes. When that wasn't sufficient, he could tap into the data feeds of any number of accompanying machines.

Given all this, Zima's art couldn't help but be original and attention-grabbing. His landscapes and starfields had a heightened, ecstatic quality about them, awash with luminous, jarring colours and eye-wrenching tricks of perspective. Painted in traditional materials but on a huge scale, they quickly attracted a core of serious buyers. Some found their way into private collections, but

Zima murals also started popping up in public spaces all over the galaxy. Tens of metres across, the murals were nonetheless detailed down to the limits of vision. Most had been painted in one session. Zima had no need for sleep, so he worked uninterrupted until a piece was complete.

The murals were undeniably impressive. From a standpoint of composition and technique they were unquestionably brilliant. But there was also something bleak and chilling about them. They were landscapes without a human presence, save for the implied viewpoint of the artist himself.

Put it this way: they were nice to look at, but I wouldn't have hung one in my home.

Not everyone agreed, obviously, or else Zima wouldn't have sold as many works as he had. But I couldn't help wondering how many people were buying the paintings because of what they knew about the artist, rather than because of any intrinsic merit in the works themselves.

That was how things stood when I first paid attention to Zima. I filed him away as interesting but kitschy; maybe worth a story if something else happened to either him or his art.

Something did, but it took a while for anyone – including me – to notice.

One day – after a longer than usual gestation period – Zima unveiled a mural that had something different about it. It was a painting of a swirling, star-pocked nebula, from the vantage point of an airless rock. Perched on the rim of a crater in the middle distance, blocking off part of the nebula, was a tiny, blue square. At first glance it looked as if the canvas had been washed blue and Zima had simply left a small area unpainted. There was no solidity to the square, no detail or suggestion of how it related to the landscape or the backdrop. It cast no shadow and had no tonal influence on the surrounding colours. But the square was deliberate: close examination showed that it had indeed been over-painted over the rocky lip of the crater. It meant something.

The square was just the beginning. Thereafter, every mural that Zima released to the outside world contained a similar geometric shape: a square, triangle, oblong or some similar form embedded somewhere in the composition. It was a long time before anyone noticed that the shade of blue was the same from painting to painting.

It was Zima Blue: the same shade of blue as on the gold-lettered card.

Over the next decade or so, the abstract shapes became more dominant, squeezing out the other elements of each composition. The cosmic vistas ended up as narrow borders, framing blank circles, triangles, rectangles. Where his earlier work had been characterised by exuberant brushwork and thick layers of paint, the blue forms were rendered with mirror-smoothness.

Intimidated by the intrusion of the abstract blue forms, casual buyers turned away from Zima. Before very long Zima unveiled the first of his entirely blue murals. Large enough to cover the side of a thousand-storey building, the mural was considered by many to be as far as Zima could take things.

They couldn't have been more wrong.

I felt the conveyor slowing as we neared a small island, the only feature in any direction.

'You're the first to see this,' the robot said. 'There's a distortion screen blocking the view from space.'

The island was about a kilometre across: low and turtle-shaped, ringed by a narrow collar of pale sand. Near the middle it rose to a shallow plateau, on which vegetation had been cleared in a roughly rectangular area. I made out a small panel of reflective blue set flat against the ground, surrounded by what appeared to be a set of tiered viewing stands.

The conveyor shed altitude and speed, bobbing down until it stopped just outside the area enclosed by the viewing stands. It came to rest next to a low, white pebble-dash chalet I hadn't noticed during our approach.

The robot stepped out and helped me from the conveyor.

'Zima will be here in a moment,' it said, before returning to the conveyor and vanishing back into the sky.

Suddenly I felt very alone and very vulnerable. A breeze came in from the sea, blowing sand into my eyes. The sun was creeping down towards the horizon and soon it would be getting chilly. Just when I was beginning to feel the itch of panic, a man emerged from the chalet, rubbing his hands briskly. He walked towards me, following a path of paved stones.

'Glad you could make it, Carrie.'

It was Zima, of course, and in a flash I felt foolish for doubting that he would show his face.

'Hi,' I said lamely.

Zima offered his hand. I shook it, feeling the slightly plastic texture of his artificial skin. Today it was a dull pewter-grey.

'Let's go and sit on the balcony. It's nice to watch the sunset, isn't it?'

'Nice,' I agreed.

He turned his back to me and set off in the direction of the chalet. As he walked, his muscles flexed and bulged beneath the pewter flesh. There were scalelike glints in the skin on his back, as if it had been set with a mosaic of reflective chips. He was beautiful like a statue, muscular like a panther. He was a handsome man, even after all his transformations, but I had never heard of him taking a lover, or having any kind of private life at all. His art was everything.

I followed him, feeling awkward and tongue-tied. Zima led me into the chalet, through an old-fashioned kitchen and an old-fashioned lounge, full of thousand-year-old furniture and ornaments.

'How was the flight?'

'Fine.'

He stopped suddenly and turned to face me. 'I forgot to check . . . did the robot insist that you leave behind your *Aide Memoire*?'

'Yes.'

'Good. It was you I wanted to talk to, Carrie, not some surrogate recording device.'

'Me?'

The pewter mask of his face formed a quizzical expression. 'Do you do multi-syllables, or are you still working up to that?'

'Er . . .'

'Relax,' he said. 'I'm not here to test you, or humiliate you, or anything like that. This isn't a trap, and you're not in any danger. You'll be back in Venice by midnight.'

'I'm okay,' I managed. 'Just a bit starstruck.'

'Well, you shouldn't be. I'm hardly the first celebrity you've met, am I?'

'Well, no, but—'

'People find me intimidating,' he said. 'They get over it eventually, and then wonder what all the fuss was about.'

'Why me?'

'Because you kept asking nicely,' Zima said.

'Be serious.'

'All right. There's a bit more to it than that, although you *did* ask nicely. I've enjoyed much of your work over the years. People have often trusted you to set the record straight, especially near the ends of their lives.'

'You talked about retiring, not dying.'

'Either way, it would still be a withdrawal from public life. Your work has always seemed truthful to me, Carrie. I'm not aware of anyone claiming misrepresentation through your writing.'

'It happens now and then,' I said. 'That's why I always make sure there's an AM on hand so no one can dispute what was said.'

'That won't matter with my story,' Zima said.

I looked at him shrewdly. 'There's something else, isn't there? Some other reason you pulled my name out of the hat.'

'I'd like to help you,' he said.

When most people speak about his Blue Period they mean the era of the truly huge murals. By huge I do mean *huge*. Soon they had become large enough to dwarf buildings and civic spaces, large enough to be visible from orbit. Across the galaxy twenty-kilo-metre-high sheets of blue towered over private islands or rose from storm-wrecked seas. Expense was never a problem, since Zima had many rival sponsors who competed to host his latest and biggest creation. The panels kept on growing, until they required complex, sloth-tech machinery to hold them aloft against gravity and weather. They pierced the tops of planetary atmospheres, jutting into space. They glowed with their own soft light. They curved around in arcs and fans, so that the viewer's entire visual field was saturated with blue.

By now Zima was hugely famous, even to people who had no particular interest in art. He was the weird cyborg celebrity who made huge blue structures; the man who never gave interviews or hinted at the private significance of his art.

But that was a hundred years ago. Zima wasn't even remotely done.

Eventually the structures became too unwieldy to be hosted on planets. Blithely Zima moved into interplanetary space, forging vast, free-floating sheets of blue ten thousand kilometres across.

Now he worked not with brushes and paint, but with fleets of mining robots, tearing apart asteroids to make the raw material for his creations. Now it was entire stellar economies that competed with each other to host Zima's work.

That was about the time that I renewed my interest in Zima. I attended one of his 'moonwrappings': the enclosure of an entire celestial body in a lidded blue container, like a hat going into a box. Two months later he stained the entire equatorial belt of a gas giant blue, and I had a ringside seat for that as well. Six months later he altered the surface chemistry of a sun-grazing comet so that it daubed a Zima Blue tail across an entire solar system. But I was no closer to a story. I kept asking for an interview and kept being turned down. All I knew was that there had to be more to Zima's obsession with blue than a mere artistic whim. Without an understanding of that obsession, there was no story: just anecdote.

I didn't do anecdote.

So I waited, and waited. And then – like millions of others – I heard about Zima's final work of art, and made my way to the fake Venice on Murjek. I wasn't expecting an interview, or any new insights. I just had to be there.

We stepped through sliding glass doors onto the balcony. Two simple white chairs sat either side of a white table. The table was set with drinks and a bowl of fruit. Beyond the unfenced balcony, arid land sloped steeply away, offering an uninterrupted view of the sea. The water was calm and inviting, with the lowering sun reflected like a silver coin.

Zima indicated that I should take one of the seats. His hand dithered over two bottles of wine.

'Red or white, Carrie?'

I opened my mouth as if to answer him, but nothing came. Normally, in that instant between the question and the response, the AM would have silently directed my choice to one of the two options. Not having the AM's prompt felt like a mental stall in my thoughts.

'Red, I think,' Zima said. 'Unless you have strong objections.'

'It's not that I can't decide these things for myself,' I said.

Zima poured me a glass of red, then held it up to the sky to inspect its clarity. 'Of course not,' he said.

'It's just that this is a little strange for me.'

'It shouldn't be strange,' he said. 'This is the way you lived your life for hundreds of years.'

'The natural way, you mean?'

Zima poured himself a glass of the red wine, but instead of drinking it he merely sniffed the bouquet. 'Yes.'

'But there isn't anything natural about being alive a thousand years after I was born,' I said. 'My organic memory reached saturation point about seven hundred years ago. My head's like a house with too much furniture. Move something in, you have to move something out.'

'Let's go back to the wine for a moment,' Zima said. 'Normally, you'd have relied on the advice of the AM, wouldn't you?'

I shrugged. 'Yes.'

'Would the AM always suggest one of the two possibilities? Always red wine, or always white wine, for instance?'

'It's not that simplistic,' I said. 'If I had a strong preference for one over the other, then yes, the AM would always recommend one wine over the other. But I don't. I like red wine sometimes and white wine other times. Sometimes I don't want any kind of wine.' I hoped my frustration wasn't obvious. But after the elaborate charade with the blue card, the robot and the conveyor, the last thing I wanted to be discussing with Zima was my own imperfect recall.

'Then it's random?' he asked. 'The AM would have been just as likely to say red as white?'

'No, it's not like that either. The AM's been following me around for hundreds of years. It's seen me drink wine a few hundred thousand times, under a few hundred thousand different circumstances. It knows, with a high degree of reliability, what my best choice of wine would be given any set of parameters.'

'And you follow that advice unquestioningly?'

I sipped at the red. 'Of course. Wouldn't it be a little childish to go against it just to make a point about free will? After all, I'm more likely to be satisfied with the choice it suggests.'

'But unless you ignore that suggestion now and then, won't your whole life become a set of predictable responses?'

'Maybe,' I said. 'But is that so very bad? If I'm happy, what do I care?'

'I'm not criticising you,' Zima said. He smiled and leaned back in his seat, defusing some of the tension caused by his line of questioning. 'Not many people have an AM these days, do they?'

'I wouldn't know,' I said.

'Less than one per cent of the entire galactic population.' Zima sniffed his wine and looked through the glass at the sky. 'Almost everyone else out there has accepted the inevitable.'

'It takes machines to manage a thousand years of memory. So what?'

'But a different order of machine,' Zima said. 'Neural implants, fully integrated into the participant's sense of self. Indistinguishable from biological memory. You wouldn't need to query the AM about your choice of wine; you wouldn't need to wait for that confirmatory whisper. You'd just know it.'

'Where's the difference? I allow my experiences to be recorded by a machine that accompanies me everywhere I go. The machine misses nothing, and it's so efficient at anticipating my queries that I barely have to ask it anything.'

'The machine is vulnerable.'

'It's backed up at regular intervals. And it's no more vulnerable than a cluster of implants inside my head. Sorry, but that just isn't a reasonable objection.'

'You're right, of course. But there's a deeper argument against the AM. It's too perfect. It doesn't know how to distort or forget.'

'Isn't that the point?'

'Not exactly. When you recall something – this conversation, perhaps, a hundred years from now – there will be things about it that you misremember. Yet those misremembered details will themselves become part of your memory, gaining solidity and texture with each instance of recall. A thousand years from now, your memory of this conversation might bear little resemblance to reality. Yet you'd swear your recollection was accurate.'

'But if the AM had accompanied me, I'd have a flawless record of how things really were.'

'You would,' Zima said. 'But that isn't living memory. It's photography: a mechanical recording process. It freezes out the imagination, leaves no scope for details to be selectively misremembered.' He paused long enough to top off my glass. 'Imagine that on nearly every occasion when you had cause to sit outside on an afternoon like this you had chosen red wine over white, and generally had no reason to regret that choice. But on one occasion, for one reason or another, you were persuaded to choose white – against the judgement of the AM – and it was wonderful. Everything came together magically: the company, the conversation, the late afternoon ambience, the splendid view, the euphoric rush of being slightly drunk. A perfect afternoon turned into a perfect evening.'

'It might not have had anything to do with my choice of wine,' I said.

'No,' Zima agreed. 'And the AM certainly wouldn't attach any significance to that one happy combination of circumstances. A single deviation wouldn't affect its predictive model to any significant degree. It would still say "red wine" the next time you asked.'

I felt an uncomfortable tingle of understanding. 'But human memory wouldn't work that way.'

'No. It would latch on to that one exception and attach undue significance to it. It would amplify the attractive parts of the memory of that afternoon and suppress the less pleasant parts: the fly that kept buzzing in your face, your anxiety about catching the boat home and the birthday present you knew you had to buy in the morning. All you'd remember was that golden glow of well-being. The next time, you might well choose white, and the time after. An entire pattern of behaviour would have been altered by one instance of deviation. The AM would never tolerate that. You'd have to go against its advice many, many times before it grudgingly updated its model and started suggesting white rather than red.'

'All right,' I said, still wishing we could talk about Zima rather than me. 'But what practical difference does it make whether the artificial memory is inside my head or outside?'

'All the difference in the world,' Zima said. 'The memories stored in the AM are fixed for eternity. You can query it as often as you like, but it will never enhance or omit a single detail. But the implants work differently. They're designed to integrate seamlessly with biological memory, to the point where the recipient can't tell the difference. For that very reason they're necessarily plastic, malleable, subject to error and distortion.'

'Fallible,' I said.

'But without fallibility there is no art. And without art there is no truth.'

'Fallibility leads to truth? That's a good one.'

'I mean truth in the higher, metaphoric sense. That golden

afternoon? That was the truth. Remembering the fly wouldn't have added to it in any material sense. It would have detracted from it.'

'There was no afternoon, there was no fly,' I said. Finally, my patience had reached breaking point. 'Look, I'm grateful to have been invited here. But I thought there might be a little more to this than a lecture about the way I choose to manage my own memories.'

'Actually,' Zima said, 'there was a point to this after all. And it is about me, but it's also about you.' He put down the glass. 'Shall we take a little walk? I'd like to show you the swimming pool.'

'The sun hasn't gone down yet,' I said.

Zima smiled. 'There'll always be another one.'

He took me on a different route through the house, leaving by a different door than the one we'd come in by. A meandering path climbed gradually between white stone walls, bathed now in gold from the lowering sun. Presently we reached the flat plateau I'd seen on my approach in the conveyor. The things I'd thought were viewing stands were exactly that: terraced structures about thirty metres high, with staircases at the back leading to the different levels. Zima led me into the darkening shadow under the nearest stand, then through a private door that opened into the enclosed area. The blue panel I'd seen during the approach turned out to be a modest rectangular swimming pool, drained of water.

Zima led me to the edge.

'A swimming pool,' I said. 'You weren't kidding. Is this what the stands are all about?'

'This is where it will happen,' Zima said. 'The unveiling of my final work of art, and my retirement from public life.'

The pool wasn't quite finished. In the far corner, a small, yellow robot glued ceramic tiles into place. The part near us was fully tiled, but I couldn't help noticing that the tiles were chipped and cracked in places. The afternoon light made it hard to be sure – we were in deep shadow now – but their colour looked to be very close to Zima Blue.

'After painting entire planets, isn't this a bit of a let-down?' I asked.

'Not for me,' Zima said. 'For me this is where the quest ends. This is what it was all leading up to.'

'A shabby-looking swimming pool?'

'It's not just any old swimming pool,' he said.

He walked me around the island, as the sun slipped under the sea and the colours turned ashen.

'The old murals came from the heart,' Zima said. 'I painted on a huge scale because that was what the subject matter seemed to demand.'

'It was good work,' I said.

'It was hack work. Huge, loud, demanding, popular, but ultimately soulless. Just because it came from the heart didn't make it good.'

I said nothing. That was the way I'd always felt about his work as well: it was as vast and inhuman as its inspiration, and only Zima's cyborg modifications lent his art any kind of uniqueness. It was like praising a painting because it had been done by someone holding a brush between their teeth.

'My work said nothing about the cosmos that the cosmos wasn't already capable of saying for itself. More importantly, it said nothing about me. So what if I walked in vacuum, or swam in seas of liquid nitrogen? So what if I could see ultraviolet photons, or taste electrical fields? The modifications I inflicted upon myself were gruesome and extreme. But they gave me nothing that a good telepresence drone couldn't offer any artist.'

'I think you're being a little harsh on yourself,' I said.

'Not at all. I can say this now because I know that I did eventually create something worthwhile. But when it happened it was completely unplanned.'

'You mean the blue stuff?'

'The blue stuff,' he said, nodding. 'It began by accident: a misapplication of colour on a nearly finished canvas. A smudge of pale aquamarine-blue against near-black. The effect was electric. It was as if I had achieved a short circuit to some intense, primal memory, a realm of experience where that colour was the most important thing in my world.'

'What was that memory?'

'I didn't know. All I knew was the way that colour spoke to me, as if I'd been waiting my whole life to find it, to set it free.' He thought for a moment. 'There's always been something about blue. A thousand years ago Yves Klein said it was the essence of colour itself: the colour that stood for all other colours. A man once spent his entire life searching for a particular shade of blue that he remembered encountering in childhood. He began to despair of ever finding it, thinking he must have imagined that precise shade, that it could not possibly exist in nature. Then one day he chanced upon it. It was the colour of a beetle in a museum of natural history. He wept for joy.'

'What is Zima Blue?' I asked. 'Is it the colour of a beetle?'

'No,' he said. 'It's not a beetle. But I had to know the answer, no matter where it took me. I had to know why that colour meant so much to me, and why it was taking over my art.'

'You allowed it to take over,' I said.

'I had no choice. As the blue became more intense, more dominant, I felt I was closer to an answer. I felt that if only I could immerse myself in that colour, then I would know everything I desired to know. I would understand myself as an artist.'

'And? Did you?'

'I understood myself,' Zima said. 'But it wasn't what I expected.'

'What did you learn?'

Zima was a long time answering me. We walked on slowly, me lagging slightly behind his prowling muscular form. It was getting cooler now and I began to wish I'd had the foresight to bring a coat. I thought of asking Zima if he could lend me one, but I was concerned not to derail his thoughts from wherever they were headed. Keeping my mouth shut had always been the toughest part of the job.

'We talked about the fallibility of memory,' he said.

'Yes.'

'My own memory was incomplete. Since the implants were installed I remembered everything, but that only accounted for the last three hundred years of my life. I knew myself to be much older, but of my life before the implants I recalled only fragments; shattered pieces that I did not quite know how to reassemble.' He slowed and turned back to me, the dulling orange light on the horizon catching the side of his face. 'I knew I had to dig back into that past, if I was ever to understand the significance of Zima Blue.'

'How far back did you get?'

'It was like archaeology,' he said. 'I followed the trail of my memories back to the earliest reliable event, which occurred shortly after the installation of the implants. This took me to Kharkov Eight, a world in the Garlin Bight, about nineteen thousand light-years from here. All I remembered was the name of a man I had known there, called Cobargo.'

Cobargo meant nothing to me, but even without the AM I knew something of the Garlin Bight. It was a region of the galaxy encompassing six hundred habitable systems, squeezed between three major economic powers. In the Garlin Bight normal interstellar law did not apply. It was fugitive territory.

'Kharkov Eight specialised in a certain kind of product,' Zima said. 'The entire planet was geared up to provide medical services of a kind unavailable elsewhere. Illicit cybernetic modifications, that kind of thing.'

'Is that where . . .' I left the sentence unfinished.

'That is where I became what I am,' Zima said. 'Of course, I made further changes to myself after my time on Kharkov Eight – improving my tolerance to extreme environments, expanding my sensory capabilities – but the essence of what I am was laid down under the knife in Cobargo's clinic.'

'So before you arrived on Kharkov Eight you were a normal man?' I asked.

'This is where it gets difficult,' Zima said, picking his way carefully along the trail. 'Upon my return I naturally tried to locate Cobargo. With his help, I assumed I would be able to make sense of the memory fragments I carried in my head. But Cobargo was gone, vanished elsewhere into the Bight. The clinic remained, but now his grandson was running it.'

'I bet he wasn't keen on talking.'

'No; he took some persuading. Thankfully, I had means. A little bribery, a little coercion.' He smiled slightly at that. 'Eventually he agreed to open the clinic records and examine his grandfather's log of my visit.'

We turned a corner. The sea and the sky were now the same inseparable grey, with no trace of blue remaining.

'What happened?'

'The records say that I was never a man,' Zima said. He paused a while before continuing, leaving no doubt as to what he had said. 'Zima never existed before my arrival in the clinic.'

What I wouldn't have done for a recording drone, or – failing that – a plain old notebook and pen. I frowned, as if that might make my memory work just that little bit harder.

'Then who were you?'

'A machine,' he said. 'A complex robot: an autonomous artificial intelligence. I was already centuries old when I arrived on Kharkov Eight, with full legal independence.'

'No,' I said, shaking my head. 'You're a man with machine parts, not a machine.'

'The clinic records were very clear. I had arrived as a robot. An androform robot, certainly – but an obvious machine nonetheless. I was dismantled and my core cognitive functions were integrated into a vat-grown biological host body.' With one finger he tapped the pewter side of his skull. 'There's a lot of organic material in here, and a lot of cybernetic machinery. It's difficult to tell where one begins and the other ends. Even harder to tell which is the master, and which is the slave.'

I looked at the figure standing next to me, trying to make the mental leap needed to view him as a machine – albeit a machine with soft, cellular components – rather than a man. I couldn't – not yet.

I stalled. 'The clinic could have lied to you.'

'I don't think so. They would have been far happier had I not known.'

'All right,' I said. 'Just for the sake of argument—'

'Those were the facts. They were easily verified. I examined the customs records for Kharkov Eight and found that an *autonomous robot entity* had entered the planet's airspace a few months before the medical procedure.'

'Not necessarily you.'

'No other robot entity had come near the world for decades. It had to be me. More than that, the records also showed the robot's port of origin.'

'Which was?'

'A world beyond the Bight. Lintan Three, in the Muara Archipelago.'

The AM's absence was like a missing tooth. 'I don't know if I know it.'

'You probably don't. It's no kind of world you'd ever visit by choice. The scheduled lightbreakers don't go there. My only purpose in visiting the place seemed to me—'

'You went there?'

'Twice. Once before the procedure on Kharkov Eight, and again recently, to establish where I'd been before Lintan Three. The evidence trail was beginning to get muddy, to say the least ... but I asked the right kinds of questions, poked at the right kinds of databases, and eventually found out where I'd come from. But that still wasn't the final answer. There were many worlds, and the chain became fainter with each that I visited. But I had persistence on my side.'

'And money.'

'And money,' Zima said, acknowledging my remark with a polite little nod. 'That helped incalculably.'

'So what did you find, in the end?'

'I followed the trail back to the beginning. On Kharkov Eight I was a quick-thinking machine with human-level intelligence. But I hadn't always been that clever, that complex. I'd been augmented in steps, as time and circumstances allowed.'

'By yourself?'

'Eventually, yes. That was when I had autonomy, legal independence. But I had to reach a certain level of intelligence before I was allowed that freedom. Before that, I was a simpler machine ... like an heirloom or a pet. I was passed from one owner to the next, between generations. They added things to me. They made me cleverer.'

'How did you begin?'

'As a project,' he said.

Zima led me back to the swimming pool. Equatorial night had arrived quickly, and the pool was bathed now in artificial light from the many floods arrayed above the viewing stands. Since we had last seen the pool the robot had finished gluing the final tiles in place.

'It's ready now,' Zima said. 'Tomorrow it will be sealed, and the day after it will be flooded with water. I'll cycle the water until it attains the necessary clarity.'

'And then?'

'I prepare myself for my performance.'

On the way to the swimming pool he had told me as much as he knew about his origin. Zima had begun his existence on Earth, before I was even born. He had been assembled by a hobbyist, a talented young man with an interest in practical robotics. In those days, the man had been one of many groups and individuals groping towards the hard problem of artificial intelligence.

Perception, navigation and autonomous problem-solving were the three things that most interested the young man. He had created many robots, tinkering them together from kits, broken toys and spare parts. Their minds – if they could be dignified with such a term – were cobbled from the innards of junked computers, with their simple programmes bulging at the limits of memory and processor speed.

The young man filled his house with these simple machines, designing each for a particular task. One robot was a sticky-limbed spider that climbed around the walls of his house, dusting the frames of pictures. Another lay in wait for flies and cockroaches. It caught and digested them, using the energy from the chemical breakdown of their biomass to drive itself to another place in the house. Another robot busied itself by repainting the walls of the house over and over, so that the colours matched the changing of the seasons.

Another robot lived in his swimming pool.

It toiled endlessly up and down and along the ceramic sides of the pool, scrubbing them clean. The young man could have bought a cheap swimming pool cleaner from a mail-order company, but it amused him to design the robot from scratch, according to his own eccentric design principles. He gave the robot a full-colour vision system and a brain large enough to process the visual data into a model of its surroundings. He allowed the robot to make its own decisions about the best strategy for cleaning the pool. He allowed it to choose when it cleaned and when it surfaced to recharge its batteries via the solar panels grouped on its back. He imbued it with a primitive notion of reward.

The little pool-cleaner taught the young man a great deal about the fundamentals of robotics design. Those lessons were incorporated into the other household robots, until one of them – a simple household cleaner – became sufficiently robust and autonomous that the young man began to offer it as a kit, via mail-order. The kit sold well, and a year later the young man offered it as a preassembled domestic robot. The robot was a runaway success, and the young man's firm soon became the market leader in domestic robots.

Within ten years, the world swarmed with his bright, eager machines.

He never forgot the little pool-cleaner. Time and again he used it as a test-bed for new hardware, new software. By stages it became the cleverest of all his creations, and the only one that he refused to strip down and cannibalise.

When he died, the cleaner passed to his daughter. She continued the family tradition, adding cleverness to the little machine. When she died, she passed it to the young man's grandson, who happened to live on Mars.

'This is the original pool,' Zima said. 'If you hadn't already guessed.'

'After all this time?' I asked.

'It's very old. But ceramics endure. The hardest part was finding it in the first place. I had to dig through two metres of topsoil. It was in a place they used to call Silicon Valley.'

'These tiles are coloured Zima Blue,' I said.

'Zima Blue *is* the colour of the tiles,' he gently corrected. 'It just happened to be the shade that the young man used for his swimming pool tiles.'

'Then some part of you remembered.'

'This was where I began. A crude little machine with barely enough intelligence to steer itself around a swimming pool. But it was my world. It was all I knew, all I needed to know.'

'And now?' I asked, already fearing the answer.

'Now I'm going home.'

I was there when he did it. By then the stands were full of people who had arrived to watch the performance, and the sky over the island was a mosaic of tightly packed hovering ships. The distortion screen had been turned off, and the viewing platforms on the ships thronged with hundreds of thousands of distant witnesses. They could see the swimming pool by then, its water mirror-flat and gin-clear. They could see Zima standing at the edge, with the solar patches on his back glinting like snake scales. None of the viewers had any idea what was about to happen, or its significance. They were expecting something – the public unveiling of a work that would presumably trump everything Zima had created before then – but they could only stare in puzzled concern at the pool, wondering how it could possibly measure up to those atmosphere-piercing canvases, or those entire worlds wrapped in shrouds of blue. They kept thinking that the pool had to be a diversion. The real work of art – the piece that would herald his retirement – must be somewhere else, as yet unseen, waiting to be revealed in all its immensity.

That was what they thought.

But I knew the truth. I knew it as I watched Zima stand at the edge of the pool and surrender himself to the blue. He'd told me exactly how it would happen: the slow, methodical shutting-down of higher-brain functions. It hardly mattered that it was all irreversible: there wouldn't be enough of him left to regret what he had lost.

But something would remain – a little kernel of being – enough of a mind to recognise its own existence. Enough of a mind to appreciate its surroundings, and to extract some trickle of pleasure and contentment from the execution of a task, no matter how purposeless. He wouldn't ever need to leave the pool. The solar patches would provide him with all the energy he needed. He would never age, never grow ill. Other machines would take care of his island, protecting the pool and its silent, slow swimmer from the ravages of weather and time.

Centuries would pass.

Thousands of years, and then millions.

Beyond that, it was anyone's guess. But the one thing I knew was that Zima would never tire of his task. There was no capacity left in his mind for boredom. He had become pure experience. If he experienced any kind of joy in the swimming of the pool, it was the near-mindless euphoria of a pollinating insect. That was enough for him. It had been enough for him in that pool in California, and it was enough for him now, a thousand years later, in the same pool but on another world, around another sun, in a distant part of the same galaxy.

As for me . . .

It turned out that I remembered more of our meeting on the island than I had any right to. Make of that what you will, but it seemed I didn't need the mental crutch of my AM quite as much as I'd always imagined. Zima was right: I'd allowed my life to become scripted, laid out like a blueprint. It was always red wine with sunsets, never the white. Aboard the outbound lightbreaker a clinic installed a set of neural memory extensions that should serve me well for the next four or five hundred years. One day I'll need another solution, but I'll cross that particular mnemonic bridge when I get there. My last act, before dismissing the AM, was to transfer its observations into the vacant spaces of my enlarged memory. The events still don't feel quite like they ever happened to me, but they settle in a little bit better with each act of recall. They change and soften, and the highlights glow a little brighter. I guess they become a little less accurate with each instance of recall, but like Zima said, perhaps that's the point.

I know now why he spoke to me. It wasn't just my way with a biographical story. It was his desire to help someone move on, before he did the same.

I did eventually find a way to write his story, and I sold it back to my old newspaper, the *Martian Chronicle*. It was good to visit the old planet again, especially now that they've moved it into a warmer orbit.

That was a long time ago. But I'm still not done with Zima, odd as it seems.

Every couple of decades, I still hop a lightbreaker to Murjek, descend to the streets of that gleaming white avatar of Venice, take a conveyor to the island and join the handful of other dogged witnesses scattered across the stands. Those that come, like me, must still feel that the artist has something else in store ... one last surprise. They've read my article now, most of them, so they know what that slowly swimming figure means ... but they still don't come in droves. The stands are always a little echoey and sad, even on a good day. But I've never seen them completely empty, which I suppose is some kind of testament. Some people get it. Most people never will.

But that's art.

Sometimes you have half an idea for a story that you hold in your head for years before you know what to do with it. Typically, you have to wait for the moment when that half-formed idea intersects with another one and the mental fireworks go off.

That's how it was with 'Zima Blue', the second Carrie Clay story that appears in this book. I'd long wanted to write a story about a robot that had become a kind of family heirloom, passed from owner to owner across many generations and centuries, with the robot becoming cleverer and more sophisticated as time goes by. I was well aware that the idea had been 'done' by Isaac Asimov in his long story 'The Bicentennial Man'. But one of the truly delightful things about science fiction is that it is far less about new ideas than it is about finding new ways to think about old ones. All you have to do is find a new spin, a new way of telling, a new truth to illuminate. Which, needless to say, is the difficult part. 'Zima Blue' sat on the back burner for years until I got the other half of the story, the new angle of attack. And I got it while taking a swim to clear my mind of the problems I was having coming up with story ideas.

Good things, swimming pools.

Since 'Zima Blue' is about the fallibility of memory, it's only fitting that I should record my own uncertainty about an anecdote in the story. Mention is made of a man who searched despairingly for a particular shade of the colour blue glimpsed in childhood, and who later finds it in the colour of a beetle in a museum of natural history. I think something like this happened to the neurologist Oliver Sacks: at least, I remember him talking about something very like it in a television programme. If I've misremembered the details, I apologise ... but I can only restate my enthusiasm for Sacks' writings, and the many moments of jaw-dropping awe I've experienced in reading his case histories. If science fiction did not exist in this universe, the writings of Sacks would fill the gap pretty effectively.

ACKNOWLEDGEMENTS

By the time this book first appeared, more than five years had passed since the idea of it was first mooted in an e-mail to me from Jason Williams of Night Shade Books. Not long afterwards, Marty Halpern (better known for his work with Golden Gryphon Press) generously consented to shepherd the book towards publication. At the time, it was a very real possibility that the book might be produced sometime in 2002, or – failing that – 2003 at the very latest.

Unfortunately, other factors intervened (novel deadlines, job stuff, real life, etc.) and I had to keep backing out of commitments to deliver the stories by an agreed date, with the result that the book – as the years ticked inexorably by – began to look less and less likely to actually happen. Thankfully, Jason (and Jeremy Lassen, his partner in Night Shade Books) kept the faith, and when I finally did announce that I was ready to tackle it again, they responded not with howls of disbelief but with gratifying enthusiasm. So too did Marty, who was as energetic and diligent an editor as any writer could ask for.

So, thanks, guys – Jason, Jeremy and Marty – not just for sticking in there, but also for valuing short fiction in the first place, and I promise that if we *ever* do another one of these ...

Alastair Reynolds
Noordwijk,
The Netherlands
May 2006

A Note on the UK Edition (2009)

When Gollancz agreed to bring out a British edition of this collection, it seemed sensible to take the opportunity to slot in the third (chronologically second) Merlin story – 'Minla's Flowers' – which had not actually existed at the time Marty Halpern and I put together the original collection. At which point, of course, we had a subtly different book on our hands . . . so why not add something else while we were at it? I wanted to include 'Everlasting', which for some reason I had never submitted to Marty when we were making the cut for the Night Shade edition (we wouldn't have had room for it if I had in any case; something else would have had to go). It also seemed right to include 'Cardiff Afterlife', a sequel to 'Signal to Noise' and another near-future piece.

It's time to reiterate my thanks to Marty Halpern for being a sterling editor on the Night Shade edition, to Jason and Jeremy for making the original collection happen, and to thank Jo Fletcher and Malcolm Edwards of Gollancz and Lisa Rogers for their enthusiasm and hard work in producing this expanded edition.

Alastair Reynolds
Rhondda Cynon Taf,
Wales
October 2008